Withdrawn

Prima Donna

ALSO BY MEGAN CHANCE

The Spiritualist

An Inconvenient Wife

Susannah Morrow

PRIMA DONNA

A NOVEL

MEGAN CHANCE

🚢 THREE RIVERS PRESS • NEW YORK

Copyright © 2009 by Megan Chance

Published in the United States by Three Rivers Press,
an imprint of the Crown Publishing Group,
a division of Random House, Inc., New York.
www.crownpublishing.com

Three Rivers Press and the Tugboat design are registered
trademarks of Random House, Inc.

Library of Congress Cataloging-in-Publication Data
Chance, Megan.
Prima donna: a novel / Megan Chance. — 1st trade paperback ed.
p. cm.
1. Singers—Fiction. 2. Brothels—Fiction. 3. Seattle (Wash.)—
History—19th century—Fiction. 4. Psychological fiction. I. Title.
PS3553.H2663P75 2009
813'.54—dc22   2009018553

ISBN 978-0-307-46101-8

Printed in the United States of America

DESIGN BY BARBARA STURMAN

2 4 6 8 10 9 7 5 3 1

First Edition

Faust

Et que peux-tu pour moi?
(Well, what can you do for me?)

Méphistophélès

Tout! Mais dis-moi d'abord
Ce que tu veux.
(Everything! But first, tell me
What it is you want.)

—*FAUST*, Charles Gounod; libretto by Jules
Barbier and Michel Carré; act I, scene 2

Marguerite

J'écoute! Et je comprends cette voix solitaire
Qui chante dans mon coeur!
(I listen and I understand this solitary voice
Which sings inside my heart!)

—*FAUST*, Charles Gounod; libretto by Jules
Barbier and Michel Carré; act III, scene 8

Prima Donna

PROLOGUE

New York City—August 1877

Behind me, I heard his gurgling, choking breath, the sound of him drowning on his own blood, and then, suddenly, it stopped altogether.

I didn't dare turn to look. I heard footsteps in the hallway outside the door, and in a panic I lifted my hands from the water in the basin, dark red now, more blood than water, and grabbed the towel, pressing it hard against my face to stop the bleeding, despite the pain that brought tears to my eyes. In the armoire there was a dark blue wool among the ball gowns of silk and lace. I had to put the towel aside to put it on, and the blood dripped relentlessly into my eyes. My hands shook so hard it took forever to make the buttons go through the hoops. I shoved my stockingless feet into boots and left them unbuttoned and looked wildly about, trying to think. Money— I would need money—but there was none, only my jewels. I grabbed what was on my dressing table, shoving necklaces and rings and brooches into my pockets, and then I yanked on my cloak, pulling up the hood to hide my loose and tangled hair, and pressed the towel again to my face and went to the door, nearly tripping over his bare feet—such lovely feet, so well shaped for a man. The sight of them startled me anew. I forced myself to look away.

Beyond the door, the hallway was silent. I stepped out, trying to make no noise. There was the elevator, but I didn't dare take it, not looking like this. Instead I took the stairs, the back ones for the servants. My boot heels clattered on the wood; the stairs were narrow and dim, and I was shaking so badly now that I wasn't certain I could make it to the bottom. I heard footsteps below me, and I drew into a darkened corner and turned my head away to hide my face. A steward hurried up the first flight and paused when he saw me. "Miss?" he asked, and I motioned roughly for him to go on, muttering something—I hardly knew what—and he hesitated, trying to peer into the dark. He could not have seen anything, and he was in a rush; he didn't delay.

I waited until he had gone by, and then I raced down, as if speed alone would keep me from discovery. The kitchen, swirling with movement, was on one side of a narrow hall half obstacled with carts and laundry bags meant for the washroom on the other side. Maids dodged about carrying glasses and linens; there was no way to avoid them. I hesitated and then I moved quickly and with purpose to the back door.

No one stopped me; most simply moved out of my way as if I were part of the dance of their hurry, and then I was outside in the dark alley, past the garbage, running, my unbuttoned boots nearly slipping off with every step. I dodged the street-lamps and kept close to the shadows, where no one could see me clearly, if they saw me at all. The only sound I heard was my own breath, and with it came the echo of his, the images that flashed before my eyes as if they were happening anew: his hands on my hips, holding me helpless ... my scream as he'd cut me ... the knife in my hand, the spurting blood. ...

I did not realize where I'd been going until I was already there. Until I'd gone blocks and blocks, until my side hurt and my whole face was a throbbing stinging ache. Past the dead-end warrens and the tenement buildings, until I stood in an alley littered with fish bones and trash piles pulsing with rats, potholed with shallow pools of emptied spittoons and chamber pots and the dregs of emptied kegs. The night was warm and the stink stung my nostrils along with the nauseating smell of my own blood.

I was before the propped-open back door of a beer hall. I heard the music from within, a polka orchestra, and the clanking of pans from the kitchen, shouted orders: *"Two fish!"* *"Get the spatzel down!"* *"Kartoffeles! Hurry now!"*

I had not stepped foot in the place for years. But I had nowhere else to go. I eased through the back door into the storage room. The shadows of stacked kegs filled the near darkness. The kitchen was beyond, men rushing about, their movements staccato and strange in the haze of greasy steam. The air was loud with the hiss of frying fish, the clank of plates, the thump of Herr Meyer's wooden leg as he moved efficiently about, shouting instructions.

They were too busy to notice me, and I was in darkness besides. I had played hide-and-seek among the kegs since I was very small, and now I found my way easily through them to the hallway that opened into the beer hall at one end, to stairs at the other.

The music was louder there, as was the talk. The heavy press of smoke and the smell of sweat and beer made me dizzy. I pressed the towel to my face, and blood seeped from it, dripping down my hand to my wrist. I waited until the hall was clear and dashed out—up the peeling and scarred blue-painted stairs, not slowing until they turned and I was out of sight to anyone below. Then I paused, waiting for a shout of discovery. There was none, thank God, but now I began to feel sick and uncertain. The door of the apartment at the top was closed, and I did not know who would open it. I did not know what my reception would be.

I knocked. Very quietly at first, and then, when I heard nothing, more loudly. I heard footsteps, rapid and light, and then the door cracked open. I saw a blue eye, dark hair, pale skin, a hand reaching around that was red and chapped from hard work—such a strange contrast on one so pretty.

"Willa." I breathed.

She frowned and glanced behind her. "*Gott im himmel*. What are *you* doing here?"

I threw back the hood. "I've had a bit of trouble—"

Her eyes grew round with horror. "*Lieber Gott*." Her voice was a whisper. "*Bitte Gott, rette uns.*"

In my dismay I pressed the towel harder. I felt again the dripping blood and I saw her gaze dart to it in fear. "Please . . . if I could come in. . . . There was . . . an accident—"

"Mama?" The voice came from behind her. A child's voice. A plump face peeked around her skirts, and then those blue eyes too widened in horror and fear. The child shrieked and burst into tears.

"Ssshhh, ssshhh, *liebling*," Willa said. She bent to take him into her arms and glared at me. She whispered something to him and closed the door and I heard her steps moving beyond, the muffled sound of her voice, and I was helpless with despair.

Then the door opened again. She stepped into the hallway and closed the door behind her, looking at me with a gaze so venomous I stepped back. "Where is he?" she demanded.

The tears welled so in my eyes that they blurred my vision. I could only shake my head.

"How *dare* you come here! How dare you bring trouble upon this house! Did you even stop to think what would happen to us?"

"I didn't know where else to go—"

"What? You mean your patrons and your Four Hundred have abandoned you?" The sneer in her voice was painful to hear. "They can bear the police better than we can, and you know it. This kind of trouble would ruin us. Papa's old now. This would destroy him."

"Willa, please—"

"You made your choice—did you think you could so easily take it back?"

"Please. I have nowhere else."

"Go to your Mrs. Astor," she said cruelly. She opened the door, stepping back inside. "Now get out of here before someone sees you."

I took a step toward her, reaching into my pocket, pulling out a necklace, pink diamonds. "Please, Willa. I can pay you—"

She recoiled as if I repulsed her. "I don't want your money. You ignore us when you like and now that you're in trouble you bring it here. Look at you! You're covered in blood! I have a child now. I can't help you. None of us can. For God's sake, think of *us*."

She slammed the door shut. I heard the turn of the key in the lock, and then the muffled cry of a child.

I had no memory beyond that. Not of going downstairs and past the kitchen, not of the alley outside. Suddenly I was in some dark tangle of buildings and corners somewhere, and I had no idea where and no idea of where next to go. I was bleeding and in pain and I needed to hide and to escape, but how to do that now was impossible. How had it never occurred to me before now that I had no friends? That I had nothing? My mind was muddy and confused and I saw things I knew rationally could not be before me. His face. The broken teapot. The knife, still greasy with capon fat . . .

It was very late now. The performance would be over. They would find him soon. They would come looking for me.

Despite the warmth of the night, my hand was frozen where it clutched the towel to my cheek. I crawled into the corner behind an old barrel and pulled my cloak more closely about me. I shook with cold all the night through. I did not sleep.

CHAPTER 1

Seattle, Washington Territory—February 1878

The little restaurant was nearly full. I slipped inside, letting the heat from the bodies and the kitchen warm me while my sodden skirts dripped into a puddle on the floor.

There was one table in the corner, and I went to it as quickly as I could, trying to ignore the men I passed, trying to hide my fear. I sat down, chilled all over again by the wet fabric of my dress beneath me and the steady trickle down my collar from my soaking hat. As miserable as it was, at least I was out of the rain. My hands were numb with cold as I shoved my portmanteau beneath my chair, glanced at the chalkboard menu on the wall, and felt the eye of every man in the place on me.

Warily, with the habit born of months, I checked their interest—anything undue, any recognition. There was none of that, but another kind of interest instead, and the shipboy's words came back to me. *"Best not to go beyond Mill Street after dark, ma'am. Them's the Lava Beds. The only women there are ... well, it ain't no place for a lady anytime."* I should have known what it would be like. I *did* know. But what other choice had I? This was the end of the world; there was no place else to run. Twice already I'd nearly been discovered; women like me did not own jewels of the sort I'd carried, and Pinkerton agents and cunning reporters seemingly never slept. But now those jewels were gone, all sold, and where else could I go where no one would expect me to be or try to find me? Where no one would recognize me or care enough about a lone woman with a terrible scar to ask questions?

An Indian with long black hair that shone oily in the gaslight approached. He wore a flannel shirt and denim trousers, along with an apron that had once been white but now was grayed and stained and filthy. He smelled of rotting fish. When I looked up at him, he spoke to me in that strange Chinook jargon I'd heard from the peddler women and about the streets and on the steamer, a mix of Indian and English words it seemed everyone here spoke but me. *"Klatawa. Halo mesachie klooshman."*

I stared at him uncomprehendingly, then I sighed. "Chowder, please."

He glared at me.

Clumsily, I opened my purse and pulled out my last twenty-five cents with fingers that could barely hold the coins. "I have money. I can pay."

"Halo mesachie klooshman."

"I don't understand."

"He's sayin' the owner don't serve whores." A man appeared over the Indian's shoulder. He had curling dark hair and a ruddy face, and I could tell by his watery eyes and his slight sway that he was very drunk.

"Tell him I just want a bowl of chowder. Then I'll go. Please. I'm so hungry. Tell him I can pay."

The man spoke to the Indian in that same language, and the Indian shook his head violently, gesturing to the door. He yelled "Go!"

The restaurant had grown silent; every man in the place

had paused to watch. A few rose, as if they meant to help—not me, but the Indian. I grabbed the handle of my portmanteau and left, tripping over my skirts in my haste, pushing by the men who crowded around me to block the door.

I ran back into the dark rain, flattening myself against a rough wall, sliding down until I sat on the narrow, slippery boardwalk fronting the building, and people stumbled over me and cursed. I closed my eyes and buried my head in my arms until my fear quieted.

I felt a hand on my shoulder, heavy—too heavy, as if it needed my support. When I looked up I saw the man who had translated for me in the restaurant. Curly dark hair, a missing canine tooth that made his face look lopsided.

"Hey, girlie."

His hand tightened on my shoulder. I could only stare at him.

He slurred, "Looks like you could use some warmin' up. I got a room near here. I been lookin' all night for someone to fuck. I guess you'd do as well as any."

I glanced away, toward the deep mud of the street and the streetlight, haloing now before my blurring eyes, and the rain pouring down like a gray curtain beyond it, where the men moved within like spirits. Then I turned back to him. He fell against the wall, squinting, as if he couldn't quite pin down where I was, and I felt a surge of revulsion and, close on its heels, acceptance. Who was I to disdain it now? How small the price was really, for warmth and someplace out of the rain. *Well, why not? It's no different than what you've done before.*

I didn't let myself think beyond that. I didn't want to think. "Yes," I said, and then, desperately, "it'll cost you . . . two dollars—and a bowl of chowder."

He smiled. "All right then. All right, girlie. Let's go. I got a room at Gray's."

He helped me to my feet, and once I was up he began to tug me after him. I said, "The chowder first."

For a moment he looked mutinous. Then he nodded and staggered back into the restaurant, leaving me to wait. He came out with a steaming bowl and a spoon and a drink he kept for himself. I lifted my veil, dodging a quick glance at him, but there registered no recognition on his face. He'd barely handed me the bowl before I dove into it where I stood, shoving the chowder into my mouth so quickly that it burned my tongue. I barely tasted it, which was probably a good thing, as the clam smell was strong and a layer of fat pooled on top, and there was something mushy and stringy and unpleasant in it.

My drunk waited impatiently for me to finish, lodging his shoulder against the doorway and slinging back his drink. When I was done, he grabbed the bowl from my hand and threw it into the street, where it broke into pieces that men trod into the mud. He took my arm and jerked me into his side, wrapping his arm around me as much to keep himself upright as anything.

The boardwalk ended abruptly, and we went into the street, which was mobbed with horses and men, dogs and whores, nightmarish and strange as they moved through the gasping flicker of streetlamps, falling again into darkness that moved and shifted with the rain so that few things could be seen and what could didn't seem quite real.

He slipped in the mud, half taking me down with him. When we righted ourselves, he took out a flask, which he uncorked and drank from before he offered it to me, and I didn't refuse it. The whiskey inside was sour tasting and rotgut, but I took a huge sip and managed to keep from choking.

Then we turned the corner, and he said, "There 'tis!" and I looked past his swaying, pointing finger to a narrow building built up on pilings, like so many of the others in this godforsaken town. I saw movement in the shadows beneath—rats or thieves or murderers or men too drunk to know where the street was. Men sat upon the sagging boardwalk before it, lolling against the door, which was crooked and barely shut.

My drunk staggered up the ramp, pulling me after him, and kicked at a man blocking the way, who fell over without a protest.

He pushed on the door. It didn't budge. He pushed at it again, and then with a great squeaking creak it opened, and we stumbled into the dark and dirty foyer of the worst hotel I'd ever seen—if that truly was what it was.

There was no desk, just a table with a sign written in a spidery hand: $1.00 A NIGHT SINGLE ROOM, 50¢ TO SHARE, and a man with a straggly gray beard snoring in a chair beside it. He didn't even look up as my companion led me to warped stairs that creaked badly as we climbed. The railing shook and rocked as if it might not hold our weight. At the top was a hall lit only by a sputtering oil lamp that cast more shadows than it relieved, and the man gripped me hard, saying, "I ain't gonna pass out, girlie, doan choo worry," as if just speaking it would make it true. I hardly cared. I hardly cared about anything now.

I was bearing most of his weight, the wall bearing the rest as we nearly fell down the hall. He counted the doors with exaggerated precision, and when we reached four, he said, "This 'un."

The room was dark, with a tiny window that let in whatever light could be had from the streetlamps below. It was almost too small for the two of us, and the narrow bed took up all the space. The smell was indescribable: a mix of stale beer and whiskey and mildew and sweat, along with the stink of piss and filthy blankets.

"Here we are," he said, falling with a grunt onto the bed, which protested loudly at his weight and nearly sank to the floor. He angled himself up on one elbow and grinned drunkenly at me and waggled his fingers. "Come on now, I'm ready for ya."

I dropped my portmanteau on the floor and took off my veiled hat, letting it fall. "Two dollars," I said quietly, and he reached into his pocket, grunting again, and drew out a frayed leather wallet. When I went to take the money, he misjudged, dropping the greenbacks to the floor. I bent to pick them up and heard something scamper across the boards beneath the bed. He grabbed my shoulder so I fell into him, the dollars crumpled in my fist.

He shoved his hand into my hair, pulling me up to kiss him, though I turned my head at the last minute so his tongue darted wetly across my cheek. He released me to fumble with his belt. In the confines of the room, he smelled powerfully of whiskey and dirty wool. He abandoned his fumbling and lay back again and said, "You'll have to do it for me, girlie."

I shoved the money into my bodice and undid his belt, jerking it loose, unbuttoning his trousers. I was clumsy and slow, and he watched me with a sort of dumb fascination. Then I sat back on the bed and waited, and he reached down into the opening in his long underwear and drew out his cock, which was soft and flopping in his fingers.

"Lift your skirts, girlie," he said, struggling to sit up, stroking himself.

I did as he asked, and when he motioned, I straddled him. He put his free hand about me, pulling me into his chest, breathing heavily in my ear. I smelled his gamy sweat and the stubble on his cheeks scraped my skin, while his mustache was wiry and coarse. There was a part of me that said I should not be here, that I would hate myself for this later, but I couldn't bring myself to heed it. There would be time to feel sick over this tomorrow; just now this was all I had.

My savior's hand slipped into the slit in my drawers, his fingers tangling in my pubic hair before they slipped away again. He was heaving and grunting, his hand pumping so hard beneath me that his knuckles were bruising my inner thighs. "Go on then, girlie," he gasped. "Go ahead and put me in. It'll be all right. It'll be—"

But he was still soft and floppy and pathetic, and I murmured, "I think you're too drunk for me tonight, mister."

"No, no," he protested, still jerking away. "Jush a few . . . more . . . minutes. . . ." Then his hand fell limply to his side, and he said, "You do it."

I eyed the door. I heard the rain pelting the roof. Looking out the window was like looking underwater. He reached into his pocket, pulling his flask out again. He took a swig and then he said, "Kiss it, girlie. I paid you for a fuck."

He passed his hand before his eyes, as if to still the room I guessed was swirling around him. He took another swig and reached for me, but he was too drunk, and his hand fell limply back to his side. He closed his eyes as he said, "Jush lay down here for a minute. Jush one minute . . . and I'll . . . be ready. . . ."

I lay beside him. My dress was so wet it was plastered to me; the cold of it pressed into my spine, but I was tired and despairing and I couldn't bring myself to move. At least I was out of the rain. The bed was narrow enough that I was nearly on top of him. Then he made a sound deep in his throat, and he was snoring.

For a moment I felt nothing. And then came the push of anxiety, and with it the thought that I had only put off the inevitable, that I had made a mistake in coming to Seattle, one more bad decision in a long line of many. I had only wanted to get lost, to be as far away as possible, but I had not thought . . . I had never thought that someday my road might take me here, that I—who had once had everything—would be prostituting myself in the flea-ridden bed of a filthy, drunken stranger. The idea was so absurd that I could not stop the bubble of laughter that rose in my chest, and I turned to muffle the sound, to bury it in the stinking blankets so I wouldn't wake him, and I was so busy trying not to wake him that it was some time before I noticed that it wasn't laughter I was quieting, but tears.

CHAPTER 2

I woke from a restless sleep, vestiges of the past lingering in a half-remembered dream: blood and fear and panic, a pawn-broker's calculating expression, someone shouting as I'd boarded the train.

The man in bed beside me muttered in his sleep. It was dawn, the gray through the window lightening, the noise in the street lessening. I did not hear any rain.

I rose as slowly and quietly as I could and eased my way to the door. The man didn't stir, or at least, no more than he had before. I grabbed my hat from the floor and lifted my bag and tried the door, which stuck and groaned when I opened it, and I paused, sure he would wake, but he only turned onto his side and muttered again, and I went out into the hallway, closing it as best I could behind me.

The hallway was silent, as dark as it had been last night. I tried not to make noise as I went down—the man with the beard was no longer in the chair, but now there were bodies lying about on the floor, all snoring and groaning and turning restlessly upon the warped boards.

My clothes were still a good deal more than damp, and my scalp and the back of my neck and my shoulders itched from bites—fleas or bedbugs or both. I shoved open the door and went out onto the ramped walk, stepping over the two men passed out there. The streets were quiet. Horses slept where they stood, and men slept where they sat, but the whores that came out at night were gone and the saloons were mostly still. A dog rooted in the gutter, tossing garbage about before he latched onto something I did not want to look at too closely and went running off. Across the street, a Chinaman peered at me through a window and then lowered the shade.

The dream still haunted me, and the world felt strange. Suspended. As if the clouds were only hesitating, gathering their strength to wrap the world in fog and rain again. I felt the stiffness of the two dollars between my breasts, and my stomach rumbled in hunger.

I passed a sleepy grocer who was just opening his stall, and when he turned away I stole two apples, and I was so hungry I ate even the cores, in spite of the lean feral dog that sneaked from beneath a building to follow me in the hopes I might drop him a bite.

"Between you and me, it's me, pooch," I told him, and after I finished the last of the apple, he disappeared.

The food raised my spirits somewhat. Just now I could pretend last night had never happened; for the moment I had the strength to keep my memories and despair at bay. Later, I knew, it would not be so easy.

I shook the thoughts away. Today, I meant to find a job, though I knew how I must look, and I had no illusions. Using my reflection in a window, I tried the best I could to put up my dark hair again, and wiped the dirt off my face with a part of my petticoat that was only wet and not smeared with mud. I did not put on the hat and veil. I no longer looked anything like the woman I'd been, and I doubted anyone in this part of town would penetrate my disguise. Still, it wasn't until I'd passed several people who didn't look twice at me that I relaxed. No one had followed me. No one had recognized me. Perhaps I hadn't failed so irreparably in coming here. I'd begun to doubt that I could disappear, but now the hope of it returned.

Before long, I reached a row of saloons—there must have been five built together, all ramshackle, all wooden; I hadn't yet seen a building made of brick or stone—Billy the Mugs, Miner's Saloon, Rough and Ready and two with no signs at all. As early as it was, they were open. I chose the Miner's first, and I stepped through the door. The floor was crooked boards covered with sawdust that sifted into the gaps between them where it wasn't clumping with spittle and spilled drink and mud. There were a few tables, and spittoons that looked as if they hadn't been emptied in a good while. A balding, older man with a paunch wiped down the bar at the back. Written on a chalkboard behind him was: WHISKEY 25 CENTS. BEER 10 CENTS. NO FOOD DON'T ASK. Above these signs, near the ceiling, was a smaller one that read: M. J. PETERS, PROP.

Sitting at the bar were three men hunched over their drinks. They glanced up idly as I came inside. Without thinking, I smiled at them. The habit was too ingrained. I regretted it the next moment, when I saw the quick light of interest in their eyes.

One of the men sitting there swiveled on his stool. "Well, well. And I was just feelin' in the mood for a poke."

"Take it outside," the bartender said. "This ain't a brothel."

I said loudly, "I'm looking for a job."

"Oh, I got a job for you," the man said, grabbing his crotch, and the others sitting near him laughed.

I ignored them and appealed to the bartender. "You need a waitress?"

"I don't use waitresses here," he said. " 'Specially ones lookin' like you."

"Now, ain't that a nasty scar," purred the one who'd wanted a poke. "That's all right, honey. I like 'em rough."

He was filthy and his teeth were rotting. I could smell his stink from where I stood. I backed away and kept backing, clear into the street, muttering a hasty thank-you as I went.

I tried every other place on the block, and into the next one over, and the replies were all the same. No one needed a waitress or anything else, most suggested I lie back on the bar and spread my legs, which was what I deserved for being both a woman and alone in this part of town, regardless of the widow's weeds I wore, which did nothing to disguise my desperation. By midafternoon, I was tired and discouraged again. I went to the last few saloons and got only a shake of the head and a suggestion to try the brothels, "*though with that scar, I don't guess they'd want you.*" I went farther up the hill, into the Chinese part of town, where carcasses of cooked ducks dripping grease hung in the windows, and the streets were lined with pens holding rooting pigs and trussed chickens and geese, and everywhere were Celestials who stared at me with unreadable eyes. I stumbled along twisted corridors between buildings that led to darkened stairs and narrow doors and the faint whiff of opium smoke that made me sick with memory. I could not stay there.

It was growing late already, and it began to rain again. The smells of sewage and drink and tobacco and sweat were so thick in the air they seemed part of the rain. Men started to appear, swarming from their workplaces, and here and there a whore. The two dollars was safe in my bodice, and I still had twenty-five cents as well, so there would be no need for a repeat of last night as long as I could find a hotel that would take a lone woman, especially one as down on her luck as I obviously was. To be inside, to give in to sleep that came without nightmares . . .

In my search I had moved steadily uphill, and now I turned the corner. Here the buildings were not crowded so closely together, some blocks nearly empty. There was another saloon, one I hadn't seen before, a flat-roofed, two-storied building on stilts that lifted it five feet from the stinking mud and sewage-strewn street, with ramps leading to its doorway. A very large sign extended perpendicular to the street, block letters spelling out THE PALACE, though the name was its only claim to grandeur. The building was as mean as any other, the only difference being a small balcony at the corner of the second story.

I nearly walked past it. It was late and I needed to find a room. I had no hope that my reception would be any different here than anywhere else. But I found myself walking toward it, going up its slippery ramp, opening the door to step inside.

It took a moment for my eyes to adjust to the dimness, and then I saw a cluster of tables and a bar and sooty oil lamps flickering weakly. I felt the gritty slip of sawdust beneath my boots. One of the men playing cards looked up idly, then glanced away again, spitting in the general direction of a tarnished spittoon and missing completely.

Then I saw something that made me pause, something I hadn't expected. Looming out of the near dark to my left was a raised platform, and above it a narrow balcony, and my senses recognized it before my eyes did.

A stage.

It was small, but a stage nonetheless, though it was empty now. The balcony above was meant for an orchestra, and I saw a large dark shape there that could have been a piano, though I wasn't certain. It was too dark.

I felt the hunger then, that yearning that had informed my days and nights since I could remember, and I told myself to walk away. But of course I could not.

I looked toward the bar, where two men stood, one washing glasses, the other leaning, though I couldn't see their features from this distance in the dim light. I had spent a lifetime learning how to recognize the most important person in a room, and by the way the leaning man was still and watching, I knew he was the one. I made my way toward him. When I got there, I settled my bag on the stool and said, "I'm looking for a job."

The man washing glasses—not really a man yet, I saw now, more a boy, and one who looked to be at least partly Indian—glanced up. He jerked his dark head toward the man I'd spotted, who straightened lazily now—*uncoiling*, I thought uncomfortably, like a snake. His hair gleamed a reddish blond in the lamplight, his mustache was heavy but well kept.

He was attractive, but as his gaze swept me, I had to force myself not to step back. This was going to be just the same as everywhere else, I knew.

"A job doing what?" he asked.

"I thought . . . as a waitress."

He raised a brow. "Does it look like I need a waitress?"

"No," I admitted.

Suddenly something crashed behind me. Glass shattered. Instinctively, I ducked. The man-boy flinched and sank behind the bar. Someone yelled, "You son of a bitch!"

The blond man cursed beneath his breath.

I twisted to see. Near the stage, a table was upended, chairs turned on their sides. Glasses rolled about splashing whiskey or beer, cards scattered across the floor at the feet of men who were jerking back to form a circle around two who grappled and punched. Someone shouted, "Ease up, boys!" while someone else said, "You get 'im, Eddie! Shove it down 'is throat!"

I heard the crack of a fist against bone, and one of them went flying into another table, sending it crashing while the men there swore and scooted out of the way. A spittoon tipped, splashing onto the floor and then rolling beneath their feet until someone tripped over it and sent it spinning into a corner.

Behind me, I heard the boy say, "Shit. This is a bad one."

"That's enough now, boys!" the blond man shouted, lunging across the floor, pushing his way into the circle.

When they saw him, some of the men watching stepped away. I saw the trepidation on their faces, which seemed odd—just another bar fight, wasn't it? But they looked frightened, and two who had been watching slunk away toward the door.

One of the fighting men was on the floor now, the other on top of him, pummeling away. The blond man grabbed him by the shoulder, hurling him back so hard he slammed into another table before he fell groaning to the floor. The man he'd been punching lay there limply, moaning, and the blond asked in a quiet, deadly voice, "Who started it?"

One of those watching pointed to the one the owner had thrown clear. "Eddie was cheatin', Johnny."

"Was he now?" The blond man—Johnny—turned slowly to face Eddie, who began frantically to scramble away, falling and tripping over himself. Johnny was on him in a moment, pulling him upright, and then his hand was around Eddie's throat.

"He didn't mean it, Johnny," one of Eddie's friends placated. "He's just drunk. We'll take him home and see he don't come back here again."

Johnny ignored him. He kept his hold on Eddie's throat, and while Eddie clutched at the fingers around his neck, Johnny leaned close. His voice was velvet as he said, "Now then, Eddie, didn't I warn you before about making a ruckus?"

Eddie tried to nod.

"You'll pardon if my memory ain't as good as it used to be. Perhaps you can remind me—didn't you promise me something not two weeks ago?"

Eddie's voice was hoarse as he gasped for air. "Not . . . to . . . cause trouble."

"But here you are, back again, making a ruckus and cheating my good customers. Can't you keep a promise, Eddie?"

Eddie's throat worked. He tried to nod. "I . . . swear . . . "

Johnny's fingers didn't ease. "Ah, I'd like to take your word, but an oath don't mean shit to you, it seems. You just proved tonight you can't keep it, and I ain't a simpleton either, Eddie, which you should've known before now."

"Johnny," said one of Eddie's friends. "Please—"

"Shut up," Johnny told him. He looked at the man squirming in his grasp. "Now maybe you want to give me a reason why I shouldn't kill you right now."

The man's eyes bugged. He pried at Johnny's fingers.

I felt the chill of dread, and I understood why those men had left so quickly. Surely he did not mean to—

"I guess there ain't one," Johnny said.

He put his other hand around that man's throat, and no one stopped him; no one said a word as he tightened his fingers. Even I said nothing, but only watched in horror. I was certain he would quit at any moment.

Eddie struggled and went to his knees. He grabbed Johnny's fingers and sent a pleading look to the friend who had asked for his pardon. That man only looked away.

It seemed to take so little effort. Johnny's jaw stiffened, and his fingers grew white as the man's face grew blue, and no one did anything at all. *He'll stop now,* I thought. And then, *Now.* But he didn't. No one protested or said a word as the man gasped for breath and struggled, kicking his feet out, and then, finally, when it seemed it was nearly over, Johnny suddenly released him. Eddie fell to the floor with a heavy thud, clutching his throat, choking, wheezing. The others backed away as if afraid his touch might pollute them.

Johnny said, "Consider this my last warning, Eddie. Show your face in here again, and I won't leave you breathing." He glanced at the man's friends. "Get him the fuck out of here."

The two scrambled to grab Eddie, nearly carrying him in their haste to be gone, and I had to remind myself to breathe again.

Johnny strode back to the bar, and the silent, careful watching of the customers broke like a spell. The men moved, shifting to other tables, coming up to the bar. I watched Johnny pour the drinks and smile and talk to them all as if he hadn't nearly murdered someone just moments ago, or as if he'd done such things a hundred times before.

I had to leave this place, and now, but my feet felt anchored to the floor.

And then Johnny looked at me and said, "Why, miss, ain't you pale," and jerked his head at the half-breed. "See to her, Duncan, before she swoons."

There seemed to be a haze before my eyes. I felt someone's hand on my arm, and I jerked in reflex before I realized it was the boy, and I was leaning on him so heavily that I would have fallen had he released his hold. He had something in his hand; he pushed it at my lips and told me to drink it. Obediently I did—it burned its way down my throat and into my chest, and I choked, and the boy—Duncan—said, "You'll be all right, miss. Not many people mess with Johnny. Guess you can see why."

His words made their way through my haze; they seemed to burn along with the whiskey. *Not many people mess with Johnny.* Of course they didn't.

But you'd be safe with someone like him.

The thought lodged in my mind and wouldn't let go, and I thought of last night, of the men in the restaurant who'd meant to gang up on me, the man I'd gone to a room with, and I knew how many more men like that there would be if I didn't find a way to protect myself.

Duncan still had a firm hold on my arm. I pulled away, saying, "I'm fine. Really I am."

He released me reluctantly and just then Johnny looked at us, and through my apprehension, I did what years of practice had taught me. He was a handsome man; it was not so hard to go up to him, to smile, to cock my head and let interest shine in my eyes. He started, and I saw when his gaze sharpened, when he looked at me again as if I were something unexpected, as if he hadn't seen me well enough the first time.

"You say you don't need a waitress," I said to him. "But I see something you do need."

His smile was slow. "Oh yeah? What's that?"

"A scrubwoman."

He laughed—it was loud and barking. He said, "Maybe I do. Maybe. And maybe something else too."

I shrugged, but I did it prettily, practiced. "Maybe so."

"Where'd the scar come from?"

"An accident."

"Oh yeah?" His tone was frankly skeptical. "Anyone but you come out alive?"

When I said nothing, he asked, "You ever scrubbed a floor before?"

"Yes."

"What's your name?"

"Marguerite. Marguerite Olson."

"Well then, Marguerite," he said, reaching behind to grab a bucket and a broom and shoving them at me. "Why don't you show me how good you are?"

I took them and went to where the fight had started. The abandoned table, the spilled drinks, the broken glass scattered everywhere. Duncan came up beside me. He handed me a scrub brush. "He forgot to give you this."

I asked, "What's the stage for?"

He smiled. His teeth were very white and even in his dark-skinned face. "Johnny had a hankering to run theaters up here. Built this up and everything, but it's only wasted. Ain't no one around to play it."

Then he went off, and I righted the table and cleaned up the mess. In twenty minutes, it was as if nothing had happened.

I took the bucket and broom back to the bar, where Johnny was standing, watching me with his arms folded across his chest.

"Good as new," I said.

"Well, Margie," he said. "Looks like you got a job."

My relief was edged with trepidation. This might be one more bad decision. This man was dangerous—but at least he was up front about it, and that was a relief. I'd had my fill of hidden motives. There were no honey-coated words, no touches meant only to persuade and distract. I imagined one always knew where one stood with him.

I smiled, hoping he would not see the stiffness of it.

He said, "Hope you don't mind hard work."

"Not at all."

"My room's upstairs. You'll stay there with me tonight."

I did not say no. To protest was a hypocrisy even I could not manage. I would go with him in return for his protection, and perhaps I could be drunk enough that I didn't care—it seemed a small enough thing to hope for. Surely God could grant me that one thing.

But after everything I'd done, I knew better than to expect it. Most people only got what they deserved, and I was sure to be no different.

From the Journal of Sabine Conrad

NEW YORK CITY, DECEMBER 10, 1870—Gideon is back from the tour at last!!! I confess I'd been quite worried, for my sister's mood had been growing blacker and blacker, and though Mama insisted he would return, I think sometimes she wondered, even though he has been Barret's closest friend since they sang together in the church choir and is not likely to treat our family shabbily. Still, his letters had been coming less and less often, and I think Willa believed she had lost him. But now he is returned and everyone is glad—especially me, because Gideon has done the most wonderful, wonderful thing!! He has arranged for me to audition with the Manchetti Company for a new tour to start in April! He says I am long past ready for it, though I'm still only sixteen, and that my voice will impress them and that if the critics like me (which he believes they will), it will perhaps open the door for me to audition for Mr. Maretzek's company at the Academy of Music after we return.

Papa was reluctant until Barret told him that Adelina Patti toured when she was younger than me, and was singing Lucia at the Academy by the time she was sixteen, and Jenny Lind

was only eighteen when she sang in *Der Freischütz,* and that
by those standards I was already too old. He said, "Would you
have her sing in the Völksstadt forever, Papa? Sabine belongs
in better places than a family beer hall. She'll make good
money, enough to buy the wagon you wish for, and much more
besides." Mama only held little Gunther close and looked worried and frowned when I said I would never be happy without
music and they couldn't mean to keep me from what I loved
above all else. Gideon told them that he was to go on the tour
as well, singing second tenor, and that Barret should go as
my manager—"Who better to watch over her than her own
brother?"—and Willa became so upset that she fled the room
and Gideon had to go after her.

I feel sorry for her—I truly do. She cannot like him going
off again so soon, though she must know he would never be
content to stay forever in Kleindeutschland and work in a grocery. Not with his talent and his handsome face. Even if his
voice is not as good as some others, he is more than good
enough, and he is surely the best pianist I have ever heard;
he truly has a gift. After two years of walking out with him,
Willa should know him well enough to know the life he wants—
even I know it, and I am seven years younger than him and
not his confidante! But Willa says she is an old maid already
(at nineteen!), though she is so pretty with her dark hair and
blue eyes it's stupid for her to think she'll never marry, even if
the worst and most unlikely happens and Gideon proves un-
true. Willa has only ever wanted to be a wife and have babies,
though I will never understand it. How can she walk these
streets and not hate the buildings so crowded they block the
sun; how can she ignore the broken cobbles and the sewage
bubbling in the gutters and the younkers gang with their flash
and their curls content to rut with their girls in the alley-
ways because they have nowhere else to go? To be nothing and
nobody . . . I think I would go mad. If not for my singing,
I surely would. We are luckier than most, to have the Völksstadt and to have our own apartment above, but what does she

think Gideon could give her if he gave up touring? Not jewels
or fine gowns. Not even privacy—they would no doubt have to
live here, and it's crowded enough with the six of us. Though
when I am gone, I suppose there will be a little extra room.

Now I am being called to sing for the families downstairs
and must go.

DECEMBER 11, 1870—Papa is still deciding whether I should
even audition for Manchetti. Part of his hesitation, I know, is
Barret. Lately Papa and my brother have done nothing but
fight over what Barret will do with his life. He has no interest in singing—he told me he only sang in the church choir
to meet girls. He does not want to work in the Völksstadt.
"Should I spend my life pouring beer, Bina, when I'd much
rather drink it, like any good Deutschman?"

I understand, of course. Barret is golden and charming
and like me. He is meant for so much more, and he is so clever
I am sure he will make a success of himself in time, and perhaps managing my career will turn out to be his special talent. I hope so.

Tonight I hid behind the door and listened while they argued about the tour. Papa said that Barret was twenty-three
years old, and no better than a younker, whoring and drinking all day, and asked if Barret was afraid of honest work?
And Barret said he wasn't, that he would make a good chap-
eron and that is true; Barret has always been so protective of
me. He beat poor William Vesey nearly senseless two years
ago when he saw me kiss him behind the nave . . . and that was
hardly a kiss at all! Barret told Papa that between him and
Gideon, who has now done two tours and who knows the
dangers, I would be watched over well, and they would make
sure I was not being cheated. "Sabine is ready for this, Papa.
I promise you that I am ready too."

Papa said he would think on it some more and I snuck up
to bed. Willa was lying awake, and when I crawled in beside
her, she said, "Why do you worry? You'll get your way, just as

you always do," and I said she had no cause to be so mean and
she said, "You've never pulled a beer in your life. You don't
smell like fried fish from serving it all day. Who always gets
the new dresses but you?"

I told her I had to look good onstage, and it was my
singing besides that made the Völksstadt so popular, and she
said, "Gideon would not be going on this tour if not for you."
I told her she was a fool to think it and she said he would stay
here if she asked him to and I dared her to do so and she went
quiet, so I know she is not so confident as she pretends. She
rolled onto her side and said that she was tired of sacrificing
for me, and I said what have you ever sacrificed? And she
said, "Everything this family does is for you, Sabine." And
then she told me that if I loved her, I would watch over Gideon
and make sure he returned to her, and I promised I would.

JANUARY 16, 1871—Today was the very best day! Gideon and
Barret took me to the Manchetti Theater on the Bowery to audition. I was wearing my best dress—the navy blue wool that
Mama let down FINALLY!! She put a border of braid about
the worn hemline to disguise it, and I wore one of Willa's hats
and Mama's gloves, though they were too big. I looked quite
the lady! Barret was nervous, as was I, and when I saw the
theater I must confess that I was alarmed at how mean it
was—just a small building that looked as if it had been shoved
between a concert saloon and a rag shop, and so ramshackle I
thought it might fall down without the other buildings to support it. There was a big placard in the window that read:

Ethiopian Opera
TWO WEEKS ONLY!!!!
Sunday Matinee!
DON'T MISS IT!!!

When we went inside, the walls were covered with posters
of past shows, including the Manchetti Minstrels, which
Gideon said would be going along on the tour, because the
shows draw bigger crowds if they're more than just opera, and
the Manchetti Company won't be doing any one opera, either,
but favorite scenes from several. There's to be a violinist too.
I hear he is famous enough, though I've never heard of him.
Owen Arriete is his name.

The theater is very small, but the prima donna is Mrs.
Follett, who I had heard of though I think she must be quite
old, probably at least forty, and she is widowed and nearly at
the end of her career. She was there, along with the tour manager, Mr. Cone (who looks like the villain in a melodrama—he
has that thin mustache and the blackest hair that's shiny with
macassar). There was also a Mr. Robert Wilson, who is the
maestro, and I liked him right away, though he is as flashy as a
younker and he had on a bright red vest and blond hair that
shone in the gaslight.

I held Barret's hand tightly, but then they all greeted
Gideon with such warmth and said, "So this is the girl you've
spoken so much about!" so Gideon was not lying when he said
he'd talked of me to them often, and I felt less nervous because of it. Then Barret handed Mr. Wilson my music, and he
frowned when he looked at it. I thought I had made the wrong
choices, a tune from the *Maid of Artois* and Zerlina's aria
from *Don Giovanni:* "Vedrai carino," which I thought were
good enough and which Herr Wirt had recommended I sing
because he had practiced me with them enough, but I told
Mr. Wilson that if he didn't like those I could also sing
Donizetti or Bellini, and his eyebrows went up and he said,
"You must be a very accomplished young lady, Miss Conrad."
Then Barret told him I had as my teacher Herr Wirt from the
Lutheran Church, and Mr. Wilson seemed impressed by that—
well, why shouldn't he be? Herr Wirt is one of the best singing
teachers in the city, even if he's in Kleindeutschland.

Mr. Wilson accompanied me instead of Gideon, but his

playing was fine enough, if not inspired. It was the very first time I'd sung on a real stage, and the sound seemed so rich and strong. When I sing at the church I always feel as if I am not myself, but something apart from the world, but today it was as if my voice had wings and was flying, and I knew this was what I <u>must</u> do—this is what I am meant for.

When I finished, Mr. Wilson rose from the piano shouting Brava! and Mr. Cone said to Gideon, "Well, Price, it does seem as if you've found our seconda donna after all." I was flushed and excited, but Mrs. Follett said I was very young and what if I was to do something absurd like fall in love on the tour and that I would have an obligation to the company and did I know what that meant. And Gideon told her he would watch out for me, and she said, "Isn't that a little like giving the fox the run of the henhouse?" which made no sense at all, because Gideon is in love with Willa and not me, but I didn't care anyway, I was so happy.

I am truly to go on tour!!!

They say I will be paid $75/month and we are to leave the beginning of April and be gone through July. We are to play in Boston, Philadelphia, Chicago, and Portsmouth and some places in between.

After the audition, Gideon said I would need a new dress, one to make the old debauched critics in the audience fall in love with me, and Barret said I was a good girl, not *eine Dirne,* and Mama would never agree to make a dress like that. But then Gideon talked of what it would be like when I was a prima donna as famous as Adelina Patti, and it was so exciting that Barret agreed I must have the dress. I was content to do whatever the two of them decided, but I do think I am certainly old enough to wear an off-the-shoulder gown, though Barret is right and Mama would no doubt suffer apoplexy if she knew I meant to do so.

Gideon took us up Broadway, and it was like another world. I had never been up so far, but it seemed to me beautiful and big and I thought how I would love to hold it in my

hand—all of it: the snarled traffic and the carriage drivers
swearing at one another and the sound of wheels and hooves
and carriage whips and the dogs in the streets and the plac-
ards and posters and notices that the wind tore from the walls
and scattered about our feet as if they were flower petals
thrown upon a stage. Even men were wearing signs there!
They all said the most enticing things, about shawls just arriving from Paris and the best perfumes and such and I wondered how it would feel to see those things every day—how
would one decide which shops to visit when they were all so
tempting? The grocers extended their bins so far out into the
sidewalks that we had to walk on the garbage mounded in the
street to get around them, but I saw ladies in silks and lace
doing so too, lifting their skirts and tiptoeing so as not to get
their beautiful shoes dirty, though I suppose they could have
afforded more than one pair, and I said to Barret, "When I'm
rich, I shan't care about soiling my shoes, as I shall have a different pair for every day." Oh! to think of it!

When Gideon stopped in front of A. T. Stewart's I was certain he was teasing. Stewart's!!! It was a castle made of glass
and cast iron, leading five stories up to a great rotunda, and
there were no things for sale in the windows, but we could see
inside, to the counters with low shelves behind them, all laden
with scarves and hats and gloves and things, and the benches
with men waiting, and clerks in their dark suits running
about and ladies in hats and flounces and pelisses turning
away one thing after another, as if there could be anything
more wonderful than what they were shown!

The porters opened the doors for us, and I stopped and
gaped like some silly fish—oh, it was so loud! The clatter of
hundreds of shoe heels, of catalog pages turning, a deep rumble that seemed to come from either above or below; I could
not tell which, but it seemed to bounce off the bare floors and
echo into the gaslit chandeliers and the stairs that went up
and up and up into the open rotunda, and then bounce back
again. It was too much for my ears and my eyes, all of it, the

salesclerks and the cashiers behind their latticed pens and
the boys running with their sales slips, as if they moved to the
music of that rumble.

Gideon laughed at me and took us up the stairs to the Ladies
floor. Barret told me not to touch anything, though Gideon
told us it was all right to touch, and after that I could not keep
from doing so. Gideon picked out a gown in rose satin with a
bodice of a lace flounce decorated with a silk rose at its center
that he said was perfect for a blonde of my coloring. Barret
said that we couldn't afford it, and Gideon said we could repay
him when I'd made us all rich. Oh, how beautiful the dress
was! Gideon was right; it became me very well, though it was a
bit big. Even Barret liked it, and Gideon said what a beauty I'd
become. He said he would have his mother, who is a seamstress
there, bring it home when it was altered and he would keep it for
me until we leave so Mama will never know. And though Barret
did not seem exactly to approve, all he said was, "You are
pretty in it, Bina." And Gideon said I looked an angel and the
audience would think so too, and Barret laughed and clapped
his shoulder and thanked him for being such a good friend to
our family, and for showing such an interest in my career.

My career!!! Soon the world will know my name, and I
have Gideon to thank for all of it.

APRIL 10, 1871—Today we boarded the train for the tour. It
was my first train ride ever, and it was very noisy and bumpy
and dirty. The cars rocked from side to side until I was almost
sick, and when I put down the window, soot and ash flew in
like snow and a live coal fell on my sleeve and nearly burnt a
hole in it! Mrs. Follett told me that if I insisted on acting like
a country bumpkin, she would have to move elsewhere and
bade me close the window again, which I was glad to do, not
because of her but because the ash was like to ruin my dress.
Everything passed by so quickly it made me think of when
I was little and Barret would chase me down the street and
I would run so fast everything was a blur.

The whole company was on the train. Here I shall list them all: the minstrels, of course, who are all men and very silly and who flirt with all the women, though not with me because Barret and Gideon told them not to. There are six of them. Then there is the violinist, Mr. Arriete, who is dark haired and very round and quiet, and his wife is like a little Dresden doll and much younger than he is, though she is as retiring as her husband. Then Mrs. Follett and Mr. Cone and Mr. Wilson, of course.

Our lead tenor is Paolo Rinzetti. He is quite nice and very handsome. He is Italian, and he has dark hair and eyes and very white teeth and he is the vainest man I have ever known, but he is very honest about it, so one cannot help but like him. I wondered at first that he had the lead tenor roles, and Gideon the comprimario ones, but Mrs. Follett prefers Paolo, and the truth is that Gideon is so fine with the different character parts—it seems so easy for him to change his voice and his demeanor to make none of them like the other—that it is best for him to do it. And I'm happier for that, because it means that he and I have duets together, which would not be the case if he were the lead.

Then there is Senor Barto, our basso, who comes from Venezuela and who does not speak very good English. He is quite old, his hair more gray than brown, and he has a nose the size of a squash, and has mostly nothing to say to me.

And here is the best part! I have a hotel room to myself in Philadelphia! Mrs. Arriete shares her husband's, of course, and Mrs. Follett will not share hers, and because I am the only other woman I have my own and the bed is to be mine alone!!! I am sure it will seem strange without Willa, but I am happy to accommodate! Gideon and Barret and Paolo must all room together, and Barret says Paolo is very messy, and I told him he was welcome to throw a pallet in my room, but as much as I love my brother, I was glad when he refused.

Then we went to the theater to rehearse before the show. It

is nearly as small as the Manchetti, but I don't care because I saw the placard out front and it was so exciting. It said:

FIVE DAYS ONLY!!!

New York City's Famous

MANCHETTI COMPANY

FEATURING

MRS. FOLLETT

IN MANY ROLES AND

OWEN ARRIETE

RENOWNED VIOLINIST

ALSO FEATURED

MANCHETTI TOWN MINSTRELS!!!!

7:00 P.M., WITH TWO SHOWS ON SATURDAY NITE,
7:00 P.M. AND 10:00 P.M.

I was not mentioned, of course, but Gideon says it's only a matter of time before my name is above Mrs. Follett's and then my name alone.

When I saw the sets upon the stage they seemed almost magic. Though I've seen them a hundred times during rehearsals, I said to Gideon, "*Gott im Himmel*, it's so beautiful!" and he told me not to speak German, that we weren't in Kleindeutschland anymore, and Barret said we weren't ashamed of being German, and Gideon said, "You don't need to be ashamed of it. Just don't advertise it. Don't give them a reason to dismiss Sabine," and Paolo said all the Germans knew how to do was make sausage, that real art belonged to the Italians, and we all laughed, but I think Gideon is right, and I am determined not to speak German again until I am home.

* * *

Oh Oh Oh!! Tonight my career began! I do not think I can
write it all without my fingers growing tired and sore! But
I shall try, because I don't want to forget one moment of it,
and it is very late and I cannot sleep at all. It feels as if my
blood is jumping through my veins!

To start at the beginning: Mrs. Follett has her dressing
room, and all the men theirs, and so I was given a shed of a
room that was obviously meant for the corps de ballet, though
I was the only one in it. The floors were warped and worn and
stained with spilled rouge. There were cracks in the walls that
let in the damp evening air, and the large mirror was cracked
too so that I looked like some gorgon with one side of my face
higher than the other. There were only two rough benches for
furniture, and one of them rocked unevenly when I sat upon
it. But it is my first dressing room!

I wore the rose satin gown and did my hair as Gideon told
me to, with some of it pinned high upon the crown and the
rest loose, and with my powder and rouge I looked quite gar-
ish. Even Barret looked startled when he came to give me a
little posy of flowers for good luck.

Then the stagehand knocked on the door and said, "Full
house, Miss Conrad," and Barret smiled at me and it was not
until that moment that I felt nervous at all. But suddenly
I was, and when Barret and I went into the wings, it was very
hot and the minstrel players were milling about in their black-
face and practicing their dance steps, the prop boys dashing
through us and leaning against the ropes that controlled the
curtains and the backdrops and people bumping into the sets
and whispering sotto voce. Even through all that, I could hear
the audience talking and coughing and the creak of the seats
as they settled, and though I'd sung before audiences many
times before, I must confess I was nervous. In the Völksstadt
there was shouting and drinking and singing along and chil-

dren running about half drunk themselves, and much of the
time the crowd was so busy talking they did not pay much attention, but this was different. It occurred to me then that
these people had paid to see us! I had never sung before a paying audience who expected good value for their money, and
suddenly I was so afraid.

The stagehand yelled out, "One minute!" and the minstrels
began lining up and Barret and I got pushed back near the
ropes. I heard the audience grow quiet and then Mr. Cone
announced us, and the stagehand pulled on the rope and the curtain whooshed open and the glare of the gaslights was blinding
and reflecting onto the faces of the audience, so I could see
them from the wings, a sea of faces, and I cannot even describe
the extent of my terror!

I started to run back to my dressing room with Barret
coming after me, shouting "Sabine!" in a hoarse whisper. Before I got far, there was Mrs. Follett and Paolo and Gideon,
looking in my distress like monsters with their heavily kohled
eyes and reddened mouths. I was sweating, and I felt sick,
and Barret said, "Sabine, what's wrong?" and I truly thought
I might vomit there in the hallway and it would be the end of
my career. How disappointed Papa would be! Barret tried to
hold me and reassure me. He kept saying, "What is it? What's
wrong?" as if he didn't know what else to say, and he was
pounding clumsily on my back and looking as frightened as I
was and not helpful at all. He gave Gideon a panicked look
I did not miss and I heard him whisper above my head, "What
do I do?" when he thought I couldn't hear.

Then Gideon whispered something to Barret and took me
into a corner and I looked into his face, and in his makeup,
with his dark hair shining strangely red in the light and his
slashing brows, he was both beautiful and terrifying. He
pulled me into his arms and held me so tight against his chest I
could hear his heart beating, and he whispered, "Sweetheart,
how can I go on myself without you?" He kissed my forehead,

and then rubbed off the rouge he'd left there with his thumb, and suddenly I was ready to go on and my nervousness seemed only a bad dream.

And then . . . oh, how to describe the most sublime experience of my life? Simply to say it was pure joy to go upon that stage, that the moment I began to sing, I was transported. I felt the love of the audience and I felt as if I were singing that love back to them as purely and sweetly as I ever had before, and when it came time to hit the A I hardly thought about it at all, but sang it as easily as I ever had. They made me sing it four times!!! Four!!!! Even Mrs. Follett was only asked to sing her best aria twice, and Paolo not at all, and Gideon's smile was so large when they applauded my part in our duet that I don't think he minded. After we took our bows, he whooped and twirled me about in his arms and said, "You did it, sweetheart! They loved you!!!"

Now I must go, because Mr. Cone and Mr. Wilson are taking us all to dinner and we are going to celebrate our success!

PHILADELPHIA, APRIL 11, 1871—I have a terrible headache from too much wine, and no sleep, and also I fear from a terrible distress.

This is what happened: after dinner, Gideon took me aside and said I had been such a brilliant diamond out there on the stage that it had hurt his eyes to look at me. I told him that I owed it all to him, and he said it was only that he understood me so much better than did anyone else. I know this is true; after all, I have known him such a very long time . . . two years at least! and he has always looked out for me. I was a bit drunk and when he smiled at me he was so beautiful I thought how lucky Willa was to have him, and—oh, I was more than a bit drunk, I think!—in an excess of passion I said that this was only the beginning, that I meant to have the whole world at my feet.

He didn't laugh. He said: "If it's the world you want, Sabine, I'll bring it to you. I promise it."

His words were still in my head as we left. I confess I was nearly swaying on the way back to the hotel, so Barret had to take my arm to keep me from falling on *meine hinterteile*—oh yes, I am not to speak German!—I mean my ass.

We all went to our rooms, but I was too excited still to sleep, and the music would not leave me and the night played itself out before my eyes. I wished for someone to talk to— even Willa would have done, with her disapproving eyes and her constant "There are other things in life than music, Sabine." Then I heard footsteps in the hall and as the whole company is on this floor I thought it must be one of us, and so I went to my door to peek out, and it was Gideon. He was barefoot, and he wore only his trousers and his shirt. I was about to call out to him when he knocked on Mrs. Follett's door, which opened quickly, as if she were expecting him, and she was hardly dressed at all! I was so startled I gasped aloud, but luckily they did not hear me, because they were kissing, and then she pulled him into her room and closed the door.

Oh, what shall I tell Willa?

APRIL 12, 1871—Today I told Barret what I had seen last night and discovered that he has known about it all along! He seemed very embarrassed and tried to explain to me that sometimes men had other women and that it meant nothing. I told him I doubted Willa would think that, and Barret sighed and said I was still very young and couldn't understand. "Things are different here, Bina. It isn't real life."

It feels the opposite to me, as if my life in Kleindeutschland was the unreal one, and I don't understand why he would keep this from Willa, who is waiting at home for Gideon to come back and marry her. But when I asked Barret if it wouldn't be best for her to know the truth, he became quite serious and said that if she breaks off with Gideon, Papa will call us both home, which I know is true, because the only reason I was allowed to go on tour is because Papa thinks of Gideon as his future son and trusts him more than he trusts

Barret. I thought of my vow to Willa, but I do not want to go home, and so I have promised not to say anything yet.

APRIL 13, 1871—The reviews are in!! I am the "jewel of the evening," and the reviewer compared me to Adelina Patti! I am beside myself with joy, and so was Barret, who brought me the newspaper, and Mr. Cone and Mr. Wilson were very pleased.

Mrs. Follett was not.

When she saw the reviews this morning it occasioned such a screaming and cursing that it brought nearly the entire company out into the hallway to witness her. I would have thought she was performing the mad scene from *Lucia* and when she saw Gideon she screamed that it was his fault for bringing me to the company, and slapped him across the face so hard she left the imprint of her hand. She called me a little whore and accused me of taking everything away from her and I called her a tone-deaf braying donkey and she lunged at me as if she would scratch my eyes out, but Barret stepped between us. Then Gideon told her she was making a fool of herself, and she said *she* was the prima donna and it was best if none of us forgot it.

That was when Mr. Cone and Mr. Wilson arrived. She told them she would not do another performance with me. Mr. Cone said she was the Manchetti Company prima donna and not to worry, and she seemed to calm then, and he escorted her back into her room and I wished I had not called her a braying donkey, because then perhaps she would not have said she wouldn't share the stage with me, and I was afraid I would be sent home.

Then Mr. Wilson said to Gideon, "You couldn't keep the paper from her until she'd had her coffee?" and I realized they all knew that he was Mrs. Follett's lover, and I was so angry I could hardly stand to look at anyone, and when Mr. Wilson said, "I'm so sorry, Miss Conrad, that you had to witness such a scene. Please think nothing of it," I turned on my heel and marched back into my room without a word.

From the *Philadelphia Eagle,* dated April 12, 1871.

AMUSEMENTS

Manchetti Company's First Night at the Periquot Theater

THE Manchetti Company performed the first of five nights at the Periquot Theater on Monday, April 10, and conquered their audience with a success hardly paralleled at any small theater in the city. Chief among the delights of the evening was the debut of heretofore unknown *seconda donna* Miss Sabine Conrad, singing various roles in selections from *Ernani, La Sonnambula, Die Zauberflöte,* and *Don Giovanni.* Miss Conrad so electrified the audience with the sublimity of her pure and luscious soprano that there was demanded four encores, each sung as beautifully as the last. Her tone is rich, consummately clear and strong and with the creaminess and range of the most lauded sopranos among us. The presence upon the stage of the young and comely Miss Conrad demands the eye as has no one since Adelina Patti, and her dramatic instincts are unparalleled even by sopranos with much more experience.

The rest of the company, including Mrs. Olive Follett, a *prima donna* of longstanding reputation, were adequate and well suited enough for their parts, and the program included the well-known violinist Owen Arriete and the Manchetti Minstrels, each of whom engaged the audience fully.

The jewel of the evening, however, was Miss Conrad, and it is to be hoped that the Manchetti Company soon realizes the depth of talent in the young lady and elevates her to the *prima donna* status she deserves. There is no doubt in the opinion of this critic that we are destined to hear very great things from Miss Conrad in the future.

The program continues through the 15th, with two shows scheduled for Saturday.

At that moment I did not care if I spoke to any of them again. But then there was a knock on my door, and it opened before I could answer. I turned to tell Barret to get out and leave me alone, but it wasn't Barret at all. It was Gideon, and he looked so wary and guilty at the same time that it was obvious he'd deceived me on purpose. I screamed "How dare you!" and ran at him. He caught my hands before I could touch him, and held me away, and that made me angry too, so I kicked him, and he let me kick him and struggle until my breath was gone.

Then he pulled me into his chest and whispered he was sorry and could he explain? I told him I didn't want to hear his explanations, that he had betrayed my sister and my family, and I didn't know how I could sing with him knowing what a liar he was.

He told me Follett had taken a fancy to him on their last tour and that he must be with her for now, because if she were to leave this tour would be over and we would be sent home. He said he was working to make us famous and that meant he must sometimes do things that he did not like to do.

Then he said that if I wished it, he would end things with Follett today, and we could go back to New York and see about getting on with another tour, though it would be difficult, as most of them are already gone for the summer, and it would be a pity because I am getting such good reviews that he thought I had a chance for an audition with Mr. Maretzek in the fall. But that could wait until next year, because the only thing that mattered now was my trust in him. He looked so repentant and sad I could not bear it.

I did not realize how important he was to the tour. How could I make a decision that would ruin things for everyone? This is such an opportunity for me as well; surely Willa would forgive if she knew? Would she really ask me to give up the only thing I love? I cannot believe she would. And to have the chance to sing on such a stage as that at the Academy of Music, before all the best of society . . . It would bring me the fame

I've wished so long for, and Gideon cares nothing for Follett—
he told me so, and I must believe him, because she is so old,
and Willa is so young and pretty. Gideon's affair with Follett
will be over the moment the tour is. He has promised it. Why
should I hurt my sister over something that will make no difference in the end?

So I told him I did not wish to leave, and that I did not
doubt him.

CHAPTER 3

Seattle, Washington Territory—February 1881

They came in as they always did, half drunk already, shaking off the rain like dogs. It was a Saturday night, which meant that the Palace was full, because Saturday was when the miners and lumbermen got paid, and every girl we had was working, alternating between the stage and the floor and the boxes lining the balcony opposite—ten of them, more than any other box-house in Seattle, each curtained on the side that faced the stage so that one could watch the show if one were so inclined, though in the two years since we'd added the boxes, I could count on one hand the number of times I'd seen that happen.

It had been my idea to change the Palace from the rough saloon it had been into a boxhouse. My first year here, I'd scrubbed the floors until my hands were raw and spent nearly every night in Johnny's room, and waited for him to tire of me. He hated my scar and the brittle coarseness of my dark hair ("What the hell d'you do to it?"), and marveled that he wanted me at all. In bed, I performed for him the way I'd been taught, a trained monkey now, willing to do whatever I must to survive, and he had marveled too at my skill. He would say,

"The men watch you, you know. There ain't no one in this place who wouldn't want to be where I am right now. Even Duncan. There's something . . . it's like you expect people to look at you—suppose you tell me why that is?"

"I don't know," I would say, and then I would wrap my hand around him and he would groan and forget that he'd asked, and then one day I asked him why he never used the stage, as he'd gone to so much trouble to build it. It had seemed to mock me with its emptiness; I hated the ghosts that paraded across it, and I knew the only way to make them disappear was to bring it alive again, though not in the way Johnny intended. He'd told me what he meant for this place to be, that he'd been partners with a man who ran a theater in San Francisco before he'd come up here, and that he was working to turn the place into a real theater. The Palace was close enough to respectable businesses that it wasn't so absurd to think it might one day be respectable itself. But it was the last thing I wanted. The danger of such a thing was unthinkable, to bring those here who might recognize me. . . . . In spite of the time that had passed, I still didn't feel safe. I never went out onto the floor without searching the crowd to see if someone watched me too closely, without wondering: *Will it be tonight that they find me?* And so I'd forestalled him. It took all my skill to satisfy his ambitions with half measures, but finally I told him of the concert houses I'd seen, of girls who took turns singing and dancing upon the stage and then worked the boxes after, and he had gone thoughtful and asked if I believed such a place could work here.

That had been two years ago. He'd said he would make me a partner if I would teach the girls to move the way I did and run them, and though I knew it was really because he was in love with me, I took advantage of it anyway. Scrubbing floors and cleaning spilled whiskey and tobacco-stained spit and the occasional blood left my thoughts too free, and I wanted not to think. I wanted to forget. So I'd mired myself in the business of the boxhouse, and mostly I liked it well enough. I was good at it. If nothing else, it kept me surrounded by people. I'd never been very good at being alone.

Now Jenny was onstage, dancing with her hoop, while in the loge above, the orchestra—Paul on the violin and Ed with a bass and Billy too drunk as usual to do anything but massacre the piano—fumbled their way through "Camptown Races." After Jenny would come Annie and Lil, who posed as two boys in top hats and trousers, with their hair cut short, and sang "Smick, Smack, Smuck" rather badly, though no one in the audience seemed to care about that. The two were a house favorite, and they were constantly leading men to the boxes, no doubt due in part to the novelty of disrobing a woman clothed as a man. Then there would be Pauline, who would gasp her way sickly and melodramatically through "Willie Has Gone to War."

Tonight, it all made me irritable. Jenny especially. When she came off the stage to hooting and applause, swinging her hips suggestively as she went down the stairs, I was even more annoyed—the girls were supposed to be selling drinks first and foremost because it was where we made the most money. The boxes were a sidelight; our percentages were much lower when the girls were off the floor. Worse than that, it was the second time tonight she'd taken that same man to the box, and I'd seen him here nearly every night the last two weeks. It didn't hurt for a girl to have her favorites, of course, but the problem with Jenny was that the money she turned in wasn't reconciling with how often she was with him, which meant she was giving away a service for free, and that was something that couldn't be tolerated.

I heard the opening of the office door behind me, and then I felt Johnny at my back, sliding his hand over my hip as he leaned over me for a glass. "Frowning, Margie? What for?"

"Jenny's not selling drinks. And I think she's sweet on one of her customers."

Johnny grabbed the glass and stepped away. "You want me to take care of it?"

I shook my head. "Not yet. I'll talk to her first."

He poured a shot of whiskey for both of us, then looked over the floor—the tables were full. Jim Ryan and Lee Blotsky, the professional gamblers who paid us a cut to run their own tables, were no doubt doing well.

Johnny swigged the whiskey. "What else?"

"Billy had Annie cornered again."

"He drunk?"

"When isn't he?"

"About time to find ourselves another piano player, I think."

"It was hard enough to find him."

Johnny's gaze never left the tables. "Surely there's someone in this godforsaken town who took piano lessons at his mother's knee. I'll have Duncan ask around." He set his glass on the bar with a little thud. "Joy's ready to leave the mop behind, by the way. She wants to take to the stage, assuming she's got any talent, which I doubt, since none of them do."

"It's hard to be a scrubwoman in this place," I said.

"You would know." He glanced at me. "You doin' all right tonight, honey?"

I felt the wariness behind his question. I met his eyes and managed a smile. "Just fine. Perhaps you could walk me home later?"

He hesitated, and that hesitation said that he'd already noted my mood tonight and knew what it meant. I shared his bed rarely now, only whenever the other girls had gone home and we were both drunk, or those times, like tonight, when I felt the heavy press of memories and I would do nearly anything to keep them at bay. Some days I just couldn't make myself ignore the ugliness around me. Some days nothing felt it would ever be right again. Today was one of them.

Johnny motioned to my shot of whiskey, still untouched on the bar, and said, "We'll see. Drink up. I'll make the rounds."

I sighed and watched as he went around the bar and out onto the floor, where he would smile and greet the customers and restore whatever order was faltering—the Palace always felt dangerous, as if violence bubbled beneath the surface, waiting to erupt, and only Johnny's presence kept it from doing so. I'd been right to align myself with him three years ago—Johnny protected what was his, and that extended to me.

I took the shot he'd left me and sipped it slowly. Not the rotgut whiskey we sold to the customers, nor the watered-down stuff the girls drank, but the best Johnny could get. It was smooth and sweet. I watched him stop at Jim Ryan's table and laugh at something one of the men there said, throwing back his head so the gaslight caught in his dark blond hair, and then I saw Sally—one of the newest girls, and Johnny's latest fancy—glance up at him from the next table over and smile, and how he smiled back before he glanced over his shoulder at me. Checking to see if I noticed, if I cared, just as he always did, though he'd never admit it.

I turned away and drank the rest of the whiskey in a gulp, waiting for Jenny to emerge from the box. I caught Lee Blotsky's eye, and he motioned me over with a subtle flick of his fingers. I pasted on a smile and went, greeting those I passed with a "Hello, boys" or a "It's good to see you again, mister" to make certain they felt welcome. It was what Johnny called casting my net. He said it was why the Palace outdid the other houses in the Lava Beds. Not just because the girls were prettier, or because we had a better eye for talent, though both of those things were true. But because, despite the ugly scar that marred my looks, there wasn't a lumberman or miner I'd smiled at who didn't think eventually he could talk me into going with him into one of those boxes. "It's the promise that matters," Johnny had told me. "The world spins on hope, honey. Just keep 'em hoping."

I was hardly at Lee's table before I felt the tension among

the men, their wary stiffness as they looked down at their cards, and I knew why he'd called me over.

I pressed myself to his back, wrapping my arms around his shoulders, smiling as I tickled his ear with my fingers. "Mind if I join you boys?"

Lee turned his face to mine. I was so close his mustache, nearly as white as his hair, brushed my cheek. "I'd be pleased if you would, Miss Margie. I could use a good luck charm, given that I've been doing poorly all night."

"What about the rest of you?" I purred. "How about a drink on the house to smooth my way?"

The others looked up; I felt the tension at the table ease. They put down their cards, and one of them gathered up the winnings as I motioned to Sally to bring drinks for the table. I loosed myself from Lee and pulled up a chair—close enough to him to imply his ownership—and seated myself with a smile, my skirts billowing about me, hoop-less, bustle-less: fashions like that were impractical here, where they only slowed one down and seemed a gross pretension, but I couldn't deny I missed them, just as I missed the petticoats and the silks and satins. . . . My own dress was only a coarse dark wool, my legs bare beneath it, because in the constant rain of winter, all stockings did was get wet and stay that way.

The melancholy came over me again. I forced it back and broadened my smile, and when Sally brought the drinks I drank mine down in a gulp and asked her to bring another. Lee leaned close and whispered in my ear, "The one in the plaid shirt's cheatin'. Keep an eye on him."

After that I made a point of smiling at the one in the plaid shirt. I flirted with him until he was flushed and fumbling with his cards, too disconcerted to play whatever tricks he'd come with. Four hands and, for me, four whiskeys later, he folded and left with a longing glance at me, and I was feeling reckless and warm with the whiskey I'd drunk, my melancholy, if not banished, then at least deadened. My job here was done, and I set down my cards and rose, squeezing Lee's pink-clad shoulder and getting a wink of appreciation in return.

I went back to the bar and leaned over it, reaching to touch Duncan's arm where he stood on the other side. "Another drink, please," I said, and though he frowned, he grabbed the bottle.

"Lee having trouble tonight?" he asked, pouring whiskey into a glass and sliding it across.

"No longer."

"Your eyes are pretty bright, Marguerite."

"Like the stars," I told him. I turned to lean back against the bar and stare out over the now-dwindling crowd. When I saw Jenny sidle up to the bar to order drinks—and about time too—I looked for her little paramour, who was now sitting at Jim Ryan's table, laughing. I poured myself another whiskey and went over to him, pressing myself to his back so he looked over his shoulder, a smile on his face that faded into confusion when he saw it wasn't Jenny.

"You winning yet, mister?" I asked him, putting the lie of interest into my eyes.

He flushed. "N-not yet, Miss M—Marguerite."

"Well then, maybe you need some luck." I turned and motioned to Lil at the next table for a chair, and reluctantly she got off her ass and gave me hers. I pulled it up beside Jenny's man, as close as I could. I put my hand on his thigh, high up near his crotch, and took a sip of my whiskey and said, "Let me see your cards."

He showed them to me nervously, and I blew on them and said, "There now, we'll see if that doesn't do the trick," and winked at Jim Ryan when Jenny's man turned back to the table. Jim acknowledged me with a subtle nod.

Jenny's miner won the next hand, of course, and the next, and I ordered two more whiskeys, one for him and one for me. When they were brought, I toasted him and we both downed the shot in a gulp. He was grinning, his eyes glassy with drink and elation from winning, and I put my elbow on his shoulder, dangling my fingers in his hair, leaning close enough that my lips brushed his ear when I said, "I've been noticing you seem to like Jenny."

I felt him shiver. He licked his lips. "Well, yes, but . . ."

I traced the seam in his trousers, up to the buttons, and he swallowed convulsively. I saw Jenny across the room. She was staring at us as she set out drinks, and I pretended not to see her and took the miner's chin in my hand. "Maybe you might come to like me better," I whispered to him. "But I'll tell you right off, mister, I don't share," and then I kissed him deeply and skillfully. When I drew away he was breathing so hard I thought he might swoon.

I smiled at him and rose. When he started to rise, I put my hand on his shoulder and pushed him back down into his chair.

Jim Ryan said, "Are you in or out, mister?"

"He's in," I said to Jim.

Jenny's man said, "But . . . don't you want to go to a box?"

I leaned down close to him again. "Like I said, I don't share. When you've proved yourself to me, we'll see," and I walked away, leaving him to stare after me.

The floorboards tilted a bit beneath my feet, but I steadied myself and went up to the bar and Duncan slid another whiskey my way with a little frown.

Just then, I felt a hand on my shoulder, and I turned to see Jenny, nearly teary-eyed with fury. "Just what were you doing with Travis?"

"Is that his name?"

"He's mine. You knew he was mine! I been his favorite for weeks."

I turned to face her, leaning back against the bar, feeling a satisfaction at her anger that only increased the warmth from the whiskey. "I know," I said, summoning up the lie of sympathy and concern. "That's why I went to talk to him. Turns out I was right to be worried over how much time you're spending with him. I think you'd better keep your distance, Jenny."

"Why?" Her little mouth pursed mutinously.

I leaned close, saying sotto voce, "He's seeing Dr. Bell, you know."

"For what?"

"He's got the pox."

Jenny's mouth dropped open in horror. "But I . . . he never said—"

"Did you expect him to confess it?" I asked. "Oh, honey, he fooled you, didn't he? What have I said? Never trust a man. I'll tell you what . . . I'll arrange for you to see the doctor yourself in the next few days. But . . . no more boxes until you do, Jenny. You understand?"

She turned bright red and nodded. I could see she didn't know whether to believe me or not, and I liked that too, that she hated what I'd done but had no way to fight it. I'd made certain of it. That miner wouldn't chase another woman but me in this place until he figured out I had no intention of having him. By then, Jenny would be gone, or onto other men.

I patted her shoulder and turned back to the bar. "Now go on. You can make it up in drinks if you work hard."

When she was gone, Duncan gave me a wry look. "Is he poxy?"

"How the hell do I know?" I asked irritably. My voice sounded low and far away, and the effort of manipulating Jenny had left me feeling mean. The soft languor the whiskey had brought turned, suddenly growing sharp edges. I felt unsettled and angry. I reached for the whiskey.

Duncan swept it away before I could grab it. "I'll go get Johnny," he said.

"What for?"

His deep brown eyes grew troubled, and even that annoyed me. I let myself sag against the bar. I felt as if the violence that lived in the Palace had somehow crawled beneath my skin—not an unfamiliar feeling of late, and one I hated, but I was beyond curing it now. The only thing that would appease it was a fight, and I was spoiling for one. I wished Jenny would come back so I could tell her what I really thought.

"Margie, maybe you better go into my office for a bit."

Johnny's voice came from behind me. I saw the relief break on Duncan's face. It only made me angrier. "I don't need to go into your office. I'm not a child."

He glanced past me to Duncan, who obviously made some sign, because Johnny nodded slightly. He took my arm and said, "Maybe we should get you home then."

His touch roused my desire. It was restless and painful; I knew already that it would not be easily assuaged. But it was better than the anger I hardly understood, and I knew too that Johnny could soothe it for a time. "Only if you come with me."

He said to Duncan, "Can you watch the place for a bit?"

"Nothing too hard to handle," Duncan said. "Marguerite already fixed Blotsky's table."

"Did she now?" Johnny glanced down at me. "It's good to see you ain't completely useless tonight, honey."

I leaned into him and whispered, "Why don't you let me show you how useful I can be?"

He sighed and released my arm, and then he went to his office to fetch my cloak and his coat. He handed the cloak to me and tucked his gun into his coat pocket. "I won't be long," Johnny told Duncan, and I said, "Don't expect him for a while."

Duncan rolled his eyes, but Johnny ignored me. He led the way to the back door, and then the two of us were outside, past the storage lean-to where Duncan slept, and down the slick steps off the narrow porch to the muddy street below.

The rain was steady but light. It was late, but music spilled from the saloon next door, men yelled drunkenly in the streets, and a line snaked from the brothel on the corner to nearly around the block. I knew from experience those things wouldn't die until dawn.

Johnny said nothing, only led me silently the few blocks to my boardinghouse. There was no welcoming light at all, the windows were dark and dead. I liked it better that way. In the dark it was impossible to see how rough it was, or the grotesque attempts Mrs. McGraw made at beautifying it: the twining sweetbriar near the door twisting from the blood-stained sawdust she got at the neighboring butcher's, the flower-pots at the corner of the ramp that held no flowers but only dead stumps of plants drowning in pools of stinking piss from dumped chamber pots.

The front door was unlocked. Johnny opened it and waited for me to precede him. The first-floor entry and the sitting room just off it were wallpapered with roses, but the stairs were dark, and the upstairs walls were unfinished lumber that sometimes left splinters in my fingers as I felt my way up. I went inside, swaying a little, falling once against the wall, and he put his hand on my arm to steady me, following me up instead of telling me good night. He meant to oblige me after all. Thank God for that.

My room was toward the end of the hall, near the toilet, which had to be on the second floor because when the tides came in, it pushed the crap right back up the pipes. I heard Tessa, who worked at the Bijou boxhouse, in the next room, heaving about and groaning. She was with someone again, a not uncommon occurrence.

I unlocked the door and slipped inside, and when Johnny came in behind me, I threw my arms around his neck and kissed him. His mustache was soft and thick. I felt the wet of his tongue against my lips, and then with a sigh, he pulled away, saying, "We need to talk."

I unbuttoned his coat. "We can talk later."

Firmly he pushed me away. "Slow down, honey." He went to the candle on my bed table and picked up the box of matches, striking one to light the wick. The candle flame flickered and danced in the tides of our breath; our shadows were elongated and strange against the walls of my narrow room, seeming to intersect even when we weren't touching. From behind the wall on the other side, Tessa's moans began to increase in intensity and volume, and whoever she was with moaned in response. The sound only increased my own hunger, and my frustration.

Johnny smiled thinly and gestured to the wall. "You get to listen to that every night?"

"Some." I started toward him. "Turnabout's fair play, don't you think? Come and kiss me."

He held up his hand to stop me. "You're having another of your bad nights."

"You could make it better."

He laughed a little. "Not for longer than the time it takes me to fuck you, Margie. You and I both know that. It's starting to affect things at the Palace. You're drunk half the time. The girls are starting to notice."

From the next room Tessa's moans had turned high and staccato, bel canto–like embellishments to an unheard tune, imitations of a coy flute, *ah ah ahahah, ohhhh!* and my washbasin shook and tipped with the final *thud thud thud* against the wall.

My skin was too sensitive. I wanted him to touch me. I wanted him to take the restless uneasiness away.

"Which girls?"

Johnny seemed impervious. "It don't matter which ones."

My anger surged back, more prickly than before. I could not keep my voice from rising. "You mean Sally." I advanced on him. "Just because she's your latest whore—"

Someone banged on the wall. From the other room, Tessa yelled, "Shut up in there! We're trying to get some sleep!"

"Perhaps you should do your fucking earlier then," I yelled back. I turned to Johnny. "I don't like her. I want her gone. If you don't do it, I will."

"Sally ain't the problem."

"The hell she isn't." I raised my hands, meaning to strike him.

He grabbed my wrists tightly. "You been looking for a fight all night. Don't tempt me to take you on."

But taking me on was exactly what I wanted. I wanted to hit him and hurt him, and then I wanted him to take me to bed and make my restlessness go away. And though there was a part of me that told me to back away, to relax, I could not listen to it. I heard myself shouting, "You and Duncan let those girls do whatever they like as long as they're on their knees whenever you call—"

His fingers tightened warningly on my wrists. "Take care, Margie."

"What's wrong?" I taunted. "Don't you like hearing the truth? Poor little Johnny doesn't like to admit a girl can twist him around her finger—"

"It's got to stop, Margie." His voice was so quiet it seemed to strip all sound from the room. He let go of my wrists and stepped back. "Once in a while ain't a problem; hell, everyone has a bad day. But lately all your days are bad ones. It's affecting business. You ain't any use to me like this, and I don't suffer anyone who's no use. Even you."

They were the first words he'd said that made their way through my anger. My agitation faded; instead what I felt was fear. Instinctively I stepped closer to him. I wrapped my arms around his neck and pressed my hips into his. "Don't say that," I whispered. "Don't say I'm no use. You know what I can do. I know you've got a use for that."

He pried my arms from his neck. "I don't got a taste for your temper tonight."

"Then I'll be good." I lifted my skirts, grabbing his hand, pushing his fingers against me. "Come on, Johnny. You know you still want this."

For a moment I thought I had him. His fingers gripped,

pulling just a little at the curls there so it stung, a punishment he knew I wanted. I pressed into him.

He leaned very close until I felt his mustache against my lips. Then he whispered, "What a fool you must think me, honey."

He pulled away. I was startled when he crossed the room to the door. I stood there, still holding up my skirts, my legs parted for him.

He stopped, his hand on the knob, and turned back to look at me. "You're good at that, honey. Better than most women ever get to be. But I'm tired of playing the whore for you."

My voice was only a breath when I said, "What do you mean?"

"You find someone else to fuck you through your tempers."

I let my skirts fall. "Johnny. No. Please. I don't want any-one else."

His smile was cold. "Sure you do, Margie. There's always been someone else in your head."

"That's not true," I said, but even I heard the lie in my voice.

"You think things through tonight. If you can't find some control, don't bother coming back in. You understand me?"

I took a deep breath. "Yes."

"No more drinking yourself stupid."

"I understand."

"Good," he said, and then, again, "Good. I'm auditioning girls in the morning. If you ain't there, I'll take it to mean you ain't coming back." He turned the knob.

"Johnny, please don't go," I begged. "Stay with me."

He only gave me a look that shamed me. "This is your first warning, Margie. Don't let it get to a second one."

Then he opened the door, and was gone.

CHAPTER 4

That night, I was plagued with nightmares, flashes of images that never stayed for more than a few moments, even when I wanted them to: a beautiful face hovering close and when I raised myself for a kiss it smiled and disappeared, turning instead into Johnny's face, into his brown eyes shifting cold and dark, and then that twisted too, becoming leering and distorted before everything went red, dripping blood into my eyes and onto my hands, which would never come clean, no matter how I scrubbed. . . .

I woke sweating, with my matted hair plastered to my face and neck and my skin crawling and pricking as if every little snag in the coarse sheets had hooked into it. These nightmares had been coming more and more often lately, and I didn't know why. Nor did I know why I could no longer completely shut them out, or why they lingered as if they meant no longer to be evaded or locked away. It had been three years. Surely that was enough time to forget?

I rose, shuddering as my bare feet hit the cold floor, and then I went to the furnace vent in the wall and put my hands to it to see if the heat was on. It was, but as usual, it had no more strength than a breath. I heard the metallic *clang clang clang* from the blacksmith's shop, and pulled aside the thread-bare brown calico curtains with the absurd ragged grosgrain ties to peer into the damp cold of late morning. Beyond the privy with its seeping pool of sewage in the yard, the gray-black smoke of the forge rose through the rain into the low-flung clouds.

I let the curtain drop into place and went to the washbasin. The water was cold, raising gooseflesh. As I reached for the towel, I was caught by the movement in the tiny square mirror nailed to the wall. What looked back at me was wavery as a spirit, a pale face surrounded by tangled and frizzing black hair, blue eyes that seemed too bright a color against the stark-ness of the rest. Because of the way the mirror was worn, the only thing that looked solid and real was the jagged pink scar striking its way from my temple along my hairline, in front of my ear to my jaw. Still bright, still raised, hardly faded or smoothed by the years. The doctor had done the best he could when he'd sewn me up, but it had been more than a day by then, and he'd told me sourly that there were worse things than no longer being beautiful; I was lucky it hadn't become infected.

I paused, putting my fingers to it, tracing its faint rise, feel-ing the numb strangeness of my touch, as if it didn't quite be-long to me. But it did. There were times when I thought it was the only real thing in my life.

"*There's always been someone else in your head.*" Johnny's words came to me like a song. "*You ain't any use to me like this, and I don't suffer anyone who's no use. Even you.*"

Tears pricked my eyes; I wiped them away almost viciously and forced myself to look more closely in the mirror, concen-trating instead on the hair at my temple, studying it as if it held the key to stopping my nightmares, to controlling my tempers, to forgetting. The distraction worked the moment

I spotted the faint gilding at the roots. At this point no one would think it anything but gray. Still, it was time to pay another visit to the druggist.

Things to do. Ways not to be alone. It was only the being alone that gave my nightmares or my memories any power. If Johnny had stayed, I would have been fine. . . . I felt the stirring of a now familiar anger.

"It's got to stop, Margie." "This is your first warning. Don't let it get to a second one."

Not today. I couldn't let my anger get the best of me today. Johnny would never tolerate it, and I had nothing else but him, nowhere else but the Palace. I knew better than to disregard his warning—the very fact that he hadn't stayed with me when he always had before was enough to show me just how serious he was.

What I needed were distractions. They were better than my own thoughts, and today there was plenty to distract me. The druggist for one. And the girls auditioning at the Palace this morning. It was enough to fill the next hours.

Quickly I dressed and pinned up my hair. I grabbed my cloak and the few coins I kept here from the bag I hid in a knothole beneath the bureau—a place Mrs. McGraw, the landlady, had not yet found in her searchings—and then I slipped into my pocket the derringer Duncan had given me and warned me never to be without. When I made my way downstairs, Mrs. McGraw was there, dusting the few pictures in the hallways, but mostly nosing into the comings and goings of her boarders, and as I reached the bottom of the stairs, she looked up with a smile that showed her missing and browning teeth. "Why good morning to you, Miz Olson. On your way to the Palace so early?"

"Auditioning girls today," I told her.

"You ain't et with us the past few days."

"I haven't been hungry."

"Are you sick then?"

"No, ma'am."

"Well, that's good. You could use some fattening up. I'll make the sausage hash tomorrow for breakfast. I know you're partial to it."

The thought made my stomach flip. I managed a weak smile and took the last step to the door. "Don't do anything special on my account. I can't say as I'll be here for breakfast tomorrow either."

"You're lookin' a bit bony—"

"Good day, Mrs. McGraw," I said firmly, stepping outside onto the narrow stoop and closing the door behind me.

I could smell that the tide was out. The stink of the mud-flats was heavy and pervasive. It was raining too, of course, the steady drizzle that was almost mistlike, hardly a rain at all, yet I knew from experience that it was almost the worst kind: it lulled one into thinking one wasn't getting wet, but seeped insidiously and with a damp chill that cut to the bone and never quite went away once it was there.

There were no boardwalks here, so I had no choice but to go into the muddy, potholed streets and dodge the horses and carts and deliverymen about the Lava Beds at this time of day. The mud splashed up my boots to my bare legs, and by the time I reached the druggist, I was as wet and freezing as I could have predicted I would be.

There was no one about but old Mr. Pollack, who took my coins for the packages of henna and black henna without comment, as he always did, though he winked at me as he said, "Good day to you, Miss Olson. Give my best to Mr. Langford— oh, and could you take this chloral to Duncan? You can sign for it."

I nodded and took the bottle, shoving the packages beneath my arm. We kept chloral hydrate behind the bar; a few drops in a troublesome customer's drink, and there were no more problems. He would be unconscious until he woke, hours later, where he'd been deposited on the ramp outside the Palace or in the mud beneath the pilings. He could count himself lucky for that; it meant Johnny wasn't beating the hell out of him, for one thing, but that wasn't the least of it. There were places in the Lava Beds where he'd be robbed or even murdered before he was dumped through a trapdoor for the tide to take away like so much refuse. More than one prostitute had taken advantage of those trapdoors as well, to dump a newborn or drown herself. There were times, especially in midwinter, when it would rain and be gray for weeks at a time and there would be almost an epidemic of bodies caught among the trestles that crisscrossed the harbor to the colliers beyond.

The melancholy was there again, and I shook my head free of my morbid thoughts and made my way to the Palace.

Duncan was leaning on the bar and drinking coffee, and a group of young women huddled close together near the stage, five of them today.

I went behind the bar and put my packages on the shelf beneath before I handed Duncan the bottle of chloral.

"Thanks," he said, putting it away.

I poured myself some coffee and took a sip. "Any of them look good?"

"I like the blonde," he said with a smile.

"Where's Johnny?"

"Not down yet," he said. He glanced toward the stairs that led both to the boxes and to Johnny's room. "He's with Sally."

He hadn't stayed with me last night, as much as I'd needed him, but had come right back to take Sally to bed. I set my coffee cup down hard. "I suppose he needs to be awakened then."

Duncan reached to stop me, but I was already past the bar and marching toward the stairs. Before I got there, Sally came flouncing down. She threw me a smug smile. "Morning, Marguerite."

I wanted to slap her. But then I heard Johnny's footsteps thudding down behind her, and I remembered what he'd said last night and I struggled to keep my temper in check. There would be time later to punish Sally. Just now, I let her go by without comment, and when Johnny reached the bottom step, I managed, barely, to keep a civil tone. "We've been waiting. The girls are already here."

He paused on the bottom step. "Good morning to you too, honey. How'd you sleep?"

This time I could not help my tartness. "No better than you did, I imagine."

He raised a brow. "You going to be pissy today, Margie?"

With effort, I shook my head. "No. I'll be good. I promise."

He glanced past me to where the girls congregated. "Is Billy here?"

"Not that I've seen."

"He was blind drunk last night. My guess is we'll have to get on without the piano this morning."

"At least then we'll know if they can hold a tune."

Johnny sighed. "Yeah. That's what I'm afraid of." He strode to the bar and grabbed the coffee Duncan pushed his way. I went up the stairs behind the stage to the orchestra loge for the sheet music Billy kept on the piano. Below I heard Johnny walk over to the girls and say, "All right then. Let's get started."

The "auditions," as Johnny liked to call them, were hardly necessary; the girls rotated so fast through this place that we were just as likely to pull one off the street. But Johnny liked the air of legitimacy the auditions had, and sometimes we were lucky enough to get a girl with a little more talent than most. Not that they needed it. How they looked was more important. Sex sold drinks.

"How many we got today?" Johnny asked. "You there—yes, you—what's your name?"

I went back down the stairs, the music in my arms. The girl he spoke to was the blonde Duncan had mentioned. Young, perhaps eighteen, and with a nervous twitch in her eye. "Sarah Wilcox, sir."

"Do you sing, Sarah Wilcox?"

She winced. "Not well. But I can dance."

"Well, we got no piano to dance to this morning, I'm afraid. But go on up there and swing your arms about like there is. Let's see what you can do."

I made my way to the table and sat down as she went onto the stage. I leafed through the music—dancing was not my interest; Johnny would know better whether she had talent or not, and it didn't really matter anyway. We were down at least two girls, and I thought we'd lose more by the end of the week; I expected him to take on all those here today.

The music was a collection of popular songs. My task was to match a girl's voice with something no one else was singing. I pulled out a few tunes now, knowing already that it was rare to find a good soprano, that most girls without experience sang with a chest voice somewhere in a middle register. I tried to match the music with a look too—there were girls like Pauline who did mournful very well, though I tried not to do too many of those. Johnny liked things to be cheery, and we sold more drinks that way, but the sad songs had a point too; they worked to calm a restless crowd and they kept the customers honest. Maudlin and sentimental made them think of their families, and they tended to be generous then and less trouble, so I liked to have a girl ready to sing something like "Willie Has Gone to War." Songs like that worked best with the young and pretty ones with expressive eyes.

Sarah Wilcox came off the stage, smiling nervously at Johnny's appreciative nod. "Now, Miss Wilcox, you know what we do here?"

"Yes, sir," she said prettily.

"And you know that once you're done onstage, you're to sell drinks. If you want to entertain our customers in one of the boxes, we'll take a cut of that too."

She nodded.

"You got any experience along those lines?"

"I done some whoring in San Francisco, sir. I just come up from there with a man, but he works the camps and ain't around much."

"He the jealous kind?"

"I don't think so, sir. He's the one told me to come here."

Johnny motioned to one of the tables. "All right then, Miss Wilcox. Have a seat, and Miss Olson here will show you around when we're done. Now, who's next?"

The next one went on the stage, a thin and mousy woman with a tremulous voice, though at least she could hold a tune, and she had a pining look I knew that some men liked. After her was the next, and then the next. They tended to blend together in my head—few voices stood out, and fewer still stayed long enough for me to know their names, and over the years I'd made connections in my head to remember them: the one singing "Then You'll Remember Me" was Emma, "Long Time Ago" for Betsey, "The Harp of Love" and Jane.

By the time the last one took to the stage, the distraction of the auditions had worn off, and I was restless. The last girl was tall, with large breasts and narrow hips, brown hair and large brown cow eyes. She was older than the rest of them, about my age, I guessed. She looked as if she would have a lower voice, and I thought of "The Bridge of Sighs" for its midrange tessitura. It was a sad song, but she had the look for it. I leafed through the music, searching for it.

But then she went onstage. She had none of the nervousness of the others, but instead a quiet settledness that caught my interest. Without preamble, she began to sing in a clean, light soprano, not the contralto I'd pegged her.

The song was "Jeanie with the Light Brown Hair." It seemed strange that I had not heard anyone sing this song in all the time I'd been here. It had been so popular, after all. But until today, no one had, and hearing it now startled me.

I knew this song; I knew every nuance available in it; I knew how it felt in the muscles of the throat, the push of it from the lungs, the quiet strength of it balanced on a column of air.

I looked away and made myself go through the music, searching for another song in her range, forcing myself to think on that alone. I fumbled through the sheets, my frustration growing as she climbed through the song. I wished it would stop. I tried hard to block it out. It was a relief when she finished, when the last note was nothing but a hush on the air.

"What's your name?" Johnny asked.

"Charlotte Rainey," she said.

"You got any questions?"

She said, "Do I got to sing? Can't I just fuck them?"

I looked up, startled.

Johnny laughed. "God help me, if I wanted to run a brothel I wouldn't have built the stage. Christ, yes, you got to sing. It helps sell the drinks. The whoring's up to you. You do it, we get a cut. You don't, then you better sell a lot of whiskey." He looked over his shoulder at me. "You got anything to add, honey?"

I shook my head, taking up the music I'd chosen. "I'll get them started."

"Then I'll leave it to you," he said. "I'll be in my office."

The girls were quiet, watching me warily as I rose and passed them the music. "I've chosen songs for all of you. You'll have a day to learn them before we put you onstage. You'll need to watch out for Billy. He's the piano player, and he's got a roving hand. If he bothers you too much, you let Duncan know." I gestured to where Duncan stood at the bar. "My name's Marguerite. Marguerite Olson. I'm the one you come to if you have any other problems. I'll take care of everything. Not Johnny. He'll just send you to me and be angry in the bargain."

They stood staring at me, looking blankly at the music I'd

handed them—illiterate, as they almost always were, and I sighed and said, as I always did, "Come in first thing tomorrow and I'll go through the music with you. Now, if you'll follow me, we'll get you dressed."

I led them upstairs to Johnny's room and unlocked the trunk near the window that held all the secondhand gowns we'd collected in the last years. Johnny's room was spartan, with only a table and two chairs and a cast-iron stove in the corner. The shelves above held a coffee can and a kettle and a few books which I knew were all that remained of his father. The bed was unmade—the sight of that reminded me of Sally, and of how Johnny had refused me last night, and when I threw Sarah Wilcox a gown and she said, "But I don't like pink," it was all I could do not to tell her to get out. Instead, I remembered Johnny's warning and forced a smile, looking back into the trunk, taking out another gown, appeasing her. "Here's a blue. Try it on and see if it fits." Then I drew out the others: a green for Charlotte Rainey, and a purple and a striped and a red for the other three. The gowns had all been altered, cut short, just below the knee, and pantaloons had been made of the extra fabric. They'd been adorned with all manner of fringe and dangling trim because it accented the movement of the girls' bodies on the stage and made them seem sensuous even if they had no more grace than a turtle. That had been my idea, and one that had made Johnny laugh with admiration when I told him cynically how to shape a woman's innocence or experience. One could dress a whore in cascades of lace and make of her an innocent, and low-cut silk and beads that shivered with every breath could turn a virgin into a whore.

"Where have you been, honey, that you know such things?"

"Why don't you let me show you what else I know...."

I looked out the window while I waited for them to dress, glancing past the railing of the balcony that abutted Johnny's room to the street below. The misty rain hadn't stopped, and

even the horses were bowing their heads as if they couldn't
abide it. It made me shiver to think of going out in it again.
Once the girls were taken care of, I had a few hours until the
Palace opened and I had to be back, and that was the time of
day I disliked the most. If Johnny sometimes filled the nights
and the mornings, the early afternoon was always empty. Perhaps I would stay around, send Duncan for a bowl of chowder from across the street, help Johnny with the accounts—

"I'm afraid it's a bit too small."

I turned at the voice, into the liquid cow eyes of Charlotte
Rainey. She looked apologetic as she tried to pull the sleeves of
the dark green dress down past her elbows.

"It's supposed to be like that," I said, reaching out to push
the sleeves back up, and it was then I saw the scar on her fore-
arm. It was large, starting at her wrist and running to her
elbow. It was ugly and strange; I'd never seen anything like it,
as if her skin had somehow melted and fused to the muscles
beneath, an unsightly deformity.

She pulled her arm gently from my grasp. "It's better if
I keep it covered."

"How did it happen?" I asked.

"I fell," she said, meeting my gaze straight on, though I recognized the evasiveness in her words; I understood it. "How'd
you get yours?"

"The same way," I told her.

She smiled; it was small and subtle, an acknowledgment
that she understood my evasiveness too, and I was surprised at
my own urge to smile back. She said, "If you don't want me
here now, it's all right. But most men don't even see it."

"Just keep it covered until they're too hot to care," I told
her. I turned back to the trunk and drew out something else, a
gown in deep red this time, with long, close-fitting sleeves.
"Try this one instead."

"Thank you," she said quietly.

After that, the other girls came up to me to fix this or adjust that, and I tended to them, but I was thinking of Charlotte Rainey. The scar intrigued me, but more than that, there was something in her manner, a straightforwardness even in her evasion, a feeling that was somehow familiar, though I'd never seen her before.

When they were done being fitted, and we left Johnny's room, and they all trailed out of the bar one by one, into the foggy rain, I could not quite keep her out of my head, and I had no idea why.

From the Journal of Sabine Conrad

JUNE 9, 1871—Gideon has become my good-luck charm. Since our first performance, I cannot go onstage without his kiss on my forehead and the rub of his thumb to erase the rouge he leaves behind. I have become as superstitious as the rest— Mrs. Follett must wear a certain pair of shoes, and Paolo must shake the hand of the man who runs the curtain rope, and Mr. Arriete must kiss his wife's ear.

The reviews continue so good that I have been given two songs apart from our regular program—Marguerite's "Jewel Song" from *Faust* and "All Things Love Thee, So Do I," which Mr. Wilson thinks will be my signature song, the same way that "Home Sweet Home" belongs to Adelina Patti. Gideon has been working every day with me to perfect them, and Follett is not happy on two counts: one, that I have been given my own part of the show, and two, that I must spend so much time now with Gideon. She has been giving me *das Auge des Teufels*—ah! no more German!!!—the devil's eye, as if she hopes to make me disappear.

Gideon has also set me to reading poetry and philosophy and literature. He says if I am to sing opera I must understand the emotions behind the stories, and as I am not likely to murder someone or have an obsessive love affair or run about in disguise, books are the best way to understand them. "You must know enough to bring those feelings onstage with you, Bina," he says. So I am studying very hard in the little spare time I have.

I also confess that I have grown used to the idea of Gideon with Follett and I think Barret and I are right to simply ignore it. This is a strange life. We in the company do not live as other people; I am quite accustomed to keeping night hours, and the day is what now seems strange. Renate Arriete joked the other day that we all had the pallor of ghosts, and strange-looking ones at that, because the kohl and rouge never completely leaves our skin, no matter how we wash.

Renate is not nearly as quiet as I supposed, and in fact has a jolly sense of humor, but Gideon tells me I should keep my distance. He says she is a performer's wife and will be jealous of the attention paid to me over her husband. I do not believe it. Our company is like a family—we are as intimate as if we are the only persons left on earth. A week does not go by without some melodrama or another, but the love we bear one another cannot be broken so easily!

Barret seems much happier too away from the Völksstadt. Yesterday after practice we snuck away to a confectioner and he bought me lemonade and a cake (though it is true he did not *buy* the cake, but flirted so with the counter girl that she gave him one for free). I felt very guilty, as I was supposed to be preparing for the show, but it is impossible to refuse Barret when he is in such a mood. I think he is relieved to be away from Papa's criticism. He was very lively and teased me until I laughed loud enough that people looked at us, though they look at us anyway—we are so alike that I think it must be quite startling to see us together.

I am so very happy! The only thing I cannot like is the way Paolo has become too nice—I feel his eyes on me all the time now, and he makes excuses to brush up against me while we wait in the wings. I have become very mean to him as a result, so that even Barret chided me for it. It is all very frustrating!

* * *

N.B. I have had a letter from Papa, who says that the Brooklyn tower of the new bridge is now complete and that they all
went to see it and found it astonishing except that it made
Willa cry to see all the couples in the crowd; she misses
Gideon and it is hard for her when he is far away. Papa asks
that I write of Gideon the next time I send a letter, as he must
be too busy to write himself. And there is a postscript from
Willa who reminds me to remember my promise.

CHICAGO, JULY 15, 1871—My Birthday!!!! I am seventeen
today.

   Mr. Cone and Mr. Wilson brought me an immense bouquet
of pink roses and they are filling my hotel room with scent and
are very lovely. But the best news of all is that Mr. Cone says
we have been asked to extend the tour through November. At
least five of the cities we have visited want us back, and the
ones we have not yet arrived at have requested that we extend
our engagements. My reviews have preceded us! He showed me
an item in the *Chicago Tribune*, which said, "Arriving today,
the renowned Manchetti Company of New York City, of which
we have heard such great praise that we find ourselves anticipating their performances with unusual impatience. There is
every expectation of a full house each night as Chicago swarms
to welcome the lauded soprano, Miss Sabine Conrad. We have
great hopes that they will consent to extend their stay in order
that everyone might have the opportunity to see her."

   I have written straightaway to Papa to ask his permission,
as has Barret, who says that Mr. Cone and Mr. Wilson are in-
creasing my payment to $100/month! I think Papa cannot help
but agree I should continue on. Even Gideon has written to
Willa—his first letter to her in months, I think. I have done as
Papa asked and reminded Gideon to write to her before now,
but he only says he is too busy with rehearsals to write more
often, which I think is not quite true, as I have seen his

weekly letters to his mother go into the post. I only really care
that he wrote her this time to tell her that he hopes she will
convince Papa to do what is best.

It makes me remember how she said she has sacrificed
everything for me.

I don't like to think of it. And it is my birthday, so I won't,
and now I must go to rehearsal.

*   *   *

N.B. I am back from my birthday celebration. Oh, what shall
I do now? Oh . . . I am too drunk to write. I will tell more tomorrow.

JULY 16, 1871—I think I may be falling in love with Gideon!

Even just to write it makes my pen shake. What a terrible
sister I am! I think I must cross it out and never admit it, but
I cannot help myself, and I write in the hope that putting it
all down on paper might somehow make my feelings for him
less. How miserable I am!

To start from the beginning: last night was our first performance in Chicago, and it was as the papers said: the house was
full and Mr. Cone was in high spirits because we had sold out.
But the crowd was restless, and I could feel their anticipation
as my turn to go onto the stage neared. First is my duet with
Gideon from *Ernani,* and as always, I gave myself over to the
music and the audience went so quiet it was almost as if they had
gone away. After I sang, there was such a chorus of Bravas!
Gideon and I were forced to encore it three times before they
would sit again. The rest of the performance was no different.
The show went nearly an hour past its usual time with all the
encores they demanded of me. I was quite exhausted at the
end of it, and Follett was glaring so fiercely I could swear I
felt the burn of it upon my cheek. She declared she had the
headache and would not go with us when Mr. Cone and Mr.
Wilson whisked us all away to celebrate my birthday. I suppose

if she had gone, none of the rest would have happened, but even now I find I cannot be unhappy that she was not there.

Mr. Cone and Mr. Wilson took us to a beer hall and it was so nice of them and so much like being at home. We drank a great deal of lager and ate fried fish, and I must have danced the polka a hundred times! Barret flirted with all the wait-resses and danced with me and we laughed at how glad we were to be here as customers and not as waiters. When the polka orchestra was done, he jumped upon the stage and to my surprise announced that "the famous Miss Sabine Con-rad, of New York City" was here, and they pushed me onto the stage and I sang the old folk songs I was accustomed to sing in the Völksstadt until some of the hausfraus were cry-ing and holding their children in their laps and I sang "Jeanie with the Light Brown Hair," which is Willa's fa-vorite song, and afterward Gideon came up to me, his face flushed and his eyes bright with drink, and he said, "I don't ever want to go back, Sabine. Tell me you don't either." And of course I agreed with him, because it's true: I wish I could stay on this tour forever.

I laughed and took Gideon's hand, pulling him close to dance with me. Then . . . I lost my balance, I think, and he caught me, and instead of letting me go once I'd regained my-self, he held me tight. I leaned into him and twined my arms around his neck, and . . . did he try to pull away? I confess I don't remember. Suddenly he was kissing me and I did not feel it was wrong at all. I felt instead that I could stay there in his arms, kissing him, forever.

But then Barret wrenched me away. I do not think I have ever seen my brother so angry. I don't remember exactly what he said to me. Only that I must think of Willa, and that he would take me home if he caught me again with Gideon that way and did I mean to ruin everything?

He is right, of course. I promised Barret to be good, and I mean to be! I do! But then I think of Willa and how she waits for him and my promise to her, and I am so jealous and guilty I can't bear it.

* * *

I have seen Gideon now, and I am more miserable than ever. I went to practice, where he was, and no one else—not even Follett or Barret—and I was so happy to see him and I meant to fly into his arms. Except that he hardly looked at me! He said nothing of last night at all, and in fact, treated me no differently than he ever has. It was as if he did not even remember, yet how could that be? I was very drunk, and I remember. Surely he was not worse than me?

I think Barret has spoken to him, and that is why he is holding himself distant. He must know as well as I that we cannot be together.

Oh, I don't know! I watched his long fingers upon the piano keys and remembered how my own had tangled in his hair, and all he could say was, "Pianissimo there, Sabine. Come, come, do it again." And quite impatiently too, as if I were a child.

And then, worst of all . . . when the practice was nearly done, Follett came to the room—which she has never, ever done before—and asked him to "promenade" with her as if it were quite the usual thing, and when he agreed, she kissed him quite insistently in front of me, which she has also never done before, and I knew she must have heard what happened and was showing that he still belonged to her. I thought my heart would break when he kissed her back and laughed, and the two of them went off with hardly a good-bye.

This is how it must be, I know. I cannot be in love with him. There is Willa to consider, and my career. Still I cannot quite make myself wish he had not kissed me.

Oh, what am I to do now?

JULY 23, 1871—I am in torment. Today Renate told me that Gideon and I were both drunk and it was nothing more than that and I am imperiling all of us with my foolishness. Follett is complaining about me, and if she leaves it will be the end for everyone.

I am trying to be good, but it is very hard.

JULY 24, 1871—Barret says that the whole company can see my misery, and there isn't a one who hasn't guessed the reason for it. I told him I was in love with Gideon and I was angry with myself, and Barret took me in his arms and was so understanding and sweet that I started to cry. When I was done he said very seriously that I must forget Gideon, that he belonged to Willa, and she meant to marry him. "She could have stopped Gideon from coming with us," he told me. "But she didn't. She knew he could help you, Bina. She let him go for you. Would you repay her this way?"

I felt so guilty when he said it, and my tears started again, and he said he was only trying to watch out for me, as Papa had instructed him to do, and as any older brother would. "You are my dear schwester, Bina, and you know I love you, but you're only seventeen—there will be other men for you, and when you find someone else to love you'll forget Gideon."

I do not want another man, but I know he is right. Gideon belongs to Willa, not to me. So I am determined to do as Barret advises. I will find another man to make me forget. I have thought of all the men of the company. Mr. Cone and Mr. Wilson are impossible, of course, as is Renate's husband—out of loyalty to her, I would not consider him even were he young and handsome. None of the minstrels will suit. Other than Gideon, that leaves only my brother and Paolo.

I am resolved: Paolo it must be.

JULY 25, 1871—Tonight I have started my plan to fall in love with Paolo Rinzetti. Before he went onstage I took his hand and smiled at him and wished him luck with such sincere sweetness as I could manage, and I was gratified when he looked quite stunned in return. Then at dinner after the performance, I sat beside him instead of where I usually sit between Barret and Gideon. He is very charming. I think it will not be hard to fall in love with him.

PHILADELPHIA, JULY 30, 1871—We are returned to Philadelphia, and Mr. Cone was very pleased to show me the new placard, which has MY name on it—now above Follett's!! It says:

THE
MANCHETTI COMPANY
RETURNS!!!

SPECIAL EXTENDED PERFORMANCES

Presenting the Incomparable
MISS SABINE CONRAD
AND
MRS. OLIVE FOLLETT

We are to be here for two weeks, and Mr. Cone believes we will sell out every night.

I am flirting with Paolo quite outrageously, enough that everyone notices. I think Barret is relieved, but he watches me very closely and I am careful not to alarm him. And although Paolo is very handsome and very nice, still my heart aches for Gideon. I know he feels the same. He's said nothing of what happened at my birthday, but yesterday after practice he told me I should not waste my time with men who could do nothing for me. I was very noble and told him that I thought I was falling in love with Paolo, and did he mean to stand between us?

He glared at me and slammed down the cover on the piano

with a loud crash—I've never seen him so angry. How jealous
he was! My heart was pounding so hard in my chest I thought
he must hear it. He came up to me and I thought he would
take me in his arms and I both wished he would and knew
I would have to reject him if he did. But he only asked me if
I trusted him to do what was right for my career and I said of
course I did and he said, "Then stay away from Rinzetti," and
then, as if he knew he should not, but couldn't help himself,
he traced my collarbone and lingered at the hollow of my
throat. His fingers were so warm. I thought I would swoon
with pleasure, and despite all my intentions, I leaned into his
hand, and I wanted him to kiss me so badly and he met my
gaze as if he meant to. But when I moved he drew back and
quite stalked away without another word!

He is so good! And I am so bad, because I am so jealous
and angry and guilty. But Willa is my sister, and I love her,
and I would not hurt her this way for anything.

So I am determined to continue with Paolo, and not to
mind his rough kisses even though he doesn't shave as closely
as Gideon so my cheeks are red and stinging and my lips are
swollen when I leave him.

AUGUST 5, 1871—Barret reminded me today that Mama and
Papa expect me to behave like a respectable girl. He said he'd
told Paolo to keep his distance, and I grew very angry and
told him I was no longer a child who needed his protection.

He said Paolo was not some callow boy who would steal
only a kiss. He said Papa would hold him responsible if anything should go wrong and he wished I would remember it.

But he must not care as much as he pretends, because
tonight as Paolo and I went out, Barret was with a girl from
the chorus. He saw us, and looked as if he might tell me not to
go with Paolo alone, but then the girl kissed him, and he
wrapped his arms around her and went with her into the
dressing room without a word to me.

AUGUST 6, 1871—Tonight, Paolo unbuttoned my gown and kissed the tops of my breasts above my corset, and I felt a little twinge of . . . I don't know what, exactly. Perhaps I am falling in love with Paolo at last!

BOSTON, AUGUST 20, 1871—I am ruined.

Barret is threatening to take me home. Paolo is gone, and Mrs. Follett, and Gideon almost so, and the whole company is in chaos and it is all my fault.

I can hardly bear to write of my folly, but I am now locked into my hotel room and there is nothing to do but think on everything that has gone wrong.

I find I must write it out to make sense of it, and I will start with our arrival in Boston, which is very hot and humid and unpleasant. Backstage is so hellish that Mrs. Follett swooned opening night, and I had to have Renate loosen my corset laces so I did not do the same, and I was still sweating and faint. It did not help that I was as big a success here as in Philadelphia. They asked for seven!!!! encores of "All Things Love Thee," which is really too much, and Mr. Cone had given me Mrs. Follett's *Norma,* which is difficult under the best circumstance, and in this heat left me nearly prostrate, though I was required to encore it thrice.

I was exhausted after the performance and I suppose that must explain some of it, because Paolo was waiting for me when I came offstage, and he took me in his arms and he was so strong that I let myself simply lean into him, and I did not protest when he kissed me there before all the others.

I saw Mr. Cone frown, and Barret shook his head at me, but nobody said anything and we went to dinner. The beer was cool and I drank quite a bit, because I was feeling sick to my stomach and I knew food would not suit. Barret made me eat some bread, and it made me feel worse than ever, so I finally said my head was aching and that I wanted to go back to the hotel.

By then, of course, Barret was dancing with some woman

he'd met there and Gideon must have been off with Follett some-where, and no one protested at all when Paolo said he would see me back, though the way they talk now, you would think they were all standing about, shouting at me to beware of him. Hah!!!

The streetlamps were lit, and Paolo said it was romantic, was it not, *cara?* and I agreed although I was concentrating mostly on trying to keep from vomiting in the carriage, and slapping his hands away at the same time. Truly all I wished to do was sleep. But then we got to the hotel, and my room felt as I imagine a steam bath must feel, and I unfastened the but-tons on my bodice and threw myself onto the bed. I heard my door close, and the window open, and I saw Paolo was closing the curtains and taking off his frock coat and his boots, and I believe I said, "What are you doing?" and he turned to me with a smile and took off his shirt so that he was quite naked above his trousers and said, "Why, making love to you, *cara.*"

I truly did not feel myself—it is the only way I can explain that I thought he meant only to do what we had done before—no more than kisses and caresses. I did not want to; really I just wanted to sleep, and I told him that I was tired and that he must go.

But he came to the bed and lay beside me, and then he was kissing me, and his hand was unfastening the rest of the but-tons on my gown and I was too tired to resist him much. I think I pushed at him once or twice but I was not very strong about it, and I did not realize what he meant to do, and the truth is that his kisses were very nice, if still a bit rough, and I have always liked it when he touches my breasts.

Then I felt his hand between my thighs, and I realized that he had quite skillfully arranged things so that my bodice was open and my corset unfastened, my chemise pulled down to expose my breasts and rucked up about my waist, and then he was taking off his trousers.

I was afraid then—but when I pushed at him he grabbed my hands, and came on top of me, pushing his tongue nearly down my throat so I could not breathe or speak. His fingers slid inside me, and I was so horrified and frightened that I froze, and did not fight him at all as he took them away and shoved his cock into me in their stead, except that I cried out because it hurt, and I tried to scramble away from him, but he pinned me down and whispered all sorts of things to me—I do not think he realized I was afraid or that I was crying, or that he hurt me. Then, I stopped protesting at all. There was no point in it; what was done was done, and so I just lay there until he grunted and went still.

He said a few things then. Things like how beautiful I was, things I think he expected I would want to hear. Then he fell asleep on top of me, and though I suppose I could have moved from underneath him, I was crying and wretched and afraid that if I woke him he would do it again, so I just stared up at the ceiling.

I don't know how long it was before Barret knocked on my door, only that it was still late night. My brother called, "Sabine? Sabine? How are you feeling?" and then he opened the door I had forgotten to lock.

I don't know exactly what he saw, but I can guess. The moon was bright, the curtains too thin to keep the light out, and Paolo and I were on top of the bed. He was completely naked, and I had not bothered to push my clothing back into place. What had happened between us would have been obvious. I saw Barret stop, and I saw a stillness come over him that I recognized from other times, when he had been required to defend my honor or my mistakes, and I felt the rage that broke over my brother like a snap in the air.

After that, I don't remember more than images—Barret yelling, and Paolo starting awake, lurching off the bed, trying to reach his trousers before Barret reached him. The crack of Barret's fists against Paolo's jaw, words hurled in German and Italian, the two of them falling on the bed so that I must scramble away, and then Gideon—Gideon—appearing in the doorway, and behind him Follett, and Gideon swearing and then lunging to tear Barret and Paolo apart, and Paolo hit

him too, and all the time Follett standing in the hall screaming, "Stop! Stop it! She's hardly worth all this!" until
Mr. Cone and Mr. Wilson came into the room and the gas was
lit and Mr. Cone made them stop. I saw how battered they
each were: Gideon with blood on his full lips, and Barret's eye
swelling closed and Paolo the worst of all, naked still, but now
with a broken nose and two eyes that would be black before
morning and blood in his mouth and some bloody, slimy thing
clinging to his shoulder that I realized dumbly was a tooth.

"What's going on here?" Mr. Cone demanded, and at the
same time Gideon said to me, "Christ, Sabine, do you know
what you've done?" and I could only stand there pulling my
gown closed over my breasts, which was very difficult, as my
corset was still unfastened and I was afraid I revealed more
than I hid.

Paolo grabbed his trousers from the floor and put them
on—very dignified, I thought, given his state—and asked what
business it was of anyone's, and since when did lovers require
permission to love? and Barret said, "Since one of them is my
seventeen-year-old sister."

Mr. Cone asked me if I was hurt and then whether Paolo
was here by my invitation?

I thought how nicely he'd put it. I did not know what to
say. He was not, and yet he was, and I knew much depended
on the reply I made, and I saw Barret's fists clench and his
fierce protectiveness, and then I saw Gideon's thoughtful,
waiting look, and Mr. Wilson's frown, and I knew what they
would all think if I told them how confusing the truth was.

And then I saw Paolo's chin come up and his assuredness
return, and in the doorway Mrs. Follett's smug satisfaction,
and there was a part of me that wanted vengeance too, and so
I said, "No. He was not."

Paolo called me a lying, stupid bitch and Barret told him
not to talk of me that way and Mrs. Follett said to me, "Will
you really claim that, my dear? I cannot be the only one who
saw you kissing Paolo after the performance tonight."

I told her I had only been excited at all the encores, and then Gideon said in a very cold voice, "Are you accusing Miss Conrad of something, Olive?" and she snapped back, "You would take her side, wouldn't you? God knows you've been as hot for the little bitch as Rinzetti is."

I would have flown at her myself then. I was gratified when Barret said, "I will not have you talking about my sister in that fashion," and Mr. Cone told Paolo, Gideon, Barret, and Follett to meet him in his room immediately, and told Mr. Wilson to send Renate to me, as I could no doubt use a woman's comfort.

They all left, and Renate came and helped me undress and lay on the bed with me while I slept, though she was gone in the morning and I was alone, and very sore, and feeling exceedingly stupid. Which was only made worse when someone knocked on the door and I knew it was Barret and told him to come in, except it wasn't just Barret, but Gideon too, and I was embarrassed.

I sat up in bed, clutching the bedcovers about me as Barret shut the door and asked how I was and his tone was so cold and mean, and I retorted angrily, "As well as someone who's been so grievously abused can be," and he said, "Leave off, Sabine. What the hell are you playing at?"

I told him I had no idea what he was talking about and that he needn't be so pious as he'd been the one who had told me I should find another man to love and I was only following his advice. Barret looked confused and then horrified, and he glanced at Gideon and asked in a strangled voice if I loved Paolo, and I told him no, of course not, and that this was all an accident, and I began to cry and Barret asked if Paolo had taken any precautions?

I didn't know what he meant, and said so, and then he swore. "Didn't you think what would happen if he got you with child? D'you really think we all sacrificed just so you could marry some second-rate garlic eater?"

I was stunned. I told him marrying Paolo was the very last thing I wanted.

Barret only gave me this terrible look and said that Papa must be contacted, and we would be lucky not to be called home, and I grabbed my brother by the shoulders and begged him not to tell Papa. I told him I wouldn't do it again, that I would do whatever he asked. I told Gideon to say something, to help me. He asked Barret for a moment with me and Barret was reluctant but I gave him my best pleading look and he said he would wait in the hall and Gideon had one minute only. When my brother was gone, Gideon sat down on the bed beside me, and took me in his arms, where I wanted so badly to be, and I sobbed into his shoulder and told him I had only been trying to forget him, that it had all gone wrong, and he pulled away and took my chin between his fingers and said, "Rinzetti was a mistake. Next time you'll listen to me. Now you must use your pretty little head. You're not a child anymore, Sabine. It's time to act like an adult and think of what is best to be done."

I asked him what he meant and he asked what I wanted more than anything and I said to sing. He said if that was true, I must not let anyone take it from me, and was I brave enough to defy my parents? "Does the world still see you as a child who must obey her mama and papa? Must the Sabine Conrad that the *Chicago Tribune* loved do so?"

Oh, what hope he placed in my heart! I clutched at him and he said that if I followed his lead he would see I became what I was meant to be. Then he stroked my cheek and kissed where my tears had fallen, and said I must be patient and trust him, and could I do that?

Trust him? How could I not trust him? If I've learned anything from Paolo, it's how true my love for Gideon is. But I didn't say that, because there is still Willa to consider, and I know I must only love him from afar. His guidance must be enough. And so, although my heart was bursting, I said only that I would be his true and faithful student.

Then he reached into his pocket and pulled out a little bottle. He said it was a Portuguese remedy, and I was to use it as a douche, and that with any luck it would "take care of" any possible child. Then he asked if I knew what a douche was and I said of course I did, and he left, but I had been lying, and I had to ask Renate, who was very good to tell me, and then I was embarrassed that Gideon had been the one to bring it and that he'd known how it must be done.

But Renate told me something else as well. She told me that Paolo had been released from his contract, and there would be a new tenor that night for me to sing with, because Mrs. Follett had gone as well, and Mr. Cone and Mr. Wilson were discussing whether or not Gideon should be released. If I am singing the prima donna roles then there will be no seconda donna and therefore no need for him, and Follett said that they must choose between her and me, and they did not pick her, and she is gone, and Gideon couldn't stop her, so they are angry with him.

When Mr. Cone came later to tell me what Renate already had, I begged for him to keep Gideon, and he told me they did not need him, and then said that we must cancel the show tonight because Follett slammed the door on Mr. Wilson's hand and he cannot play. So I asked him why Gideon could not take Mr. Wilson's place at the piano and Mr. Cone said it was a good idea. Gideon was not happy as I expected. He said he would not be their trained monkey, that he was a singer and did they think he had studied all these years to not take his own place upon the stage? But in the end he agreed.

In spite of what I told Gideon, I am still nervous about what is to come. I am ashamed over what happened with Paolo, but to pay such a price as this . . . I could not bear to lose everything now that I know what it's like to sing this way. I cannot go back to what I was. But I have never disobeyed Mama and Papa, and if they send for me to come home, I wonder if I can be as brave as Gideon expects. I intend to be! Oh, I do! But I am afraid. Gideon could not stop Barret from sending the letter home, and now there is nothing to do but wait.

CHAPTER 5

Seattle, Washington Territory—February 1881

That night, the Palace was full, the way it always was when word got around that we had new girls. Even when the girls weren't yet ready to perform, the novelty lured the men in, and that was good, that was what I liked, because it kept me busy and made it easy to ignore the agitation that lurked just below the surface, ready to leap up whenever Sally challenged me with too bold eyes or when Emma faltered over the words of her song and then broke into laughter onstage and I saw her pupils were tiny as pinpricks from the laudanum she'd been drinking. The new girls helped too; I had to show them around and introduce them to the customers and make certain they were holding their own. Sarah Wilcox would do fine; she was an adept flirt, and Duncan was nearly falling over himself to help her. The three I thought of as Girl one, Girl two, and Girl three were adequate enough. Girl two spilled four drinks out of nervousness, and Girl three had a braying laugh that seemed to echo through the saloon and set my teeth on edge whenever I heard it. And as for Charlotte Rainey . . .

I'd been aware of her the moment she stepped into the Palace, and that awareness hadn't eased since. It was because she was so tall, taller than the others, and easy to spot in the crowd. And too, she walked with a kind of proud dignity that drew the eye, though she wasn't cold—she smiled readily and I saw her laugh with real gusto more than once. She went to the boxes three times that night, and each time the men were grinning when they returned. And she was good at selling the drinks too.

I was leaning on the bar, watching her, when Johnny came out of his office. He came up to me, leaning close to say, "How're the new girls tonight?"

"Some better than others. Sarah should do well."

"I see Duncan's kept a close eye on her."

"She'll be in his bed before the week is out," I agreed.

"What about the others? What about that one?"

I followed his gaze. "You mean Charlotte."

"She seem a bit long in the tooth to you?"

"I believe she's about my age," I said dryly.

He smiled. "Well, you ain't a whore."

My discomfort pricked. Deliberately, I said, "No one seems to mind it. She's doing very well. Her drink totals are as good as Annie's."

"Good," he said. I heard the intake of his breath, slow and wary. "How you doing tonight, honey? You seem good."

"Oh, but I've been warned I'd better be. And you know how well I follow direction."

"Margie," he said quietly.

I shrugged away from his hand where it rested on my hip. "I'm fine, Johnny. You can fuck Sally tonight without worrying that I'll be pining for you."

"I don't mind you pining for me."

"You seemed to mind it last night."

"Not the pining," he said. "What I mind is the fact that you don't."

He stepped away then, moving to Duncan, whom he spoke to for a moment before he poured himself a glass of whiskey and went back into his office. I felt the urge for a drink myself, but I remembered his warning and left it. As always, Johnny left me feeling somehow *less than,* as if he expected more from me, as if I failed him in ways I didn't understand. I disliked the feeling, but more than that I disliked the loneliness it left in its wake. He wouldn't be coming with me to the boardinghouse tonight, and I would be alone, and the rest of the night seemed to race pell-mell toward that conclusion, the hours spinning by in a blur of color and sound until suddenly it was nearly 4 A.M. The girls and the orchestra had gone home, and the newest scrubwoman was cheerlessly cleaning up, and it was time to make my weary way back to the boardinghouse and my cold and empty bed.

Johnny was nowhere to be found, and it occurred to me as I grabbed my cloak from his office that I hadn't seen Sally leave either. They must have gone off to his room when I wasn't looking. It wasn't that I was jealous—Johnny had had his favorites before, and the truth was that I was mostly relieved at it, because I knew he loved me, and I didn't want the responsibility of having to love him back. But not having the guarantee of him frightened me. Johnny at least was easy; he understood me, he knew his place in my life and the role I meant him to play. If he'd really meant what he said about not obliging me any longer, what was I to do without him?

Duncan was shrugging into his coat as I came out of the office. "You ready to go, Marguerite?"

I nodded and put on my cloak and together we went out. The light from the nearby streetlamp seemed to shiver and shift in the rain. It was a moment before I saw the shadow within it, the person lurking in the corner where the lean-to butted up against the saloon, and I went still in sudden fear. *So this was to be the night....*

Duncan stopped, one hand on my arm, the other sneaking to the gun he kept in his pocket. "Who's there?"

"It's only me," a voice said, and then the shadow lengthened and grew as the person stood and stepped from the corner.

It was Charlotte. She was wearing a threadbare coat, too big, obviously once a man's, and no hat. Her hair was plastered to her head, dripping into her face. Her eyes were enormous, her lips colorless with cold. I swallowed my relief. Not tonight, after all. Thank God.

"I got no money yet," she said. "There's no place else to go."

Duncan said, "You can't stay out here. Johnny won't have it."

"Look, I only need tonight—"

"Sorry, but you got to move on." Duncan was adamant.

"Where the hell should I go?"

"That ain't my problem."

She nodded and began to move off, and suddenly I remembered my first night in Seattle, the cold wet and the despair that had led me to sell myself for a bowl of chowder. I thought of her today in Johnny's room, that evasion, that understanding, and all of it tangled with my fear of going to my empty room, of being alone, and I found myself saying, "You can come with me."

Duncan jerked to look at me. "What?"

"She can come home with me," I said again, and then, at his disbelieving expression, "I didn't put all this time into training her today just to have her murdered in the street."

Duncan shrugged. "Whatever you want. Come along then."

Charlotte fell into step beside me. "Thank you," she said quietly. That was all, just *thank you*, but it was sincere and she didn't grovel and I didn't regret that I'd made the offer. Instead I felt comforted. I didn't ask myself why that was; all I cared about was that I wouldn't be alone.

None of us said much on the walk to the boardinghouse. We sloshed quickly through the mud because the night was cold and wet and still full of other, less benign shadows. Charlotte was shivering so I could feel it. When we reached McGraw's, Duncan let us go with a "Good night, ladies," and then, as I stepped back to let Charlotte go first up the ramp, he touched my arm and asked, "You sure? You never done this before."

"I'm sure," I told him. Then I patted the pocket where I kept the derringer. "I've got a gun if she gets too hard to handle."

His white teeth flashed in the darkness as he laughed. "I won't worry then. Good night, Marguerite."

I hurried after Charlotte to the door. "This way," I told her as we went inside and I led her up the stairs to my room. I unlocked the door and she was still shivering as she went inside. The room was cold as it always was, not even the breath of the furnace to heat it now; it had been banked for hours. At least Tessa was quiet in the room next door.

Quickly I hurried to the bedside table and lit the candle. "You'd best get those wet clothes off so you can get warm. Though I guess it might take a while in this place."

She nodded and slipped out of her coat before she sat on the edge of the bed to take off her boots. She cursed softly as she fumbled with the laces. I knelt on the floor beside her and batted aside her dead cold hands and made short work of it, though the laces had been broken and knotted many times. I eased them off her feet. Her stockings were soaking as well.

"How long were you out there?" I asked.

"Only a few hours," she said. "Johnny told me to go around two, I think, when things started to die down."

"Your drink sales were good tonight. Better than some of the girls who've been there a while."

"The work ain't hard."

"You don't think so?"

She shrugged. "I've done worse."

I got to my feet, and she rose as well, reaching back to try the buttons on the gown. I gestured impatiently for her to turn. She still wore the dress I'd given her at the Palace. Even as cheap as the satin was, the rough skin of my fingers caught on its smoothness as I undid the buttons one after another. It was as wet as her coat had been; I peeled it from her shoulders to reveal her corset, the pale skin of her back, which the candlelight burnished to a smooth gold, seemingly unblemished by the gooseflesh I felt there. She bent her head forward, her muscles flexing beneath the soft down of fine, light hair at the nape of her neck that trailed down her spine to disappear beneath the grayed muslin of her chemise, as old and cheap as mine. When I loosened the laces of her corset I heard her sigh at the release the way I always did.

I stepped back. "Take off your stockings and get into bed. You'll find it's best only to wear them at the Palace. They'll just stay wet otherwise."

"I know," she said, pulling up the skirt of her chemise to loosen her garters, rolling the rough dark stockings down her legs. "I was just trying to keep warm. I used to live in Portland."

"It rains there too?"

She tilted her chin to look at me, obviously amused. "More than here, I think."

"I didn't know that was possible."

She draped her stockings over the dresser, and then she took down her hair, plaiting it into a thick, fat braid with clumsy fingers. She motioned to the bed. "Which side?"

"What?"

"Which side is yours?"

"Oh. I don't care. Just climb in before you turn to ice."

Obediently, she crawled beneath the blankets which were old and thin but for the thicker wool of the Hudson's Bay blanket, which Johnny had given me the first night he'd brought me here and for which I'd been grateful ever since. She burrowed in, shuddering, the sound of her breathing a steady and comforting sound in the silence.

I took off my own boots and undressed, hanging my cloak and dress on the peg beside the door, and took down my hair, not bothering to brush it, twisting it into a rough braid, and by the time I was done her shuddering had stopped and her breathing had become soft and heavy. She was already asleep, but when I lifted the blankets, she shifted and muttered, making room for me, as if she were used to doing that too, and I crawled into bed beside her, careful not to disturb her.

Her body had warmed the bed even in that short a time; she was a soft presence beside me, perfumed with rain and dirt and the soft musk of her sweat. If I closed my eyes, I could almost imagine that it was another time, another place. Almost.

THE NEXT MORNING I woke to the sound of splashing. I jerked up, startled at the unfamiliar noise until I saw her at the basin, her shoulder blades jutting sharply beneath the straps of her chemise as she bent to wash her face. My sleep had been deep and even, untroubled as it was whenever someone else was here. I felt rested for the first time in days. I lay back upon the mattress, staring up at the ceiling, waiting.

She said, "Sorry. I tried to be quiet."

"What time is it?" I asked.

"Nearly noon, I think."

"This is later than I've slept in some time." I stretched and got out of bed, going to the window, easing the curtain back to look outside at another gray and misty day.

"You were good to let me stay here," Charlotte said. "I'll be gone as soon as I get dressed."

"To go where?"

"I don't know. It don't matter. Someplace cheap."

"Perhaps here," I heard myself say, letting the curtain drop back into place. "I'll ask Mrs. McGraw."

"How much is it?"

"Four dollars a week, extra for meals. But I wouldn't pay the extra. There's better food to be had at almost any other place in the Lava Beds."

"D'you think I can make enough at the Palace to pay that?"

"From what I saw last night, you should do so easily."

She nodded. She undid her braid and brushed her hair with her fingers, and then twisted it up again with the pins she'd taken out last night.

"Don't you have a brush?" I asked.

"No," she said quietly. "I left Portland . . . quickly."

I had gone to the basin to wash, and now I paused at the words that were, like so many other things about her, too familiar. I told myself not to ask. It was none of my business; it was easier if I didn't know. But I heard myself saying, "Will trouble be following you up here?"

Her expression hardened. "No."

Suddenly the scar on her arm seemed very red and even more obvious than it had before. I wondered if it had anything to do with her leaving Portland. It looked to be old, older than mine, though how could I know that really?

I turned to the basin, tamping down my curiosity, remembering how much I'd hated the questions, how much I still hated them. I washed and left her to dress in quiet, back in the Palace satin. I wondered what had happened to the dress she'd had on when she arrived.

When I dried my face, she said, "Would you mind?" and turned so I could do up the final buttons, which I did quickly. Then she said, "Thanks again. I won't forget I owe you."

"Why don't we see if Mrs. McGraw has an empty room?"

She hesitated. "I don't want to be a burden."

"It's no burden," I said. "Just let me get dressed."

She waited, and I dressed quickly, and led her out of my room and downstairs. Mrs. McGraw was in the kitchen, peeling potatoes for what was certain to be a heavy and greasy supper. When we came through the door, she paused, setting aside the paring knife, wiping her hands on her already filthy apron.

"Why, Miss Olson, good afternoon to you."

"I was hoping you might have an empty room for a friend of mine. This is Charlotte Rainey, who's just started work at the Palace."

She peered at Charlotte with sharp and rather beady eyes. "The Palace, eh?"

"I hired her yesterday. She's new to Seattle."

"Well, you know I'd always take someone you're vouching for, Miss Olson, because I don't take no one who don't got a personal recommendation, but there's no room just now. That nice Mr. Clemmons down the hall says he's going as soon as he sells his silks, but who knows when that'll be? Maybe a week, maybe more."

Charlotte said, "Thanks just the same, Mrs. McGraw."

Mrs. McGraw frowned. "I'd be happy to have you, Miss Rainey, if you can wait a bit. God knows I hate to lose a good renter."

"But I need a place now. I can't be sleeping on the streets."

"Maybe Miss Olson could put you up for a few days," Mrs. McGraw said, looking at me pointedly. "That way you'd be ready to move in just as soon as Mr. Clemmons moves out. Why, I'd even charge you only fifty cents more instead of my usual dollar for sharing."

I had been surprised at my disappointment when there had been no room, and now I found myself surprised once more at Mrs. McGraw's suggestion. Not because she'd made it, but because I considered it. Usually I spent as little time in my room as possible, because I hated the quiet of being alone, the sound of my own breath, of my body moving about the space. To have Charlotte there, even for a short time . . . Hadn't I slept last night? Had I felt even a single moment of that disquiet that had lately been my most constant companion?

I said, "How generous of you, Mrs. McGraw," at the same moment Charlotte said "No."

I turned to her. "Why not? It's only for a time. This place is better than most. At least Mrs. McGraw washes the sheets."

"Of course I do!" Mrs. McGraw said in outrage.

Charlotte shook her head. "You already done enough."

"We'll accept your offer, Mrs. McGraw," I said quickly.

Mrs. McGraw smiled. "Well then, that's just fine. I'll keep Mr. Clemmons's room for you, Miss Rainey. I'm sure you'll find it to your satisfaction."

"Thank you," I said to my landlady, and then I went out, Charlotte following more slowly.

It wasn't until we were back on the stairs that she said, "I don't understand."

"What is there to understand? I've just managed to keep Mr. Clemmons's room for you and give you a place to stay in the meantime."

"But that's what I mean. Why'd you do it?"

I turned on the stair. "Because I wanted to."

She met my gaze. "What d'you want?"

"I don't know what you mean."

"There ain't no such thing as kindness without purpose," she said. "And the other girls warned us about you. They said you never did anything without a reason. They said sometimes you could be cruel."

I tried not to feel pain at her words. "Yes. That's true."

"Then what's your reason now?"

I was disconcerted, confused, a little angry. I told myself to take it all back, to send her on her way. I'd changed my mind; I didn't like her at all. But I heard myself meeting her honesty with my own. "I sleep better when someone's there."

She stared at me for a moment, and then nodded as if my answer satisfied her. "Well, all right then. But just so we're clear . . . you can do what you want with me at the Palace, but here . . . I won't play your games. I ain't afraid of you."

I grabbed hold of the railing to steady myself. "Good. I don't want you to be."

CHAPTER 6

The other girls were waiting at the Palace when we arrived, holding their music tight in their grimy hands as I led them upstairs into the orchestra loge.

It was crowded with all of us. Usually there were only three in our "orchestra," and with the piano, there wasn't much room for more. Billy had left it a mess, as always, the lid over the keys up, the ivories sticky with spilled whiskey or beer, one key stuck fast until I hammered it loose. The girls hovered close around me, and one by one I took them through their songs.

I was no kind of accompanist, but all I needed to play was the melody line, one single note after another, and that was easy enough. I'd been doing it regularly for two years now, as I could count on one hand the girls who'd come in already able to read music, girls who'd played instruments as children. Most were like the five huddled around me just now, and I'd got quicker at matching up the notes with the right keys, though I still paused and fumbled.

They didn't need to know the songs well; that would come with time. All they needed was to be able to follow a melody

plausibly enough. I was done with the first four within an
hour and a half, and one by one they'd left the loge until now
I was alone with Charlotte. I'd left her for last. I would have
said I'd done so unthinkingly, but when she seated herself on
the piano bench beside me, I realized I'd done it purposefully,
that I liked her, and that troubled me and made me short, so
I banged out the melody of her song with impatient little
strokes.

She either didn't notice or didn't care. She frowned intensely at the music as if she could read it, and I had the impression she was trying somehow to hook the notes with the
sounds of the keys, unlike the others, who had wanted nothing more than to learn the melodies and the words and leave.
Charlotte was slow and thoughtful, but she knew the song before we'd gone through it twice.

I said, "Very good. You've sung to music before?"

"No. Not ever."

"Well, you've learned it better than the others in half the
time." I laid the sheets upon the folio of music on the piano's
top and rose. Charlotte stayed seated.

"Is there something else?" I asked.

She looked up at me. "Those things you say: that legato
and pianissi—whatever it was—"

"Pianissimo."

"What do they mean?"

I was uncomfortable. Had I really used those words? When
had they sneaked back into my mouth? How had I not noticed? "Smoothly. Softly."

"You a music teacher before you came here?"

In the two years I'd been teaching girls the songs, not a one
of them had ever asked me a question like that. Their uninter-
est had made me too comfortable, I realized suddenly. And
now I found myself nonplussed and uneasy.

"I'm a music teacher now, of a sort," I said roughly. "You
aren't the only one who needs help, you know. None of the

girls here read music but Annie." I hurried to the stairs. "I've
got things to do. You'd best get ready to work."

I WATCHED HER at the Palace that night, the way she dipped
and smiled, the equanimity with which she took the men to
the curtained boxes, her implacability when she returned, un-
moved, unblemished, seemingly untouched. It was clear she
was going to be a favorite. When she went onstage that night,
she sang the song I'd chosen for her easily, forgetting only
some of the lyrics, which was not at all unusual for a first
time, and at the end of it the applause was almost as great as it
was for Annie and Lil. My uneasiness with her questions had
faded; I could no longer remember why they'd disturbed me.
They were harmless enough—in fact, it seemed odder that no
one had asked them before now.

"Duncan says she stayed with you last night," Johnny said
as Charlotte came down from the stage. "Getting a little soft-
hearted in your old age?"

"She was trying to sleep on the back stoop," I told him.
"What else was I to do? Send her up to your room?"

"How about sending her on her way?"

"She's the best of the five you hired. I didn't want to
lose her."

I felt Johnny scrutinizing me, though I didn't look at him.
He said, "Well, it seems being a Good Samaritan suits you,
honey. You ain't so riled up today."

"Not yet," I told him. "You keep it up and you might force
me to it."

He laughed, and then he poured himself a whiskey and
went back into his office, and I wondered why I hadn't told
him that Charlotte would be staying with me for a while. I
hadn't told anyone. When Duncan asked if she'd found someplace, I'd told him yes and nothing more. I didn't want to explain myself. The truth was that I wasn't certain I could.

I went about the Palace that night soothing aggravated poker players and moving from table to table, and tonight it was easier than it had been for months; tonight I had no trouble laughing and smiling and flirting. The work I'd done to control Jenny had been effective. She had seemingly lost as much interest in her favorite customer as he had gained in me. It was second nature to keep him in the line that formed forever in my wake. After a month or two, he'd grow weary of it and disappear, and I would not think of him again, just as I'd forgotten so many others.

I hardly spoke to Charlotte at all; it was almost as if we didn't know each other, as if we moved in different orbits, and when the place died down and we went about closing up, it felt both strange and reassuring to know she would be coming back to the boardinghouse with me, that I wouldn't be alone.

When I called her over as Duncan readied to walk me home, he gave me a questioning look. I said, "Charlotte's staying at Mrs. McGraw's now too."

I waited for him to ask if she was still staying with me, but he didn't. Duncan had never been the curious type; he simply took everything in and accepted it. There had been times when I admired that, when I thought how nice it would be if nothing mattered. But I was not made the same way. The only numb thing about me was the scar on my face, and even that sometimes hurt, as if the memory of how it had been made had never quite left it.

We went to the boardinghouse in silence. Duncan said good night at the door. Charlotte yawned as she went up the stairs and was still yawning when we entered my room. I went to light the candle, which sent our shadows flickering about the walls, making it somehow seem smaller and more intimate than even it was.

"It was a long night," she confessed as she undressed. "I don't care for the singing."

"It didn't show."

She let me unbutton her and then shrugged out of the satin, leaving it crumpled on the floor. "I'd give my soul to bathe."

"Saturdays only," I said. "And it'll cost you fifty cents."

"Well, I'm saving so much on the room I guess I'll pay it." She laughed and plaited her hair, and then she went to the basin and washed with quick efficiency—her face and beneath her arms, raising her chemise to wash between her legs. Then she rinsed her mouth, spitting into the chamber pot she dragged from beneath the bed. "But this is a sight better than where I was living before, I can tell you that."

"In Portland?"

"Yeah."

I waited for her to volunteer something more, but she didn't, and I slipped off my own dress and went to the bureau, where I'd put away the packages I'd bought at the druggist's yesterday. How intimate we were, washing in front of each other, undressing, and yet we were strangers, and I felt it in what she didn't say, in what I didn't volunteer.

She asked, "You been in Seattle long?"

"A few years," I said. I took out the henna and laid it on top of the dresser.

"You been with Johnny all that time?"

"Yes."

She went to the bed and lifted the blankets, slipping between them. "The two of you are partners."

I nodded. I unknotted the twine on the packages, pulling it loose, then unfolding the paper on the first one to reveal the green powder within.

"I saw him with Sally," she said.

"She's his new favorite."

"But he watches you."

"Johnny and I have a history," I said. "But that part of it's over. Mostly, anyway."

"Annie says he's in love with you."

"Annie says a lot of stupid things."

Charlotte laughed sleepily. "Yeah, she does, but that seems true enough to me." She moved a little, the mattress creaked and shifted. "You coming to bed?"

"In a while. There's something I need to do yet." ·

"All right." She turned over, a shuffling of blankets, her soft sigh.

I went to the window and lifted it just enough to pour out the water she'd washed with, hearing it splash into the mud below, and then I poured the henna powder into the basin and mixed it with water until it was a grassy, muddy paste. I glanced over my shoulder. Charlotte was quiet, her eyes closed. I took the basin over to the dresser so I would disturb her less, and then I began to scoop the paste into my hair. It was cold and unpleasant, but I worked diligently, massaging it into my scalp, along my temples, into the hair at my nape. I didn't need a mirror; I had done this the same way so many times I could do it by feel alone.

"You look too young to have gray hair," Charlotte said.

I started. I'd thought she was asleep. "It starts early in my family."

She sat up, ghostly white in the near darkness, the candle flame playing over her skin, glinting in her hair. She was out of bed in a moment, coming over to me before I realized what she was about. "Let me help," she said, and then, before I could protest, she was dipping her fingers into the paste and her hands were in my hair.

"Don't," I said. "Go back to sleep."

Her voice was very soft. "Let me do this."

And so I let her. Charlotte's fingers were strong and steady; they felt good against my scalp, working through my hair. I could not remember the last time someone had touched me this way, without meaning to have something in return.

When she was finished, she asked, "How long does it stay on?"

"Half an hour," I told her, and then, when I saw her yawn again, "Go on back to bed. I can finish it. There's no need for you to stay up."

She shook her head. "I don't need much sleep. A couple of hours." She sat on the bed. "Whoring'll train you to that."

"How'd you come to it?"

Bluntly, without preamble or hesitation, she said, "I ran away from my husband and trusted a man I shouldn't have. How'd you come to the Palace?"

Her question was so direct it took me by surprise, and then I cursed myself for asking her anything, for the quid pro quo it accorded her. I shrugged, trying to make it seem casual, a simple answer to a simple question, when nothing was that simple at all. The memory surged back; with effort I pushed it away. "I was looking for a job. Johnny gave me one."

"As his partner?"

"No. I scrubbed floors and shared his bed," I said, and my words held a bitterness I hadn't expected and didn't want her to hear. "The partnership came later."

"You must've been some fuck." When I glanced sharply at her, she smiled knowingly and said, "Well, ain't you? No man makes a partner of a woman unless she's got her hands around his balls. Else why not just put you to work on the stage?"

I felt a flicker of anger—too much, too quick, and with effort I suppressed it. This was no longer my old life, and Charlotte was only partly wrong. "It was just a saloon then. To make it a boxhouse was my idea."

"How'd you come up with that?"

"Johnny means to make the Palace a theater. This way is close enough that he forgets what he really wants."

Charlotte frowned. "Why d'you want him to forget it? A theater sounds pretty good."

I faltered. A careless answer on my part, a too perceptive question on hers. I searched for a plausible lie. "Because

Johnny isn't thinking. Look around you. You think a real theater could make money here? With phrenologists a quarter a
ticket? Or temperance and woman suffrage lectures? No acting
troupe's been to Seattle in more than a year. They don't even
come to Squire's."

She snorted. "Squire's. Is it really an opera house?"

"That's what the sign says."

"Why the hell did they build it?"

"I don't know," I said, trying not to remember how it had
drawn me those first days, how I'd gone out of my way to
walk by it, how I'd hoped each time to see a placard for an
opera in its close-set windows, how I'd been both disappointed and relieved when there was nothing. Once I'd stood
so long outside the dry goods store leasing its bottom floor that
the clerk came out to ask me what I wanted.

"I guess a city's always trying to be finer than it is," Charlotte said. "So you were the smart one. And Johnny listened to
you. That ain't like a man."

"He's not a fool. Don't ever make the mistake of thinking
he is."

"Believe me, I don't."

"In any case, it worked. We make money, and Johnny gets
to pretend he's an impresario, for what it's worth."

"You regret it?"

"What makes you ask that?"

"You sounded angry."

Henna dripped at my temple and I wiped it away impatiently. "Did I? Pardon me. What the hell do I have to be angry
about? I run whores for a living. Isn't that every girl's dream?"

"Some girls."

"Well, it wasn't mine."

"No? What was yours then?"

I took a deep breath and closed my eyes. "I don't know.
Something different."

"At least you ain't spreading your legs for two dollars."

My laugh was short and hard. I regretted it almost the next moment, because when I looked at her, she was staring at me as if I'd just given her some clue to a mystery she was trying to figure out. Nervously, I said, "So what about you, Charlotte? You mean to marry your way out like some of the other girls?"

She snorted. "No."

"You can't expect to work at the Palace forever?"

Her mouth cracked in a smile. "Don't worry, Marguerite, you won't have to worry about a sixty-year-old whore."

"That wasn't what I meant."

"I don't think about the future. One day at a time is hard enough."

That was something I understood.

When it was time, she rinsed the henna from my hair and applied the black, and once the paste was in my hair and the air was filled with its mashed-pea smell, she rinsed her hands. But they were covered with the blue-gray stains I knew would not fade for days, working up the discoloring of her scar like a shadow growing with the passing of the hours. She went back to the bed to wait, curling up on the mattress, and within a few minutes she was asleep. I watched her there, breathing slowly and evenly, her arm crooked beneath her face, and thought about the things she'd said, the things I'd told her that I hadn't meant to say, and I wondered about her, who she was, what she thought of me. It was the first time in three years—or even before that, really—that I'd felt such curiosity about someone. I'd never asked a single question about Duncan's past, and what I knew of Johnny's was because he'd told me, not because I'd cared enough to know. The other girls in the Palace . . . well, they were just whores I was meant to manage; I could hardly be bothered to re- member their names.

It had been a long time since I'd revealed something about myself to another person, and I didn't like it. I didn't like the essence of her, or the way it clung to me. I didn't like the way her breathing eased my loneliness.

But neither did I want to dispel it.

When the half hour was up, I rinsed the black henna from my hair and toweled it dry and then I quietly lifted the sill to pour the water out. She shifted and murmured in her sleep, and I went still until she settled again, looking out at the sky, growing paler now with the faint light of dawn.

I put up my hair and then gently crawled into bed. She turned and eased close, in her sleep searching for warmth, pressing her chemise-covered legs against mine.

MY DREAMS WERE tossed and vibrant, a closed gate, beyond its cast-iron rails a city I knew very well. I was shivering and cold, waiting, and I didn't want to be there; I was afraid. At first I was alone, and then my brother stood beside me, whispering: "It would be best if you ran, you know." And I meant to. I meant to run. But my feet were stuck fast, and then the gates began to open, and he was gone, and it was too late. Far too late—

I woke with a gasp, clawing at the bedcovers in fear. It was a moment before I realized Charlotte was beside me, opening her eyes sleepily at my movement, frowning.

"What's wrong?"

"A bad dream," I said. I crawled over her, suddenly desperate to get out of bed. The light that shifted through the crack in the curtains was bright, and with unsteady hands I opened them. There was a good wind blowing through the treetops on the hills above the tideflats, breaking up the overcast so that the peak of Mount Rainier sat like an illusion in the sky, its foot still shrouded in clouds so it looked as if it were floating, rather like Wagner's Valhalla.

I remembered the first time I'd seen it—not until weeks after my arrival here, when one day the perpetual gray had lifted and the Mountain had appeared so suddenly and huge that I was convinced I was seeing things. There it was, giant and snow covered, looming above the black treed hills to overlook Seattle, so large that it seemed the town was nestled in its hollows, as if one could walk through the forest and come upon its slopes after a short trek, though Duncan told me it was sixty miles away. The blue-gray of glaciers and shadowed crannies sculpted it; the sunset colored it blue and gold and pink. They called it Rainier in Seattle, though Duncan told me the Indians had another name for it—Tahoma—and that to them it was a god.

The next day the rain came again, and it was gone, but now I knew it was there, veiled by clouds. I'd begun to think of the Mountain as a benevolent watcher, a good omen, though today even that could not soothe me. The dream had brought the edges back again. I was uneasy, uncomfortable in my skin, feeling the constant need to move about, as if I were running from that gate in my waking life too.

Quickly I washed and dressed. I wanted out of this room and into the air, where the wind could blow me about, but as I went to the door Charlotte said, "Where are you going?"

"Out," I said sharply.

"D'you want some company?"

I turned back to look at her. There was only one thing I knew that softened those edges, and even then it was only as temporary as Johnny had said it was. When I was in a mood like this it was better for everyone to keep distant.

"No," I said bluntly, opening the door, stepping into the hallway. "I'll see you at the Palace."

I closed the door firmly behind me, and the moment I did, I found myself regretting that I'd told her to stay. I forced myself to go down the stairs and out through the front door. She would discover soon enough the woman that the girls at the Palace had warned her of, and that was better. That was how it should be.

The air was cold and brisk; there was the sense of movement in it that suited my restlessness, the low clouds scudding
across the sky, the creak of the ropes holding swaying signs,
the smoke from the foundry and the mill blowing away in
wisps instead of gathering to glower over everything. The
Mountain's peak disappeared and appeared again; the branches
of the firs and the cedars waved about like feathered arms; the
already bent tops of the hemlocks bowed deeper. My skirt and
my cloak tangled about my legs as I walked down the ramp
and into the street, making my way toward the waterfront,
where I hoped the distraction of the busy harbor might soothe
me for a time. I wanted to see the water capping in the wind
and the fattened sails of the schooners and the clippers, the
plungers skirting the water like tiny seabirds before the steamer
wheels.

It was not far to Commercial Street, with its businesses
more respectable than those farther down on the sawdust: the
Gem Saloon and Schwabacher Brothers dry goods and two
butchers, the Miner's Supply and the three-storied, elegantly
embellished Squire's Opera House with its overhanging balus-
trade. Today I could not bear even to look at it. I started down
the street toward the wharf, where the mill spewed its black
smoke into the air.

I was halfway there when I heard someone calling my
name. I looked over my shoulder to see her: Charlotte, running
toward me, her hair still in its braid trailing out behind her.

I stopped. She raced up to me, skidding to a stop, her boots
sliding through the mud. Her cheeks were flushed and she was
breathing hard.

"What is it?" I asked. "What happened?"

She bent over, pressing her hand to her stays to catch her
breath, and motioned for me to wait a moment. Then she
gasped, "I'm coming with you."

I didn't know whether to feel warm or irritated; I felt a little of both. "Just leave me the hell alone."

"Look, I thought . . . you been a friend to me and I—"

"I don't make friends with whores." The words were out of my mouth before I could call them back, that cruelty in me gaining hold, tainting everything, a meanness that matched the sharp edges inside of me.

She stopped short.

I kept walking. She would leave me alone now, as I'd warned her she should do. The next time—if there ever was a next time—she would listen to me.

I reached the mill. On the wharf, men hurried about like ants, shouting to one another beyond the growing pile of saw-dust that eventually would be spread on the tideflats. The whir of the saw was loud in my ears. I dodged off the board-walk, turning onto the wharf. The tide was out. I jumped the three feet to the rocky beach below, sliding a little on rolling pebbles.

The wind was cold and whipping, the water slapping upon the rocks, gray with the reflection of the sky. The trestles lead-ing to the colliers crossed the shallow tideflats like black stitches; beyond, Elliott Bay was dotted with steamers whose smoke tangled and spread in the wind, schooners and the little private plungers speeding, dipping, and dodging across wakes, and everywhere canoes maneuvering across the choppy water with sinuous grace. I watched them, wondering where they were all going, and for a moment I let my own soul fly with them—I didn't care what the destination; only that it was away from here.

It was a moment before she came up beside me, before I re-alized she had not gone after all.

I stared at her with bewilderment and suspicion. "Didn't you hear me?"

"I heard you just fine."

"Then why are you still here?"

"What was your nightmare about?" she asked.

I looked out at the harbor. "Nothing. I don't remember."

She was quiet, which was a blessing, but after a moment I relented, I said, "It's best if you keep your distance, Charlotte. I . . . I can't always control it."

"Control what?"

"Just . . . sometimes everything . . ." I trailed off, shrugging in frustration, unable to explain how it felt, how the moods came, how when they did I honestly didn't care that I was hurting people, how my anger was all that mattered. I felt oddly exposed and shamed at it. I felt the heat move into my face, and I dipped my head, unable to look at her.

She stood there beside me, close enough that her loosened hair whipped against my cheek in the wind. She didn't say anything more, and neither did I, but I felt some hardness within me soften and give way; I felt her solace like a whisper.

From the Journal of Sabine Conrad

SEPTEMBER 20, 1871—I am not with child. This morning I had my monthly visitor. <u>Thank God</u>!!!

But I have had a letter from Papa telling me I must leave the tour and come home, as he says I have shamed him and he is angry at both Barret and Gideon—they cannot watch me as well as his own eyes and I am obviously not the daughter he thought he had raised. He has sent train tickets for me and Barret, and says Gideon can of course make up his own mind what to do but that he must do a great deal of explaining if Papa is to allow him to see Willa again.

There is a postscript from Willa berating me for being the cause of Papa's bad humor with Gideon, and telling me that I must convince him to come back with me and Barret because she is beginning to wonder if he loves her even a little bit. And she tells me again to remember my promise to her.

Barret says we must go home, that he is worried for me and he thinks this life is not good for either of us. He says, "On tour it's too easy to forget what's right and wrong," and that I am forgetting who I am. I screamed at him that I knew perfectly well who I was, that I was no longer some immi-

grant's daughter, but <u>Sabine Conrad</u>, and that I didn't want
to live without performing, and he said, "There's still the
Völksstadt," as if it should be good enough for me when even
he disdains it, and I wanted to hit him, I was so angry.

Then he told me it was my own fault and now I must take
the punishment and I said it had been his idea that I go after
Paolo so he was equally to blame. He looked so guilty and tormented then that I felt horrible. He is my brother and I love
him best and I don't like to fight with him. So I forgave him
and went into his arms and told him now that Mrs. Follett is
gone, we have a responsibility to stay because I am the tour's
prima donna. Mr. Cone decided two weeks ago to cut the duets
in favor of arias because the audiences so love me, and so
I sing alone, without a tenor to partner me. It is clear the audiences come to see me, and if I were to leave, the whole company must disband, so there is much more than just me to
think of.

Barret is afraid to go against Papa so plainly, but I told
him he was of his majority now and Papa cannot order him
about like a child, and anyway we would be forgiven when
Papa saw how much money the rest of the tour brings in. He
could not disagree with that! He saw the sense in my argument finally, and so he has agreed to join Gideon and me in
standing up to Papa.

Gideon has said not to worry; that if I stood firm, Mr. Cone
and Mr. Wilson would fight to keep me, though they don't
know what they can do legally, because we are past the dates
of the original contract, and Papa's agreement to extend the
tour is only in a letter. But he tells me to have hope, and not to
bend, and so it shall be.

SEPTEMBER 22, 1871—Today terrible news! Gideon received
word that his mother has died. In spite of my own worries,
I was very sad for him, but he told me she had been ill and
under a doctor's care for some months. This was very surprising to me, as he had said not a word about it, although

I suppose there is no reason he should speak to me of it. I have never met his mother, though I know she was a seamstress at Stewart's and Willa had told me his mother had such high hopes for Gideon's music career, and that she was all he had because his father abandoned them when Gideon was born, so he did not know him at all.

He is leaving us for a few days to attend to her funeral, and I am very jealous (though I have no right to be) that it will be Willa at his side, comforting him.

That, along with everything else, has put me in a very bad temper.

SEPTEMBER 27, 1871—It is settled—I am not going home!

In the end it was not Mr. Cone or Mr. Wilson, nor Barret, who changed Papa's mind. It was Gideon. While he was home for his mother's funeral, he visited Papa too and arranged everything.

He was gone three days, and I thought of him every moment, and of Willa with him. I was at rehearsal with Mr. Cone and Mr. Wilson when he showed up at the theater, dusty still from the train and so grim that it squeezed my heart to look at him. He told them he'd spoken to Papa and that the tour could continue, and then he gave me the letter from Papa, which I burned, because I could not bear to read again the things Papa had written. How unfair he is in accusing me of being selfish and thoughtless and Barrett of being weak. And as for Willa— Gideon has broken things off with her. He told me so when I said that it was a pity his mother had not lived to see him and Willa wed, and he said that his mother had not been anticipating a wedding, and there was something about the way he said it that made me think she had not known anything of Willa at all, and then he told me everything was ended.

Now, of course, Willa is very angry with me. She says I vowed to bring him home—did she want me to drag him there by the ear? How could I promise he would love her forever?

He is twenty-four, after all, a grown man who knows his own mind.

But I do feel guilty too, because later, when I asked Gideon what his reason was for ending it with Willa, he said, "Why, because of you," very quietly, as if he didn't like to admit it, and I confess I could hardly breathe for joy. It isn't over between us! Oh, perhaps I _am_ selfish, and I do not like to hurt Willa, but is it so very bad of me to love him as I do?

NEW YORK CITY, DECEMBER 10, 1871—It has only been six weeks since the tour ended, but my yearning for it is a torment. We have put up at a small hotel just off Broadway, better than we can afford, but not quite good enough for society, so Gideon says we should try not to stay long. He & Barret share a room and I have my own, which is very small but comfortable enough. I find myself sleeping far too late in the morning and staying up far too late at night, still used to the hours of the tour, though there is nothing now to keep me busy. I miss singing every night—practicing is not the same. To see the tears, to hear the applause . . . I would even take the Völksstadt just now, though Gideon will not hear of it.

When we returned, Renate and Mr. Arriete offered us rooms at their home, but Gideon told me that she only means to use me, now that I have grown more famous. And she did ask if I might keep her husband in mind for future tours so we could be together again. I thought it was out of love for me, but Gideon says I am too naive for my own good. So I refused her. I felt terrible about it, because she seemed so hurt, but Gideon said it was all an act and I trust that he knows better than I do.

Also, Mr. Cone & Mr. Wilson offered to manage me, but I told them Barret was my manager and I could not abandon him. Even if Barret hasn't the experience to know what to do with me, he is good at listening to Gideon, who does, and Barret is trying to learn all he can. Gideon is full of plans for all of us. In spite of how late the two of them stay out at night, it doesn't seem to affect Gideon in the daytime, when he writes letters for Barret to sign on my behalf and chases down Mr. Maretzek, who has leased the Academy of Music for next season's opera, to try to secure an interview. Gideon never leaves without a book of my favorable notices in his hand. Barret tags along, though I think he doesn't feel very useful. I asked Gideon if he could at least try to give Barret more to do, but he reminded me of the mess Barret had made of the affair with Paolo and said it had taken all his skill to salvage things, and that he was not quite ready to trust Barret again with something so important as my career, but he would if I wished it.

I had not thought of it that way, and of course Gideon is right. But I did feel a little guilty—Barret has dedicated himself to managing me, and even if he has been well rewarded for it, I cannot just dismiss him. So I asked if perhaps Gideon could think of one small thing for Barret to do, and he smiled and said he would.

Gideon was worried, when we arrived home, that news of my affair with Paolo would have got out, which would have been very bad for my chances of securing an audition with Mr. Maretzek, as society would not approve, and would shun my performances, but it seems Paolo didn't return to New York City and so my reputation is unblemished! But Gideon has not been able to get work with any company because of the things Follett said about him, and so we must depend on me. He has been frustrated and cross, which is one of the reasons, I suppose, that he and Barret go out every night.

But I also know it is because of me. It's very hard to be so close to each other, and never speak of it or act upon it! Sometimes when he looks at me I feel as if my heart must burst from my chest. I tell myself that soon we will be together, and I can be his equal in patience for now. If he must go out with Barret every night rather than give in to temptation, then I mustn't complain.

He means to cheer Barret too, I know, as he's been low

since we came home. Sometimes I see my brother looking at me as if I am a puzzle he cannot figure out, and he is always staring out the window toward Tompkins Square. He asked me the other day if I missed it. I told him no, and he asked me if I was going to be angry at Papa and Willa forever. I answered him that it was they who were angry at me. Papa wouldn't speak to me when I went to the Völksstadt after we returned, in spite of the fact that I'd sent him all but a very little of the money I'd earned and I saw the new settee it had bought upstairs. He told Barret that he wondered how he had the hodes to look him in the face after failing so badly. Mama said it was best if we stayed away for a time, and Willa . . . I can still feel the sting of her hand against my cheek.

No, I don't want to go back there. I don't know if I will ever want to go back, though I suspect that Papa will soften after a time, even if Willa never does. But now, with Christmastime approaching and the city growing festive—yesterday it snowed—I do miss them, even if I am mostly relieved that I am away. But now I hear Barret and Gideon at the door and I must go—

* * *

N.B. I am to audition for Mr. Maretzek!!!!! Gideon has secured it, and he and Barret brought me home a Christmas stollen to celebrate, and we ate every bite of it and drank wine and Gideon kissed me in congratulations (or so he told Barret, but the kiss did not feel like only a congratulatory kiss) and I am now a little drunk and very happy. The audition is next week. Gideon tells me I must sing Pamina and Rosina and that I must practice every day before the audition because I have become a bit breathy and my shoulders raise too high and so I am not as beautiful singing as I could be.

DECEMBER 16, 1871—This morning I had the audition with Max Maretzek. I had not been inside the Academy before, and only the stage was lit, but the gold trim of the boxes and the curtains glimmered in the light, and it was so big! So much bigger than I'd thought, with the shadows disappearing into the boxes above and into space below that seemed to extend so far out I could not imagine where it would end, like a huge cave, with every voice echoing up into the rafters and suspended there. Mr Jarrett, the business manager, was there as well, and Barret and Gideon, who played for me. I was very nervous, though I had been practicing, and I knew the arias flawlessly. Still, Pamina especially is very difficult to sing, as it is mostly in the middle voice and pianissimo and a lament too, so that one must act so solemn and bereaved. Before I went onstage Gideon kissed my forehead and then rubbed his thumb, though there was no rouge to rub away, and whispered *"In boca al lupo"* for luck.

Once Gideon began to play, I forgot to be nervous. I was to sing "Ich bin fuhls" first, and then Rosina, and Gideon added my favorite Zerlina too because I do it very well, and he believes the ingenue parts are the ones I am best for just now. Barret smiled up at me, and I sang for him, and my voice sounded so magnificent there that the passion came over me as if it were newfound. I forgot all else until the last notes died away. I was a little stunned when it was over, so I failed to see the expressions on Mr. Maretzek's and Mr. Jarrett's faces.

They said nothing except "Thank you, Miss Conrad," and I was certain I had failed, but Gideon told me it was how they always were, and to be patient. So I am trying to be, but I'm not very good at it. Gideon says that if they want me, we will know it by the end of the week, which seems far too long to wait.

DECEMBER 18, 1871—I've heard nothing yet, and I'm in despair! The audition only made my longing for the stage worse! I told Gideon this morning he must arrange another tour for me or we will all starve, and he snapped at me that he was looking for a company every day and what else should he do?

His tone surprised me, so I broke into tears. Though both of us knew he should not, he took me in his arms and whispered he was sorry, but that the wait affects us all and the two of us must support each other and not let anything come between us. And I said, "Not anything?" and he looked at me and such a communion passed between us!!! I knew he wanted to kiss me, and oh how I wanted it too, but I meant to be noble and turn away—it has only been a few months since he broke with Willa after all. But in the end I could not. There was no one there to see or stop us, and his lips were so soft and yet so forceful too. I could not have pulled away for the world, and he was the one who had to stop it. I was so breathless and confused and longing. . . . I begged him to forgive me, and said it was so hard to live with uncertainty and Barret esp. does not bear it well. He has come home every night quite drunk.

Gideon said that Barret didn't have the faith in me that he did, but that we shouldn't hold that against him. He said that Barret forgets the dreams we had, but he never will, and he hoped I wouldn't either. Which I never shall!!!

DECEMBER 20, 1871—It's almost Christmas. Barret sent Mama a note saying where we were staying, but we've heard nothing from them. I do not think I shall go even if we do.

Barret is still drunk this morning. He is lying on the end of my bed, curled up like a babe, laughing at what he says is a strange pattern on the rug.

DECEMBER 25, 1871—Christmas Day—I write this very late. It is near two in the morning, and the moon is very bright, so I don't even need a candle. The snow piled in the gutters is too dirty to reflect the moon's shine, but at least it's cold enough that the stink of shit and rotting garbage isn't as strong as usual. When the horses piss on the street it freezes immediately, leaving little pools of ice to slip on when you cross, and it is so cold that my fingers are still stiff, though we returned to the hotel hours ago.

I find I would rather write about these things than what happened today, but I can't sleep either and so perhaps writing things down might help.

The day started out well enough. Gideon and Barret came to my room in the morning and Gideon gave me a soft pair of expensive kid gloves—he says he bought them when we were on tour and has kept them for me all this time. They fit perfectly. He helped me try them on, as they are very tight, and when Barret wasn't looking he kissed the underside of my wrist and whispered that he would give me a proper Christmas kiss later, and I was trembling at the thought of it. For Barret he had a leather wallet "to keep the money in when Sabine sings at the Academy," and a bottle of brandy "for celebrating," though we've not heard from Maretzek yet. Barret gave me a bag of toffee, which I love, and to Gideon he gave candied orange peel, and I had for them each a knitted scarf that I bought from some old woman who was selling them near the Washington Market—not the best or softest wool, but the colors were pretty: blue for Gideon and green for Barret.

There were none of Mama's pfeffernuesse or springerle or Papa's Christmas ale. Just coffee, and not very good coffee at that, and day-old sweet rolls that Gideon fetched from the bakery down the street the night before. I was thinking that the only flaw was that Mama and Papa and the others weren't with us, when there was a knock on the door, and Papa stood there, come to bring Barret and me to Christmas dinner.

I was very happy, thinking we would all be together, and Papa had forgiven us, but then I saw the way he was looking at Gideon, as if he couldn't stand the sight of him. When I said I wished to invite him, Papa refused, and Gideon said it was all right, that we should go on. I felt terrible leaving him there, especially as it is his first Christmas without his mother. I asked him had he any other family to spend the day with and he said Barret and I were his only family now, so I felt doubly sad—it doesn't seem fair that I should be forgiven when he is not, especially when, without him, I would not have a career. I told Papa this as we were walking, and he said if I wished to talk about Gideon then I should go back, as he would not tolerate mention of him.

It felt so good to be home that I forgot Gideon for a while. I had missed it: the smell of beer and smoke and fried fish that has seeped into the walls, so it is always there, like the quiet beat of a drum below a melody; the sound of Mama humming as she cooked sauerbraten and baked apples; Gunther playing with his new Christmas top. The only thing that marred it was Willa, who offered her cheek to Barret and laughed with him, but only gave me a cold stare and said Happy Christmas as if I were a stranger she must be polite to.

Willa has a new beau, Mama said. A German like us, a good, solid boy who will inherit his father's grocery one day. Mama said Willa was happy, but she said it with a sigh and a sidelong glance at me, as if she thought Willa might never be truly happy again and it was my fault.

Papa gave us some of the Christmas ale he'd brewed and we drank it with springerle that was dry in my mouth. By the time Mama served up the sauerbraten, Barret was so drunk that he dragged his shirt cuff through his plate and knocked over a chair. Papa stared at him with disapproval that only grew worse as the evening went on and Willa looked at me as if that were my fault too. Then, after Barret broke into a loud guffaw over some stupid thing Gunther said, Papa asked him since when had his oldest son become so dissolute, and Barret told Papa that he was old enough to do as he pleased. They said some horrible things to each other, and Barret kept drinking until he could barely stand upright and his eyes were glassy and his nose red and I said it was time we should be getting back to the hotel. Then Willa said to me that she wasn't surprised Barret had become a drunk, given that he must take responsibility for my bad behavior, and that I was no better than *eine Dirne* who must have every man she sees and I lost my temper and said perhaps she should look to herself for the reason that Gideon no longer loved her.

Then Papa exploded that he would not hear that name in his house, and I yelled back that Gideon had made my career possible and they should be grateful to him. Papa said, "Grateful? For what? For taking my daughter on a tour that taught her to forget her good upbringing?" He said the daughter he had raised would not have betrayed her own sister or made herself into a whore. I yelled back that none of them understood me at all, and he spat at me that it was true, and that he had no wish to understand a girl who so easily and thoughtlessly sullied her family's good name. Then he told Barret and me to get out, and I was glad to go.

Mama was crying, and Gunther calling out after us, and it was dark and cold and starting to snow, and Barret could not walk without help. I had to support him while the both of us slipped on the ice and he was laughing and stupid and then he fell on his ass, nearly taking me down with him. He lolled back on a mound of garbage, falling through the layer of ice and snow that disguised it, laughing like some mad idiot. I was so angry I cursed him in German, and he said: "No more German, Bina, remember?" and then he began to sob.

I had never seen him like that. Never so drunk, never so sad. His crying was so gulping and loud that someone opened their window and called out to ask if he was all right and when I said he was only drunk they said to shut him up, he was waking the baby. I tried to grab him and pull him to his feet, but he grabbed my hands instead and I lost my balance and fell into him, and he put his arms around me and held me so tight I could not move, and cried into my hair. He kept saying: "What are we doing, Bina? What are we doing here? This is all wrong. We should be at home." I told him home was the hotel now, with Gideon, and Barret said we should not stay with Gideon, that he was not what he seemed.

I was very angry with him then. I pulled away and pushed at him so he went deeper into the garbage, and I said coldly that Gideon had done everything for me. Then I walked away, though I knew better than to walk alone at night in this neighborhood.

Barret ran up behind me, falling into me to stop himself, hard, so I stumbled, and as we passed through the halo of a streetlamp, his tears glistened like trails of light on his face. He kept saying he was sorry for failing me, that he meant to take care of me and he would not fail again.

Then we were back at the hotel. He would not come up with me, though I begged him. He said he wanted a drink and went staggering off like a man meaning to fall down at the first comfortable place. I ran up the stairs to Gideon's room and I pounded on the door like a mad thing until he opened it. His eyes were heavy and he was holding a book, and he looked so beautiful in that moment, so safe, that I launched myself at him, crying into his chest, not realizing until his arms came around me and he pried me gently away that his shirt was open and I had been pressing my face against his bare skin. "What happened?" he asked me. "Where's Barret?"

I could not tell him everything; I only told him that Barret was drunk and mad, and that Gideon must go after him or I was afraid we would find him tomorrow dead in some ditch, and he threw his book aside and grabbed his coat from the hook beside the door and told me to go to my room and stay there, buttoning his shirt as he hurried down the hall.

That is all I know. Neither of them have returned, and I've been listening very closely. I have not heard a single step. I have put the gloves Gideon gave me on my pillow, where I can see them and touch them, the softest kid, the purest white. And I intend now to think of them as a good luck charm, because only a lady of society would own such a useless thing as white kid gloves. It means that Gideon has faith that I will be hired to sing at the Academy of Music. It means he thinks everything will work out, and we will be rich and successful and as lauded as I was in Philadelphia and Boston and Chicago. Even Barret was happy then.

CHAPTER 7

Seattle, Washington Territory—March 1881

It took longer than Mrs. McGraw had predicted for Mr. Clemmons to leave. After three weeks, he still wasn't gone, though Mrs. McGraw said he kept promising he would go. "I'll have that room for you yet, Miz Rainey," she said, and Charlotte gave me a troubled glance that had me reassuring her that I didn't mind.

Truthfully, I didn't. I had grown used to her; the sound of her breathing, the warmth of her, as much a part of the room as the rickety bureau or the faded calico curtains. At the Palace, we were as separate as two women could be; I barely spoke to her there. I still hadn't told Johnny or Duncan that she was staying with me, and I tried to ignore her. Having favorites only made me vulnerable. But at night I felt myself drawn to that settledness in her, and though I never said it to her or anyone else, I found it hard in the morning to wake, to be separate again.

March had come in mild—the lamb instead of the lion—and the Mountain showed itself more often than not, as did the Olympics across the Sound—the mountain range standing stark and white and blue, craggier than the Cascades that Rainier belonged to, older still.

The first real sunny day after the long, gray winter had a restorative effect on everyone. When I went to the Palace that afternoon, my arms full of new gowns that had been altered by the seamstress, the girls were smiling and bright. My own mood was good as well, but it had little to do with the sun, and much more to do with the pile of dresses I carried.

Johnny was in his office, but Sally was lolling about at the bar, and when I said, "Time to get ready, Sally." She gave me one of the smug looks that had become more frequent, a look that said she didn't have to do anything I said because she was fucking Johnny.

"I'll be there in a bit," she said casually.

I smiled back at her. "You just take your time."

She frowned, but I kept walking, pushing open the door to the dressing room with my hip. The room was small and crowded, especially now, when all the girls were here and getting ready for the evening's entertainment. They sat about on the rough benches, powdering themselves and brushing their hair and rolling up their stockings, leaning over one another to see into the single, spotted old mirror. Today they were laughing and joking, which was rarely the case; another reason to thank the good weather.

"New dresses!" squealed Jenny as I came inside, and Lil and Annie spun around from the mirror to see. I glanced at Charlotte, pinning up her hair, and felt warm when she smiled.

I let the dresses fall onto a bench in a rustle of satin and cheap silk and lace and fringe, and the girls swarmed around me like bees. "No new ones until the old ones are in my hands," I directed as I disentangled the gowns. "I'm taking them to be cleaned and mended."

They surged away, grabbing up gowns and pantalettes from the benches, all trying to shove them into my hands at once, and I laughed.

"Here's a pink for Jenny," I said, taking her old green.

She snatched the pink from my hands, pressing it to her chemise-clad breasts. It made her cheeks look flushed and pretty, a good color for her. There had been some strain between us since the incident with her lover, and this was my way of making it up to her. When she looked up at me with shining eyes I knew she'd accepted my tacit apology. "Oh, thank you, Marguerite!"

"It will look good on you," I said, and then they were all crowding around again.

"Could I have the blue?"

"I'll take the purple!"

"Oh, Marguerite, thank you! Thank you!" As if the dresses were diamonds. Still, I smiled at how well they loved me at this moment. Benevolently, I handed out the others, including the one I'd had altered especially for Charlotte, a bronze silk with lace added to the sleeves to lengthen them so they covered her scar, and her nod of appreciation was worth the pains I'd taken.

They were all dressing in their new finery—if it could be called that—when Sally deigned to enter the dressing room. There was one gown left, one I'd bought with her in mind, and it had taken some effort to find a yellow in such an unappealing grayish mustard. I could not imagine who had created the color, because I could not imagine a complexion it would favor. There wasn't a girl in the Palace who would look good in that yellow, but Sally, with her pale skin and hair, would look especially horrible in it.

"This one's for you," I said, holding out the silk, trying not to smile when she drew back in dismay.

"Oh, not that! I'll just wear the old one."

I shrugged. "As you wish."

"I'd rather. Yellow makes me look sallow." She shuddered and went to her peg, lifting her gown from it.

I folded up the yellow very slowly.

Her gasp was loud enough that the other girls looked up. Sally held out her old dress. There was a huge, gaping rip in the bodice, a clean cut nearly severing the gown in two. "Look at this! Who did this? It's ruined!" Her eyes narrowed as she looked at me. "You did this, Marguerite, didn't you?"

I gave her my best innocent expression. "Why would I ruin a perfectly good gown?"

"Because you're jealous of me. You hate me with Johnny. Admit it, you do!"

"I don't have any claim on Johnny," I said coldly. "He can fuck who he likes. But I will say his taste has got worse over the years."

"You bitch!" She lunged at me, her eyes flashing.

Charlotte stepped in front of her, grabbing her arm. "Careful, Sally."

"Get out of her way," I snapped at Charlotte. "Let her try to hurt me. Then we'll see who Johnny really favors, won't we?"

The other girls went silent. Charlotte glanced at me, and then she dropped Sally's arm and stepped back. Sally was breathing hard, her face mottled with anger.

I held up the yellow. "I guess you have no choice, Sally, do you?"

She made a sound deep in her throat, a muffled, aborted scream, and threw the ripped gown on the floor. "I'm going to tell Johnny!"

"You do that," I said calmly.

She stormed from the room, letting the door slam behind her, and I looked at the other girls and said, "Hurry up. It's nearly four."

Then I followed Sally out. The bar was starting to fill; Jim Ryan and Lee Blotsky were already at their tables, shuffling their cards. Billy was leaning against the bar before he went upstairs to the piano—from the looks of it, he was already drunk. Johnny stood talking to Duncan. When Sally screamed, "Johnny! Johnny Langford!" he turned with an irritated expression.

"She's making me wear yellow!" Sally screamed.

Johnny frowned and looked past her to me. "Margie? What's this about?"

I stepped up to the bar. "Sally doesn't want to wear the new gown I bought her."

Impatiently, he said, "I don't got time for this, Sally. You do what Margie says."

"You always take her side!"

Johnny gave me a look. "Margie, take care of this."

"I'm trying," I said sweetly.

"I can't wear the yellow!" Sally threw herself at him. With little effort, he grabbed her by the shoulders to hold her away. "It's ugly! I won't wear it!"

"Then don't. And you can get the fuck out of here while you're at it." There wasn't a person in that bar who didn't hear the danger in Johnny's voice, and Sally was no exception.

She looked at him, and then she looked at me, and I saw the helplessness come into her face, and then the hatred, but I didn't care. When she said mulishly, "I'll wear the damn yellow," and marched past me, I had to hide my smile.

Johnny said, "Damn whores," and turned back to Duncan.

As I went back to the dressing room, Charlotte stood at the door, looking at me with an expression I couldn't fathom. When I passed her, she said, "She'll be lucky if anyone looks twice at her in that dress."

"Oh, I don't know. There's always someone too drunk to see straight."

"Christ, Marguerite, she was right: you *are* a bitch."

The word startled me coming from Charlotte, and the way she said it brought both shame and anger, and because I hated the shame, I let the anger swell. "Next time she'll think again before she crosses me."

"How'd she cross you? So she takes on airs once in a while because she's fucking Johnny. What do you care?"

I glared at her. "It's time Sally understood who's in charge around here. Do you need the same lesson?"

She didn't back down. "Didn't you ever learn to share? You got everything and she's got nothing. She don't even got Johnny; everyone knows he belongs to you."

"I've got everything?" I laughed in disbelief. "Is that what you think?"

"Don't you?"

"Go to hell. You don't know anything about me."

"You're right, I don't. But that ain't for lack of trying. I never met anyone who keeps everything so close as you."

I noticed the curious looks from the nearest tables, and I turned back and leaned close to her, deliberately lowering my voice as I said angrily, "If you don't like it, you're free to go. See if you're treated so well at the brothel down the street."

"At least a brothel's not pretending to be something it ain't," she returned. She met my glare with an equally hot one of her own, and then she turned on her heel and went into the crowd.

I was still angry as I went back to the bar. Johnny came up to me just as Billy played a song that was completely different from the one Betsey was singing. She faltered and threw a panicked look in my direction, and then, thankfully, Billy passed out, and the violin and bass continued on without him.

Johnny winced. "Christ. Who's been giving him whiskey?"

"He was drunk when he came in. Didn't you see? We haven't given him a drop."

Johnny poured himself a drink. "This is what happens when a man tries to bring a little culture into a hellhole. No wonder I never get society down here for anything but a surreptitious fuck. I think I'd sell my soul for a real attraction, but no, Squire's gets *Faust* and I get Billy puking over the piano keys."

All I heard was *Faust.*

"*Faust?*" I repeated blankly.

"Yeah. Some opera company's decided to try their luck out here next week. We'll see if they can sell tickets enough for one show, much less five."

I forgot Charlotte and Sally and everything else. The music went through my head without my beckoning it: the hammer blows of the overture leading into the beautiful harp, the Jewel Song—"Ah! je ris de me voir"—the quartet, the duet with Faust, "O nuit d'amour".... To hear it again ... I was caught up in the daydream of it until all I saw were the gas footlights blaring in my eyes; all I smelled were the beloved scents of rouge pots and sweat and perfume—

"You want to see *Faust,* Margie?" Johnny's voice was quiet, sinuous, tempting as a serpent's. When I glanced up I saw how closely he was watching me. He reached into the pocket of his vest, pulling out two pieces of thick yellowish paper. "Yesterday the marshal gave me two tickets when I paid him his monthly 'license' fee. It seems he don't appreciate the opera."

"You're going?" My voice came out in a croak.

"Maybe. I'm thinking about it. God knows I need something to remind me what the hell music really sounds like."

He held out the tickets for me to see. The writing upon them was bold and black.

FIVE NIGHTS ONLY!!! Special Seattle Engagement!

World-Famous INEZ FABRIZI COMPANY Presents

Gounod's FAUST

A DOUBLE cast of STAR performers!

WEDNESDAY NIGHT, 7:00 P.M.

"I—I can hardly believe it," I managed.

He fluttered the tickets at me. "What d'you say? Want to go?"

A touring company of *Faust* in Seattle—there was a time when I would have laughed at the very idea, when to see it would have been unfathomable. But now it seemed to brighten a corner of the darkness I lived in, though I knew it was dangerous to go. The kind of people who would be at this opera were exactly the kind of people I should avoid. One could not get lost among respectable people. Someone like me could not stay hidden. They read the newspapers and went to operas and theaters and read reviews and gossiped at their soirees and their dinners. They were the kind of people who had loved me once, who might still love me well enough to recognize me even through my disguise.

But more than that, I'd kept my hunger asleep these last three years; I was afraid to waken it. And Johnny was clever. Who knew what he might see in me while I watched *Faust?*

Yet the desire to hear it again—to hear *anything* again—was overwhelming. I could not resist it, and I had never been good at denying myself. I would have done anything for those tickets, and I didn't care if Johnny knew it.

"Yes, I want to go," I told him. "Yes."

AFTER THAT, I could not stop hearing it. "Ah! je ris de me voir" rang in my head all through that night; I no longer heard Billy's obscene attempts at playing the piano, nor the singing. I could not have said how the hours passed or what happened within them. Later, as I lay in bed staring up at the ceiling, it was as if I watched the whole opera unfurl before my eyes.

"Look, I'm sorry for what I said. You can stop punishing me."

Charlotte's quiet voice broke into my thoughts; the visions scattered like rose petals across a stage. In my excitement over *Faust,* I'd forgotten all about our argument that afternoon, and now I realized she'd taken my preoccupation for anger.

"I'm not punishing you," I said.

"You ain't said a word to me all night."

"I've been thinking of something else, that's all."

"What? Or is it a secret?"

I winced at her bitterness. "It's no secret. Johnny said he'd take me to see *Faust* next week, and I've thought of nothing else since."

"*Faust*? What's that?"

"An opera. There's a company coming to Seattle to play at Squire's."

"I thought you said no opera ever played there."

"None ever has before now."

"You like opera then?" she asked. "You know this *Faust*?"

"Don't you?"

"I never saw it. What's it about?"

"Faust sells his soul to the devil in return for eternal youth and pleasure, because he wants to seduce a young woman he's come to fancy. She falls in love with him and then he abandons her. She has his child and in a fit of madness kills it, and she's hanged for the crime. Satan tries to damn her, but she begs forgiveness for her sins, and the angels redeem her and take her up to heaven."

"What happens to Faust?"

"Nothing, I suppose. The curtain falls."

"So she pays for loving him, and he don't pay at all." She made a cynical little laugh. "Ain't that the truth of it."

"Well, he did sell his soul to the devil, remember. He no doubt ends up in hell."

"Yeah, but he got to make the choice, didn't he? He knew what his reward would be. What choice did she have?"

"She had a choice," I said quietly. "She shouldn't have believed him. She was a fool to do so."

She was still for a moment. I heard her steady breathing in the darkness. "What woman believes the truth when she's told it?" she asked, and her voice had changed; there was suddenly something so unbearably sad in it. "I don't think I like the story much."

"But the music is wonderful," I said, and then, because it was late and I was tired, and our conversation had lulled me into sweetness, I hummed it for her; just a little bit, a measure or two of the ballad of the King of Thule that led into the Jewel Song, and the feel of the melody vibrating in my throat was both strange and so familiar it brought tears to my eyes. I felt her go still and silent; I felt the reverence of her listening, and I knew that too, I remembered it with a pang that made my voice catch and trail off.

She sighed. "That was lovely. Does Johnny know you can carry a tune like that?"

How stupid I was. "No! God, no. And you mustn't tell him. Promise you won't tell him." I grabbed her hand, squeezing her fingers hard.

"You're hurting me."

"Promise me. Promise you won't say anything to Johnny."

"All right, all right," she said, and when I released her fingers, she rubbed them angrily. "I don't understand you. Why should that be so damned secret?"

"I just . . . I don't want him to know."

"Why the hell not?"

"He would . . . he would put me onstage."

"It ain't so bad. Took me a while to get used to it, but now it's all right."

"I can't go up there," I whispered.

She turned to me, her eyes dark as pitch in the candlelight. "There's something more, ain't there?"

"It's late. We should go to sleep."

"You used to sing on a stage, didn't you?"

I said nothing.

"You did," she said. "And you said it was your idea to turn the Palace into a boxhouse. Did you sing in one of them before you came here?"

I could have denied that I'd ever sung, but she would have known it for the lie it was, and she would be hurt, and I did not want to hurt her. "No. I've never sung in a boxhouse."

"Then where?"

I measured my words carefully, not wanting to reveal too much, nervous even at this. "I sang in a beer hall when I was young."

"A beer hall? So you do have talent."

"My father owned it."

"Even so. Johnny don't know this?"

"I've never told him. It's better that way. I don't want him to nag me about it. And I don't sing any longer in any case." I was growing uncomfortable now; I wanted the conversation to change.

"Why not?"

"I fell out of practice."

"How hard is it to fall back in?"

"Too hard," I said and felt the tears well in my eyes, the sadness I could not bear for her or anyone else to see. "I'm tired, Charlotte. Good night."

She murmured a good night. I heard her disappointment, but I couldn't salve it. Not now, not tonight. I rolled onto my side, away from her, so she wouldn't see me cry.

From the Journal of Sabine Conrad

JANUARY 9, 1872—I am to sing at the Academy. They want me for next season, to change off with Pauline Lucca and Clara Louise Kellogg for the Italian: *L'Africaine, Faust,* and *La Traviata.* I would be glad but it is so far away, and cannot help with funds for now. All of New York City is entranced with Christine Nilsson, she is singing Lucia at the Academy and then will leave and return in late February and in the meantime there is the Philharmonic and some Italian company doing English opera and they have no need of me.

Gideon says that the soprano with the Mulder-Fabbri Company at the Stadt Theater is ailing, and they've asked me to audition as her understudy for *Der Tannhäuser.* He does not want me to do it, as he fears Wagner will strain my voice, but I have insisted as we need the funds too much. Even if I get that, it is only for a few weeks, and so we must arrange another tour for the spring and summer. Barret said we should arrange concerts here in the city, but Gideon told him most schedules are tied up for the summer already, and they argued about it until Barret stalked off somewhere, and Gideon went to find him. Barret is my brother and I love him, but

Gideon has been in the business longer and he knows it better. Yet when I say that, Barret accuses me of being disloyal and worse. I don't know why he looks at me so sorrowfully or what he means when he says he is failing me.

I wish I knew what could be done—Gideon says that Barret will only be a problem for us and that I cannot afford to have a drunk for a business manager, even if he is my brother. But that is exactly why I cannot let him go, either. We are the only family each other has just now, and I know he means well and would love him even if he didn't. I could never send him away.

FEBRUARY 14, 1872—Tonight I had the night off, as too many in the Mulder-Fabbri Company are ill and there is to be no performance at the Stadt. Barret asked if I would go to dinner with him, just the two of us, and then he smiled and said it would be a family dinner. It had been so long since I'd seen that smile! I thought what fun it would be because he was in a good humor, which is so rare lately.

But then Gideon came home with tickets to the New York Circus, saying I deserved a treat. He had bought a ticket for Barret too, and I was so excited—I had thought Barret would want to go, as neither of us had been to the circus before. But Barret said I had agreed to go to dinner with him alone, and I must choose.

Well, what could I do? I was torn, because as much as I'd looked forward to dinner with my brother, I've never seen the circus and I have so little time with Gideon that's not spent in rehearsal or practice. My heart wanted to be with him, and I felt so guilty for wanting it above Barret. Oh, why couldn't Barret understand that and just come along? We could go to dinner together any night!

He got that hurt, disappointed look in his eyes. I _had_ promised, but it was all so unnecessary! It was only dinner, and he was being so contrary only because he is angry with Gideon. I _know_ Barret would have chosen the circus any other time, so it was unfair of him to make me feel so horrible.

Gideon said not to let Barret spoil things and the truth is that I was so excited to go it was easy to forget about Barret once we were there. There were so many people! The main event there was called: the "Mirthful Equestrian Pantomime of: Ride a Jack Horse to Banbury Cross to see an Old Lady on a White Horse." Of course the lady was not so old, and she did the most amazing tricks on that horse, who was not that white, but who cared? I held my breath every time the tightrope walker swayed, and grabbed Gideon's arm so he laughed. He bought me a ginger cake and ale and said he liked to see me this way.

Afterward, we stood outside and looked across the street to the Academy of Music, whose lights were very bright, and carriages gathered out front with drivers in livery slapping their hands against the cold. Gideon whispered to me that they would be coming to see me in only a few months. "Imagine it, Sabine. Imagine how they will hold their breath to see you. They won't believe such a voice is real, they'll wonder if it wasn't an angel from heaven they heard instead."

Oh, how I loved his words! After that, I couldn't bear to let the evening end, so we walked to the Bowery, though it was starting to snow. It was a long way, but I hardly cared, and the noise from the saloons and the theaters and the screech of streetcar brakes and the wheedling cries of the men hawking amusements was like music that seemed to float down with the snow. It was the most romantic night. Gideon took my hand and tucked it into his arm and pulled me close into his side. We stopped at the crowd standing around a man selling patent medicines. His face was so strange in the haze of kerosene torches and the freezing clouds of his own breath that I laughed, and Gideon pulled me into the alcove of a darkened doorway and kissed me so passionately I forgot to breathe. Suddenly I understood why the younkers and their girls had never cared whether people saw them. I didn't care either. I could have kissed him this way all night on a stage in front of a circus crowd and it wouldn't have mattered.

He drew away, but he took my face in his hands and looked into my eyes and said, "Sabine." He made my name sound like a high A rising, my very own angel's voice, and he smiled at me and drew me out again into the street.

Before I knew it, we were climbing the stairs and standing before my door. He said good night; I grabbed his arm, pulling him back to me so hard we fell against the wall. I think I said "Don't go," but I wasn't sure, because before I could finish, he was kissing me again.

And then his door opened, and Barret stepped out to see us there.

I felt a great shove, and then Gideon was gone from me and I was reaching for air. He and Barret fell hard onto the floor. Barret pounded on Gideon, who was first only holding up his hands to shield his face, and then he fought back, and I was screaming at them to stop. The hotel manager came up and told us we must leave, that he wanted us out of the hotel by tomorrow, even though we were paid through the week—the money must go to repair a hole in the plaster they made.

Barret ended up far the worst and lay flat out on the floor. He was drunk, of course. I smelled the liquor on him. Gideon dragged him into their room and laid him on the bed. Barret was muttering again about failing me and saying things like "Don't, Bina. Don't do it," and not making much sense as I tugged off his boots. I was so angry at him. He had ruined this perfect, perfect night, and I wanted to hit him myself. I put my face in my hands and cried, and when Gideon touched my shoulder I just couldn't bear to look at him. I didn't want the look on his face to make me forget the one I remembered from earlier, when he had gazed into my eyes and said my name in a voice like an angel's. I told him to go, and when he left, my tears dried up and I felt very calm, as if this were all a dream I was watching from faraway. I cleaned the blood off my brother's face, and when I turned to go he grabbed my wrist and opened the eye that wasn't swollen shut. He said that Gideon wanted to be rid of him so he could have me all to himself, and I called him a fool and tried to pull away, but he held me tighter. "We should leave," he said. "You and me. We can go back to Kleindeutschland. Papa can get you a tour. Herr Wirt could help. Please, Bina. You should leave while you can."

I said I was staying, but I was too angry to care if he left.

He said he would stay too then. He said he needed to protect me, and I laughed meanly and asked him, "Protect me from what?"

He didn't answer. He fell asleep, and I left him there, snoring.

FEBRUARY 15, 1872—Barret walked me to practice today because Gideon was auditioning. (I can only say this here, but please God, let them choose a different tenor!)

People stared at Barret as we went, and well they should because he looks terrible. Both eyes are black and one he cannot open enough to see through, and he kept rubbing his shoulder, which is hurt from going through the wall. He was sober, and I begin to wonder if that is such a good thing, because he asked me very roughly if Gideon had already taken me to bed, and I felt myself go red and told him no in as offended a voice as I could manage, because it would not do to tell him that I wished Gideon had!

He was very sorry then, and he asked me if I remembered the afternoons on tour when the two of us would sneak out to the confectioner and weren't those the best times? He said we could do the same thing today if I would skip practice, and he gave me the smile I love but it was lopsided because of the swelling.

Of course I do remember, though it seems very long ago now and I am no longer a child but a woman with responsibilities. I told him I could not, that Gideon would not like it, and Barret said that the last he'd heard, he was my manager and not Gideon, and he should be the one to say whether I needed practice. He said again that Gideon meant to come between us and I told him that I was tired of this argument, which I am.

And I am also tired of how sad Barret gets when I tell him this. When he let me off at the door to the theater, he sighed and kissed my cheek and asked would I please be careful and remember the things he'd said, and I kissed him back and said I would.

I went to the back practice room, where Gideon was waiting at the piano. He was distracted and tense, which meant he had not got the role, and though I was relieved, I went to him and pressed myself against his back where he sat on the bench and leaned down to kiss his hair and say I was sorry. He twisted around, and caught me about the waist, and pulled my leg up so my foot was on the bench and my skirts fell back.

I could barely speak. He traced up my stocking to the ribbons of my garters, and his fingers slid beneath to touch my bare skin. He asked me if Barret was upset with him, and I was too mindless to do more than nod, and he leaned over to press his lips where his fingers had been. I thought I would swoon; the pleasure of it was too much. He moved his mouth as if he wanted to touch every part of those few bare inches, and when I gasped he raised his eyes to me and said that Barret wanted to tear us apart and I must not let him. He said my brother was jealous of how close we were, and of how well Gideon understood me. I felt his lips move against my skin and my thoughts grew all muddled, but I remembered what Barret had said, and I felt a twinge of doubt that made me thread my fingers through Gideon's hair and hold him still. When he asked me what was wrong, I told him I thought Barret was worried that he would seduce me and leave me.

Gideon laughed then, and pulled away, and said it was hard to concentrate while I was around, but he supposed we must, and I wished I hadn't said anything at all because all I wanted was for him to keep kissing me.

MARCH 6, 1872—There is to be no tour this summer because Mr. Mulder has asked for me to stay through the end of the season and by then it will be too late. So we are to stay in New York, which is both a relief and not. I'd hoped that a tour would keep Barret from drinking too much, but now there is no help for it, and I cannot make him stop in any case, though I've told him often that I wish he would. He only says he wishes I would do as he tells me too.

Gideon has got us rooms at another hotel—the Farthingale, which is down the street and two blocks over from the Townshend. The rooms are small and not as nice, and the hotel is closer to the Bowery, which is no good for Barret. I see the whores lingering about when we come back late at night, but when I told Gideon my worry, he said that Barret would find trouble wherever we went.

Then he kissed my jaw and undid my dressing gown and unhooked my corset and murmured that I did not need my brother anymore, not when he was there to watch out for me instead, and his mouth was hot against my nipples—oh my God, just to think of it now turns me to liquid! I want him so I cannot think. Since the night at the circus, things have grown more heated between us. But it is only caresses and kisses; he never does what I most want him to do.

I wonder if he waits because of Barret? I think if my brother ever learned how Gideon touches me when he is not around he might kill him.

Or perhaps . . . could it be that Gideon still thinks of Willa? It has been seven months since it was ended, so surely it can't be that. Maybe he doesn't wish to cause more estrangement between me and my family, who all seem to dislike him now. . . .

Oh, I hardly know! and I am tired of guessing! All I know is that my mind is full of him, and beyond that and the music there's room for nothing else, and I find myself confused sometimes, so that when I look at Barret I think Gideon is right and I should send him home, and perhaps if I do, Gideon will come to my bed at last.

But I can't do that. Gideon doesn't know the brother I know late at night, when Barret stumbles into my room to be sure I am safe and alone, or the way he lies on the bed beside me and strokes my hair, as if I were still the small sister who followed him around the alleys like a little dog. "Don't worry," he says to me nearly every night. "I am here to protect my own dear schwester." And before we both fall asleep I tease him that he must not speak German. How could I possibly send him away?

AUGUST 1, 1872—I am now eighteen and a soprano at the Academy of Music! Rehearsals began today. Mr. Maretzek is very demanding. Kellogg and Lucca sometimes don't show up for rehearsals, though I am expected to attend every one, and in the evenings I practice still again with Gideon, who serves as my accompanist and teacher (though of course we still hold to the fiction that Barret is my manager). Gideon has not stopped auditioning, though I live in terror every time he goes—I think I would die if he left me to be some other girl's tenor!

OCTOBER 4, 1872—I am a success as Marguerite! The reviews said I added a "saucy innocence" as a contrast to Kellogg's more restrained interpretation, and that my voice had "a lyric genius rarely encountered and which portends greatness for Mme. Conrad's future." !!!

Lucca herself congratulated me after the performance, though she also made a point of asking where my "pretty repetiteur" was. She is a bitch, actually, and I know she has her eye set on Gideon. He only laughs when I say it and says I have nothing to worry about, but still I don't trust her.

Barret is seeing one of the girls in the chorus. Her name is Dorothea, and she is only seventeen, but very blond and pretty. She has gone out with us after rehearsal three times now, and Barret seems smitten. The best part is that it has turned his attention from me for a time, which is such a relief.

OCTOBER 26, 1872—This afternoon I came home after a costume fitting to find Gideon sitting in the hallway outside his and Barret's room because Barret was inside with Dorothea. They were rather loud too, as I could hear her moans. Gideon looked exhausted and said he had just returned from an audition for the Layler Company and I told him to come into my room to wait until Barret was done and then I told him he should not bother with auditions anymore as I was doing well enough for us all.

He went to my window and seemed so sad. When I asked him why, he told me that this wasn't what he'd expected for himself. He had wanted to make a name in his own right. I told him he was making a name for himself, as my manager, and he laughed and said Barret was my manager. I told him everyone knew it was really him, and that he had a talent for it and was very clever besides. He has learned so much about the business these last years. He watches so carefully and Barret has not half his ambition or skill. I believe he could make us both rich, and I told him why shouldn't he reap the rewards, as he has been the one to set it all in motion? He could be a famous impresario if he wanted. Then I said that I needed him, and I could not bear it if he went away. He got the most brilliant look in his eyes and asked, "Do you mean it?"

I confessed that I loved him, and once I said the words I was so horribly afraid, because he said nothing, and then I was reassured when he kissed me, and I thought at last I would have what I've wanted for so long. When he led me to the bed, I tried to undo his trousers, but he stopped me, and I was so frustrated I slapped at him, and he whispered, "Patience, sweetheart." He put his hands up my skirts and then he was touching me just as Paolo had done, but it wasn't the same, it was . . . I thought I might burst, and I twisted and gasped and he kissed me into silence and suddenly I could not keep myself still. I grabbed his hand to keep it there and cried out—I could not help myself. It was as if my body belonged to him and not me, and I wished it would go on forever. And when it faded he said, "Do you really love me, Bina?" and I kissed his face the way he kisses mine and said yes, yes. Then he said he meant to plant a claque in the audience the night Kellogg performs to boo her on my behalf, because the best prima donnas have rivalries. It keeps them in the news even if they aren't singing. He said I must start one with Kellogg.

I teased him that I would prefer to start one with Lucca, and he said Kellogg was the better choice, as she did not yet have Lucca's status. Pauline Lucca is ambitious and would hurt my career if she could, because she is jealous of my talent. I told him it wasn't my talent she was jealous of, and he said if that was the case, it was better that he flirt with her. "Keep your enemies close," he said.

I told him that I would scratch her face off if she touched him. He kissed me and asked did I think he cared for her at all? It was for me he would flirt with her, because Lucca would do her best to keep me from having a rich patron like August Belmont or Leonard Jerome. I don't care about such old men, but he asked did I see the jewels Adelina Patti wore in all her photographs? Did I not remember that Jerome had a private theater built for her? Did I not want such things myself?

I told him again I didn't care and he whispered that I must flirt with one of them for us, just as he must distract Lucca for us, that we all must do things we didn't like to make our fortune. And then he began to move his fingers upon me again until I could not think, and said, "You'll be more famous than any of them when we're done," and I gasped and said yes yes yes.

So I have agreed. But now the idea troubles me and I think I must tell him I cannot flirt with one of those men when I am in love with him, and that I want him to have nothing to do with Pauline Lucca either.

DECEMBER 3, 1872—I would like to kill Pauline Lucca!!!! Yesterday I came out of the dressing room to see her giggling with Gideon in a corner behind one of the scene flats, and they were far too close and he was bending to whisper something in her ear. They looked so intimate—oh, I could stab her heart out!!!

So last night, when I was onstage, I looked directly for the Jerome box, and while I couldn't see exactly who was there through the footlights, I sent them my most brilliant smile and did not look away as I sang.

This morning I received a dozen pink roses. I put them in a vase in my dressing room, and when Gideon came in and asked who they were from, I told him Leonard Jerome and hoped he would be jealous. But he only smiled, so I turned back to the mirror and quite deliberately asked where Barret was, because I needed my manager to pick up my pay at the intermission, even though Gideon has been doing that for months now.

Then I did see the anger I wanted, and I felt a little satisfaction. But it didn't last long, because Gideon brushed his lips against my bare shoulder above my gown, and when I shivered, he whispered, "When you punish me, you only hurt yourself, Bina."

He left then, and his words made me even more angry, and I thought of how Lucca had pressed close to him. I threw the vase of roses on the floor so the water and shards of china and flowers went everywhere, and then I stomped on the flowers too for good measure.

When I returned to my dressing room after the performance, it was all cleaned up, and there was another vase on my dressing table, with more pink roses, as if my temper had never happened at all.

CHAPTER 8

Seattle, Washington Territory—March 1881

The night of the performance of *Faust*, I dressed in the black widow's weeds I'd first worn to Seattle, still serviceable, though rusty and a bit musty smelling. I had not worn the gown or the veil since, and it felt strange to put them on again, to remember the woman I had been then.

When I walked into the Palace, Charlotte put her hand to her mouth in surprise. "Damn, I never would've recognized you. I don't guess society'll turn up their noses at you now."

I wanted to laugh, remembering how this same dress had not kept me from being thought a whore. But I'd been a lone woman then, stinking of desperation. On Johnny's arm, in Squire's Opera House, it would look respectable enough.

Wryly, I said, "Oh, they wouldn't dare snub us in any case. It's businesses like the Palace that fill the treasury, you know. Without us, they'd have to tax themselves."

She glanced past me, toward the stairs. "My, who knew Johnny dressed up so good?"

She went back into the crowd with a smile, and I turned to see Johnny. He looked so the respectable Society man that

I was startled: his coat was dark and well brushed, his vest gold and black striped, and he wore a hat and a tie. The girls on the floor fawned over him as he approached, and he smiled at their compliments and shrugged them off.

"Don't you look the proper widow, honey," he said when he finally got to me. "You look like you did the first time I saw you. You should have told me you needed a new dress."

"This one does just fine," I told him, though I didn't say it was the veil that made it so. I didn't quite trust my disguise among society; better to be half hid. "But you . . . you could almost be a stranger."

"Haven't had occasion to wear it in a while. I'd almost forgotten how to knot the tie. You like it?"

"I don't know. I feel I hardly know you."

He leaned close to brush his lips against my ear. "I feel sure familiarity will come to you before too long. Let's go before we're late."

He took my hand and settled it in the crook of his arm, and then he called out a good-bye to Duncan, who nodded an acknowledgment. "I hope nothing happens tonight beyond Duncan's capabilities," Johnny said as we went out the door. "I don't like leaving him alone."

"Paul will help if he needs to," I said.

"If he can get down from the orchestra in time." Johnny patted my hand. "I'm going to try not to think about it. You suppose this Fabrizi Company is any good?"

"I doubt it."

He laughed. "So do I."

The gas streetlamps had been lit, and as we approached Commercial Street, there began to be carriages—not the kind I would have seen in New York, with their crests and liveried footmen, but beaten, ancient broughams splashed with dried mud, and one or two open landaus, their wheels caked with sawdust and manure and their sectioned tops fastened back though the night was cool and moist. There were even a few

wagons. Women in satins and laces, and men in frock coats
and morning coats stood waiting on the boardwalk, top hats
gleaming darkly in the blaze of light falling from the opera
house windows.

Many of them greeted Johnny as we came upon them,
and I bent my head and huddled nervously into his side,
trying to seem inconspicuous. It was true what I'd said to
Charlotte. Johnny, for all that he ran a business down on the
sawdust, was well known in the city and respected. God
knew the Palace contributed more than its fair share to
the city coffers. But I had not really realized how much
attention he would gain tonight, and I ducked my head and
murmured hellos, glad for the veil that softened and blurred
my features.

"Don't be shy," he murmured to me at one point. "It's about
time they knew who you were."

The doors opened, and we joined those going inside, past
the closed doors of the dry goods store on the bottom floor,
and up the stairs. I had supposed Squire's would be a small theater, and as shabbily built as most of the other buildings in
Seattle, though from the outside it was nicely appointed. But it
was much grander than I'd expected. It seemed Seattleites had
high aspirations after all—the stage was very large, and the
house must have seated near to six hundred, with twelve boxes
on either side.

The footlights rimming the stage had been lit. I smelled
gas and perfume and the faintly mildewed scent of the
heavy green velvet curtains separating us from the stage as
the heat from the lamps shone upon it. In a narrow pit,
the members of the orchestra began to tune their instruments. Talk and laughter filled the auditorium as the audience entered. There was the usual shuffling of feet and
the rustle of satin and taffeta and the quick swish of fans,
the creak of seats straining to accommodate. I felt a sharp
anticipation.

I had no illusions—I knew I would not see an unparalleled performance coming from a company willing to trek to the outpost that was Seattle—but I craved the sound of that music, the romantic story, the battle between good and evil where the stakes were high and the moral easy to identify, so unlike real life, where those fights were subtle and small and you never realized you'd fought them until they were over.

Beside me, Johnny leafed through his program, his top hat settled on his knee, his hair shining golden in the reflected light. "Now here's something I'd forgotten. It's your namesake here."

I glanced down at the page, at the character name I knew already perfectly well.

"Your ma an opera lover?" Johnny asked.

"I don't know how she came up with the name," I said stiffly.

"Well, let's hope you don't share this Marguerite's fate." He closed the program and glanced around. "Looks to be a full house tonight."

"It seems Seattle's growing hungry for culture."

"Maybe it's time to contact some of my old friends in San Francisco. What kind of show d'you think would go up here?"

I shrugged. "Anything by Verdi. No one dislikes Verdi."

I knew the moment the words were out of my mouth that I'd made a mistake. Johnny's gaze sharpened. "Verdi? You know something about opera?"

I scrambled for safety. "Everyone knows Verdi."

He looked at me thoughtfully for a moment, and I wished I'd kept quiet. I turned away, looking up as the bejeweled and best of Seattle society took their seats in the boxes, and when the lights flickered off their opera glasses, I looked away and down, my excitement and anticipation fading in anxiety. I had been a fool to come.

But then the lights went dim and my nervousness slipped away as everyone quieted. I held my breath, waiting for the first notes.

The orchestra began the overture. The music was mysterious and eerie, and I found myself on the edge of my seat, leaning forward, my breath caught as the curtains opened with a swish, revealing Faust at a table, preparing the poison he was about to drink, and from the moment he called out for the devil and Mephistopheles appeared in a showy burst of smoke, I was lost in sensation and words and music and a story so compelling I forgot where I was, who I was with, everything but the opera, which seemed to climb into my throat and lodge there, urging me to sing it.

For three years I had kept away from this. Now the intensity with which I'd missed it hit me like a blow. My soul drank the music, and when the intermission came and the curtain fell, I blinked my way back into time, bewildered, for a moment not remembering where I was, and I could not speak for the weight of my memories. My face was wet with tears I hadn't realized I'd shed. Surreptitiously, I wiped them away.

But Johnny saw them. Of course he did; he noticed everything. When I turned to him I saw how he watched me, the puzzlement that was in his expression, and I tried to smile and said, "It was very moving, wasn't it?"

I waited for him to comment on my tears, to say something like Charlotte would have said, to disarm me with his notice, but he only said, "I'm waiting for Valentin to die. One of the most well-deserved deaths I know."

"Well deserved? But he was only defending his sister's honor."

"Well deserved for damning her to hell. She was stupid, but stupid ain't a crime. Not yet, anyway. A bit over the top, old Valentin."

"I didn't realize you had such a soft heart," I said.

Johnny gave me a wry smile. "Don't fool yourself. Why don't we get some lemonade, or whatever the hell else they're serving in the salon? I don't suppose I can count on whiskey."

He rose, holding out his hand, helping me to my feet.

The crowd was hard to get through, and the talk was loud, and I could see little beyond Johnny's broad back. When he stopped short just within the salon, I almost plowed into him.

He was shaking some man's hand, a man I didn't recognize, who was about Johnny's age, but dark haired, and wearing the impeccably cut flash of the nouveau riche. On his one side stood a young man who was nearly a copy and obviously his son, and on the other another man with a broad expanse of shining forehead and dark hair curling over his large ears. Johnny turned, pulling me up beside him to introduce me to Mr. Bartholomew Perkins and his son, Theodore.

"Charmed, Miss Olson," Mr. Perkins, senior, said, bowing perfunctorily over my proffered hand. I felt like an imposter, such a shabby copy of my old self that I was embarrassed.

"And this is Thomas Prosch," Johnny said. "You've heard of him, no doubt. Owner and editor of the *Intelligencer*."

"Co-owner," Prosch corrected.

I had to resist the urge to turn and run. A newspaperman. It was all I could do to smile, to say how pleased I was to meet him. I pulled nervously at the veil, wishing it were longer, thicker, hoping it blurred my features enough.

"Well, what do you think of it?" Perkins asked.

"A sight above what I expected for these parts," Johnny said.

"I'm afraid I'm not much of a connoisseur," Prosch confessed—and I was relieved.

Perkins said, "The orchestra is not the best, of course, and the tenor playing Valentin is only adequate, still . . . the Siebel is delightful, don't you think? One doesn't expect to find a mezzo of that quality in a troupe like this."

Johnny looked bored. "She's a bit throaty for my taste."

"I was just telling Father that it does one good to hear something better than fiddle playing in this place at last," said the son earnestly.

"Seattle ain't about to get the best companies. But the fact that they're here at all is something."

"A man of your experience ought to know," Perkins said. He turned to Prosch. "Will there be a piece about it in tomorrow's paper?"

Prosch tapped the pocket of his suitcoat. "That's why I've brought my notebook. You can all rest assured I shall use your comments quite unashamedly."

They laughed. I managed a close enough approximation; at least I hoped no one noticed how strained it was.

"Well, it doesn't compare to the best," Perkins said with a sigh. "I once saw the most sublime production of *Faust*. It's been several years ago now, of course. In Philadelphia. The girl who played Marguerite was quite the most stunning soprano I'd ever heard. At the time I thought her better than Adelina Patti, though she was still so young. Just a child."

My fingers tightened on Johnny's arm. When he glanced at me, I forced my hold to loosen.

"Of course, she grew up to be the renowned Sabine Conrad, so it turned out I was quite right."

Johnny said, "Quite a talent. I saw her once in San Francisco. So many damned people there I couldn't get close enough to look at her, but I'll never forget that voice."

I was stunned. *Johnny had heard Sabine Conrad.*

Prosch said, "Can you imagine if she ever turned up again?"

Johnny snorted. "Just let it be on my doorstep. Hell, the tickets I'd be able to sell...It'd turn the Palace legitimate overnight."

"Why is that?" the young Perkins asked.

Prosch said, "The whole city would pay to see her, no matter where she sang. No one knows what happened to her. She disappeared after the scandal."

"Scandal?"

I squeezed Johnny's arm again, feeling faint. "The heat is really too much—"

Prosch went on. "A terrible thing. It's been . . . what? Three

years? Four? And, you know, people still talk about her.
I know someone who hired a man just to look for her. And a
reporter friend of mine in San Francisco has dedicated his career to finding her again."

This time, I tugged hard and insistently on Johnny's arm,
and when he looked at me with a frown, I managed, "My
head . . . Forgive me, but—"

"Pardon me, gentlemen," Johnny said politely. "But the lady
requires some lemonade."

"Of course, of course, we hardly meant to keep you,"
Perkins said. "Enjoy the rest of the performance."

Johnny pushed through the crowd, and I was relieved when
we left Perkins and his son behind. But before we could get to
the lemonade, the ushers were calling people back to their seats.

"They're starting again," I said, turning back, pulling
Johnny with me.

"You don't want the lemonade?"

"I'm feeling much better already."

"You sure about that, honey? You looked ready to swoon."

"I was overcome for a moment. I'm all right now."

He nodded, and though I don't think he completely believed me, he led me back to our seats. I was grateful
when the lights faded and the music started up again. But
Mr. Prosch's words stayed with me through the rest of the
opera, and I never again regained my sense of wonder as it
went on. The music seemed full of false notes, banal and sentimental suddenly, and the tenor truly was unbearable, the
soprano playing Marguerite seemed too brightly innocent and
sweet—there was no nuance to her at all, and her embellishments during the Jewel Song were too ornate and rather silly,
her despair as she lingered in prison, condemned for killing
her child after Faust deserted her, almost hysterical. Only
Mephistopheles felt real to me. His fiendish bass lingered in
my ears when all else fell away, and when Marguerite sang her

song of redemption to the angels, and they carried her to
heaven as Mephistopheles and Faust cowered before them, I
realized the ending for what it was: a fantasy of the basest
kind. I knew already: angels did not redeem women like
Marguerite.

CHAPTER 9

Johnny reached into his pocket for a cigar and a match, which he struck against the rough outside wall of a barbershop. He paused to light his cigar, and I waited as he puffed it to life, wrinkling my nose at the smoke that clouded before my face. The night was full of the sound of carriage wheels thudding over the streets, distant whoops and hollers, a dogfight.

When he began to walk again, I fell into step beside him. Johnny said, "You always surprise me, honey."

"Really? I would have said I was anything but surprising."

He inhaled and let the smoke out in a cloud. "Take the opera, for example. You know *Faust* like someone who's seen it more than once."

"No, I—"

"You were keeping time."

"I was what?"

"Keeping time. You know that music inside and out, Margie. Don't lie to me about that, at least. I don't doubt my own eyes."

"I . . . have a good ear. That's all."

"I don't dispute that." He flicked off the ash from his cigar. "So how'd you develop this 'ear'?"

"I don't know. I've always had it."

"That's how you know Verdi."

"Yes."

He was quiet. His footsteps—and mine—seemed too loud on the boardwalk, thudding and echoing in a night already heavy with sound.

"It occurs to me that we don't know each other very well," he said finally.

"Does it matter?"

He went on as if I hadn't spoken. "Now, there're some things. . . . I know you like it a little rough, and hell, I ain't averse to a little pain myself if it makes the pleasure better. But there ain't much that you let yourself enjoy, honey. I always figured you were punishing yourself for something. Am I right?"

I was startled into silence.

"Suppose you tell me what that is."

Still I was mute; I had no idea what to say.

"Does it have something to do with him?"

"With who?" I whispered.

"Whoever it is you got in your head. The one I can't dislodge."

"Oh, Johnny . . ."

He held up his hand to quiet me. "You enjoyed tonight. At least at the start. That's what surprised me. I don't think I've ever seen that in you. Hell, you looked like you were staring into heaven, and I found myself thinking: now, if she looked at me like that when I was fucking her, I would give her anything she wanted." He laughed ruefully. "I suppose we all got our vanities, don't we?"

I could not answer him. I should never have let him take me to the opera. I should never have gone. I'd known I was taking a risk, and now the two things I'd been most afraid of had happened: my longing for the music was so strong I didn't know how I would live without it again, and Johnny's curiosity about me had sharpened. I should have listened to my instincts; I should have denied myself the pleasure.

Johnny said, "Three years we been together, Margie, and I know hardly more about you than I did at the start. I thought I stopped wondering about you a long time ago, but tonight's been . . . a revelation."

"The past is the past," I said softly. "I never ask you about yours."

"Because you don't care—that's the difference. What you want from me ain't what I want from you."

I looked away. How stupid I'd been.

Johnny laughed shortly. "You see? You don't even ask: 'What is it you want from me, Johnny?'"

"I know what you want."

"Do you?" He stopped walking for a moment to look at me. The cigar lit his eyes weirdly; I found myself taking a step back. "Were you like the Marguerite in *Faust*? Is that why you took her name?"

"It is my name," I said, but my voice quavered, and I knew he heard it.

"Where'd the scar come from? Did he give it to you?"

"That's none of your business." I walked on. In two steps, he was beside me, his hand on my arm, gentle enough that I could have kept going, but I stopped.

"Did you never think to move on, honey?" His voice was unbearably tender. "You say the past is the past, but I don't think you left it behind. How long you planning to wait before you start living again?"

His comment pricked. I found myself saying meanly, "Why don't you admit what it is that bothers you, Johnny? I don't love you—that's what this is about. That isn't going to change; we both know it. What's so wrong with the way things are now?"

"Because I'm your partner, and you're keeping secrets."

"You have your own secrets."

He went quiet, and I was grateful until he said, "Tonight got me thinking. Maybe it's time to do what I intended in the first place and make the Palace a real theater."

"Just because an opera company managed to fill Squire's one night doesn't mean Seattle's ready for anything else."

"Hmmm. Maybe. Or maybe it is. Maybe we should take a trip down to San Francisco, see if we can't convince a couple troupes to make the trip north."

"It would be a waste of time. Who would come here?"

He tapped off a growing ash. "You know, I'm starting to think you don't want me to make the Palace legitimate. Why is that?"

"I'm only being cautious. We have a good thing now—"

"It could be better."

"Are you so certain? It couldn't hurt to wait a little longer—"

"We were the first boxhouse in Seattle. We're the most successful because we took a risk. Who's to say this wouldn't pay off the same way?"

"It's too soon. We can't afford it. What about our regular customers?"

"What about them?"

"We'd lose them."

He shook his head thoughtfully. "I don't think we would. Not all of them anyway, and we'd have a whole new crowd to take their place. It'd take—what?—a few months, maybe, until the profits came up again. We could survive it. I'm ready to do this, Margie."

"Johnny—"

"We could add footlights to the stage, get rid of the chaises in the boxes. Turn the bar into a salon. There'd be no more whores, no more temper tantrums over yellow fucking dresses." His voice had gone low and vibrant; he gestured with his cigar, the lit end glowing brightly in the darkness. "We'd run a melodrama or two, maybe even an opera of our own.

Can't you see it, Margie? You and me, proprietors of the best damn theater in the city."

His words were seductive. I could not help picturing it. A theater the equal of Squire's or better. Singers who could sing. Musicians who could play. The ambitions that I'd forced dormant shivered and stretched. In my ears rang *Faust*, tempting, cajoling. . . .

But then I remembered what Prosch had said about people who still searched for Sabine Conrad, reporters who meant to find her, and I knew I could not keep hidden here, not if the Palace were a theater. There were so many people I'd left behind, players, singers, managers. Sooner or later, someone who'd known me well enough to recognize me would arrive. And then what? How could I escape myself then? How could I keep myself safe from everything I was?

I swallowed hard and shook my head. "I don't think it's a good idea."

He gave me a sidelong glance. "You afraid?"

"Of course I'm afraid. Of losing money."

"You sure it ain't more than that?"

"What else could it be?"

"I don't know." He made a little laugh. "I wish to hell I did."

He threw his cigar into the middle of the street and took my arm, pulling me close, putting his hand to my chin so I could not look away. "I want to do this, Margie, and I want you to help me. I could go ahead without you, but I'm likely to make a mess of it. I need you beside me. I don't know why, but you understand this business like no one I've ever seen."

Everything felt dangerous, unbalanced. I did not want to think about this. I wanted things to remain as they were. And so I did what I had always done. I curled my arms around his neck, and when he stiffened a little, I rose on my toes and kissed him. He didn't respond at first, but I did not relent; I knew what he liked, and soon his mouth moved on mine; his hands crept to the small of my back and then lower. I drew

back, teasing, pressing my lips against his throat, above the unfamiliar high collar, the smooth cold silk of his necktie. I unknotted it, looking about for a place, a corner, a shadowed
alley. I slid my hand down his chest and pressed my hips to
his. "Over there," I murmured. "No one would see—"

Johnny curled his fingers tight about mine, stopping me.
"No, Margie."

I let my other hand fall to his trousers. "Come on, Johnny.
Let me thank you for taking me to the opera."

He smiled. "Oh, you can thank me all right, but it don't distract me, honey, if that's what you mean to do. I'll fuck you if
you want, but when we're done, we're coming right back
around to this. It's time for you and me to move into something
new. You know it as well as I do. It's time to turn the Palace."

I jerked away, surprised and angry.

He raised a brow. "Oh, don't tell me you changed your
mind. What a pity. And here you got me all excited."

"Go on home to Sally, then," I snapped.

"I think I just might do that," he said. "But you and me, we
ain't finished with the rest of it." He took my arm; when
I tried to pull away, he tsked at me. There was a smile in his
voice when he said, "You put me in mind of a little girl who
didn't get a treat. Come on now, let's go home. We'll talk about
this tomorrow. Just now you got 'til McGraw's to change your
mind about taking me to bed."

THE CANDLE WAS lit, and I watched its shadow against the
walls while in the next room, Tessa and her partner's rhythmic
gruntings kept time to the duet between Faust and Marguerite
that repeated itself unendingly in my head. How many times
I'd sung that duet. How often in these last years I'd tried to
forget it, to forget everything. I'd closed my heart to it, and
I had not realized until tonight how much that had cost me,
not until Johnny had uttered his proposition. *Faust* had raised

my hunger again, and now I heard Mephistopheles's terrible, derisive laugh, calling me a fool, calling me worse than that.

I was relieved when Charlotte came home—anything that robbed me of my thoughts was something to be grateful for. She came inside and sent a frown in the direction of Tessa's room before she looked at me in surprise. "I thought you'd be asleep."

"I couldn't sleep."

Charlotte sat on the edge of the bed and bent to unfasten her boots. "Was the opera good?"

"As I expected."

She slipped off one boot and then the other and rose, going to the basin. On the other side of the wall, Tessa screamed out and went still. In the silence after was the smooth gurgling splash of water as Charlotte poured it. "Thank God that's over. You'd think she got enough of it at the Bijou."

"You never wish to bring someone back with you?" I asked.

"No."

"Do you ever . . . enjoy it?"

She shook her head. "It's a job. D'you enjoy running whores?"

I didn't think she expected an answer, and I didn't give one.

She dipped her hands in the water and brought them to her face, tilting her head so the water dripped from her jaw, her chin. The dim light against her skin made her scar look like a deep purple shadow. She hesitated, and then she splashed her face again and reached for the ragged towel. "Something happen between you and Johnny tonight?"

"Why do you ask?"

"He was in a bear of a mood when he got back."

"*Faust* inspired him. He wants to turn the Palace legitimate."

"You said he's wanted that a long time."

"He has."

She sat again on the edge of the bed. "So what's stopping him?"

"I don't think it's the right time."

She sighed and lay down beside me. Her hair straggled into her face, and I rose onto my elbow and smoothed it back. Her skin was soft and warm. Once I'd touched her, I couldn't stop. I found myself stroking her hair the way I would a child's, and she let me, and I had the odd sense she knew it soothed me better than it soothed her. "What did he say to that?" she asked softly.

I was distressed enough that I found myself confiding in her. "He said I was afraid. That I was holding on to the past."

"D'you think he's right?"

"I don't know."

She laughed a little. "What is it you want, Marguerite?"

A hundred things, I thought, and that troubled me, that the thought came so easily, that upon its heels rushed everything I'd had once, everything I could not have again. *Music. Adulation. Footlights.* I saw myself dancing across a stage, admiring the paste jewels sparkling around my wrist—a gift from the devil and from Faust—falling easily into a seduction that could only end with death, unredeemed. . . .

I shook the thoughts away. Her hair was fine, but thick too. It gave and sprang back beneath my fingertips. "I have everything I need."

She closed her eyes and sighed. We were quiet for a moment, and then she said, "It wasn't an accident, you know. Not like I said."

"What wasn't?"

"My scar." She raised her arm for me to see as if I might have forgotten it. "He pushed me into the fire. He meant to do it. He said he was sorry after, but he meant to do it all the same."

"Who did?"

"My husband."

She was so matter-of-fact, so unemotional. It was as if she were talking about someone else. "Why?"

"He was a mean son of a bitch. I didn't see it at first, you know. He was handsome, and when I married him I thought it was just about the best thing that ever happened to me. And then one night he came home drunk and threw me against the wall. My fault . . . I burned the stew. And he was so nice after . . . well, you can guess what happened after that. Only the stew wasn't to blame the other times."

"Some men are—"

"Yeah, I know. Some men are just like that. But I never saw it until it was too late. And you know the real hell of it was that I loved him. He said I brought out the worst in him, and I believed it."

I stopped stroking, though my fingers lingered in her hair. That familiarity again, though I couldn't quite grab on to it, I didn't know why.

"And then"—she took a deep breath—"and then one night he came home and he was pretty rough, but I got pregnant so I guessed it was worth it. I thought it would change everything."

"Did it?"

She shook her head. "I knew I had to get away or he'd kill me, and maybe the kid too. So I went to this man I'd met. He'd said he was a traveling peddler and I believed him, though I never saw him selling shit. He told me he'd take me out of town and to pack a bag. So I did. But then Tracy came home from the camps and found the bag and . . . well, he threw me into the fire."

She lifted her arm, twisting it so the scar stood out in bright relief in the candlelight. "I went into a fever. When I woke up, the doctor said I'd never have another baby again. So I went to the peddler and asked him to take me out of town."

"Oh, Charlotte—"

"I ain't finished," she said abruptly. "He took me out of town, all right. And I was so grateful to him that when he said I had to pay him back for my expenses, I said I'd do whatever he wanted. So he fucked me there in the wagon. And then he took me up to a mining camp and sold me to whoever could pay, and I was still so damn grateful, because he said he'd protect me and take care of me. . . ." She made a little sound of disbelief. "But it wasn't more than six months before I got sick and he left me to die, and when I found out he was gone, I wished I had. I didn't see how I could go on without him. That son of a bitch. I think if I saw him now I'd stab him through. At least I hope I would."

I didn't know what to say. "I—I'm sorry."

She shrugged. "It don't matter. I don't think about it much."

"How can you not think about it?"

She met my gaze. "It's behind me now. Thinking about the past only fucks things up. What can I do about it but go on anyway?"

Slowly, I said, "You think I should help Johnny turn the Palace."

"I think you should do what makes you happy. Whatever that is. You mean to live in the past forever?"

"It's just that . . . it's not what I'd hoped for."

She laughed shortly. "Christ, Marguerite, ain't no one gets exactly what they want. I never meant to be a whore, but at least now I don't got to go with anyone I don't want to go with. I got a roof over my head and plenty to eat."

"It doesn't seem enough," I said bitterly.

"What are you waiting for?"

"What makes you think I'm waiting?"

"Ain't you?"

"I—"

"Suppose you tell me what you're afraid of," she said softly.

And I found myself admitting something I didn't even know. "What if it isn't enough?"

She laughed again, this time in pure amusement. "Oh, Marguerite. You got to make it be enough. How else can you go on living?"

From the Journal of Sabine Conrad

NEW YORK CITY, FEBRUARY 26, 1873—I am quite exhausted—today I sang two performances as Kellogg is feeling poorly and not in her best voice, so I must stand in for her. When I came back to the hotel there was an invitation for me to one of Caroline Astor's weekly dinners!

It is what we've been waiting for! All my longing glances to Mr. Jerome's box, as well as my very good notices, have had the effect we hoped. Mr. Jerome sends me flowers now once a week, and last time there was a pair of small pearl earrings tucked away in the blossoms, and his note said: "Please be kind to me, Miss Conrad, when I call upon you." Though as yet, he has not made an appearance (something I confess only here that I am happy about. It's easy to flirt with someone from afar; I don't know if I can pretend to like him in person. But Gideon says to remember that I do this for our future, and so I will do my best).

But the dinner! Gideon was so happy he danced me about the room. It means I have gained society's attention and I am deemed important enough to attend <u>Caroline Astor.</u> If she likes me, all of the rest of society will come knocking on my

door. I am so excited and nervous over it—how am I to know
how to act in high society? Oh, I wish I could take Gideon
with me, but I am the only one invited, and it says nothing of
bringing a guest and Gideon says angering Caroline Astor by
bringing him would be folly.

Of course I don't think of taking Barret now. It would be
too big a temptation for him, as he is trying for Dorothea's
sake not to drink so much, though he does not seem quite himself lately. Last night he and Gideon went out. When Barret
stumbled into my room it was past two and he was drowsy and
smelling of something odd—I don't know what it was, some
kind of tobacco, I think. This is the second time now he has
done this, and when I ask Gideon he only says that my
brother's behavior stains my career, and that no one finds him
nearly as charming as he once was and half the time he
doesn't show up at meetings so Gideon must make up for him.
I said I thought Barret was better with Dorothea, and Gideon
said I could believe what I wanted but that Barret hardly deserves the love I bear him or the dedication Gideon devotes to
watching over him.

I must go now, because Gideon has me studying for the
Astor dinner. These are the subjects I can discuss: food, wine,
horses, yachts, cotillions, and marriages. Of course I know
nothing of any of these things, but I suppose if they wish me
to give my opinion on the best beer and fried fish in the city,
I could accommodate them.

MARCH 5, 1873—Tonight after my performance the usher
told me the Astor carriage was waiting outside the backstage
door for me. Sitting right there in the alley with the Astor
crest and livery! Gideon helped me dress and nearly pushed
me out the door, and I was giggling with excitement and
nerves when he kissed me for luck and told me to remember
everything he had said. But once I was in the carriage I was
sure I would forget it all, and I wished he was with me, be-

cause I was so nervous I thought I would be sick. Then
I looked down at my white kid gloves—at last, an occasion to
wear them!!—and my new gown of pale reseda green that
Gideon had made me buy for the occasion and I thought: I am
Sabine Conrad. They want to meet me! and I knew all would
be well.

Then I truly began to enjoy myself. The carriage was so
beautiful, the springs smooth as if they were liquid, the seats
fine leather, and there was a good brazier so I was warm. How
luxurious it all felt! I have determined that I will have one
myself just like it someday.

The house was beautiful, with lights in every window, and
there were fourteen of us there. The women were dressed elegantly, but they were all older than me, and I felt very young
and pretty. I noticed how the men looked at me, the way
Gideon sometimes does, as if he would like to eat me alive, and
I felt not nervous at all, but something else entirely . . . as if
I were a queen, or . . . not a queen, exactly, because it was
quite obvious that Carolyn Astor was that, but . . . perhaps a
princess. I could tell they were nervous to meet me: to think it!
Mr. Ogden Goelet, who is richer than Croesus, nervous to meet
me! I confess it quite turned my head! They all wanted my
favor. I am so glad I went!!

The dining room was lovely, and there were paintings hung
throughout from golden cords. I was seated between Mr. Goelet
and a Mr. Martin, who were both very, very attentive—one
would think I had not the strength to cut my own duck or pour
my own wine!!! There was a gold dinner service that seemed
too fine to eat upon. Mrs. Astor was as courteous as could be
and asked me how I liked New York as if I had not lived here
all my life, but Gideon had told me not to mention Kleindeutschland under any circumstances, and so I smiled and
said that I found the city very exciting. Mrs. Astor wore five
strands of perfectly matched pearls with a diamond clasp. She
is not a handsome woman, but she is very commanding, and

one can see why all of the city is in awe of her. Whenever she raised a subject, everyone fell over themselves to comment on it and then talked it through until it was quite dead and she looked bored beyond reason and then waited for her to raise another.

But she is a great lover of opera. She said she thought I would make a perfect Rosina or Pamina especially, and that perhaps it was time to bring Mozart back to the Academy. I didn't tell her I'd already sung those parts on tour. At the end of dinner, she called me a lovely girl and asked would I sing something for her guests, and so of course I obliged. One of the other ladies played the piano—not very well, so I had to cover up her mistakes with my own embellishments, but they enjoyed it tremendously. I sang "All Things Love Thee," and "Jeanie with the Light Brown Hair," and Amina's aria, "Come per me sereno," and they called me "beautiful" and "sublime."

In all, I think I was quite a success!!!

When I got back to the Farthingale, Gideon was waiting up to hear. Barret was off with Dorothea somewhere. Gideon came into my room and helped me unbutton the gown, and I began to tell him everything, but he was hardly attending to me. He seemed half asleep, and he smelled of whatever it is that seems to inhabit Barret's skin now. It was so disappointing I felt like crying. I snapped at him that I was sorry I was boring him, and perhaps he preferred to go back to bed, and at that he came back to himself. He grabbed my hand and said, "Only if you come with me," and pulled me into his lap so we sat together on the chair. He told me I'd done well and that Mrs. Astor's good opinion was my way to true success, and then he kissed me long and well, until I was nearly dizzy with it, and I hoped. . . .

But no. We heard Barret stumbling about in the hall, and Gideon took his hand from my breast and said reluctantly that he must go back to his room, and he left, though he looked so longingly at me as he went that I was quite breathless!

MARCH 10, 1873—I was mentioned in the society page yesterday as having attended one of "Mrs. Astor's coveted weekly suppers." And also "the talented prima donna is the new toast of the Four Hundred." Gideon has said we can no longer stay at the Farthingale, that we must move uptown because now that I am of society I cannot be seen in such mean circumstances. He has got us rooms at the Fifth Avenue Hotel, which is fashionable and far too expensive for us, but Gideon says to make money one must look as if one has money, and that for my upward flight we cannot be seen as being fast or cheap, and the Fifth Avenue is very respected.

Barret says I should be saving my money instead of squandering it on rooms in some hoity-toity hotel, but Gideon gave him a look I did not understand and said that Barret was good enough at spending my money that he should not complain when I meant to make more of it, and Barret looked at me as if he expected me to agree with him, but I pretended not to see. Perhaps Barret is right, but to live in the Fifth Avenue Hotel! Gideon must know what he is doing, and I had no wish to challenge him, as it would only start another argument. They are not fighting as much as they used to, but I think it is only that they aren't doing so in my presence, because they know it troubles me. And we still all pretend that Barret is the one managing me, though of course he has done hardly anything of the kind for months and months.

I received a card from Mr. Jerome asking me to go driving with him tomorrow afternoon. Gideon sent the messenger back with my acceptance.

* * *

N.B. Barret and I got a letter from Mama telling us that Willa is going to be married in June! I am so happy!!!! Oh, not for Willa so much (forgive me please, God, for saying it), though I am happy for her, of course, but because now there is no more need for guilt. Willa is recovered from her hurt, and

Gideon and I are one step closer to professing our love to the world! Of course, there is still Barret to consider, and Mama and Papa, but surely soon they will realize that Gideon is my one true love and we belong together!!!

Barret and I are "cordially" invited to attend Willa's wedding. I told Gideon I thought it was a sign of forgiveness, but he disagrees, saying only that Mama and Papa wish not to be the subject of gossip among our neighbors if their famous daughter and their oldest son do not attend Willa's wedding. Of course when Barret heard this it caused another terrible fight between him and Gideon, and Barret has stormed off again.

MARCH 11, 1873—This has been the most wonderful, wonderful day! I have had my heart's desire at last! I am—no, no, not so quickly. I must start at the beginning.

First: In the morning, Gideon moved us into our new rooms at the Fifth Avenue Hotel, which is the busiest and most elegant place—the only thing I've seen better is Mrs. Astor's dining room! I could not believe he meant for us to stay there, and I'm afraid I agreed with Barret that it must be too expensive. There is a lovely clock tower outside, and the hotel itself is made of white marble and is six stories tall, and there is an elevator!!!!—the first one in the city, Gideon told me. It was actually a bit frightening to ride in it, and I felt a little sick, but it is much better than carrying bags up flights of stairs.

The lower halls have several reading and sitting rooms, with spittoons placed about that are so highly polished and clean that they look like decorations. There is even a Ladies' Parlor on the second floor, which Gideon says I can go to alone if I wish.

We could not afford a suite, of course, but our rooms are perfect. Barret, of course, was very glum—when we came into my room he went to the window, which was bordered by heavy chintz drapes with velvet ones beneath, and asked Gideon quite sourly if it was really necessary to pay for two sets of curtains. Gideon asked what would Leonard Jerome think if he came to pick me up at the Farthingale, and Barret said it was better that Jerome did not come at all.

It all came to another argument, where Barret said he couldn't like me going driving with Leonard Jerome, who is married, and considered fast, and did Gideon intend that I become Jerome's whore?

That was when I told them both to be quiet, as I do not want to be evicted from the Fifth Avenue Hotel before I have spent a single night there.

Gideon had to leave then, and I knew by the way Barret paced the room that I was about to get another lecture, which was true. He asked me did I understand what people would think of me if I went driving with Leonard Jerome? I told him Gideon said that all prima donnas had patrons, and I did not see the harm, but he said I was too willing to trade my virtue for jewels and society. I told him my virtue was long gone, and he snorted and said that soon the whole world would know it too, and I cried and told him to leave because he was spoiling everything.

He said he would serve as my conscience, as no one else would, and there were better ways to have the fame I wanted— I did not have to choose this way. And then he begged me to do as he wished for once. "This isn't you, Bina. All these trappings, rich patrons . . . You don't need any of it. Your voice is enough."

I didn't say anything, because Barret does not understand how this world works, and he no longer trusts Gideon, and what can I say to that except that I do? Barret did not leave until Mr. Jerome's man came to retrieve me at three o'clock promptly. Even then I was not certain he would let me go. And I determined not to think about my brother when I saw Mr. Jerome's smart barouche.

It was drawn by two pairs of sleek and well-matched horses. Truly beautiful animals, and Mr. Jerome admires them a great deal and cares for them excessively. On our way to Central Park he took me by his stables, which he is greatly proud of. I have never seen such a thing as that—it is paneled in black walnut and is <u>carpeted</u>!!! His horses live so finely that I could not help but think of all the people crushed into tenements in Kleindeutschland, and I thanked God I no longer must live there. I very much prefer the luxurious lives of Mr. Jerome and his set!

Central Park was so full of carriages—broughams and landaus and sulkies and other barouches—that it was difficult to move more than sedately, but that, I suppose, is the point. Mr. Jerome and I were the center of attention, and he kept me laughing and entertained throughout. At one point Mr. Belmont drove up beside us and told me that he was enraptured by the "sublimity" of my voice. He said how unusual he found it that Mr. Jerome had acquired such a stunning companion, and Mr. Jerome said that Mr. Belmont was not the only man in the city capable of charm. I laughed at both of them.

I admit I flirted quite outrageously with Mr. Belmont as well, which made Mr. Jerome strive to outdo himself with compliments. He is really a very handsome man, for someone so much older. He has a huge drooping mustache and sleepy eyes. He said he would like very much to see me on the stage of the private theater he had built onto his mansion some years ago (for Adelina Patti, I know, but he didn't tell me that). Should I need to practice new roles or anything else, he said he would place it entirely at my disposal.

It was an exhilarating afternoon, and I was quite full of myself when Mr. Jerome deposited me back at the hotel. I must admit that all this attention is <u>inspiring</u>!

I was only in my room a moment when Gideon knocked upon the door—Barret was gone somewhere, but Gideon had been waiting for me. I told him of the day and my flirtation with Belmont too and Jerome's offer of his theater, and Gideon got a look on his face I had never seen before and said, "Don't enjoy it too much, Sabine," and when I asked why shouldn't I, he said what a little hoyden I'd become, and pressed me to the wall and whispered that I was splendid, and that I would be a prima donna like no one had ever seen, but that I mustn't forget who I belonged to, and his words sent a shiver through me, and though I'd felt alive and beautiful driving in the park, I had not felt like this. I had never felt like this. And then Gideon was kissing me possessively and passionately, and I could not wait anymore! I pulled at his tie until it came undone and fell to the floor, and then I put my hands to his shirt and he pulled away and said we must go to dinner in the dining room, just the two of us, as my reward. But that wasn't what I wanted.

The day had made me brave. I looked into his eyes and then I—oh, I can't quite believe I did this even now!— I pressed my hand to his cock through his trousers and said I had in mind a different reward, and he was to be it.

I loved the look on his face! As if he had come too close to a fire meaning to be burned, and was both surprised and excited by the pain. I knew then that I would have him at last. He said, "Well then, I suppose I must oblige you," and turned me around to undo the buttons of my gown. He kissed the nape of my neck and whispered that we must keep this secret, that if Jerome found out it would all be over, that everything we'd worked for would be ruined, and I gasped that I would tell no one, and my gown came down around my shoulders and fell to my waist, and his hands came to my breasts and I was so impatient for him that I tore at the hooks of my corset in a fury to get it off. His breath was so warm against my throat. He said not Barret either, and I agreed. He touched my nipples and said, "Promise me," and I said yes yes, whatever he wanted. I didn't care. I would have given him anything. I would have done anything.

Then I was naked, and he was still fully dressed, and he pulled me to him and the feel of his clothing against me was strangely exciting and I pressed like a wanton against him and I liked it. When he laid me on the bed and stood back to look at me I put my arms over my head and arched so he could see me better, and I thought how bad it was, but I liked that too.

He went to lock the door. Then he came back and undressed and didn't take his eyes from me as he did so. I had never seen him naked, and he was so beautiful I lifted my arms to him and demanded that he touch me. But he only smiled and shook his head as if he meant to make me wait, and pulled something from his trouser pocket and unfolded it— something very strange, like thin rubber or . . . I didn't know what it was, but when I asked him he said "a precaution," and drew it over his cock and then—finally!!!—he came down beside me and I was in his arms and kissing him and he was between my thighs and inside me, and I wrapped my legs around his hips and drew him deeper, and I was no longer Sabine Conrad but whatever he wanted me to be, only pleasure made just for him, only sensation.

Have I ever loved <u>anything</u> this much?

Only singing. And Gideon is like my voice made flesh. How would I live without either one of them?

MARCH 26, 1873—I have now gone driving with Mr. Jerome three times, and I am in the society pages again. This from yesterday: "It seems all society can talk about recently is the entrancing sight of our favorite emerging diva driving in Central Park in the company of a well-known horseman. Can it be a new infatuation?"

Mr. Jerome sends flowers to my dressing room every day. And yesterday I received orchids from Mr. Belmont, who writes that I must not let Mr. Jerome command all my time, and might I have occasion to dine with him one night next week? Gideon has instructed me to refuse Mr. Belmont's invitation, but gently, and to hint that I regret it very much. He says that we don't wish to offend him, but neither do I want to look fast by pursuing both him and Leonard Jerome at once. "Save Belmont for if Jerome loses interest," he says.

Barret hates it, and makes me feel so guilty and a little ashamed, though I've done <u>nothing</u> to merit it. When I went to their room I found him sprawled on the chaise there, and he was sweaty and disheveled and lazy, and his pupils were so tiny he did not look like himself. He had the paper on his lap, and when he saw me he tossed it to the floor and told me that Gideon was turning me into *eine Dirne*. At first I thought he must know about me and Gideon and I was afraid and trying to decide what to say, but then he kicked at the newspaper and said that if Gideon had his way, it would only be a matter of time before I was fucking Jerome, and I was relieved. If he thinks that, then he must not know our secret, because if he knew he would realize that of course Gideon cannot want me in Jerome's bed! It is all too stupid! I told him it was only an innocent flirtation. Barret said that Jerome's wife and daughters live in Paris now because of his well-known dalliances with opera singers and everyone knew it. I told him that I did not like the way he spoke and then I left.

I have been invited to two balls and three suppers this week. Gideon is deciding which I should attend.

MARCH 28, 1873—Leonard has sent me a lovely golden locket on a chain and a brooch set with small rubies. Gideon is not impressed and told me to refuse Leonard's invitation to a private supper, that it wasn't yet time for that. I asked him what we were waiting for, and when he didn't answer I told him what Barret had said.

Gideon asked why my brother would wish to hurt me that way? And then he put the locket about my neck so it was the <u>only</u> thing I wore, and brought me down to straddle him on the chair, and I knew that it is truly as Gideon says, that my brother means only to hurt me because I am so happy and growing so successful.

But still I wish I could make Barret believe that Gideon truly loves me and means for me to have the best. I wish I knew how to convince him.

I went to supper at the Stevenses', which was very enjoyable. I sang Pamina and, of course, "All Things Love Thee."

MAY 1, 1873—Everyone has gone. Some to Newport for the summer, and others on their Continental Tour. Leonard stays in the city. He has given me a lovely bracelet set with sapphires and diamonds, and a matching necklace.

I have been in the society pages every week now. Last week they printed an item telling of how Clara Kellogg and I fought backstage over a costume—it was quite true, though not as large a fight as they described. Now everyone calls us the Rival Ritas, due to our shared role in *Faust,* and there is much jockeying about of hostesses trying to decide which of us is more the thing so they know which to invite to their supper.

Oh, how I will miss the parties now the season is over, though one thing I will not miss is that bitch Lucca, who has—thankfully—gone off to tour Europe. I do not think I could bear another evening of watching her throw herself at Gideon. I wish sometimes our love was not quite such a secret. But, of course, I know that to reveal it would mean the end of society, and of Leonard, who is really quite dear and whom I should miss very much, and I doubt Mrs. Astor would deign to invite me again to her suppers. To the world's eyes, Gideon is only my accompanist. They have no idea how much he has given me, and how I owe him everything.

It is not fair that Gideon does all the work and it is Barret whom society thanks. Of course none of us reveal the truth. Barret is still my manager in name and so must sign my contracts. The theater owners and impresarios put up with him because they must; Gideon says they would tolerate anything to get me, but it will not last forever. I am frustrated beyond measure with Barret. When he is not drinking, he is very nice, though that happens far too seldom now. But for the meetings Gideon arranges and forces him to be sober for, he only lies around all day. Even so, he is my brother and I love him, and so I will not hear of putting him aside. What would he do without me? Especially now, because I have not seen Dorothea for some weeks, and he will not discuss her and so I think they might be over. Gideon says it's best to leave him be, because as long as he is in his room he is not about costing me money and reputation.

I think a change of scenery for all of us is warranted, and Gideon has booked me on a tour—a concert tour, with me singing alone—to start after Willa's wedding. We go to cities all over the country—as far as San Francisco! When we return I am to sing with Strakosch's troupe for the Italian opera at the Academy. He is quite the impresario now. The days until we leave cannot pass quickly enough for me.

JUNE 8, 1873—After what happened at Willa's wedding, I wonder if Mama or Papa will ever speak to me or Barret again.

The day before, Gideon begged me not to go. He said that with Barret there, something was certain to go wrong and he didn't want me hurt. But I told him I was glad to attend my sister's wedding because it meant she was no longer in love with him. He grimaced and said that was a long time ago, but he is only trying to make me feel better because he knows that sometimes I cannot help but feel guilty.

I wished I could bring him, but of course he was not invited, and I did not wish to remind Willa of him. I was a little nervous, though I did think Willa would have forgiven me by now. I truly thought it would not be so bad. Oh, how wrong I was!

Barret did not look well. He was pasty and his eyes were red rimmed, as if he had not been sleeping, and I scolded him for that and for the fact that his necktie was not tied correctly and his shoes were unpolished. He was in a nasty mood and told me to leave him alone, and so we weren't speaking much when we arrived.

At first, it was lovely. Mama asked me to sing a hymn, which I did, and Willa looked beautiful in blue, which matched her eyes and went well with her dark hair. She is so very pretty. Her new husband is nice enough. His name is

Frederick, and it is obvious he loves Willa very much. Barret whispered to me that Willa was already expecting, though I saw no sign of it, and truly Frederick seems so staid that I cannot imagine he has any passion in him.

When we arrived, Willa kissed my cheek, but she did not quite look me in the eye, and Papa was distant, though Mama kissed both Barret and me, and Gunther ran into my arms—he is so big now! Twelve years old, and a handsome dark-haired boy who looks like Papa.

Papa closed the Völksstadt for the day so we could hold the celebration there, and he had one of the polka orchestras come in to play. I was very surprised when Willa sat down beside me. She complimented me on the hymn and asked if I was well and I told her of the upcoming tour and my successes at the Academy and in society, and she pretended not to be impressed and looked about the room as if I bored her, and then she asked if I'd seen Gideon recently.

I could tell that she still loves him! I know that look in her eyes, and I was taken with a most fierce jealousy and I told her (though I shouldn't have) that Gideon and I were in love and he was in my bed nearly every day and often more than once. And then something came into her face, and I realized that Willa hates me. I think she would like nothing better than to see me fail. She said, "Well, you must be satisfied you've got what you wanted, Sabine," and then she went off to dance the polka with her new husband.

I was furious with her. She is _married_ now!! How unfair that she thinks she can still lay claim to him and that I must feel guilty _forever_! And I was angry with myself too, because I'd given in to my temper and told her what was supposed to be a secret, and I knew Gideon would not be at all happy about how childish I'd been. And then I thought perhaps Willa would tell Mama and Papa, and that would be _disastrous_!!! So I went to find her. She was drinking beer and her eyes were very bright and she asked what I wanted in such a nasty voice that I nearly left it be. But I tried to be mature, and I told her I had exaggerated what I'd said about Gideon. And she asked me what I'd exaggerated, the fact that he loved me or that I was playing the whore with him? And then she walked away before I could answer and I was angrier than ever and wished I'd never said anything at all. I feel sorry for Frederick, because Willa has only settled for him and she is just the kind to resent that and I think they will be very unhappy together.

I had been having a good time, but after that, I wanted to go home, and I went to find Barret, but he had disappeared. Papa came up to me and asked where was my brother—was he off drinking again?—and he seemed very angry and I was angry too and told him Barret was not drinking much anymore, and he should not be so quick to judge his son. Papa said I was not blameless. My selfishness had driven Barret to drink and despair, and would no doubt lead to his death as well. It was a horrible, horrible thing to say.

Then I heard a commotion at the back of the hall, in the kitchen, and I felt sick to my stomach, because I just knew it had something to do with my brother. There was a crowd gathering there, and I pushed my way through it to see that someone had indeed found Barret.

I am not sure what could have been worse than what I saw. They were in the pantry, Barret and some girl—no one from the wedding party, but obviously a whore (I have no idea where he found her; he must have gone out into the street), and Barret's shirt and trousers were unbuttoned and his tie loose and the girl was lying there beside him with her skirt up to show her cunny. She was looking at everyone gathering around as if they were strange creatures that had suddenly appeared before her, and her eyes and Barret's too had almost no pupils at all.

I have never seen Papa so angry. Not even at Christmastime. He yelled at the whore to cover herself among decent people, and then he went to grab Barret, but Barret reached for a bottle that was beside him. I realized he'd been drinking, and I was so angry and despairing myself, until Papa yanked the bottle from his hands and threw it on the floor so hard it broke and everything spilled out, and I smelled laudanum.

Papa grabbed him and threw him against the wall, and Barret fell to the floor again, and I knelt beside him. He smiled at me and said, "There you are, Bina," as if he didn't know where he was, and I tried to pull him to his feet. He was like a dead thing.

Papa told two of his friends to get Barret out. I put my arms around my brother and told them to leave him alone. They were afraid to touch me and they looked at Papa, who seemed ready to explode. He told me to step away from Barret and I said I would stand by my brother and then Papa said Barret and I deserved each other, and we were not welcome in his house again, and then Barret laughed and Papa's friends grabbed him and half carried him to the back door, where they pushed him out so he went stumbling, and Papa turned to me and asked if I would go on my own two feet or did I need help too? And I hurried out into the street after my brother. Willa was crying on Frederick's shoulder and Mama's face was white. Papa's friends slammed the door shut behind us. I don't know what happened to the whore.

Barret was just lying there in the middle of the alley among the trash and fish bones as if he were dead. He groaned when I turned him over and said I would get my dress dirty and I told him I didn't care. To my horror, he began to cry. He said he wanted to die, that he thought about it all the time, and then he asked if I would say his eulogy. I told him he wasn't going to die and I tried to pick him up. He grabbed my arm, and asked me not to say just the kind things at his funeral that didn't matter. He wanted me to say what no one else would know about him. "I've thought about it, you see, Bina," he said. "It's not the big things that make us who we are, but the things we don't show anyone. . . ."

I was crying too. I told him that Gideon and I would take care of him, and at that he tried to prop up on his elbow and I saw him working to form the right words, and he told me that

Gideon brought out the worst in me and I was letting him and I was better than that. I hate that he feels this way, but I don't know how to comfort him anymore. "I've tried to stop it," he said. "I've tried to stop you, but I can't. Don't let him ruin you, Bina." I finally got him to his feet and hooked his arm over my shoulders and grabbed up my train with my other arm, though it was already filthy from dragging in the street. It must have taken me an hour to get to Broadway and hail a cab, and even then the driver wouldn't take us until I gave him money in advance.

I was very cross then and I told Barret what a fool he was to get a whore at Willa's wedding and one who brought laudanum too, and he said, "It wasn't her who brought it." He told me Gideon had given it to him. I said he was talking nonsense. I know very well Gideon is as concerned about Barret's habits as I am. Why would he do such a thing?

Once we were at the hotel, I had the driver go up to fetch Gideon to help me get Barret inside, and when he came down and saw Barret unconscious in the cab, he gave me such a look, as if he had expected it and hadn't he told me before? He and the driver took Barret up to the room and Gideon told me to follow at a good distance so no one would see me with them, which I did.

Gideon asked me what had happened, and I told him, also that Barret had said Gideon had given him the laudanum, which he denied. He said Barret was too drunk to even remember his name half the time, and asked me, "Who do you believe, Bina? Me or your brother?" and I cried and said that of course I believed him. He held me, and then he brought me down on the bed to lie beside him and cradled me and stroked my hair. His voice was quiet in my ear. "Your family doesn't believe in you. Not like I do."

I thought of Willa, who wanted to keep me from him, and Papa, who blamed me for Willa's hurt and Barret's dissolution, and Barret, who thinks so little of me now that he calls me a whore at the slightest provocation, and I know Gideon is right.

CHAPTER 10

Seattle, Washington Territory—March 1881

When I woke the next morning, Charlotte's words were sharp in my ears, and Johnny's too and I knew what they said was true. The past had such a tight hold on me I could hardly breathe for its grip, and I knew at last the time had come to learn to live with it, and that Johnny's suggestion to turn the Palace legitimate might be just what I needed. The idea still frightened me, but to have something back of what I loved, no matter how small, to no longer live in weariness and joylessness . . . it was too much a temptation to deny.

And I told myself that this time everything would be different. I didn't love Johnny, and that kept me safe. I could lead him where I wanted. He trusted me, and he would listen to my advice. In the same way I'd appeased his ambitions by suggesting the boxhouse, I could slow this plan to my pace. I could protect myself with half measures that satisfied us both.

I could have some kind of a life again.

The next morning, when I went into the Palace and Duncan warned, "Johnny ain't in a good temper this morning," I gave him the smile that had charmed more men than I could count, and even though he should have been used to it, he flushed and dropped the glass he was drying so it shattered on the floor.

"Is he in his office?" I asked.

Duncan bent to pick up the glass. He nodded, mumbling something unintelligible, and I knocked on Johnny's door and stepped inside. Johnny sat at his desk, marking figures in a ledger. He looked up. "It's about time."

I hung my cloak on a hook. "You could have sent for me if you wanted me here earlier."

"Would you have come?"

I seated myself on the edge of his desk and leaned forward to brush his lips with my own. "I'm at your beck and call, as you well know."

He frowned. "What the hell are you in such a good mood for?"

"I've been thinking about what you said last night. About turning the Palace into a real theater."

"And?"

"And I think we should do it."

His frown disappeared in surprise. "You do?"

"I do. I've been thinking about the best way to go about it."

He hesitated, and then said, "I got a friend in San Francisco owns the Luxe Theater. Thought I'd send him a letter, see if he has any acts that might be interested in coming up here."

"Not yet," I said firmly, ignoring my quick panic. "It's too soon. You can't ask anyone to play this stage. It's barely a platform. We'll need to make it at least look like a theater, and for that we need money. So unless you've got a pile of gold sitting in that safe under your desk . . ."

"You know better than that, honey." Johnny sat back in his chair, tapping the end of the pencil against his mouth.

"We'll need investors. Rich people who have nothing better to do with their money than spend it. City fathers, merchants, the mayor, people like that."

"Go on."

"We'll get together a list—you should do that, you know everyone. More important, you know their secrets."

He smiled a little.

"Figure out who will give us money. Then we can start to make changes. Then we can talk to San Francisco. We'll get some of the smaller acts up here. Limit the whores to the floor and the boxes, so we've got real talent on the stage for a change and the rest is just a service we offer. That will keep our regulars around until we're ready to lose them."

Johnny said, "Not a bad idea, honey. Not bad at all."

"But the money has to come first," I said.

"That could take a while."

"It's not a race, Johnny. Better to do this right."

He nodded slowly. "All right. I'll see what I can do. But I don't suppose it could hurt to write San Francisco anyway."

"We need the stage first."

"Building this place up will take months. Investors will need to see more than footlights," he pointed out. "They get nervous with their money. They'll want to know real entertainment is waiting in the wings."

"The last thing we want is for a troupe to come up here and discover they're playing in a glorified brothel. We'll never get a second chance."

"I'll just advise Tom that you and me are changing things up here, and to keep an eye out."

"Don't mention me," I said quickly—too quickly; Johnny's eyes narrowed suspiciously.

"Why not?"

"I . . . because . . . because I'm a woman. He might not look kindly on your partnering with me. He might think you aren't serious."

"Hmmm." Johnny went quiet and thoughtful.

"Your friend won't want to deal with me anyway. You know

that. He'll just assume I'm involved because you're fucking me. He won't listen to anything I have to say, and he won't trust you if it looks like you are."

"I suppose you're right about that."

"I am right." I slid off the edge of the desk and stood. "So we're agreed? You'll look for investors first?"

"We're agreed," he said with a nod.

"Then I'll get back on the floor."

I was at the door when he said, "Margie—"

I glanced at him over my shoulder. "Yes?"

"What the hell made you change your mind about this?"

"I just saw the sense in it," I told him. "And I guess . . . neither of us wants to work a boxhouse forever."

He nodded and waved me away, but there was a thoughtfulness in his expression that sent a little frisson of discomfort into me. I told myself I was imagining it. I'd just given him what he wanted. What else mattered?

Now THAT I'D said yes to Johnny, things seemed strangely different, as if I were looking through a glass into another world. The Palace was ugly, I knew that, but tonight it did not seem so irredeemably so; tonight when I looked at the stage I didn't see the splintery and warped platform or the rickety steps leading to it. Instead I saw what it was going to be. I found myself mulling over how the footlights would be placed and whether we would get the fittings to turn their colors from yellow to green or blue or red. How we would build wings to hide the steps leading to the orchestra loge. Whether the drop curtain should be blue or green or crimson.

That night, the shadows were not so very dark as I'd thought, the men not coarse and rude but simply honest laborers looking for a little fun, ready to laugh and be teased, and the girls were more likely to break into a smile, as if they too sensed that something had changed. They missed fewer notes; even Billy's playing improved nominally.

The place stayed full a long time that night, and it was closer to dawn than to twilight when the crowd finally lessened enough that I could take a break. I stepped out the back door and onto the stoop and breathed deep. Cool air, but not cold, and tinged with damp from the harbor but not from rain. It would be spring soon. The sun would not be unwelcome.

The back door creaked behind me. I turned, expecting it to be Duncan coming for another keg, and was surprised when it was Charlotte instead, her hair frowsy and falling from its pins.

"I thought I saw you come out here," she said.

"Is something wrong? Do I need to go back in?"

"No, no, nothing like that." She sighed and came up beside me, crossing her arms over her breasts, shivering a little. "It's dying down. Johnny just told me I could go home if I wanted." She sat down on the edge of the stoop. "You seem happy tonight. The whole place feels it."

"I don't think it's just me. There's something in the air."

She tilted her head at me. "Oh, it's you, believe me. When you're a bitch the whole place feels that too."

"How sweet."

She shrugged. "What happened today?"

"What makes you think anything happened?"

A heavy, impatient sigh.

I sat down beside her. "It's your fault, in any case."

"My fault?"

"I decided to do what you suggested. I'm going to help Johnny remake the Palace into a real theater."

"And that's what's got you so happy?"

"Yes." I turned to look at her. "Shouldn't it?"

She laughed a little and shook her head. "If that's all it took, why the hell did you wait so long?"

"What you said made the difference," I admitted quietly.

"You and Johnny . . . you were both right. About my living in the past."

"So what're you going to do? Apart from getting rid of the whores."

"We're not getting rid of you. At least not yet."

"I don't see much fucking going on in places like Squire's."

"Don't fool yourself," I said wryly.

"Oh yeah?" The faint glow from the streetlamp on the corner glanced over her face, softening the sharp outlines of her cheekbones, her nose. She teased, "How do you know that, Marguerite? Let me guess . . . you and Johnny do it there at *Faust?*"

"Don't be absurd."

"All right, so what did you mean?"

I wasn't surprised at the question, what was surprising was the lack of fear I felt at it. Perhaps it was only that I was in a good mood. The past seemed far away for once, too far to hurt me, and she had been honest with me about her own life. Didn't that create an obligation to answer with mine? And I wanted to tell her something. Not the truth . . . or at least not the whole truth, because I knew it would change the way she felt about me and I was afraid of that. But something else. Surely there was something else I could tell her, something small, something to show how much her friendship meant to me.

I found myself saying, carefully, anxiously, "I traveled theaters all over the country with him."

"With who?"

"A musician. He was a pianist." I let out my breath slowly, relieved when the words caused no pain, when they were as simple as they sounded. "I met him when I was very young and I fell in love with him."

"Was he famous?"

"A little," I said. "No one you've heard of, I'm sure. I think you'd have to have worked in the business to know of him."

"Ah." She leaned her head back, looking up at the sky, which was nothing but a hazy darkness above our heads. "What happened?"

"It ended, that's all."

"Bad?"

I nodded and tried not to think of it.

She said, baldly and irreverently, "So that explains it then. No doubt the two of you fucked your way through every theater in America."

I laughed and she laughed with me until Duncan stuck his head out the back door and said Johnny was looking for me, and we went back inside.

MY LIFE WAS moving on, whether I went with it or not, the things I'd agreed to put into motion. Johnny spent nearly every night speaking with men I didn't know, men wearing suits and vests and hats, who looked nothing like the miners and lumbermen who were our usual customers. The Palace had always had its share of respectable merchants and businessmen slumming, but none of them had ever looked it over with such interest. I stayed out of their way mostly, as I stayed away from the respectable parts of town in general. Once or twice Johnny came downstairs dressed in the suit I hadn't seen until the night of *Faust,* and he'd give me a wink and leave the Palace for some meeting or another, and I felt both anticipation and anxiety at how quickly he worked the plans I'd put into his head.

And my friendship with Charlotte progressed just as quickly, as if now that I'd opened the dam, the flow could not be contained. I found myself telling her things. Some things were small enough that they could be detached, they could be said, and with each saying the tight, hard knot of my memories loosened a little more. I told her I had a nephew I hardly knew and a sister I no longer spoke to, and Charlotte said families were strange things, bound together by blood but not nec-

essarily by affection. I told her I had a brother and my parents
wanted nothing to do with me, and she said her father had
been such a mean son of a bitch she'd spent every waking
hour hoping he would die. And so it went on, truths and half-
truths and omissions all bound together, so I could not always
remember what I'd said or how I'd phrased things, but it was
becoming easier to breathe, and my nightmares were easing,
occurring not so often now.

Then, one day in early April, as Charlotte and I walked
back to the boardinghouse room after a breakfast at nearby
Miller's Restaurant, she asked, "How did you meet him? Your
musician? In the beer hall?"

The memory came unbidden. The door opening, a gust of
air through the smoke, my brother's bright hair shining, his
laughter as he turned to the dark-haired young man who'd
come inside with him. The calling of orders back to the
kitchen, the beer foaming as Papa drew a glass from the keg,
the music from the polka band onstage. And then Willa moving through the crowd to take his hand.

Talking about him was not easy—I could not think of
what wouldn't be dangerous to say. But to tell her nothing
would offend, and so I cast about for something and landed
on *The Barber of Seville*. Warily at first, in the event she would
recognize it, I lied. "He'd watched me from afar for some
time. He said he'd admired me, but he never dared to speak
to me because I was so young, and my brother was very protective of me. And his father and my father had been enemies
for years."

The day was warm for the time of year, and bright and
beautiful enough that it made it easy to forget the muddy
squalor of winter. The Mountain shone so whitely it was hard
to look at without squinting. We passed a lilac tree in someone's yard, and I snagged the branch and snapped a blossom
from it, holding it to my nose, closing my eyes for a moment
to breathe deeply of its scent.

"Enemies?" she asked.

"Rival beer hall owners."

"So how did you meet?"

I smiled, thinking of the scene in *Barber* as we'd played it onstage, a painted balcony, myself perched on a ladder behind, gasping in delight at an impromptu serenade. "He sang to me. One night, he stood below my window and sang to me. I think I loved him from that moment."

"It sounds like a fucking fairy tale."

"It was very romantic. When I called out for his name, he didn't tell me his real one, because he knew Papa and my brother would keep him away."

"Such an honorable man," Charlotte said sarcastically.

"It wasn't like that. He wanted to meet me and he knew they would object. What was he to do?"

"How about walk the hell away?"

I twirled the lilac stem between my fingers, watching it spin. "When Papa advertised for a music teacher for me, he came in disguise and pretended to be one."

She snorted. "And then you ran off with him."

"How did you know?"

"Ain't that how all those stories go? Hell, it's even how mine went."

We climbed the ramp to the boardinghouse door, and then up the stairs to our room. The sun filtered in through the faded curtains, and the little room was hot. Charlotte pounded on the sides of the window to force it up through the swollen sill, and I laid the lilac sprig on the table before it. The sprig seemed to swell in the sun, exploding with scent. The hot metal smoke of the foundry next door came in, along with the faint blood smell of the butcher's on the other side, but the lilac was so fragrant it held sway over the rest.

I fell back on the bed, crossing my arms under my head.

She stood at the window, looking out. "And it ended the way all them stories do, didn't it? You ran off with him, and things weren't the way you'd thought they would be."

"That didn't happen for a long time. We were happy for a while."

Charlotte's glance was penetrating. "Is he the one gave you that scar?"

Would I have answered that? Could I have said anything true about it at all?

I don't know what would have come out of my mouth; I was hardly conscious of thinking, only that she was watching me as if I might for once give her some truth she wanted, and I wished nothing more than to keep that look upon her face, the look that told me we were friends, that she trusted me.

But the knock on the door startled us both.

"Miz Olson? Miz Rainey?" Mrs. McGraw's voice was harsh as a seagull's caw.

"One moment!" I rose and went to the door to open it.

Mrs. McGraw stood in the hallway, her face wreathed in an anxious smile, her browning, missing teeth hard to look away from. "Oh, I've got good news, Miz Olson! Mr. Clemmons is moving at the end of the week, so Miz Rainey can have his room, just as I promised."

I stared at her in stunned surprise. "Mr. Clemmons? Are you . . . are you certain?"

"He gave me his notice this morning. Ain't that good news? Now you needn't share."

"Yes," I said slowly. "That's good news indeed."

"Thought I'd tell you right away. I know it's been a trial, waiting this long, but now you can have your room to yourself again."

I nodded, but I didn't hear her words any longer, only a slow buzzing, and when she said her good-byes and left us again, her footsteps clattering down the warped boards of the hallway, I closed the door and turned back to Charlotte, who was looking as stunned as I felt.

"Mr. Clemmons is leaving," I said, as if she hadn't just heard the same words I had.

"Your own room back at last," she said, smiling weakly. "I guess it'll be a relief."

The lilac bloom was fading in the harsh sunlight; its scent was suddenly unbearable, too sweet, almost rotten. "A relief," I agreed.

From the Journal of Sabine Conrad

JUNE 11, 1873—Today, flowers from Leonard, along with a small box from Tiffany with a diamond pavé barrette. Very beautiful, though Gideon turns his nose up at it and says "Jerome had best do better than that if he wants to keep Belmont at bay."

Leonard also pens that he must leave town for a few days and so will not see me before I go on tour, and the clip is "for good luck." Gideon has me write him back to say that I shall think of him, and hope that his affections do not diminish in the coming months, as mine will not.

All nonsense, of course.

SAN FRANCISCO, AUGUST 20, 1873—The tour has been a resounding success. I have been too busy to write, and now we are in San Francisco, where I can hardly move without being nearly assaulted by a mob. They have thrown flowers at the stage every night, and I have sung so many encores I must drink warm honeyed water each night to soothe my throat. There have been too many dinners and toasts and prominent people to remember them all. I have received jewels in nearly every city—a diamond star with a ruby in the center, a pearl fan, and three diamond rings—oh, and a brooch in the shape of a butterfly and studded with jewels of every color, from a French marquis who was visiting New Orleans and happened upon my performance and came every single night. My notices have been too many to mention and all good. But here in San Francisco, I am more adored than I could have imagined!

Last night there was a crowd gathered at the backstage door when I came out, which is not so unusual, except that they had unfastened the horses from the carriage that was to take me back to the hotel so that they could draw me there themselves!!!! "We shall act as your horses, Miss Conrad," said one young man, and then they harnessed themselves and took me through the streets of San Francisco. Oh, I never laughed so hard, and even Gideon was moved by it. When I arrived at the hotel, they waited below, shouting and refusing to leave until Gideon said I must say something to them, so I stood on the balcony and threw flowers and Gideon whispered in my ear: "Look at them. They'd eat you alive if they could, sweetheart."

Barret is becoming known as quite the impresario for arranging this tour. Even the newspapers mention him as being the force behind my success, which is ironic, because it has all been Gideon. Everyone in the business already knows this, of course, though none of us say it, and the papers can only state what is publicly advertised.

AUGUST 22, 1873—I have insisted on having our photographs taken—me and Barret and Gideon together—in a little shop near the hotel. I wore the double strand of pearls that Gideon bought me for my nineteenth birthday (how old I am now! I shudder to think it!). I sent the one of me and Barret to Papa and Mama (in the hopes that they will remember how they love us), and Gideon had the one of me alone made into some cartes de visite for us to hand about, but my favorite is the one of Gideon and me together. I have framed it and my own copy of me and Barret, and I mean to put them on my bedside table in every hotel I stay, but I confess I put the one of me and Gideon forward so I can see it better. We look like we belong together, and he teases me every time he sees it and says that now I will not forget him. As if I ever could!

NEW YORK, SEPTEMBER 24, 1873—We returned home earlier than we meant because of the disaster the world is so suddenly in thanks to Jay Cooke & Company's bankruptcy, and because Gideon could not get all of my money from the bank and Chicago is in such disarray that there was no coin to be had at all. I read of two suicides in the newspaper. On Friday there was a terrible mob in Broad Street that was so large no traffic could move, and on Saturday the Exchange shut down trading. Gideon says either we will recover quickly or the banks and insurance companies will be ruined and we will go into a depression and thank God I was paid in coin and not cheques. He says he will never accept cheques again. He rescued as much of my money as he could, and thankfully, we finished most of the tour before the worst hit and it was very lucrative. I have a great many jewels, and Gideon says that many of the rich are still rich enough to buy me more, and the opera season will go on regardless, because those who are most affected by this panic will not be the ones buying subscriptions anyway. Gideon has spoken to Mr. Strakosch, who is not worried, and says that the Italian is so well liked we should have no fear for audiences. It seems Mrs. Astor will get her way about Mozart, because *Don Giovanni* is to be sung in October, and I am to do Zerlina instead of Christine Nilsson— she is Donna Anna this year.

I returned to find four letters from Leonard waiting for me, along with a pair of golden earrings and a brooch, and I hear that Belmont is buying stocks as the prices hit bottom, so he cannot be too badly off either.

OCTOBER 23, 1873—The newspapers say Mme. Nilsson and I are to be considered the "finest sopranos in the United States today, and one might be tempted to say the world"! Well, that should show P. Lucca and Clara Kellogg too! I confess I had not been looking forward to singing with Christine, as she is so fine, and I thought I would suffer in comparison, but she is very generous, and it has been a pleasure.

Gideon has asked me to speak with Leonard about financing a new tour this summer, one with a troupe put together by Gideon himself, as his experience now with Mr. Strakosch has made him see that becoming a true impresario—as I once told him he should be!—is the way we will make a fortune.

Barret told me that Gideon will have to think twice if he believes I will condescend to head a troupe. He says it is my career we should be worried about and not Gideon's, and Gideon should focus his energies on getting me a position at Covent Garden or La Scala or the Theatre Italien in Paris. Adelina Patti and Christine Nilsson are both recognized worldwide and I should be as well, and though I can't deny I would like to go abroad, there is time enough for that. If Gideon grows very powerful and influential, it can only help me too.

NOVEMBER 4, 1873—Barret has told Gideon I will not head his troupe, which made me angry because he had no right to do so. Gideon was so furious he did not come backstage as he always does before I go on, and I was desperate without his good luck kiss and I didn't perform my best. Leonard, of course, did not seem to notice. When he came to my dressing room after, he said I was as lovely as ever, but I declined to go to supper with him and went back to my rooms, where I am now and am very dispirited. Barret has gone off somewhere, and I have not seen Gideon at all.

NOVEMBER 6, 1873—Gideon has been gone <u>two</u> days! I have been so miserable and sick I could not go on, no matter how they all begged me. Where is he? Has he abandoned me? I've been staring at our picture for hours in the hopes I can somehow wish him back to me but he does not come and I HATE

Barret for doing this to me. I would kill him if he were here,
but of course he has disappeared as well and left me here on
my own.

I would do ANYTHING to have Gideon back. <u>Anything</u>.

NOVEMBER 7, 1873—Tonight Gideon returned. He sleeps beside me now as I write this, and to look at him gives me a terrible pain and longing at the same time, because it is nearly
dawn and soon he will wake and ask me to decide.

When he came back, he looked tired and distraught. He
told me that he had something to show me and to dress in my
plainest gown and come with him. I was so happy to see him
I didn't question him at all, and then he told me to wear a
cloak and a veiled hat, and took me out of the hotel and called
a carriage. When he gave the driver a direction, the man
protested, but Gideon offered him a bonus, which he could not
refuse, of course, not in these terrible times. I asked Gideon
where we were going and he would say nothing, only to wait
and see, and he was so terse and angry that I was afraid. For
a moment I thought he meant to take me back to Kleindeutschland, but we didn't go there. I didn't know where we
went, the way had so many turns. When he rapped on the ceiling of the carriage to tell the driver to stop, I thought he had
made a mistake. There was nothing before us but saloons and
concert halls—we were somewhere off the Bowery, I thought,
but I wasn't sure, and certainly in one of the worst parts of
the city. The buildings were all grimy and run-down, and
there were drunks and men lurking in the shadows who eyed
us when we came out of the carriage, which drove off quickly.
Gideon told me to be quiet, and to pull the hood of my cloak
over my head, even though I was already wearing a hat and
veil, and then he took me to these narrow dark stairs between
two saloons that went down into a basement, and knocked
sharply on the door at the bottom.

It was opened by a Chinaman wearing a black cap and
tunic. When he saw Gideon he opened the door farther, as if

he recognized him. When the door closed behind us, the Celestial said, "Back here," and led us down the hallway toward a dim, flickering lamp shaded by a red scarf, so the place looked eerie and strange. As we drew closer to the light, I began to smell smoke—not tobacco, but something else, and I recognized it as the same scent I had smelled on Barret before, and on Gideon sometimes too. A little flowery, or even sweet, like burnt sugar but very heavy and odd.

At the end of the hallway, the Chinaman turned, and there were two doors, one of which he opened, and then he stood back and gestured for us to go inside.

The room was large—the main of the basement—with damp stone walls, and there were two other lamps turned down very low, all with scarves like the one in the hallway, and pallets with men lying upon them. Other men were huddled about smaller, open-flamed lamps that sat about on low tables. The room was so heavy with that smoke it made me dizzy.

Gideon took my arm and led me past men who gazed blankly up at us, smoke curling from pipes loose in their hands, and I knew already what I would see before Gideon stopped, and I was looking down into the open-eyed face of my brother, slack mouthed, his eyes nothing but iris, while a Chinaman sat at the table next to him, boiling something tarry-looking on a needle, a fat, pulsing glob of what I realized was opium.

I said his name, and Barret turned his face to me and smiled and then he saw Gideon and he said, "Where'd you go to? Have another smoke." His voice was so slurred, and he looked so dissolute, so awful. Nothing like the brother I love. I think he hardly realized who I was or that I was even there. Gideon whispered to me that this was where Barret came every night, and sometimes in the afternoons, and then he said with so much contempt it startled me, "Is this what you'd choose over me to manage your career, Sabine?" This, as if Barret was hardly human, and it was true, he didn't look human lying there, but grotesque and unreal, waxy and drooling and so lost in dreams he seemed to have forgotten we were there almost the next moment.

I felt as if my heart were breaking, and I feel it still now, because of course I know the choice I will make, and I hate Barret for forcing me to make it.

NOVEMBER 8, 1873—Today I told Barret that I was giving control of my career and my money to Gideon, and that I have made Gideon my manager in name as well as in deed, and that I will have no more need of my brother.

It was a terrible scene. First Barret raged until I thought the hotel manager would come, and then he railed at Gideon, who wisely stayed away, and then he cried. He sobbed so I thought my own heart would tear in two. He said I was making a mistake, that I would destroy myself without him. Then he said it was Gideon who had introduced him to the opium to begin with—to which I said that even if that were true, it was not Gideon who made him keep smoking it.

Barret asked what would he do now, and I told him I didn't know, but I still loved him, that I would always love him, because he was my brother. Barret called me some terrible things. He said I was not fit to be a Conrad, and that I had besmirched our family, and that I was a whore willing to do whatever I must to be famous, including killing those who loved me.

I left him then. I was crying. I am crying still.

NOVEMBER 9, 1873—I can hardly think.

The world feels like a terrible dream. I wish I could wake up.

My brother is dead. Someone in a room down the hall heard a gunshot early this morning, and the hotel manager broke open Barret's door to find him there. He had shot himself in the head. I did not even know he had a gun.

Gideon and I were at Delmonico's when he died, drinking champagne.

CHAPTER 11

Seattle, Washington Territory—July 1881

As the spring faded into summer, the stink of the sun-baked sewage and putrid mud of the tideflats was tinged with the fragrance of roses and sweetbriar and the blackberries that tangled at the fences of every yard and bordered the roads at the edges of town. Johnny went coatless, and both he and Duncan wore their shirtsleeves rolled up over their forearms, and men came into the Palace covered with sweat that soaked their long underwear, only adding to the stench that worsened twice a day, when the tide was out. The fish oil the peddling Indian women combed into their shining hair smelled so rank in the sun it was hard to stand near them. Smoke from the sawmill and the forges climbed into skies cleaner and bluer than any I'd ever seen, and dust rose from the streets to blanket everything. The Mountain loomed, some days hazy, some days so sharp and chiseled it looked as if someone had drawn it onto the sky with gray-blue ink.

And I could not stand those late and early hours between leaving the Palace and going back again. Now that Charlotte had her own room at Mrs. McGraw's, my own became unbearable. I felt the lack of her within it. I had never liked being alone, but now my solitary hours there seemed worse than ever. In my need to spend as little time with myself as possible, I began to eschew sleep. I went to bed just before dawn and woke only a few hours later, and then I went to her room and waited until she woke and asked if I cared for some breakfast as if she were unsurprised to see me there, as if she expected it. And I suppose, after I had done this nearly every morning our first week apart, she did.

Even Johnny noticed it. One night, as we both leaned on the bar, watching the action, he said, "What's got into your craw about the tall one?"

"Her name's Charlotte," I said. "And I don't know what you mean."

He shrugged. "You been watching her. Afraid she'll steal us blind if you look away?"

"Charlotte wouldn't steal anything," I said—a little too hotly, I realized, too late, as Johnny frowned.

"You sound like you got an affection for the girl."

"She's a friend. Why should that be so odd?"

"A friend?" He laughed. "You ain't ever had friends."

"Well, I do now."

He made a sound deep in his throat, doubt and disbelief, and then he exhaled and said in a low voice, "I think I might have our fellow. I'll know better in the next day or two, but he seems interested enough in our prospects."

I was both relieved and dismayed at the change of subject. That Johnny had found an investor so quickly surprised me. I'd thought the search might take nearly a year. I'd hoped it would.

Johnny's gaze narrowed. "That don't make you happy?"

"Who is it?"

"New money," he said, pouring us each a drink. "Eager to find a way to show Daddy he's a smart boy."

"Are you certain he has what we need?"

"Certain enough. You want to meet him?"

"Should I?"

Johnny laughed a little. "You're my partner, ain't you? Tell you what, I'll arrange a little dinner for the three of us, how's that? If he's on the edge, I guess the two of us can figure out how to push him over."

I took a sip of my drink. Again, I felt that mix of apprehension and excitement, the little stir of yearning. I thought of a curtain, footlights. "Just tell me when, and I'll be there."

Johnny drank the rest of his whiskey and slammed the glass onto the bar and said, "That's my girl. I'll schedule it. You got any special plans for the next few days?"

"What plans would I have?"

"How should I know? What about with your tall friend? I'd hate to interrupt any sewing circle."

"Go to hell, Johnny."

He laughed and backed away from the bar, and he was still chuckling to himself when he went into his office. I didn't know how to feel about the fact that he knew about my relationship with Charlotte, whether to feel pride because I'd never thought myself capable of friendship before now, or vulnerable because Johnny had never failed to use a weak point to his advantage, and Charlotte felt like a weak point, something I should protect.

That night was warm and sultry, strange for July, which was as often cloudy and cool as not, and as Charlotte and Duncan and I stepped out from the Palace, I had a sudden thought, and I turned to Duncan and said, "You don't need to see us home tonight. Charlotte and I are going for a walk."

He frowned. "Ain't a good time for walking, Marguerite. You know that."

"I've got my derringer."

He snorted.

"We'll be all right," I assured him. "You go on to bed. And wasn't that Sarah I saw waiting by the bar?"

He agreed quickly then, and left us there by the back stoop, and Charlotte turned to me with a little smile and said, "A walk? Where the hell to?"

"Down to the harbor," I said.

"We're as likely to get raped and murdered as make it there in one piece."

"I'm willing to take the risk," I said.

I felt the curiosity in her glance. "Why? What's got into you?"

"It's a beautiful night, and I'm not tired yet." All of which was true, but there was something else too, the need to have more of her, for just a little longer. I was not ready to go to the boardinghouse, where she would go to her room, and I to mine. I wanted to keep her with me for a few moments more.

The movement in the bay was constant even through the night, the lamps of the steamers set upon deep shadows as they moved through the darkness, reflecting upon the water like stars set in a rippling firmament. I made a blind descent down the bank, slipping a little on stones I could barely see, hearing them roll and rattle to the barnacle-covered ones on the beach below. There was an abandoned wharf just beyond, and I stepped up onto its loose, splintered boards and went halfway down its length before I sat.

Charlotte sat beside me and drew off her boots, sliding to the edge of the dock, trailing her feet in the water, sighing. She lay back, looking up at the sky. "That feels good."

I took off my own boots, easing my feet into water that was cold even in summer, feeling the gentle nudge of a tentacle-less jellyfish—scores of them floated about the dock like clear, gelatinous bubbles—and then the tickle as it fluttered its edges and drifted away.

The smell of coal smoke from the steamers was heavy on the air, salt and seaweed and tar, from somewhere something rotten. I heard the small splash of her feet below the sight line of the wharf. Her presence eased my apprehensions and my fears, yet even as those lessened, another kind of fear came, familiar, the same I'd felt before, with him. That longing that went beyond friendship or sex, a fear that had everything to do with love, with the dread of losing it.

I found myself saying, "I miss you."

I couldn't see her expression in the darkness. "Oh hell, Marguerite. Things change. It ain't always bad. It just takes getting used to."

"I don't want to get used to it."

"You sound like a spoiled kid."

I pulled my feet from the water, my knees to my chest, drawing away from her. "Forgive me. I'm sorry if I don't know how this is supposed to work. I've never had a friend. I don't know the rules."

"You can't mean it. You must've had friends before. What about your sister?"

"I told you I don't speak to her. We were rivals, not friends."

"Your brother then."

"My brother . . ." I closed my eyes. It was too hard to think of him. I shook my head mutely.

"There must have been someone."

"You're the first to make the attempt. Virgin territory, as it were." I tried to laugh and failed miserably. "You'd best take care. I understand it can be dangerous."

She slid closer to me, her skirt catching in the splinters of the boards. The wharf rocked. "What about your piano player? There must have been good times at the start, weren't there?"

"Yes, of course," I said impatiently. "But it didn't last. Nothing ever does."

"So what happened?"

I searched for what to tell her. Another bit from *Barber*, perhaps. Or *La Traviata*. I said, "His father asked me to walk away. He'd arranged a marriage for him with a woman who could do something for him, and said I should step aside so he could be as famous as he was meant to be."

"And you said no."

"Why would I say no?"

"I ain't never seen you do anything without getting something in return."

"Well, I did this time," I said hotly. "I would have done anything for him."

Charlotte laughed. "I ain't wrong to say it, and you know it. All right . . . so this time you played the martyr and left him. I guess it *was* true love. What then?"

I went on, sulking at first, then, as she listened more intently, I forgot my irritation. I added more from *Barber,* another piece of *La Trav* here, one from *Figaro* there. I told her how I'd left him, how he'd followed me. How we'd come back together, how we grew tired of each other.

"He had affairs," I said. "He was never faithful."

"Well, he was a man. At least you never married him."

"No," I said, and the word carried with it a sadness I'd forgotten, one I hadn't expected. I let it fall into the darkness, and she let it lie there, untouched, neither of us picking it up to explore it.

She threw her head back to look up at the sky. "A pretty night, ain't it?" she asked, and then she began to hum, low in her throat, "Roll on Silver Moon." When she mangled a note— too quiet; she couldn't reach it—I couldn't help myself. I joined in. Very softly, correcting. I closed my eyes; I tried not to think of her beside me as the hum turned into words, as I began to sing: " 'Roll on silver moon, point the traveler on his way. . . .' "

She went still and quiet and I could have stopped too; I should have stopped. But my voice took on an odd sort of power in the night, and I could not stop singing. I could not stop until I'd finished the song, until I climbed to the final crescendo: " 'I never never more with my true love will stray by thy soft silver beams, gentle moon.' "

When I opened my eyes, it was to find her staring at me. She said, "Sing something else."

Had she complimented me, I would have stopped, I would have put it away and locked it tight. But instead I broke into "Long Time Ago," a light, comic tune that required no effort at all, even from my unpracticed throat, and though I had known I missed the singing, I had not truly realized how much. It felt as if something had been restored to me, something I had loved and never expected to see again.

When I finished, Charlotte clapped her hands and put her fingers to her mouth, whistling as if she were in an audience, and I bowed where I sat, deeply from the waist, gracefully opening my arms in thanks as I'd been taught. *"There's seduction in a bow, Bina. The finishing touch—it tells them how much to love you."*

The words from the past startled me. For a moment I could not find myself, I did not know who I was.

But then Charlotte said softly, "Don't. Don't ruin it."

I called myself back with effort. "What?"

"Whatever you were thinking just then—don't think it. You were happy when you were singing."

"Charlotte—"

"I ain't never seen you like that. D'you know this one?" And she began to sing "Ständchen," though she sang it in English. "Serenade." " 'Murmur low and sweet through the leaves, the night winds moving. . . .' "

The happiness I'd lost for a moment bubbled up again inside me. I sang with her, and the night was suddenly so beautiful my heart ached with it. Charlotte lifted her foot, splashing water that sparkled and glowed, though there was no sun to reflect in it, and she stopped singing in a rush of startled breath. "Oh! Look at that! Phosphorescence!"

She plunged her foot in again, swirling it, and the water came alive with light that shimmered against her skin, as if she'd set off sparks.

"It looks as if the stars fell in," I said.

Charlotte arched her foot and made the water dance, creating a waterfall of light from her bare toes, and together we laughed like little girls at the wonder of algae that made its own light in the summer water, and I felt something inside me shift, a lurch of memory, and one I'd forgotten—a girl on a beach in Cuba, lifting her skirts and petticoats to run barefoot in the surf, laughing with happiness as she did so, bursting with it, while nearby a man laughed in reply as he took off his coat and sat on the beach to watch her, the wind ruffling his dark hair.

From the Journal of Sabine Conrad

JANUARY 10, 1874—I have not been sleeping well, and Gideon said this morning that I must not let Barret's death continue to haunt me, as Leonard told him that it made me poor company. Leonard has sent: one gold tiara studded with diamonds and pearls; an ivory and silk fan painted in the Japanese style; three rings: one emerald, one amethyst, and one ruby; one sapphire brooch in the form of a beetle with diamond eyes. He has written a note with each one saying that he misses our drives together, and to please say I have not abandoned my most ardent friend.

Gideon says the jewels are not enough, that if we are to put a troupe together to tour this summer we must start now, and Leonard must finance it, and I can grieve all I want, but I mustn't lose sight of our future. He says Barret is still controlling me even into death, and do I mean to thrust us into poverty because of my brother's selfishness?

Sometimes I hate Barret so much for leaving me to feel as guilty and horrible as I do. At night I hear his words— that I am not myself, that Gideon is ruining me, and I hate that I even allow such thoughts into my head. Barret never understood. I can hardly bear the moments I'm not with Gideon, and he has been everything that is patient and kind. He has held me more nights than I can count and let me sob into his shoulder until we are both wet with my tears. How can I doubt him?

I have not written about Barret's funeral because I cannot. It was horrible, and Papa and Mama both blame me for his death, I know. They barely spoke to me, and they accused me with every look. Willa, of course, kept her distance, because I brought Gideon with me and she is heavy with her husband's child. But I felt how she blames me too. None of them understand. No one understands but Gideon.

Gideon whispers that I don't belong in that world anyway. He reminds me of the dreams we share and says that this is the beginning, and once we have the troupe together we will be in control of our future. We will decide what shows we produce and where we play, and I will have the chance to show my talents to their best advantage and become the diva I should be.

When he says things like that, I feel much better. He reminds me that it is only a matter of time before I convince Leonard to give us the money we need, and the truth is that I do love the attention that Leonard and Belmont and the others lavish upon me. Next Wednesday is the French Ball held by the Cercle Français de l'Harmonie at the Academy of Music. It is to be a masked ball, and I confess I cannot help but look forward to it. I am tired of being so sad.

JANUARY 11, 1874—Today I had a visit from Willa.

How wretched it was! I had not expected her, and when the boy came to ask if the manager might send her up, I was in bed with Gideon. It was near eleven, and though we had been up very late the night before after the Hamilton soiree, I knew Willa would think me very decadent indeed to be sleeping the day away (though, in truth, I hadn't been

sleeping). I told the boy to have her wait for me in the Ladies'
Tearoom, but he said she insisted on a private interview.
Gideon kissed me and said he would stay and that it was time
my family understood there was no separating us now.

There was no time to dress, so I put on a chemise and
dressing gown, and Gideon pulled on his trousers and a shirt,
but no coat or vest, and the bed was unmade behind us, even
though I pulled out the screen, so I knew Willa would see right
away how intimate we were, and I was nervous to face her.

I was right to be so. When she came through the door, her
gaze went right to Gideon, and I saw the longing that came
into her eyes in the moment before he came to stand behind
me and put his hand on my shoulder. When he touched me,
her expression went hard. But worse still was that Willa was
no longer pregnant. She'd had the baby, and I hadn't known.
No one had sent a note or told me anything. When I asked
her, she said she had a little boy who looked just like his
father, and that she'd named him Barret after her brother—
her brother, as if he was nothing to me—and that she hadn't
told me because she wanted him not to have anything to do
with me.

I started to cry, though I tried to hide it from her. Gideon
squeezed my shoulder and asked her why she'd come, and
Willa said she was on an errand from Papa. When I said how
strange it was that he'd sent her instead of coming himself,
she said Papa had no wish to see me, that I was selfish and
willful, and Barret was dead because of me and none of them
could forgive that.

She must have known how much she hurt me. I grew angry
and said very sarcastically that shame hadn't kept Papa from
taking the money I sent him. She reached into her bag and
brought out a small stack of bills tied with string and set it on
the table—it was why she'd come, to return the money I'd just
sent Papa, the first since Barret's funeral. "Don't send any
more," she said flatly. She said Papa didn't want anything

from me, that he wanted her to tell me I was no longer his
daughter.

I said Mama could not feel the same, and Willa said she
did. That since I so obviously wanted to be free, my family
would release me. She glared at Gideon and said she hoped
I was happy with my choice.

Then she left.

When she was gone, my tears left with her. Gideon made to
comfort me, but I told him I had no need of comfort. I was
cold deep into my heart, and so angry it stays with me still—
I think it might never go away. I saw the confusion come into
his face, as if he didn't know what to make of me, so I kissed
him and made him take me to bed once again because sometimes I can only forget things when he is deep inside me.

If my family wishes to have nothing to do with me, I am
happy to oblige them. I hope they still feel that way when
I am very rich and very famous, and they are still crowded
into a tiny apartment above a beer hall in Kleindeutschland.

JANUARY 15, 1874—It has been twenty-four hours since I've
slept, and I am still so awake and stimulated I wonder if I will
ever sleep again! The French Ball was truly the most lascivious
thing I have ever experienced. It is so bacchanalian I'm surprised the city hasn't put a stop to it, but then, how could they?
The people who were there . . . well, I think they wouldn't
admit to it in the light of day, but I spotted several very rich men
despite their masks and costumes, and of course Leonard was
there and August Belmont too, and all kinds of women I'd
never seen before (and NONE I recognized from the Four
Hundred) and some I hope never to recognize in society, because how would we look one another in the eye? What a balm it
was for my unhappiness these last weeks! For a few hours I
confess I forgot everything.

Gideon had our costumes made, and when I saw what he'd
done I did not think I could wear such a thing in public. He'd

made me into a Turkish harem girl, with flesh-colored tights beneath thin silk pants and my bare stomach showing beneath the long fringe of a <u>very</u> revealing corset-like top. I told him it was too indecent to wear and he said it would be nothing compared to some of the other costumes. It was, however, quite beautiful, all in gold and that color of blue that looks very nice on me. He went as a harem guard—which I said I believed were eunuchs and he pulled me close and asked would I like to see how much of a eunuch he was and I laughed.

I had sapphires at my ears and throat and several bracelets on my arms, and my hair was down and Gideon had a hairdresser weave jewels into it so that every time I moved they thudded against my back, and I wore a blue silk mask too. Then we went out in the cold night, and I felt quite naked beneath my cloak. We teased each other in the carriage so that by the time we reached the Academy I was so inflamed for Gideon I wanted him to take me back to the hotel and to bed. But he told me that my distraction these last weeks had annoyed Leonard, and that tonight I must lure him in again. He said too that I should be careful, because these balls were known for their excesses, and though he would keep an eye on me, I must remember what I was about. Then he said he would reward me later if I were very good, and I laughed and promised I would do what he asked, but I was unprepared for how truly debauched the night was!

There must have been two thousand people there, crowding the floor and the pit and the boxes; so many it was near impossible to get through the lobby, and the music from the orchestra onstage was loud and there was champagne in every person's hand. And the women! There were many that were almost naked, far more so than I was. I saw another woman with a harem costume, only her corset was cut out to show her rouged (!!) nipples, and there were two men I saw who had painted phosphorescent paint onto their chests so they shone and glowed in the gaslight. There were a hundred satyrs and nymphs and a dozen Cleopatras and Caesars and scantily dressed Marie Antoinettes

and lion tamers and Napoleons and gypsies. Everyone was
drunk, and in our costumes and masks, we were not ourselves,
but strangers who did not bear responsibility or consequence. I
saw men leading women into darkened corners and it was like
being in the back alleys of Kleindeutschland, passing the
younkers and their girls and turning away in embarrassment,
though some I passed motioned for me to join them. At first I
was shocked, but then Gideon pushed champagne into my
hand, and after a few glasses I stopped being shocked at all.
Twice Gideon had to tell me I must not look at him that way, and
when he led me upstairs to a box, I thought he meant for us to
have our own private spot, but he drew me into the shadows
and kissed me hard and told me that he meant to find Leonard,
and I was to wait there for him.

I drank my champagne and went to the railing to look over
the crowd. In the box below there was a woman lying over
chairs shoved together, with her legs spread and her skirts
pushed up while the two men she was with took turns mount-
ing her. I was both embarrassed and titillated—I could not
look away, and I wished only that Gideon would return, because my skin felt too sensitive and my breasts felt tight and
I thought I might burst if he did not touch me.

Then I heard the curtain open behind me and I smiled and
deliberately did not turn, but waited for him to come up behind me. I felt his bare hands on my naked waist, and
I arched back against him and twined my arms around his
neck, and it wasn't until then that I realized it wasn't Gideon
at all. I gave a little gasp and turned to see a gladiator, and
I thought it must be Leonard, whom Gideon had sent to me,
but then he said, "How beautiful you are, little nightingale,"
and I recognized his eyes behind his mask and the words
he said, because he'd called me that before. It was August
Belmont. I remembered what Gideon had told me, that I must
not encourage him because Leonard would be angry, but I was
very drunk, and I let him kiss my breasts and my throat and
closed my eyes because to be adored is a heady feeling, and also

because (I confess it!) I expected Gideon back any moment, and I thought this would make him just a bit jealous and I like him that way.

And then Gideon did come back with Leonard, and both Belmont and I heard their talk, which was very loud, as they came into the box, and August stepped away like a gentleman, though his fingers lingered just long enough on my breast for both Gideon and Leonard to see what we'd been doing. I saw the glitter in Gideon's eyes, and in Leonard's too, and I smiled and became quite suddenly the most feted woman at the ball—three men in a box, all of whom wanted me, and only their own honorable natures keeping them from doing what was going on in the box just below. I must admit it all felt very dangerous. Then Gideon led August away on some pretense I don't remember, and Leonard and I were alone. I apologized for my distraction lately, and said I hoped he was not too angry with me. Then he kissed me in a way he never had before, open-mouthed and deep. He said he would call on me next week. Oh, I was quite drunk by this time, so I pressed my hips to his and said I looked forward to it, and for just a moment I thought perhaps I'd gone too far, but of course he is too much a gentleman to do anything too improper.

Then Gideon came back and we called a carriage, and I could not wait until we reached the hotel to have my reward. To think of what we did in that carriage makes me blush now. When the driver stopped we had to hurry to return our clothing to its proper places, though I'm sure we both looked very disheveled. I wanted Gideon again when we reached our rooms and we stayed up all night, and today I am sore and have a terrible headache, but I don't regret one moment.

Perhaps just one moment. This morning came the most beautiful necklace from Leonard. It is diamonds and pearls and emeralds, and I am certain it cost a great deal. When Gideon saw it, he said quietly, "What did you promise him?"

and I said only that I'd told him he could call on me this week.

I know what the necklace means, of course. And I know Gideon has been waiting for it, because it means Leonard is very close to giving us the money we need. All that remains is for me to give him what he so clearly wants, and though I know it is what I must do, and that I do it for Gideon and myself and for the future we both want, I cannot help but feel a little sick at the thought that Gideon is so willing to share me when I am not inclined in the least to share him. I wish he would tell me not to go. I wish I had not pressed into Leonard that way at the ball, or let him kiss me quite so intimately. And I remember Barret's warnings and the things Willa said, though I try very hard not to.

Gideon is my only family now. He is all that matters. To think of what we will do with the money . . . I suppose it will not be so hard, and I like Leonard well enough. And after that, it will be over, and I shall never have to do it again.

JANUARY 22, 1874—I have received Leonard's invitation to a private supper at his club. Along with it came a very beautiful snood of gold and diamond and pearl.

I have accepted. Gideon seems satisfied, and though I drank a glass of champagne with him, I begged leave to retire early; my stomach is very upset.

JANUARY 25, 1874—It is done. I have fucked Leonard Jerome and he has given us ten thousand dollars as an investment in our new troupe, which is to be named the Price Company.

I am more persuaded than ever that I did the right thing. I went to the Club at ten o'clock, as Leonard instructed, and (because a child would ruin everything) I took one of Gideon's "precautions" from the drawer in the bedside table. I was not sure if Leonard had his own now that the Comstock laws have made them so very difficult to get; Gideon must have a prescription to procure them, and since Leonard is married with children I did not know if he could do the same.

He had taken care to bring all the best foods that the kitchen could provide—we had oysters and wine and roast capon that he cut and fed to me from his fingers, and sweet grapes and strawberries which came from someplace faraway that I cannot remember. I did not eat very much, as my stomach was still upset, but I did not turn away the wine, and by the time he led me to the chaise I was drunk and relaxed and not at all averse to him and when I closed my eyes I imagined his kisses were Gideon's and the only thing that spoiled the illusion was the brush of his very big and bushy mustache against my skin. I did not have to offer any precaution after all, as Leonard had his own, and I was relieved for it, because I was not sure how I would explain it, given that that part of my relationship with Gideon is still secret and I was fairly certain that Leonard may have believed I was still a virgin— I know he doesn't suspect anything at all about Gideon. I have told him Gideon is like a brother to me, and he has not questioned it, which is good, as I think he would not want me if he knew exactly how unlike a brother Gideon is!

I made convincing enough moans I think. In any case, he seemed satisfied and called me all kinds of endearing things afterward. I was relieved when it was over, and all I wanted to do was go back to my own room and sleep, but I pretended to be quite disappointed to leave him, and when he wrote out the cheque and gave it to me, I felt I might be sick, and I had to work to keep my smile, which was strange, as the money was what I had wanted most of all, and now that I had it I was out of sorts. I was near crying as Leonard's carriage took me back to the Fifth Avenue.

By the time I reached the hotel I was angry with the world, and, as Papa used to say when I was a little girl, wanting to fight the air because it was too easy to breathe.

I went to Gideon's room to give him the money. I thought I would just leave it on his bedtable, as it was very very late—

after three a.m.—and I thought he would be asleep. I both
wanted him to be and hoped he would be awake, because
I knew I would not be able to sleep, and I wanted someone to
snap at.

He was not in bed. There was an oil lamp burning low and
he was in the bathtub, and he looked almost as if he were
sleeping there. His hair was wet and slicked back from his
face, and his arms were dangling over the sides, and when
I saw him I loved him and was angry with him at the same
time, and I could not move but only stared down at him until
he opened his eyes—which were as sleepy as if he'd been smoking opium—and said, "You're back."

I took Leonard's cheque from my purse and held it out,
letting it flutter down so that he must catch it with his wet fingers before it landed in the water. He sat up a little, and
looked at it, and then he said, "I don't like cheques."

I told him very sarcastically that I thought Leonard
Jerome was good for it, and he let it drop on the floor and said
I had made our futures, but he didn't sound happy, and when
I knelt down beside the tub and told him I loved him, he
pulled me close to kiss me. Then he said, "You stink of him,"
and I said wasn't that what he'd wanted?

Then he grabbed my shoulders and pulled me into him so
hard I fell into his chest and halfway into the water. He told
me to take off my dress, which was soaked now to the waist. It
was the blue-striped silk, which looks very well on me, and
which he'd told me to wear tonight. It buttons down the front
and he likes to watch me take it off. I supposed he thought
Leonard would like it too, though I hadn't been able to bring
myself to tease Leonard the way I liked to tease Gideon, and
he'd taken the gown off himself and made quick work of it.
When I thought of that, it made me angry again, and I shoved
each button through its loop very roughly and peeled it off,
and once I was done Gideon made me take off everything and
when I asked him why he said he was checking for damage to
his property and I grew so furious I stripped to my skin and

pointed to the red mark above my breast where Leonard had kissed too hard. I meant to make him angry and I did. He grabbed my wrist and jerked me into the tub and it was too small and awkward and water spilled out all over the floor. He was very rough with me—but I was rough with him too. I bit his shoulder twice hard enough to leave a mark and I hoped rather viciously that it would scar, though it has faded to just a bruise, and I have a bruise too, very large and painful, on my hip, where he'd gripped me so hard when he spent himself that I gasped and cried out my own release. It embarrasses me now to think how loud I was, because Gideon had to clap his hand over my mouth to muffle me.

This morning it was as if none of it had happened, and he has gone downstairs to put the cheque in the hotel safe until the banks open. On Monday, we are to commence looking for the rest of the Price Company, and he is to start arranging tour dates, and he has promised me that our future is very bright indeed.

CHAPTER 12

Seattle, Washington Territory—July 1881

Two days later, Johnny pulled me aside and said, "I've scheduled dinner with our investor for tomorrow night. At the Occidental."

"The Occidental Hotel? Isn't that a bit uptown for us?"

"It's where he feels comfortable, honey, and my guess is we'll fit in just fine. Wear the widow's weeds. There ain't time to get anything new, and it makes you look respectable enough."

"With the veil?" I asked.

Johnny shook his head. He ran the back of his finger down my scar, making me shudder, and gave me a smile that reminded me that I'd once seen him almost kill a man with his bare hands. "No veil. Best if he knows who he's dealing with. A little fear don't hurt."

"Afraid of me?" I laughed a little shakily. "Oh, I doubt that."

"He won't know how you got it, now will he?" Johnny asked. "Maybe he'll think I gave it to you."

I stepped away, and Johnny laughed and said, "Just bring your charming self to the table, Margie. And make sure it's the charming you, not the Medusa."

"Who enraptured men with her gaze, as I recall," I said.

"We need him alive and ready to hand over cash. Not turned to stone."

He left me to go into his office, and I stood at the bar and watched the floor. Charlotte sauntered up, smiling, and when I smiled back at her, she said, "I got a surprise for you."

"What?"

"You'll see," she said, and then she stepped away again, her hips twitching beneath the satin frock, and I watched her go and found myself humming—something that had been happening far more often in the last two days. I had guarded even against that; my voice was the most recognizable thing about me, and I could not take the risk. But she had not recognized it, and I began to think, *why not?* It was only humming, after all, and silly little songs, and surely it was safe enough. And it loosened something inside me, a tentative joy I had not felt in a very long time. "*You were happy when you were singing,*" Charlotte had said, and I knew that was true. Perhaps the truest thing about me, if she could have known it.

THE NEXT MORNING, Charlotte swept into my room like a storm. I woke, startled at the noise of the door bouncing against the wall. Before I could comprehend it, she had jerked open the curtains so the sun filled the room, and I blinked, my eyes watering at the sudden light.

"You overslept," she said. "I expected you in my room an hour ago."

I peered out the window. The sun was high in the sky; it was past noon. I sat up, pushing back the hair I'd neglected to braid the night before. "I'm sorry. Had we some plan for today?"

"It's time for my surprise. Get up. Get dressed!"

Dutifully I rose, stumbling to the ewer, pouring water to wash. "What are we doing?"

"It wouldn't be a surprise if I told you, now would it?"

I dressed quickly, and she took me from the boarding-house and past the blooming sweetbriar twined about the rail, into the street. The day was already hot and shimmering. The Mountain was hazy, as if we viewed it through the dust rising with our every footstep, and men wiped the sweat from their faces with their neckcloths as if it were much later in the day. There was a group gathered about the Puget Sound Ice Company buggy, leaning close to feel whatever cool air there was as the delivery man unloaded the chunks of ice with large metal pincers, dropping wet sawdust to the street.

Charlotte led me without hesitation down one block and up another, and then we were climbing the steep hill of Mill Street's skid road to the Occidental Hotel and then onto Jefferson.

"Where are we going?" I asked, trying to catch my breath. There was nothing up here, only half-cleared lots and houses and the Brewery.

"It ain't much farther," she said. Before long, she stopped before the Gothic-styled clapboard of Trinity Episcopal Church, with its arched windows and door and wretchedly ugly bell tower that could be seen from the Lava Beds.

Charlotte smiled. "Here's your surprise."

"A church?" I frowned and started to turn away. "Charlotte, I haven't set foot in a church in . . . a long time. I've no wish to hear a sermon, and—"

"Don't you dare walk away," she said, stopping me. "We're going inside."

"Why? Are you worried for my mortal soul?"

"Yeah, that's exactly right." She rolled her eyes. "Christ, Marguerite, you think I got any interest at all in getting you into a sermon?"

"I don't understand."

She took a deep breath. "A customer of mine said there was a choir here. I think you should join it."

"Don't be ridiculous."

"I already talked to Mr. Anderson. He's the master of the choir. We're here to see him."

"Charlotte, I can't sing in a choir."

"Why not?"

"Why would they have me? This is *Trinity*. Society comes here."

"You said before they wouldn't snub you."

"It's not that—"

"Too late. I already told him what a beautiful voice you have. He wants to hear it."

I shook my head. "I can't. I'm sorry. I know you meant well but I can't."

She stepped over to me. "D'you remember that night on the wharf? You remember what I said?"

Reluctantly, I said, "That singing made me happy."

"At least talk to him. He's waiting to see you."

She looked anxious, and I felt an uneasy guilt. I did not want to hurt her or to spoil her obvious pleasure in her surprise, but neither could I do this.

"Just talk with him a moment," she pleaded.

He was only a choirmaster. What could it hurt to talk to him? I didn't have to agree to stay, or to sing, and it would please her. So I nodded. "I'll speak with him. But only that."

Her smile broadened. "All right."

I sighed and followed her inside.

The nave was quiet and dim, lit only by the sunlight coming through the windows on one side and making the stained floors and the well-tended, uncushioned pews glow. The altar was hung with a purple and white silk cloth and flanked by candlestands. The risers for the choir were behind it, and a small upright piano was at one side.

I had not been inside a church for some time, and now— as I'd feared—it brought back memories from so long ago it seemed another world. I remembered the pounding chords of the organ and the organist who sprawled across the keys as if he and the instrument were one. I remembered the heavy robes hanging in the wardrobe, smelling of sweat and must, decades old, raising dust motes to float in the sunlight that always made someone sneeze whenever they were put on. . . .

I heard the sound of boot heels. A neat woman in brown came from a doorway near the altar, bearing a feather duster. She stopped when she saw us, and said, "Oh—good morning, ladies," and made to turn away as if to give us the privacy to pray, but Charlotte hurried forward.

"Pardon, ma'am," she said. "We're here to see Mr. Anderson. About the choir."

The woman turned back again, obviously delighted. "Oh yes, of course. Please, come this way." She skirted around the corner, disappearing into a doorway on one side of the altar, and with a quick glance at me, Charlotte followed.

I came more slowly. I followed them, passing the choir robes hung in a shallow alcove—purple, worn satin—to a hall that led to two doors. The woman stopped before one of them, rapping sharply.

"Mr. Anderson! I've someone here to see you!"

"Come in, come in," said a deep voice, and she opened the door and ushered us into a small office, closing the door behind us. Inside was a tall, stooped man sitting at a table; behind him were rows of shelves lined with hymnals and sheet music. A jumble of music stands and a leaning piano bench were jammed into a corner. Next to them was a small bookcase littered with sheets of music scribbled upon with spidery handwriting. There was a narrow case on a shelf above it—I recognized it as similar to one from my own past, and I knew it held a triangle or perhaps chimes. Beside that was a row of golden bells. There was not much room to stand. Charlotte and I were so close to the table that served as his desk that our skirts brushed up against it.

Mr. Anderson glanced up, his blue eyes watery through the

thick glass of his wire spectacles. His nose was long and beak-like, his hair gray but still abundant except where it receded sharply at his temples.

"Ah yes, Miss Rainey," he said to Charlotte. He glanced at me. "This must be the friend you spoke of."

"Miss Marguerite Olson," she said, introducing us, and I took Mr. Anderson's proffered hand. His glance slid down my scar before sliding unobtrusively away.

"Miss Olson, I'm delighted," he said. "Miss Rainey tells me you have an interest in joining our choir."

"I'm afraid she spoke too soon."

He raised a wiry, rather unkempt brow. "You don't wish to join the choir?"

"Oh yes she does," Charlotte put in.

"Have you ever sung in public, Miss Olson?"

I hesitated. I would have said no had Charlotte not been standing there. "As a child," I said, the half lie only, the one she knew.

"And not since? But there's no need to be afraid. You won't be alone. There are ten others in the choir. We rehearse on Sunday, after we sing at the morning service."

"You see? That won't get in the way," Charlotte said.

Mr. Anderson peered at me with his watery eyes. "Do you read music, Miss Olson?"

Charlotte spoke before I could. "Yes. She chooses the music for the girls at the Palace."

"The Palace," he said slowly, and I thought I was saved.

"The boxhouse," I said in relief. "I'm Johnny Langford's partner. So you see, Mr. Anderson, I am sorry to waste your time—"

"That ain't a problem, is it, Mr. Anderson?" Charlotte asked quickly. "She ain't a whore."

"We are all lambs of God, Miss Rainey," he said. He looked at me. "As are you and Mr. Langford, Miss Olson. Your . . . position . . . holds no impediment to the choir."

"Oh, but—"

"Miss Rainey led me to believe you wanted to join," he said. "Please don't let any nervousness you might have keep you from trying. The choir here at Trinity is well regarded in the city. I flatter myself that I have some skill in bringing voices together to form a pleasing whole. We've recently purchased a pipe organ—we'll be lengthening the church to make room for it later this year. So, you see, I have high ambitions for the choir."

"A pipe organ," I said, startled by the announcement, by what it meant: Seattle had a church large enough to buy a pipe organ, large enough to support one. "Have you someone to play it?"

"Yes indeed. My wife, whom you saw this morning, has the talent." Mr. Anderson folded his hands. "Might I have the honor of hearing you sing, Miss Olson?"

I met Charlotte's gaze; she was staring at me with anticipation and pleasure.

She said quietly, "What makes you happier than singing?"

It was tempting, although it shouldn't have been. Mr. Anderson reminded me of my old master, Herr Wirt, at the Lutheran Church in Kleindeutschland, and my memories of standing on those warped wooden risers as he directed me, and taking lessons with him after, his exactitude, his surety, filled me with warmth and pleasure. I'd been fourteen when I started with the Lutheran choir, and after only a few months I was singing solos in the old church, the robes hanging, too large, over my hands, my voice rising to fill the nave, strong and sure and sweet, until it seemed almost to color the stained-glass windows, while my parents watched from the pews and my brother stood singing only one away and Gideon three down.

"Will you sing, Miss Olson?" Mr. Anderson asked.

Caught by the rosiness of the memory, I found myself saying yes, and he smiled and escorted us back into the nave where the piano was. He sat on the bench and pulled it close and opened the lid over the keys and then looked at me expectantly. "Shall we start with 'Rock of Ages'? I assume you know it."

I nodded. Charlotte settled herself in the pew, and I stood by the piano and waited for him to start. Though I knew a moment of fear when I thought he might recognize my voice, I told myself I could sing the song simply and cleanly, the way I would have sung it if I were truly Marguerite Olson, if the only training I'd had was that of a talented child. When he played, I let my voice loose, singing the song easily and well and without even one-tenth of my strength to do so. This was no aria; this had no notes I must reach inside myself to meet. This was pure pleasure, and I sang it that way.

Mr. Anderson's wife—the neat little woman in brown—appeared from a door to stand and listen. She clasped her hands together before her in a rapt expression of gratification, and when I was finished, she applauded. Charlotte joined in with her, and I felt myself flush; I could not help my smile.

"You're very kind," I said.

"And you will be a very welcome addition to Trinity Choir," Mr. Anderson said. He rose from the bench, coming to me, taking my hand between his, clasping it hard. "You will sing, won't you, Miss Olson? I cannot tell you what a disappointment it would be to lose you now that I've heard your voice."

Some things had not changed after all. My own vanity had not. It stretched and preened like a pampered cat beneath his words and Mrs. Anderson's expression. And the delight I'd taken in singing made it hard to resist.

"I will," I said.

"Delightful," he told me. "Then we shall see you this Sunday, the twelfth."

"This Sunday is the seventeenth," his wife put in gently, and Mr. Anderson started and said, "Good heavens, is it? Ah yes, today is already the fifteenth, isn't it?"

The fifteenth. Of July.

Mr. Anderson smiled and went on. "Well, Miss Olson, I look forward to introducing you to the rest of our choir. Come to the service if you like. Practice begins just after."

"Thank you," I said. "I will."

We took our leave, and when Charlotte and I were on the steps outside, she said, "Is something wrong? You looked sick of a sudden."

"Nothing," I said. "It's just . . . today is my birthday."

"Your birthday?" She laughed. "Well, happy birthday. How old are you?"

"Twenty-seven." Old. I was old. Too old for the ingenues I'd loved. Only Donna Annas and Queens of the Night for me now. The thought was so absurd I laughed. As if it mattered at all, as if I would ever take to the stage again.

Charlotte laughed with me. "Well, there you go. And look at that, I got you a present without even knowing. I hope you like it."

I smiled at her. "I do like it. I like it very much."

And then I remembered Johnny.

CHAPTER 13

"Dear God, what was I thinking?" I said to Charlotte as we made our way back home. "I can't do this."

"Why not?"

It was not just Johnny, it was the people who came to that church, who sang in that choir. People I'd spent three years avoiding, for good reason. This was beyond foolish, and I knew it. But I couldn't say that to Charlotte, so I said the most obvious, the thing she would understand.

"What if Johnny finds out?"

"How would he find out? He don't go to church."

"Others do."

"Who would know him? Who would tell him?"

"Anyone," I said helplessly. "Do you think it's only miners and lumbermen who come to the Palace? Johnny knows everyone."

"So he finds out. What will he think, except that you've turned to God?" Charlotte clasped her hands and looked woefully up at the sky. "'I repent of my terrible ways, oh Lord, and must do penance by singing in Trinity's choir.'"

"You've chosen a wrong profession. You should have been an actress."

"You should've seen your face. The music is what makes you happy. Anyone can tell that."

I could not deny that I *had* loved it. Those few moments, singing to the piano that Mr. Anderson played, regardless that it was a simple song, was singing to music, and now that I'd tasted it again, I didn't really want to give it up, despite the risk. And here was Charlotte, making it so easy to tell myself it was all right to do something that made me happy when I had not been for so very long. To take my life back again . . . I could not take it back, not really, not completely, and in fact, there were parts of it I didn't want back. But I could do this. I could sing in this way. Hidden. Among others.

"I'm a fool," I told her.

"And an old one too," she teased.

I laughed with her, but I could not forget the danger so easily. My apprehension stayed with me as I readied for the dinner with our potential investor. The choir was just one more thing to add to the lies I was already telling Johnny—perhaps the most dangerous one of all. The fact that I was singing in the church when I had not even told him I could sing well enough for the Palace's stage would raise questions—and he would want the answers. Now that I was well away from the church and those few moments of pure happiness, I knew singing there could only hurt me. How long, truly, could I keep Johnny from discovering it?

I tried not to think of it when I met him at the Palace that evening. When he came down from his room, dressed again in the suit and vest with the silk tie, I was transported to the night we'd gone to *Faust*. The arias slammed back into my head, impossible to dislodge until he came to me and took my arm and said, "You in a good mood, honey?"

"I won't be Medusa tonight," I said rather tartly.

"I'm counting on it," he said.

It was not a great distance to the Occidental Hotel from the Palace. The hotel was one of the best in the city, a long, storied building with a peaked roof sited in the midst of the triangle created by the butting up of Commercial to Front Street. From its second-story balcony, the hotel had the best view in town of the many accidents that occurred at "the throat," as it was called—wagon overturnings and careening carriages certain they could make the treacherous corner without incident were legion.

The setting sun had blazed through the westward-facing windows earlier in the evening, and the restaurant was hot. The tables were full, mostly men, undoubtedly travelers and businessmen, and I felt their stares as Johnny led me inside and spoke briefly to the waiter, who led us to a table in the corner by the window, where sat a man I'd never seen before.

He was long-limbed and elegant, with red hair and a full set of whiskers, though he was quite young—I would have guessed younger than me. He wore a deep blue coat, and his necktie was a large swath of bronze silk about his throat, his watch chain large and looped and ostentatious. In New York he would have been the grossest kind of parvenu. I was intimidated at first—it took me a moment to remember that he was nothing new; ambitious men like this had been second nature to me once.

He rose when we came to the table and Johnny introduced him as Blakely Davis. I offered my hand, and he bowed deeply over it, and smiled when I said how pleased I was to meet him.

"The honor is mine, Miss Olson," he said. His gaze flickered over my scar; he was too polite to stare, but I knew he noted it by the way he glanced quickly at Johnny—undoubtedly making the connection Johnny had wanted him to make.

I took the chair between them, easing it closer to Mr. Davis, giving him my best smile, gratified when he seemed a bit taken aback by it. "Have you been in Seattle long, Mr. Davis?"

"A few months only," he said. "But I've found it quite to my liking. I mean to stay."

"Davis acquired an interest in a mining concern," Johnny said.

"From my father," Davis acknowledged. "I came out here to oversee it."

"You have a generous father," I said.

"Oh, not so much as one would imagine."

The waiter hovered. Johnny ordered wine and whiskey.

"It's not every son who gets a mining company handed to him."

"Not a company, I'm afraid. Merely shares. But I daresay they've turned out better than anyone expected."

"And as a result, Mr. Davis is looking for investments," Johnny said.

"Mr. Langford tells me you may be interested in our enterprise," I said.

Davis looked thoughtful. "Perhaps."

"Do you enjoy entertainment, sir?"

The wine came, and the whiskey. Johnny poured for each of us, handing me the wine, though I would have preferred the other. Still, I understood; whiskey was not a woman's drink.

"I like to be entertained as much as any man," Davis said.

I laughed and took a sip of the wine. "Ah, but all men are different, Mr. Davis. Have you a preference for minstrel shows or farce? Or perhaps you've a melodramatic turn of mind?"

"What I have, Miss Olson, is a money-making turn of mind," he said. "And I must admit I'm intrigued by the proposal Mr. Langford has set forth. But you understand, I must be careful with what investments I make. I'm not so wealthy that I can afford to lose money."

"We don't intend to lose money," Johnny said firmly, curling his fingers around his drink. "Were you at Squire's for the opera a few months ago?"

"I regret I was out of town."

"Full houses every night. I tell you, Seattle's overdue for good entertainment. How many temperance lectures or juggling dogs can one man see? What I want, Davis—what *we* want—is to provide entertainment that's . . . entertaining."

"You see, that's what has me concerned, Langford. The Palace is not exactly known for its quality entertainment now. Why should I believe you can provide anything different?"

"Because I say we can," Johnny said bluntly. "And I do what I say I'll do."

"No doubt you mean to, but—"

"You accusing me of lying, Davis?" Johnny's voice had gone silky.

"Of course not. But I—"

"What Mr. Langford *means* is that we understand your concerns," I said, glaring at Johnny and putting my hand on Mr. Davis's arm. "Frankly, there's no one who wouldn't have them. But you must understand, Mr. Langford and I are ready to change with the times—as we have always done. After all, when we started the Palace, this town was nothing but lumbermen and miners. The boxhouse was considered farsighted then. Seattle wasn't ready for a real theater. It is now."

Johnny eased back in his seat. Mr. Davis glanced down at my hand on his arm. I did not move it. Instead, I pressed a little more warmly until I felt him relax, and said, "We do have some experience in this kind of thing. Before he came up here, Johnny helped run a theater in San Francisco."

"What about you, Miss Olson? You said 'we.' You've had experience with theaters?"

I felt Johnny's glance, though I avoided it. Instead, I met Mr. Davis's gaze and held it. I smiled and began a quiet, back-and-forth motion with my finger over his suited arm. "I once kept company with a traveling musician, sir. I have quite . . . intimate . . . knowledge of such matters."

He swallowed.

"I think we would make good partners, Mr. Davis. You seem an intelligent man."

"I would hope so."

"And I can see in your face a certain sensibility. Have you ever been read by a phrenologist?"

"Once. Yes, once. Some time ago."

I leaned forward. "I'm certain he must have found the finer natures most pronounced. I believe I can see them myself. You have a refined countenance, sir."

He looked down modestly. "I believe he did say I was very developed in sublimity."

"And spirituality too, I'm certain."

"Why, yes. How perceptive you are, Miss Olson."

"It hardly needs perception, Mr. Davis. Your physical attributes are obvious for anyone to see." I pressed closer until I could feel the warmth of his trousered leg against my skirts. He did not move away. "I do not think we could ask for a finer partner. I think I should always be assured of your honesty. How peerless you would be in advising us!"

"I would hope always to be of service," he said, very modestly, though he was turning pink. Perhaps it was the heat, though when his gaze came to mine, I saw desire there, and I smiled demurely and dropped my eyes and didn't stop my caress on his arm.

"I'm most certain you would be," I murmured.

Davis glanced across the table to Johnny. "However did you find such a charming creature, Langford?"

"She wandered into my place one day like a lost dog," Johnny said wryly, and when I looked at him, his expression was glittering—a little dangerous, a little amused. "But she's proved herself useful enough. Ain't no one better when it comes to smoothing things over."

Davis turned to me. He was pink as a lobster, clashing

terribly with his beard. "I imagine so. You have a very invigorating presence, Miss Olson."

I let my eyes sparkle. "Why, Mr. Davis, how kind you are to say it."

Johnny said, "As you can see, Davis, Miss Olson's talents are something to behold. I expect her to be quite useful in procuring the right acts for the Palace. Have you any doubt she could win over the most reluctant manager?"

Mr. Davis shook his head vigorously. "None at all."

"Then will you invest in us?"

I glared at him again before turning back to Mr. Davis. "Mr. Langford is impatient, but I should so hate to rush you into such an important decision, Mr. Davis. Especially on an empty stomach."

"Then let's order dinner," Johnny said.

"We'll have strawberries after," I said, smiling. "Have you ever had strawberries and champagne, Mr. Davis? Why, I shall feed you one from my own hand. A more delicious combination would be difficult to find."

"Fed from such a lovely hand as yours, how could it be otherwise?" he said.

THE DUST FROM passing carriages lingered in the air, hazing the glow of the streetlamps; if there were stars in the sky, they were impossible to see through its fog. Dinner—and the wine served with it—rested comfortably in my stomach. I felt soft and languid. Though Blakely Davis had not yet said he would invest, I was certain he would.

"Strawberries and champagne," Johnny mused. "Where the hell did you come up with that?"

I shrugged. "It worked, didn't it?"

"Honey, I'm surprised he didn't fuck you there on the table. Or that you didn't let him."

"He's of no interest to me other than as an investor."

He shook his head. "That ain't what he thinks, I promise you."

"Do you think he'll invest?"

Johnny chuckled. "At the very least."

"You wanted me to be charming."

"Well, you were that."

"I thought you'd almost ruined everything. I had to do something to fix it."

"Damn, I swear to God I never saw anything like what you did to that man."

"Don't be absurd. It's what I do every day at the Palace."

"Not like that."

I took a deep breath. "Just like that."

He was quiet. We walked in companionable silence for a while, our boot steps echoing on the hard street, raising little clouds of dust. As we got deeper into the Lava Beds, the noise from the night increased, the now familiar sounds of shouting and shooting and laughter.

Johnny said, "You never told me about the musician."

I felt a little flutter of anxiety. "Didn't I?"

"I'm pretty sure you didn't."

"It was a long time ago."

"Well, it explains *Faust*, don't it?"

Softly, I said, "Whatever I know can only work to our advantage. Does it matter how I came to it?"

"No," he said, and then, again, "no, I guess it don't." He stopped, and when I stopped with him, he took my arm and pulled me close. His eyes were burning in the darkness. I thought he would kiss me, but instead he only said, "We're going to make this work, ain't we, honey? We're going to have our theater. You and me, together."

His voice was thick with a raw kind of desire I recognized, that yearning for something more, something bigger. I felt the past at my back like a menacing shadow, the piercing nip of my own ambition, and for a moment, I was afraid. But when

I drew back, he cupped my chin in his hand, his fingers hurting where they pressed into my jaw, and he said, "We're partners, ain't we?"

"Yes, of course."

"Then I want you to promise me one thing."

I tried to pull away. He held me fast. "What?"

"That you will not tell me another fucking lie."

The danger of him was so thick I could not move. Immediately the choir came into my head, the things I'd told Charlotte, the lie of my own life, and I swallowed and whispered,
because he gave me no choice, "All right."

He released me. And I knew then I must refuse the invitation to sing in Trinity's choir. The risk was too great; I could
not afford it.

From the Journal of Sabine Conrad

MARCH 10, 1874—These last weeks we have been auditioning singers for the company, which is very taxing work. Although Gideon has done most of it, I must be there sometimes so we can find the voices that best showcase mine. I am astonished at how many singers are managed by their husbands, and I think it very stupid of them, as one wonders why they could not find a proper manager. I think it much better to be like Gideon and me, who do not need marriage vows to bind us.

But now, finally, the Price Company is complete. For tenors, we have signed Adriano Torriani, whom Gideon and I both saw at the Manchetti, believe it or not! and Yuri Blanov, who has just come to this country from Russia. There is also Jose Herrera, who will do the comprimario parts and understudy. For sopranos there is me and Amelia Maresi, who has sung for Strakosch's troupe. Leila Svensson (who is very young and pretty) is our mezzo and understudy. Our basso is Taddeo Nannetti.

Gideon says we will add more as the tour commences, but that this is the core group and will do quite satisfactorily for now.

Leonard has graciously allowed us to rehearse in his theater, and he comes to watch and seems happy with his investment. Gideon is much harder on me when Leonard is there; today he told me I was forcing in the *passaggio*, which I was not, and that my trills in the *cantabile* were too harsh. Leonard told him that I was perfect, and Gideon asked stiffly if Leonard would prefer to be the maestro, and I had to whisper to Gideon to take care and make excuses for him to Leonard after.

Leonard has since given us two more cheques. One would hardly know the city is in such despair by the way he spends his money and the parties that are held nearly every night. He squires me about everywhere now, and we are known as a very amusing couple. Gideon says nothing, though I know he does not like it. But he is so busy now arranging tours and choosing our program that he has little time left for me. Without Leonard, I'm sure I would do nothing at all!

It would be perfect if not for Gideon's distraction and the fact that Leonard expects me in his bed. Still, it avails us the money we need, and when the tour starts, Leonard will find some other soprano to adorn his arm, and everything will be back to the way it was.

MARCH 16, 1874—Gideon has decided we will perform *La Trav*, *Aida*, *Don Giovanni*, and *Lucia*, and will possibly add others, depending upon the reception of the tour. An ambitious program, and he is very nervous, but I have told him he has chosen such popular operas that we cannot help but draw the crowds, because although the streets are thick with beggars and "To Let" signs are posted in windows everywhere, the rich are still rich in every city. Also, *Aida* is so new that no one outside of New York has seen it in America, and so they will all be curious because everyone loves Verdi.

He has settled dates in many cities, including Havana! Amelia Maresi and I have toured often enough that it is nothing new to us, but Leila Svensson is so fluttery and anxious that Gideon has had to schedule rehearsals for her alone. She is such a stupid girl. If she did not have such a good voice to complement mine I am certain he would let her go before we even leave.

MAY 13, 1874—We are a success in Brooklyn! Though I had not let Gideon see it, I _was_ worried, because the economy is so bad and I was afraid the crowds would be small. But, as he said, I am becoming so well known that people will spend their savings to see me. We sold out every night, and the newspaper notices were very good. One said: "Now that Mr. Price's artists have been shown to the public, we are free to congratulate the impresario on his ear for talent and his genius for production."

We leave tomorrow for the tour, and I was relieved to say good-bye to Leonard. He looked very sad, and gifted me with an exquisite necklace of pink diamonds and a bracelet to match, which may be my favorite of all the gifts he has given me. He tells me to write to him (which of course I shall have to do, as Gideon must send him percentages), and he looks forward to my return in the fall. I have not told him that I don't know if I will be returning in the fall, or that even if I do I doubt I shall be his lover. He looked so distraught at the thought of my leaving that I was very sweet to him instead.

NEW ORLEANS, JULY 15, 1874—Today is my twentieth birthday, and we are back in the French Quarter after spending six days in Havana, which was stranger and more delightful than anyplace I've ever been. There were men outside the backstage door every night, and when I came out they threw flowers and ribbons and swore they loved me and every time I passed they reached to touch me. One man even cut off a small piece of my hair as I went by and then held it up for all his friends to see and told me it looked made of spun gold and he would keep it forever.

Gifts came to my room every day—jewels and flowers and pretty ribbons, and I have given some to Amelia and Leila too, because there are too many for me to have alone. (Though I have lost one of my favorites—a jeweled ivory fan—and cannot find it anywhere.)

I enjoyed Havana very much, but I love New Orleans too, because here they love Gideon as much as they love me. We have been feted at the homes of the very best of Creole society, and I have grown very jealous at the way all those dark-eyed women flirt with him and he is very charming in return—almost too much so, I think. But he deserves this, because he has been so very brilliant in conceiving this tour, and everyone in the company loves him. I hate how secret we must be, and I long for the world to know what we are to each other. But Gideon only laughs when I say this to him and says not yet, that we are not yet secure enough. Then he kisses me and asks how much I like pink diamonds. I confess I like them very, very well indeed.

AUGUST 10, 1874—Gideon has been so distracted and tense of late that everyone feels it. I don't know why it is so, as we are nearly selling out each venue we play. But he has hardly spent any time with me, and I am very anxious over it. Last night, I begged him to take me somewhere just to have fun, and he was very impatient and said he could not be squiring me around everywhere as he was too busy trying to make our dreams come true.

I was very hurt. Sometimes I miss Barret. Oh, not the fights, but the way he would come to my room and talk with me. Without him or Gideon to distract me, the days seem very long.

SEPTEMBER 4, 1874—Yesterday Taddeo threatened to leave the company. He and Gideon fought during rehearsal over something stupid. Amelia told me that Taddeo has been in love with me since before the tour began, and that he has been looking for an excuse to leave because I hardly look at him and he is heartbroken.

I was surprised—Taddeo has always been a gentleman, and I love playing Donna Anna to his Don Giovanni because he is so passionate. I didn't realize he was so passionate because he was in love with me. Amelia said she thought Taddeo could be moved by any appeal I might make to him, and as the rest of the company liked him very much, would I make the attempt?

So I did. It took some time and much pretty talk, but I flattered Taddeo into staying. But Gideon was very angry. He said I had no right to interfere with Taddeo without talking to him first, that he had let him go and had been auditioning bassos for the last three hours and hired two, so that now he had three and what was he to do with them? I told him to let one of the new ones go because I liked singing with Taddeo, and he said he would not keep a singer who spent his hours making calf-eyes at me and asked how exactly had I convinced him to stay?

He was very offensive. I was so angry I broke into tears, and I could tell Gideon was very frustrated. When he took me into his arms I stayed very stiff and angry, and then he whispered that he was sorry, but the company took a great deal of his time and patience, and he must be able to trust that I was not working against him. Which I did not mean to do! I told him Amelia had asked me to speak to Taddeo. Gideon said that the others in the troupe would not watch out for me the way he does. He says I don't realize how important I am and how people will try to use me.

I felt very stupid then, and told him I would be more careful, and he kissed me and was very gentle and loving again.

* * *

N.B. When I went to dress for dinner I saw that the earrings I'd left on the dressing table were gone. I have searched everywhere for them. Gideon says I must have mislaid them, but they were very large emeralds and I do not see how I could.

ST. LOUIS, OCTOBER 10, 1874—Besides the fan and earrings, my golden locket is missing, and two brooches and one
of my favorite rings. Gideon says perhaps it's the maid, but
I snapped at him that there was a different maid in every
hotel, and I doubted they were in collusion. He does not seem
to think it matters, but I am extremely frustrated.

OCTOBER 15, 1874—Last night I told Gideon that I thought
Leila was stealing from me, and he said I must be mistaken,
and why would she do such a thing? I told him that I saw how
she flirted with him and he said I was acting like a jealous
wife, and I asked him if I had a reason to be jealous. He said
no, of course not, and then I said I wanted him to prove it by
letting her go.

He said he wouldn't punish her for my stupid suspicions
and that if I didn't believe him then I must not love him
and that he had more reason to be jealous of me and Taddeo
than I did of him and Leila. Then we had a terrible fight.
I screamed at him and he told me to mind my voice and I told
him to go to hell. He slammed his hand against the wall and
went out, and when he left I lay on my bed and cried until
I was quite hoarse, and my voice was completely gone. Amelia
had to sing for me, which only made everything worse. It is at
times like these that I need to sing, because I can lose myself
in it and it soothes me as nothing else does.

I fell asleep, and when I woke, he had come into the room.
It was late, after the performance, and he sat down beside me
and handed me a jewel box. He said he had meant to give it to
me next week, but he wanted me to have it now. It was a
brooch, a circlet of filigree studded with sapphires to look like
the night sky, with one large pearl to serve as the moon and
stars made of diamonds—six of them; one for each year we had
known each other, he said, because we had met on October 25th
the year I was fourteen (how had he remembered that when
even I had forgotten?!), and he said he would have one added
each year from now on.

It was so romantic and beautiful that I burst into tears. He took me in his arms and kissed them away, and then he helped me pin it on, and said he was sorry, that he did not mean to make me unhappy, but it hurt that I didn't trust him, and I said I did trust him, that I had been a fool, that of course Leila could stay.

Much later, after he had fallen asleep beside me, I stared at the brooch where I'd put it on the bedtable so I could see it and thought how many more stars might be added to it, until it is an entire universe of diamonds.

ST. LOUIS, FEBRUARY 25, 1875—Again in St. Louis! This tour seems to be dragging on forever, with all its extensions and added dates, and I think I am not the only one wearying of it. I am very worried about Gideon. He is working so hard, and the demands of the company are so much that I hardly see him, and when I do he is too exhausted to do anything but fall asleep. All these petty things consume him, and he is more impatient with me than ever when I tell him how I miss him. He has not come to my bed in two weeks. If I were his wife, he would not ignore me this way, and that stupid Leila would not be so quick to look at him the way she does. But I know what he would say if I were to mention it. No famous prima donna is managed by her husband. And I suppose too that a woman must obey her husband's commands no matter how famous she is, so it is best this way. But I think that Gideon and I should buy a house together when we return to New York, with servants who don't change and furniture to my taste. I have been happy at the Fifth Avenue, but I'm going to be twenty-one this year, surely I should have something of my own?

I asked Gideon what he thought of such an idea and he said now was not the time. He thinks we must begin looking at Europe. He's been making inquiries of impresarios there, trying to win me a role at Covent Garden or the Theatre Italien or even La Scala. I told him that of course I longed to go to

Europe, but why not buy a house in Manhattan as well, something to return to? He said it was an additional expense we did not need, as this tour was costing a great deal, and our finances could not bear a house just now, which surprised me greatly. I had thought we were becoming quite rich, but I admit I am not very good with such things; I have always been satisfied to leave them to Gideon, and he knows better than me.

DENVER, MARCH 22, 1875—I am the "Queen of Denver." My dressing room and the hotel are both filled with flowers, and Taddeo brought me a lovely ruby and pearl brooch that someone threw upon the stage for me, though of course Leila asked him how he knew it was meant for me and not for her or Amelia. Taddeo (bless him!) told her I was the only one who had deserved it, and she grew very angry and broke a mirror.

Afterward Gideon said I must not provoke her so. I said that he had always told me that rivalries increased the public interest, and here was one he could exploit if he cared to, and he said, "Damn it, Sabine, think of me, will you," and I said I was always thinking of him, and I did everything he wanted me to do, so perhaps it was time he did something for me and sent Leila packing before I took it into my head to go instead.

I regretted my words immediately because I saw I'd hurt him. He said that he had dedicated his life to making me happy. Then he said he'd had a letter from an impresario in Paris—one Alain DeRosier—who was planning to be in America next year and would like to hear me, and I forgot all about Leila.

But as soon as Gideon was gone I resented that he had turned everything to my fault, and had not really listened to me and pooh-poohed my idea of a house. I have been thinking lately that he does not wish the best for me so much as he pretends he does. He always finds a way to dismiss my complaints and suggestions, and I am growing very dissatisfied, which is a feeling that has consumed me lately, and I don't know how to stop it.

I begin to long for Europe. Barret was right; I cannot be as famous as Adelina Patti without it, and besides then it would be just Gideon and me alone again. If I cannot be his wife in name, it will at least be as it was. He could devote himself to me and leave all the little frustrations of running a company behind.

SAN FRANCISCO, APRIL 22, 1875—We are in a great deal of chaos. Everything was arranged for us to perform at the Royal Theater, but when we arrived yesterday, the owner of the theater, whose name is Mr. McAlester, told Gideon that he had decided to cancel our booking in lieu of a company who is asking for a lower percentage of ticket sales.

I have not seen Gideon so angry in a long time, though he was very calm, and threatened to sue because we had signed contracts saying we were to perform here during these dates.

It was all very bad, but I noted how Mr. McAlester kept looking at me as if he could not quite believe I was standing before him, and so I put my hand on his arm and said in my most soothing voice that I thought we could come to some agreement, perhaps over dinner and some wine? Mr. McAlester stammered and blushed, but he agreed. I thought for a moment that Gideon would protest, but in the end we went to dinner and I flirted with Mr. McAlester quite shamelessly. I know Gideon did not like it, but he was as ruthlessly engaging as he always is, and because I am still suspicious of Leila and him, I admit I did try to provoke his jealousy a little.

Afterward, Gideon said he would have to consider either going to a different theater or taking his company out of San Francisco altogether, and Mr. McAlester said we could always try Seattle. Gideon said that Seattle was where culture went to die, and he had been thinking more of Sacramento. Mr. McAlester asked Gideon to have a drink with him after they escorted me back to the hotel.

So, I was put out of the way. I was in bed reading much later when Gideon came into my room. He loosened the drawstring of my nightgown, and kissed my breast and murmured against my skin that Mr. McAlester had asked for a private audience with me the next evening, and would I consent to go?

It had been weeks since Gideon had touched me this way, and my longing for him had only been growing and growing. He said how desperate our money situation was, and how much we needed this booking, but I only wanted him to kiss me. So of course I said I would meet McAlester.

When Gideon was falling asleep, I whispered to him that I was so happy he belonged to me, and he roused and kissed me and said we belonged to each other, and that I must remember it always.

APRIL 24, 1875—Last night I went to sing for Mr. McAlester— whose Christian name I don't know even now. He has a small house near Telegraph Hill, and there are many lovely things within it, and when I arrived I saw the dinner he had laid out and the fine china and silver and all the little touches in the decor and I thought he must have a wife or sister or mother to have done it for him, but he said no, he was quite alone.

It was not until we were halfway through the main course that I realized he had meant it literally. There was not even a servant about, and a thought began to grow in my mind that I resisted. But when dinner was over Mr. McAlester listened to me sing with such divine attention that I was reassured it was all he wanted.

But then he began to talk about how he might be willing to rethink his percentages if I could convince him. I knew the whole company was counting on me, and The Royal is a fine theater, and every other is already booked. I remembered what Gideon had said about how expensive the tour was, and how he was paying the company only to sit about, and I thought of the house I wanted to buy in Manhattan, and I told Mr. McAlester that I was quite certain he would come to see our side of things, and then I unbuttoned my gown.

I let him fuck me there on the carpet before the fireplace. He agreed to Gideon's terms, and I made him sign a piece of paper to that effect, and then I left. I felt like a whore—this wasn't as it had been with Leonard, but was so purely business without any charm or liking to disguise it, that I was repulsed and angry.

I pushed the paper beneath Gideon's door, but I didn't wake him. I went into my room and I vomited in the chamber pot, and then I took the bottle of brandy Gideon keeps there because sometimes a hot toddy soothes my throat, and I drank it until my trembling stopped and I thought I could sleep.

Then I dreamed of Barret. His eyes were clear and gleaming and knowing, and he said that he knew what I was even if no one else did, and I could run from it all I liked but in the end I knew it too. He asked if there was anything I wouldn't do to advance myself and Gideon. "Will you give up your soul, Sabine?"

MAY 7, 1875—Mr. McAlester has asked us to extend our stay (oh yes, he is doing very well even with our higher percentages, as Gideon told him he would—I wish one could write sarcasm as easily as one could say it). But Gideon said no, and I was relieved. Though the crowds love me, and I am called the Angel of San Francisco, the city no longer holds the charm it once had for me. I dislike the theater—though the acoustics are nice enough, I must pass Mr. McAlester nearly every day and now and then he paws me as if he thinks I would consent to lie down with him on the backstage floor.

What is worse than all that, however, is the fact that Gideon and I are barely speaking. I practice with him every day, of course, and he is how he always is when in a temper of this sort—very exacting and most unfair. I am straining, my *legato* is not *legato* but *staccato*, the *cadenza* is excessive, & etc. I would ignore him as I always do, except that I am angry with him. I have done everything he wished for me to do, so I don't know why he should be so furious with me. We come together at practice, and glare at each other over the dinner table and I would hate him with every part of myself if I did not yearn for him so badly to love me again that I cry myself to sleep every night.

MAY 10, 1875—How is it possible to love someone so much and yet hate him equally? It's true what Gideon once told me, that when I punish him I only hurt myself.

Last night, our last performance, was the best house we'd had. I was so moved by the audience's cries, and feeling in such charity, I vowed I would speak with Gideon tonight and do my best to mend things with him.

But then I was in the wings, taking bouquets from the stagehand before I went out to take my final bow, and I saw Gideon and Leila in the corner behind the curtain. She was clinging to him, and he was kissing her, and I went cold and faint. The stagehand had to push me out onto the stage to take my bow, and I must have bowed and smiled & etc., but I don't remember any of it. All I remember is coming offstage and Gideon coming to help me with the flowers, but before he could I gave the bouquets to the stagehand and turned to Yuri, who was coming offstage too. He came to kiss my cheek in congratulations as he always does, and I turned my face and met his lips, and he, like the full-blooded Russian he is, took advantage and kissed me back. I grabbed him to keep him from pulling away and kissed him very deeply. He was laughing at the end, and he bowed and said, "My dear Sabine, you have made certain I will have very sweet dreams!"

Gideon was very angry. He deserved it, so I did not feel the least bit sorry, not even when Yuri left and Gideon grabbed my arm and asked me what the hell I thought I was doing? I wrenched away from him and said he should look to his own behavior. By then, everyone backstage was staring at us. I didn't care, but he is too aware of what others think, and he told them curtly to go to dinner, and then he took my elbow hard and whispered in my ear that we would speak in my dressing room. He told the stage manager there would be no backstage visits tonight, and that I would wave from my balcony in the morning before we left.

When he closed the door of my dressing room, I turned and slapped him as hard as I could and screamed that he was fucking Leila and I wouldn't have it and I went to slap him again, only this time he caught my wrist and said very low and quiet to watch my voice. I told him I'd seen him kissing her tonight, and he said it was _her_ kissing _him_, and that he'd been only trying to console her because she was jealous of how many encores I got, and she had taken advantage.

I called him a liar. I said she was in love with him. He said he couldn't help it if she was, and that he hardly went around fucking every woman who was in love with him when the one he most wanted was me. But he said it as if he hated that it were true, and then he backed me up until I fell onto the chaise. My bustle sprang and bit into my back; he pushed up my skirts and unfastened his trousers and then he was inside me. I dug my nails into his back and shoulders; I wanted to cause him pain. My release when it came was unsatisfying. We were both so angry it seemed the air was quivering.

He made a sound deep in his throat and got up as if he could hardly wait to be gone. And then he walked out and left me there, and I buried my face in the stinking cushions of the chaise and _once again_ sobbed until I lost my voice.

I don't care if I never see San Francisco again.

CHAPTER 14

Seattle, Washington Territory—July 1881

All the rest of that night, and through Saturday, I told myself I would not sing in the choir. And then, when Sunday morning arrived and Charlotte came to walk with me to church, I told myself it was only right to tell Mr. Anderson in person I'd reconsidered. Charlotte and I hovered outside the doors, which had been kept open for the faint breeze. As I watched the women in satins and taffetas and calicos, men in morning coats and frock coats—Seattle's upper class, along with the usual merchants and storekeeps and butchers—I grew more and more convinced I was making the right decision.

Then the choir came out and I saw how their voices blended—Mr. Anderson was right when he said he knew how to make a chorus. They harmonized beautifully, no one voice standing out, and they looked a piece in their purple satin robes. And if I felt a wistful longing and thought that no one would pick me out from the others, all I had to do was remember how Johnny had looked Friday night to remind me of what was at stake.

We drew back into the corners as the service ended and the congregation filed out of the church, and the preacher with them, all of them lingering about the narrow yard while they said their good-byes in the mellow late morning air. Then Charlotte and I slipped inside.

The church still smelled of perfume and tobacco. The choir mulled about; most had already taken off their robes and laid them over the back of the pews. Mrs. Anderson was bustling about, picking them up, shaking them out.

Mr. Anderson was leafing through piano music. He glanced up when we approached. "Miss Olson! Miss Rainey!" he said with real enthusiasm. "Come, come! Let me introduce you to the rest of our choir."

I grasped Charlotte's hand and pulled her with me. "Mr. Anderson," I began. "I'm afraid—"

"Here they are!" He walked to where a group of men and women waited. They were talking and laughing among themselves, obviously well acquainted. I had no choice but to follow him. "Ladies and gentlemen," he said before I could stop him, "I would like to introduce our newest member, Miss Marguerite Olson."

They looked up with interest, and I felt my attempt at refusal die in my throat. I could not embarrass him now, in front of all of them.

"We've been in dire need of a soprano since Mrs. Davis left last spring," said a dark-haired man with sparkling dark eyes who Mr. Anderson introduced as Dr. Robert Marsdon. "Dare I hope that's the part you sing?"

"She's a soprano," Charlotte interjected. "You're lucky to have her."

But for Dr. Marsdon, the names of the others slipped by me: there was a tall, thin merchant with sandy hair, two older men, one grizzled in a morning coat and well-tailored vest, obviously prosperous, and a fourth who was a dark-haired butcher.

As for the women: two were young, the debutante-aged daughters of a Mrs. Audrey Lapp, who was bedecked in ruffled taffeta and a widow's bonnet; one was a spinster, who wore deep puce and held her chin very high—I thought her name was Isabelle Wright. One other was the wife of the butcher. They all looked at me with interest, but it was—thankfully—only that which comes upon meeting a new colleague, and nothing more.

"Do you join the choir as well, Miss Rainey?" Mrs. Lapp asked.

Charlotte shook her head. "No, ma'am. I ain't much interested. I'm only here as a friend."

Mrs. Lapp peered at me, and I bent my head, uncomfortable beneath her gaze. "Have you been in Seattle long, Miss Olson?"

"More than three years now," I said.

"And only just now come to church?"

Mr. Anderson interjected himself smoothly between us. He had a pile of hymnals, which he passed out to us. "Shall we begin? I'd like to work on a new song this morning. If you will all turn to hymn forty-two."

I took the hymnal into my hand. I would practice with them, as it seemed I had no choice, but only for today. Once it was over and Mr. Anderson was alone, I would speak to him. For now . . . I threw a nervous look at Charlotte. She only smiled at me and withdrew, sitting beside the merchant's wife in the pew to watch. Mr. Anderson directed us into position— I was made to stand between the young Deborah Lapp and Miss Wright, who were the only other sopranos.

As we took our places, I felt Miss Lapp's gaze touch upon my scar, but she was too well-bred to say anything. Miss Wright was not so circumspect. "What a terrible scar, Miss Olson."

Mr. Anderson saved me from answering. He had seated himself at the piano, and now he laid his hands upon the keys, and we all went still.

I was skilled at this; I'd had to learn new music almost constantly, and this was easy for me. I did not falter as he played

the melody, though those around me did, and as a consequence, my voice rang out far too loudly. It startled me, and
I was uncomfortable when Dr. Marsdon turned from his place
down the riser to look at me. I felt the glances of the others as
well, and I made myself look straight ahead, to Charlotte, who
smiled in encouragement, and forced myself to sing more
quietly—to blend was my goal, I reminded myself. The habit of
being distinctive was one I could not indulge.

When the song was over, Mr. Anderson took us each
through the parts, the contraltos first, and Miss Lapp leaned
close to whisper, "What a divine voice you have, Miss Olson!
I've never heard finer!"

I smiled at her, but the compliment unnerved me. I had to
restrain the urge to leave the church. It was only for today,
I reminded myself, and then Mr. Anderson came to the sopranos and took us again through our part in the song, and I concentrated on the sounds of the voices beside me—Miss Wright's
strong clear soprano and Miss Lapp's softer, more girlish one.
Deliberately, I tuned myself to them. I contoured my voice,
I brought it to blend—softer, a little breathier. In my head
I heard the terse instruction: *"No, not that way! Breathe deeper—
from the diaphragm, yes, yes!"* and I ignored it as I had never done
before. I made myself into what they expected me to be, a
woman who could sing, but who would never set the world
aflame.

After that, despite my intention, I began to relax. I began to
enjoy it. As we went through that hymn again, and again, and
then once more, and then moved on to the others the choir already knew, I found myself smiling. By the end of the practice,
I felt as if a press inside of me had eased; I could breathe again,
and yet I had not realized until now that I had not been. I had
not felt the press until it was gone.

And suddenly I did not want to refuse this.

I let Mr. Anderson hurry away, and knew I would regret it,
and yet I simply could not make myself go after him. The

pleasure the singing had brought was too much; already I was thinking how to keep it secret, how to manage it. I doubted any of these people knew Johnny personally. And as for my being recognized . . . I'd seen already how anonymous they were standing in matching robes, how none of them stood out. I could make myself disappear among them. I could blend my voice and do my hair to mostly cover my scar and stand in the back. No one would guess who I really was. And Johnny would never have to know.

There was a part of me that knew this was reckless, that sneered at such wishful thinking, but in the end, the truth was only this: I wanted to sing in the choir, and I wanted it badly enough that none of the rest mattered.

When Mr. Anderson dismissed us, Miss Lapp stepped with me down the riser and said, "I'm so glad you've joined us, Miss Olson. Why, I think I was afraid to sing out until I heard the strength of your voice!"

Charlotte came up to us then, smiling. "That was lovely."

"Quite lovely indeed," Dr. Marsdon said at my shoulder. "I would have said we needed two sopranos to complete the choir, Miss Olson, but you have filled the void admirably."

"You're very kind," I said.

"Wherever did Anderson find you?"

"You can thank me for that," Charlotte said. "I heard her sing and insisted she come."

He turned to her. "Ah. So you're a member of the congregation?"

Charlotte laughed. The sound was rich and full; I did not miss how it arrested him. "I hardly—"

"I think you'll see Miss Rainey every Sunday now, Dr. Marsdon," I interrupted quickly as Charlotte looked at me in surprise.

Marsdon smiled. It brought out well-established laugh lines on his face. He was not so young as I had supposed. "Then I shall look forward to it."

When he'd gone, Charlotte said to me, "I ain't much for churchgoing, you know that. Or d'you mean to reform me?"

"I doubt I could," I teased. "But I've no intention of coming here to sing without you."

"Don't tell me you're nervous?"

"As it happens, I am. I suffer terribly from stage fright."

She laughed again. "You do not!"

"I could never go onstage without a good-luck kiss," I told her honestly.

"But you're too old now to need your papa's blessing."

"Yours will do." I led her to the door and out into the day. I had not realized how hot the church had been until we stepped outside. "Besides, I think Dr. Marsdon might find his Sundays much better decorated if you're there."

"Don't tease."

"I'm not teasing. Did you see the way he looked at you?"

"I saw the way he looked at *you*. The way all the men do. That scar of yours makes you mysterious. Hell, if you were a whore, you'd make a fortune."

I ignored that. "It wasn't me he was looking at when he said he looked forward to next Sunday."

She put her hand on my arm to stop me. "Don't, Marguerite. Please."

I pulled away. "You're being foolish."

"I know you meant to keep me from saying where I was from. But I'd rather he know the truth. Then he'll leave me alone—or he'll come down to the Palace and pay me for a fuck. Either way's fine with me."

"Charlotte—"

"Next time he asks, I'll tell him."

"You will not," I said. "Did you think I was trying to save you from embarrassment in there? Only Mr. Anderson knows about the Palace, and I'd like to keep it that way. The last thing I want is for any of this to get back to Johnny."

"Oh." Her voice was small. "I forgot about that."

"Please don't forget again."

"I won't," she said, and there was something in her tone I'd never heard before, some little irritation that unsettled me. "You can be sure of it."

CHAPTER 15

Johnny was impatient and short waiting for Blakely Davis's decision about investing. I was not. Nothing could progress until we had the money in hand, and the longer it took, the better.

But a week hadn't passed when Johnny called me into his office.

"I got a letter from that son of a bitch." He held the pages out to me, dangling them between his fingers as if they were noxious. Mockingly, he said, "He sends Miss Olson his most sincere regards."

"What else does he say?"

"That he's thinking about our offer. That he has to go to Chicago for a few months, but he hopes to come to a decision when he returns. That's what I get for dealing with Daddy's boys." Johnny threw the letter to his desk. "Dillydallying shit. Why the hell should we wait for him? What does it matter what the place looks like? If I had Adelina Patti here right now, you could be damn sure people wouldn't give a damn whether or not there's a drop curtain."

"But you wouldn't get Adelina Patti with a stage like this."

"How can you be so sure?" His eyes narrowed. "We offer enough money, who knows who we'd get? I say to hell with Davis. Let's get acts in here now. We can rebuild the place later."

I leaned forward, bracing my hands on his desk. "When does Davis leave? Can we meet with him again before?"

"I don't think it's me he wants to see."

I straightened. "Is that what you want? For me to see him alone?"

Johnny met my gaze. I saw the flash of something in his eyes, a little jealousy, perhaps; I wasn't certain. "No, I ain't saying that," he said irritably. "Let's try this my way, honey. Maybe we don't need Davis. I should get an answer from San Francisco any day."

I didn't like how quickly he was moving, or the way he'd wrested control. Desperately I tried to think of a way to wrest it back. "What if I convince Mr. Davis to invest now, before he goes?"

Johnny shrugged. "You do what you want. I'm tired of waiting."

I left Johnny's office frustrated and bad tempered. I'd had him well in hand, and now that idiot Davis had ruined everything with his hesitation. When Duncan looked up from the bar and said, "You all right, Marguerite?" I snapped, "I'm going out."

I nearly ran back to McGraw's. Once I was there, I dressed again in the widow's weeds, again without the hat and veil, and then I made my way to the Occidental Hotel. I didn't let myself think of what I was doing, or of my intentions. At the desk, I asked for Mr. Davis's room, and when the man there told me the number, I went up the stairs and knocked on the door.

The door opened. Mr. Davis was in his shirtsleeves. In surprise, he said, "Miss Olson?"

I gave him my best smile. "Do you think I might speak with you a moment?"

"Here? In my room?"

I licked my lips. "Why not?"

He looked startled and uncomfortable and then he said, "Let me fetch my coat, and we'll go downstairs," and I was momentarily disconcerted. This was not what I'd expected.

I stepped inside his room. When I went to close the door, he stopped it with his hand so that anyone in the hallway might see us. A little chivalry which I was impatient with. I was here; best to get this over with.

"Will you invest in the Palace, Mr. Davis, or must we find another partner?"

He stepped back. "How very . . . straightforward you are, Miss Olson."

I nearly laughed at that. "Mr. Langford tells me you're going to Chicago."

"Yes. The day after tomorrow."

"And you might not be returning for some months."

"That's true as well."

"We can't wait forever, Mr. Davis. Surely you understand. I came here today in the hopes that you might make a decision before you leave."

He stroked his beard thoughtfully. "I . . . see."

"And"—I took a deep breath—"and I wondered if there might be something you want from us. In return for your agreement."

Now he frowned. "Something I want from you and Langford?"

"Or from me. In particular." I met his gaze boldly.

And he did something no other man in my experience had ever done. He said, "I think you mistake me, Miss Olson."

The response was so unexpected I blinked at him. "I . . . mistake you?"

"I have every intention of investing in your enterprise," he said. "And I require nothing in return but the percentages we've agreed upon."

I felt a twisting, sharp relief, and something else too, an almost paralyzing sickness that I had been so ready to do this again, that I had only thought of getting what I wanted; I had never considered that there might be another way.

"Miss Olson, are you quite all right?" Davis's voice came to me through a fog.

"Yes, of course."

"I mean no insult, of course—"

"None taken."

"You are a charming woman, and I would be honored—"

"Please, Mr. Davis, say nothing more."

"I imagine it was Langford who asked you to come here."

I peered up at him in confusion.

"He is . . . determined, by all accounts. As a partner, I have no qualms about that. It seems to me Langford prospers when he chooses to. However, it troubles me to think that a fine woman such as you might find herself . . . compelled."

I laughed. "Johnny has no idea I'm even here, Mr. Davis. I'm hardly compelled, as you say. He's an impatient man, but you'll find him fair, as long as you don't cross him."

"Have you ever crossed him, Miss Olson?"

I tried not to think of why I was here, or of the choir, or of the things I hadn't told Johnny. I tried not to think of what he might do if he discovered any of it. Uncomfortably, I said, "We have an understanding."

"Ah." Mr. Davis looked thoughtful. Then he became very officious, and it was as if the rest of the conversation had never taken place. "Well then, Miss Olson, shall I write you a cheque?"

I PUT THE cheque in my pocket and felt a little thrill of victory as I did so. I didn't bother to go home and change but made my way back to the Palace. Duncan glanced at me in surprise when I came through the door. "You got another opera to go to?"

"Where's Johnny?"

He jerked his head toward the office door.

I wrenched at the knob and went in, surprising Johnny as
he bent over the books, an unlit cigar clenched between his
teeth.

"What is it?"

I reached into my pocket and took out the folded cheque,
letting it fall to the desk before him. "Surprise."

He grabbed it before it landed, unfolding it, staring at it for
a long moment.

"Where the hell'd you get this?"

"Where does it look like?"

He set the cheque onto the desk slowly—too slowly. There
was something in his face I recognized, though it wasn't an expression that belonged to him, and the memory flashed back.
A bathtub, a cheque sailing through the air, a bodice soaked
through.

Angrily, I said, "Are you accusing me of something?"

Johnny said, "Whoa, honey—"

"I asked him for the money straight out and he gave it to
me. He'd already decided to give it to us. I didn't have to do
anything."

"Margie—"

"What do you think I am, a whore? How dare you—"

"Margie, shut the fuck up." Johnny stood, frowning.
"Suppose we back up just a bit. Why don't you tell me what
happened?"

"Not if you're going to assume I fucked him."

"Did I say that? I don't recall it."

"You were thinking it."

"So you a mind reader now?"

"If you're going to be jealous every time I have anything to
do with another man—"

"Stop right there," he said, coming around the corner of the
desk. "First off, I don't give a damn how you got the money.
What you do is your own business. But I got to protect what's
mine, honey, and I can't do that if you lie to me."

"I'm not lying."

"You sure about that? I would've said you went out of here this morning riled up and ready to fuck Davis if you needed to."

"It was what you wanted."

He laughed. "Damn if you ain't delusional, honey. You should know by now it'd be the last thing I want."

I frowned. "What do you mean?"

"You know what I mean." He stepped closer.

"Johnny—"

"I want a partnership."

"We're partners already. Nothing's changed."

"Something has changed," he said. "You have."

"I'm just the same."

He looked at me thoughtfully. "No, honey, you ain't. These last couple months . . . something's different. I wish to hell I knew what it was, but you know, I'm willing to let it be. I've been waiting for you to settle. Seems to me as if maybe you finally have."

He leaned down to kiss me with a gentleness I'd never felt from him. Johnny had always been a skillful enough lover to know what I'd wanted: sex that was both an appeasement of loneliness and a punishment for past sins, and nothing more. But this . . . this was not that. It was troubling, but not unpleasant.

I let him kiss me. When he drew away, he brushed his thumb over my cheek. "What d'you think, honey? You ready to try a partnership that ain't only business?"

"Maybe," I said, and was surprised to hear myself, to hear an answer that wasn't no, but something else, something truer, something unexpected. "I guess that depends."

"On what?"

"On whether you can take me as I am. No more questions. Leave the past alone."

His hand came behind my head, holding me in place as he spoke against my lips. "Agreed." He kissed me with a skill that had me clutching him even as I sensed there was something missing, something I could never have again, something I wanted quite desperately, though I could not bring myself to think of what it was.

That night, as I lay in his bed and listened to his soft snoring, I sang hymns in my head, practicing, longing, and all I could think about was the choir.

CHAPTER 16

On Sunday, I went into the choir room with the others, pulling on the musty satin robes, clasping closed the braided trim at the front. Up close, they were more worn than I'd realized, frayed at the hem and cuffs and sour-smelling beneath the scent of the sachets Mrs. Anderson had hung on every hook.

"Miss Olson," Dr. Marsdon said when we bent to gather our choir books, "your friend, Miss Rainey—"

I looked up into his brown eyes, smiling when he faltered. "Miss Rainey?"

He cleared his throat. "You said she might be in the congregation. . . ."

"Near the back, Dr. Marsdon," I said. "I should think you'd be able to find her quite easily."

He nodded, flushing beneath his pale skin as we went out with the others and took our places on the risers.

I had sung on stages in front of hundreds—even thousands—before. I knew audiences intimately; I knew the sound and the feel of them; I knew how to manipulate them with a bow or a smile or a note strung to the gallery gods in the topmost seats.

And yet here, where there could not have been two hundred faces, I was intimidated. I sat on the back riser beside Miss Lapp, and heard the congregation shuffle and cough. I saw their interest in the sermon wax and wane, their eyes shifting in search of distraction, their curiosity as they spotted me, more than one piercing look. I averted my eyes and—but for Charlotte's—tried not to meet anyone else's.

When we rose to sing, it was a relief. And as I sang I forgot the audience's curiosity and my own nerves. To sing was what I'd been born to do, and even as I mixed my voice with the others, altering it, blending it, I felt that singular joy I'd always felt, that emptiness always within me easing, healing.

When the service was over, Mr. Anderson took me aside. "My wife and I are having a small luncheon for the choir this afternoon. We'd be delighted if you and Miss Rainey could join us."

I smiled my declination, but before I could say anything, he said earnestly, "It's meant to welcome you to the choir, Miss Olson. You are a most hoped-for addition."

After that, I could not say no, and so I brought Charlotte with me, up the street to the foot of First Hill, where the Anderson house stood with three others on a block otherwise filled with brambles. The house was a standard whitewashed clapboard, with a front porch and a screened lean-to and a fence twined with sweetbriar and a huge rhododendron in the corner, its blossoms long since fallen away. A tethered cow stood in the side yard, grazing.

Charlotte and I had walked, and so were the last to arrive. Wagons and horses and one carriage—Mrs. Lapp's, I assumed—had parked on the street out front. There was a table set in the yard, and the other members of the choir were gathered around it, helping themselves to fried chicken and oyster stew and salmon and corn bread. They welcomed us warmly; Mrs. Anderson was quick to get us each a plate, and to pile it high with food, and then we went to sit with others on the blankets they'd spread.

I saw the way Mrs. Lapp marked us, leading her daughters to a blanket some distance from ours. I leaned close to Charlotte, pulling at my chicken with my fingers. "Mrs. Lapp does not like how curious her daughters are about me. I think she wishes Deborah didn't stand so close on the risers. She'd probably move her if she weren't a soprano too."

Charlotte raised her eyes to follow my gaze.

I said, "And the merchant's wife doesn't know quite what to make of me."

"She don't like your scar," Charlotte said, bringing a bit of chicken to her mouth. "It makes her nervous. She said so when we were sitting together at practice. She asked me what I thought happened that made it."

"What did you tell her?"

"That you'd probably murdered someone."

I felt myself pale.

Charlotte laughed. "It was a joke, but I think she believed me."

I bent to my plate and tried to smile. "No wonder she keeps her distance."

Just then, I saw a pair of boots appear before us. I glanced up to see Dr. Marsdon; just behind him was the butcher and his wife, all holding full plates. "Would you ladies mind if we joined you?" Dr. Marsdon asked, and I picked up my plate and scrambled back, making room for them. Charlotte was less nimble, but she eased to the edge of the blanket, and I did not miss the fact that Dr. Marsdon sat beside her.

The butcher and his wife sat down in a bloom of skirts. She leaned forward to say, "Miss Olson, I must tell you that the choir sounds so different with you in it! I'd not realized how much we missed our third soprano."

I smiled and thanked her. After that, I said little myself but listened and nodded as the conversation drifted to the conversion of Squire's Opera House to a hotel and all the other ways the city was changing, and I found myself laughing easily and well, as I hadn't done in years. I leaned back against the fence, and the day turned drowsy with the hot sun and a faint breeze. I felt included and innocently so—I was Marguerite Olson here, a member of the choir, and nothing else. I wanted nothing from them; they wished nothing of me but to sing with them, and there was relief in that, an easy kind of joy, a kind I had never known and had never thought to want before now.

As SUMMER FADED, I lived my double life. For all except those few hours on Sunday morning, I was Marguerite Olson from the Palace. But those few hours colored the rest. Mr. Anderson was the only one who knew of my association with the Palace, and he was very discreet. I had no fear the others would stumble upon me there—they were not the kind to frequent the Lava Beds; I doubted they would ever set foot in the boxhouse. And so the choir became my solace; I did not worry about Johnny or anything else when I was there.

My time in the church made it easier too to endure the time I spent alone. When I wasn't with Johnny, I no longer felt the need to go to Charlotte's room in those few hours after dawn; instead I lay in bed and relived my time upon those risers, the sheer joy of singing again. I hummed or sang softly to myself and listened to my voice ease into the corners of my tiny room, filling those corners where before they had held only shadows.

Charlotte seemed to enjoy it too. Dr. Marsdon had continued his attentions to her, and though she claimed to want nothing to do with him, I saw the sparkle in her eyes when she came with me to church each Sunday; I knew she looked for him.

One Sunday, after practice, I said to her, "You and Dr. Marsdon were quite cozy just before he left."

Charlotte became pensive. "He asked me to go with him for ice cream."

"Then why aren't you walking with him?"

"You know why," she said.

"He admires you a great deal, Charlotte."

"Enough to excuse that I'll fuck any man with two dollars?"

"He wouldn't have to know."

"I don't like living in secrets. In fact"—she took a deep breath—"in fact, I think it best if I don't come with you anymore."

"But I need you there!"

"For what? Don't tell me you still got stage fright."

"I don't know. I wouldn't like to try." I grabbed her hand. "Please, Charlotte. I need to see you in the audience. I look for you every time."

"You don't really need me. You just tell yourself you do."

"I don't know how I would get through the day without you, to tell the truth."

She gave me a wan smile. "Don't let it get out. Half the girls in the Palace are jealous of you; I don't want them jealous of me too."

"Jealous," I repeated. "Of what?"

She rolled her eyes. "Of how lucky you are."

"Lucky?" Her words made me pause. When I thought of everything I'd once had, everything that had happened . . . I could only view my life now in terms of absence; I measured only by what was missing.

"Well, ain't you? You're Johnny's partner. You could get any man in the place to give you whatever you want. A man like Robert Marsdon . . . you could even have him if you wanted."

"Oh, hardly." I choked on the word. "And believe me, I don't want him."

"Why not?" she asked reasonably.

"I don't want anyone."

"Why? You never planned on getting married or having kids?"

"Dear God, no."

"Not even with your musician?"

"It wouldn't matter if I had," I said angrily. "That was a lifetime ago. He means nothing to me now."

Charlotte's smile was small and cryptic.

"What?" I demanded. "Why do you look at me that way?"

"Because I never saw a woman so bound not to see the truth of things."

"You want the truth, Charlotte? Here it is: I run whores and fuck a pimp, and my best friend is a prostitute likely to die of violence or disease before she's much older. Is that truth enough for you?"

She said calmly, "Your pimp loves you, as does your whore of a friend. You got the voice of an angel. You ain't living in a gutter, and you got friends who go to church every Sunday. You're lucky, Marguerite. And you ran away from your old life, so it couldn't have been that good. Stop pretending it was."

I stared at her, startled by her words, by the truth of them. I turned away from her and took a breath to calm myself. "How did this conversation even begin? All I wanted was for you to keep coming to church with me."

She said, "And I will. A little longer. But don't ask me to do what I can't. Robert Marsdon's got to know the truth about me sooner or later. It'd be kinder to be sooner."

"I think he'll manage to withstand it whenever he knows," I said bitterly.

"Kinder for me," she said.

THE FOLLOWING SUNDAY, I watched as she smiled softly and shook her head at Robert Marsdon after practice. He walked away, his disappointment showing in every line of his body, and I thought of her words and how I should not require this of her, of how selfish I was. It *was* unkind, and the fact that it had never occurred to me until she'd said it sobered me. Just as it sobered me to think of the other things she said. She was right, and I knew it. I had run away and made a new life here. I *was* Marguerite Olson. I had found a measure of happiness I'd never thought to have again. The choir filled so much of that emptiness inside of me that I wondered: if I could just hold on to the joy I took in those hours, could I spin them into something new—a whole cloth where before there had been nothing but separate threads?

I was quiet and contemplative as we went back to the Palace.

"You all right, Marguerite?" Charlotte asked.

"No," I said. "I was wrong. I shouldn't make you come to church when it troubles you so to see him."

She gave me a puzzled look.

"You don't have to come with me anymore. And . . . tell him the truth the way you want."

"Tell him the truth?" Now she looked stunned. "But . . . what about Johnny?"

"Let me worry about Johnny."

Charlotte hesitated. "Are you sure?"

"I am." I hid my apprehension in a quick smile.

She smiled back, but it was uncertain. "I think I'll keep coming to church, if you don't mind. And I won't say anything to Dr. Marsdon."

"But I've just told you—"

"I know what you told me. And I'm glad. But now that it's my choice, I think I'll just keep on for a while."

"Not because of me. Please."

This time her smile was real. "Hell, the sermon's good for my soul, and I like to hear you sing. And I guess . . . Dr. Marsdon'll get tired of me eventually. There ain't no need to embarrass him."

"If you think so."

"I do," she said.

IT WAS A few days later that the letter came from San Francisco. I was in Johnny's room, and he came inside, holding it, and said, "Got an answer from Tom at the Luxe."

I stopped in the middle of unhooking my corset, and he smiled and said, "Don't stop that on my account."

"What does he say?"

"My, my, such curiosity." He glanced over the words, as if reading them for the first time. "Let's see now. First, that he don't know nothing about you."

I sank onto the bed, my worst fears realized and relieved in the same moment. "I thought I told you not to mention me."

"I was curious."

"You promised not to ask anything more about my past."

He came down beside me. "That was after I'd already sent the letter." He undid the last hooks of the corset, and he eased it aside. His hand was very warm. "You can't fault me for that. Don't you want to know the rest?"

I tried to smile away my discomfort. I lay back, pulling him with me. "Tell me."

"He's got an interesting idea. He wants to set up a circuit. The Luxe and us and a theater in Portland. One or two others, maybe. That way, we got more to offer any touring companies. It ain't a bad idea."

"No, it's not," I agreed.

"He's going to make a few inquiries."

"Good," I said. "That's . . . good."

"It's happening just like we hoped," he said with satisfaction, kissing me. "We'll be the most famous theater north of San Francisco, just see if we ain't. You and me are something together, Margie."

And if those words held an uncomfortable echo, I told myself not to listen. I told myself it didn't matter. I kissed him back and let him keep me up into the morning and remembered what Charlotte had said. I told myself this was the life I'd chosen.

From the Journal of Sabine Conrad

NEW YORK CITY, OCTOBER 13, 1875—Gideon has leased the Opera House for the season, but he is not happy because subscriptions are down. He says it is that way all across the city, and I believe him, because one sees broadsheets advertising new auctions for the possessions of bankrupts every day. Tramps are camped out in every doorway, and Gideon has forbidden me to go about without an escort.

In spite of this, we've had respectable enough audiences. Gideon has told me that he is thinking of adding *Die Zauberflaute,* if I feel I could do the Queen of the Night, which is very demanding, and which I have not attempted before, because I have always done Pamina. Gideon says Amelia can do Pamina, and as I am the prima donna of the company, the Queen is right for me, even though it means I will be playing Amelia's <u>mother</u> when she is older than me! Gideon wants it for the impresario from France to hear, and he thinks it will boost subscriptions if I can be ready by January, so I have agreed, and we've set about practicing it. But Gideon is at his most unpleasant right now, and practice is my least favorite part of the day, if only because it so obviously illustrates how much his affection for me has changed.

I know much of it has to do with his worries over money. The orchestra's pay is going up & etc. etc. When I asked him again about buying a house he told me not to mention it to him again, though of course we are still staying in the Fifth Avenue Hotel, and so I think we are not as desperate for funds as he pretends. He says that financially everything depends now on getting to Europe and that it is our best hope for the future. I hope he is right. I begin to despair that things can ever be good between us again, and I can't help but think that if we could be apart from the rest of the company—and that wretched Leila—in a place that was just our own, perhaps everything would be better. So I am determined to be the most lauded Queen of the Night ever, and to persuade this impresario beyond all doubt that I am the best prima donna in America, and worthy of the Theatre Italien.

NOVEMBER 8, 1875—Tonight Leonard Jerome came to the performance. I had not seen him since we returned, though I heard rumors he was squiring about the new soprano performing at Steinway Hall, and I admit I was relieved that he'd found someone to replace me, as I was afraid if he had not, I would have to take up with him again because the money is so very helpful. But when Leonard came backstage after, I was very glad to see him. He is as charming and handsome as ever, and he brought me a gift of pink roses, which he knows I love, and he sat on my chaise and I gave him champagne and we laughed for some time. He told me I must feel free to use his theater for practice, as he so particularly loved to hear my voice within it, and then he asked me—oh, so very casually, as if he thought I wouldn't notice it—about Leila.

At first I was jealous, but then I thought how well this could avail me. Europe is not settled yet, and who knows when it will be? So I told him of her and intimated that she was looking for a protector of her own. "She's so very young, you know," I told him, "and quite naive." And then I said I thought she would benefit from a wise man's mentoring, in the same way I had benefited so well from his.

He said nothing more about it, but I feel quite certain he will act upon my hint, and though I feel a little guilty over it, it is not too much.

NOVEMBER 19, 1875—Leonard sent Leila flowers after the performance Thursday night—white roses, oh how charming! As if she is as innocent as she pretends—and sent me pink ones too, of course, because he does not wish to offend. This morning I told Gideon I wished to practice the Queen at Leonard's theater, because the sound was so very good there, and that perhaps Amelia and Leila could come along to practice as well (which is of course the whole purpose, though I didn't tell him that).

He said I didn't need Jerome any longer, and that he'd prefer I didn't see him, and I said we were just friends now, and he'd offered the theater and I saw no reason not to take advantage of it. It took me an hour to convince him, which I was glad to do, because it means he is jealous and that means he still loves me. Finally, he agreed, because with Amelia and Leila there it was quite obvious I had no intention of a private tête-à-tête.

As I anticipated, Leonard was there to watch, and he was just as taken with Leila as I meant him to be, and she with him—especially after I told her how happy I was to see him, and how intimate our relationship had always been and how I hoped for it to be that way again. She will do anything to thwart me. She spent the afternoon flirting with Leonard, and he was very receptive. My only fear was that Gideon would notice, but he kept closer to me than he has in some time, as if he thought I might sneak away with Leonard while he wasn't looking.

Afterward he told me that I was not to go there again,

because Leonard had already done everything we needed for him to do and he had been amply repaid for his investment.

Then he took me to bed and was very attentive—much more so than he has been recently. And though I know he will not like at all my plans for Leila, in the end he will see it's for the best. And once we are in Europe, none of it will matter anyway.

DECEMBER 2, 1875—Tonight after the performance, Leila said very loudly to Taddeo while I was standing there that she was on her way to a private dinner with Leonard Jerome. Of course she meant for me to hear, and I saw her watching me quite surreptitiously and I pretended to be very dismayed, but it was all I could do to keep from dancing back to my dressing room.

DECEMBER 18, 1875—Today Yuri told me that Mr. Mulder was auditioning for a mezzo-soprano. So I wrote a note to Leonard telling him that, as Leila's friend and supporter, I felt that Gideon was favoring me at her expense, and so she was not perhaps getting the stronger mezzo roles she deserved. I suggested that, as her very special friend, perhaps he would be so kind as to mention to her that the Mulder-Fabbri Company was auditioning. I asked him not to tell Leila that I had said so, beause if Gideon found out he would be angry. I also told him I had some experience with Mr. Mulder and Mme. Fabbri, and I knew they would be especially kind to her.

JANUARY 18, 1876—Gideon and I had a terrible fight. Today Leila told him that she was leaving the company for Mulder. I, of course, could not help my joy over it, and I suggested we go out to celebrate, which was exactly the wrong thing to say, because he was furious. I told him there were a hundred mezzos to be had, and he said Leila had the perfect tone to complement my voice, and where would he find another like her? I said that was a pretty thing to say, and why not just admit he missed fucking her since she'd taken up with Leonard Jerome.

For a moment I thought he would hit me, and I stepped back, and when he saw it he grew even angrier and asked how I could possibly be afraid of him, when he'd dedicated his whole life to me. Then he accused me of deliberately managing things to send Leila away, which I admitted I'd done because I hated her and I'd been asking him for more than a year to get rid of her, and how could he say he'd done everything for me when he had not done the one thing I most wanted?

He slammed out of the room then, and I have not seen him since.

I do feel a bit guilty over it. But what else was I to do?

FEBRUARY 1, 1876—Gideon has found a mezzo to take Leila's place, though he says Sarah does not match me as well. But I like her better because she is married and unaffected by Gideon's charm.

Gideon is still consumed by the business affairs of the company. I think my getting rid of Leila surprised him—it makes me wonder how he did not see my misery before. God knows I made no secret of it. He comes to me more often now, yet sometimes he seems so far away I cannot reach him, and my yearning for Europe and escape from all the cares that surround us now is so great I wonder that I can bear another day with the company.

I am growing to dislike my room very much. I am there too much, and I'm often lonely. Gideon does not like me spending time with the rest of the company, and there is no Barret and no Leonard to squire me about town. I am not to go out alone because of the tramps and the too-ardent attentions of those who love me. The only adoration I see is in the evenings when I sing, and it is not enough—not when I am used to so much more. I have even been extending my practice times—which is saying a great deal, because I have never liked practice. But it gives me time with Gideon and I am so desperate for his attention that it is the only way to have it, even if he is mostly lost in his playing and not paying much heed to me.

I think I would do almost anything to have my life as it used to be before the company. Oh, to take these worries from him and make him happy again . . .

When will that damn impresario from France arrive?

FEBRUARY 14, 1876—Today Gideon gave me a beautiful card of gold tissue with quilled paper roses that said: "To My Valentine, who holds my heart," and he had written below: "Even when all of Europe is at your feet, her devotion will not come close to measuring the depth of mine." He also gave me a strand of pearls interspersed with rubies. It is very, very beautiful, and I liked it so much that I put it on and took off everything else to thank him, and he was very appreciative. It was almost as it used to be, and afterward we ordered up a private dinner and ate it in bed. When I teased him over his good humor, he said the French impresario, Alain DeRosier, is due to arrive in the city next week. We will open *Die Zauber-flaute* in his honor.

FEBRUARY 29, 1876—Last night I met Alain DeRosier. I think I will see Paris at last!

Gideon told me DeRosier was planning to be at the performance, so I sang particularly well (though I don't think the Queen of the Night is my best role—she is not in the opera very much, and she is very regal and icy, and I am much better suited to the warmth of Pamina, but the role does better showcase my skill, so I know Gideon was right to choose it). The audience would not allow me to leave the stage until I'd sung "Der Hölle Rache" three times, though Amelia and Taddeo and Adriano sang the good-bye trio four.

I was backstage in my dressing gown, taking off my makeup, when Gideon brought M. DeRosier back. He carried such a large bouquet of lilies it hid his face, and when I took it from him I was quite struck by how handsome he is. His hair is darker than Gideon's and he wears it rather long, so it brushes his shoulders, and his eyes are a strange sort of greenish brown that is very pretty. He is a little taller than Gideon, but they have much the same form, both slight and athletic, though M. DeRosier is a bit of a butterfly in his style—his clothes are very well cut and close-fitting, with a great deal of color. His vest was all greens and golds and his necktie was a great swath of golden silk and his watch chain was adorned with tiny keys, some with jeweled heads and others with strangely elaborate pins—one had the shape of a bird. When I asked him what they opened, he smiled quite prettily with very even white teeth, and said, "Why, I hope they open your heart, mademoiselle." Which of course made me laugh.

After I'd dressed, we went to dinner, just the three of us, to Delmonico's. M. DeRosier and Gideon are very like kindred spirits, I think—I have not seen Gideon so relaxed or laughing so much for a very long time, which made me happy too, and as a result I was quite animated, and I saw that look in Gideon's eyes that makes me grow warm.

M. DeRosier said he means to go to Chicago and Boston too in search of singers to bring to Paris. He intends to base himself in New York for several months—but he said that if I am any indication, perhaps it will not take him so long as he thought.

I found him so charming, though he is a little too familiar, as handsome men are when they know their attentions are not unwelcome. When dinner was over, we all three went back to the hotel and had some more wine until I said I truly must go to bed or I would be unfit for singing tomorrow, and he asked what he and Gideon would do without a beautiful woman to look at? But his appeal did not dissuade me.

I think we shall all be a great deal in each other's pockets. I only wish Barret were here to see it—he could not be at all unhappy over this, when it was what he so often urged me to do.

MARCH 22, 1876—Tonight Alain wished to go gambling, so Gideon and I took him to Vons on Twenty-eighth Street. I had never been there before, but Gideon had. It was the most luxurious place I could have imagined. From the front, it seemed to be any large mansion, though its blinds were drawn, but when we went inside it fairly dazzled the eye with mirrors and cut glass and gilt everywhere.

Gideon was doing quite well; Alain not so much. He asked me to sit beside him and bring him luck, and when I did he drew me close and whispered that everything had changed for him since he'd met me. At one point he touched me beneath the table, and I could not help glancing to Gideon to see if he'd seen, but I don't think he had, though his mouth was very tight and he would not meet my gaze, and so I knew he was angry but would not say anything because too much depends on Alain.

Then Alain began to win, and Gideon to lose, and after he lost his fourth round he slapped his cards onto the table and rose, saying he needed some air, and left me and Alain alone. He was no sooner gone than Alain leaned to whisper that I had beguiled him, and he nuzzled my ear. I should have slapped him away, I suppose, as it made me rather uncomfortable, but it is always lovely to have the attention of a handsome man, and Gideon would tell me to be nice to him, and so I smiled and let him do it and leaned closer to encourage him. I said, "I cannot imagine I should capture you better than your French *mademoiselles*," and he said it pierced his heart that I should think him so fickle, and that the women in France were nothing compared to me. I told him I was looking forward to seeing for myself. I hoped he would tell me then when he planned on our departure, but he only smiled and said, "Here comes your watchdog now," and I saw Gideon coming across the room. I told him Gideon was not my watchdog and that I was a free woman who could do as she liked, and Alain said he was glad to hear it. But he moved away from me when Gideon came near, and I know he did not believe me. In truth I did not believe myself, but his words made me remember Barret and the strange dream I'd had in San Francisco, and I was uncomfortable and troubled until I made myself forget it.

JULY 16, 1876—Last night was my birthday. I am now twenty-two, which feels ancient as the sphinx, and New York is as hot as I imagine the desert in Egypt to be. Everything is sticky and humid, and the hotel is stifling but no less than the air outside. Everyone who is anyone has long since departed to Newport or the Continent, and I wish we were gone with them. At least to France. But Alain says he is not ready to return, and so we wait. Gideon and Alain wanted to take me out to celebrate my birthday, and though I was tired and irritated by the heat I agreed. We went to a beer garden that had a small area outside lit with lanterns, where we could hear the music and the air was cooler. We stayed until it was very late, and Alain had his arm about my shoulders. I knew Gideon was growing jealous and I thought I should make Alain stop. But so much depends on him that I didn't like to anger him, and it was my birthday and I admit I liked the attention, and liked imagining what Gideon would do to me when we got home.

Then we left. We tried to call a cab, but there were none to be had, and Alain and Gideon were so drunk and laughing so loudly and leaning on me as we walked that I suppose no driver wanted us anyway.

But then . . . we passed a whore. I don't remember much about her, except that she had dark hair. Alain asked her how much she cost, and she said it would be three dollars for him and another three for Gideon and extra if they wanted her together, and he said, "What about the three of us?" and she smiled and gave me a look that made me feel both aroused and sick, and suddenly I was imagining it—all of us in one bed tangled together—and Alain leaned close with his wolfish face and said, "Shall we buy her?" and I looked at Gideon. He was intrigued, I could tell, and for a moment I could not breathe, because I knew if he said yes that I would go along with them.

I would do whatever he wished and I knew I would regret it later. I knew I would be sick and ashamed. But I also knew I would not say no.

I don't know what he would have said, because then Alain seemed to think better of it, and he laughed and turned back to the whore and said not tonight, and we walked on. And though he teased and flirted with me the rest of the way home, and I laughed with him, it was all pretense, because I was tense and afraid, and I didn't know why.

He kissed me good night and left us at the hotel door. Gideon and I went up to my room and neither of us said a word. It felt the way it does sometimes before we have a terrible fight, but I didn't know what it would be about. I thought Gideon would say good night and leave me. But when I opened my door and stepped inside, he grabbed my arm and pushed the door closed so hard it slammed. Then he pressed me to the wall and kissed me as if he might devour me, and I did not know whether it was jealousy over Alain or the temptation of the whore that made him that way and I didn't care. He took me so roughly my head banged against the wall and we were both very loud—it embarrasses me now to think of how careless we were; anyone passing in the hall might have heard. And then when it was over I whispered to him that I knew he'd wanted the whore, and he said no, that he had been pretending for Alain's sake, and I wished I hadn't brought it up. But I could not help myself. I asked him would he have done it if Alain hadn't changed his mind, and he looked at me and asked if I would have and I said yes. I told him I would have if he'd wanted me to, and then suddenly I was crying.

He was quiet and then he picked me up and carried me to the bed, and I wound my arms around his neck and buried my face in his chest and felt wretched, though there was no reason for it. We hadn't bought the whore, and he was with me and nothing terrible had happened. He lay down beside me and pulled me into his arms and my love for him filled my chest until I couldn't breathe and it was . . . like a torment. Not peaceful at all, but . . . uncomfortable, and this morning when I look at him asleep beside me, I am confused and afraid.

AUGUST 3, 1876—Today I found Gideon and Alain lying about on Gideon's bed in the middle of the day, and the whole room stinking of opium. They were both sweaty and disheveled and their pupils so tiny that they might have had only irises for eyes. I was so stunned to see Gideon this way—especially after what had happened to Barret—that I stood there unmoving.

When he saw me he said to Alain, "Look how beautiful she is," and Alain nodded and dragged on the pipe and agreed that I was an angel, and they both laughed as if it were the most clever thing ever said.

I lost my temper and threw the water pitcher at them so water splashed everywhere and they had to scramble to avoid it. Gideon fell off the bed in his attempt to escape it, but he couldn't, and his hair was soaking wet and dripping water to his shoulders and he tried to get up to grab me but he was too drunk on smoke to manage it, and he fell back again. Alain just laughed and laughed, though he was wet too, and I walked out and left them to each other.

AUGUST 4, 1876—Gideon has apologized to me very prettily. He said it was a mistake, and that Alain had wanted it, and he had given in, though he knew better. He says he never meant to upset me. He says plans for Paris are moving forward. Alain has all but agreed we are to go.

He drew me into his arms so that I lay upon his chest, and he stroked my hair and told me how Paris would be, how we would stay in some wonderful hotel off the Champs-Élysées, and how the crowds at the Theatre Italien would be on their feet begging me to sing encore after encore. "It will be as we always dreamed it, Bina," he said. "Everything will be better when we're there, I promise." I could hear his heart beating, and it was like a song just for me, and I wish I could believe him.

CHAPTER 17

Seattle, Washington Territory—January 1882

It was pouring, the wind blowing so the rain slapped onto the warped floor of the balcony and against Johnny's window, sudden bursts of it that invaded my consciousness slowly until I was fully awake, and then I lay there, listening to the rough but beautiful song of the storm and feeling warm and snug in this bed, with Johnny asleep beside me.

I glanced over at him. One arm was thrown over his eyes, his breathing deep and steady. I was growing used to being here again, and for the most part, I liked it, though I kept my own room at McGraw's. Johnny had been asking me to give it up. "Why pay for it when you ain't ever there?" and I understood what it meant to him. Proof of a commitment, the admission that I was here to stay.

It wasn't that I didn't mean to make it. I did. My life had become settled in a way I'd never expected. I did my job at the Palace and slept with Johnny and lived under his protection. The idea of the theater circuit was taking hold—Johnny's friend Tom had convinced a theater in Sacramento to join, and Johnny had brought in one in Vancouver. Blakely Davis's money had bought a crimson curtain, currently on order from a shop in New York City, and a new stage. Workmen were adding gas footlights now. Charlotte and I had grown even closer in these last few months, and the choir at Trinity was my solace and my satisfaction. All in all, I was content, and if some days I felt restless, well . . . those days were fewer and farther between, and I knew that one day they would disappear. One day, I would learn to love this life the way I'd once loved the old one.

But until then, I kept my room and told myself and Johnny I would let it go soon. Soon.

I felt him stir beside me. He rolled over with a groan and kissed me and murmured, "Quite a storm out there."

"The perfect day for lying abed," I told him.

He laughed deep in his throat. "Now don't that sound inviting. But we got auditions today."

"What does it matter? We take them all. Just say they're hired and be done with it."

"We need the best ones on display tomorrow," he said. "I'm still hoping to find one with talent."

I sighed. The owner of a theater in Portland was coming up to see what we'd done. Whether or not The Orpheus would join our circuit depended on his good opinion, and I was weary of it already. "Will you really need me there?"

Johnny smiled. "I ain't a fool, honey. After how you convinced Davis, I need you whispering in Portland's ear. I'm betting he won't be able to resist you."

"You're only saying that because I'm in bed with you."

"Ummm." His hands came to my hips. "I'll say whatever it takes to keep you here."

"Then say there won't be auditions today. I can already predict how it will be: two mezzos and one soprano with a thready voice and all three of them flirting with you as if I wasn't there."

"Jealous, honey?"

I met his gaze, arching my shoulder a little, cocking my head flirtatiously, an unthinking habit. "Of course I am."

He looked at me thoughtfully.

I felt the danger then, the fragility of what we'd made. He'd kept the promise he'd made me: he never asked any questions. Maybe because he didn't want to test if I would keep my promise not to lie. I didn't know myself if I could. I knew what it cost him to tell himself I was nothing and nobody, that I belonged to him alone.

I wanted to tell him the truth. Some days it weighed so heavily upon me I couldn't breathe. But I couldn't do it. Not yet. Things were progressing quickly—too quickly for me, though the whores were still jockeying between the stage and the boxes, and there was still the little matter of Portland. But Johnny's enthusiasm never waned; he would have given anything for a decent act to start off the new Palace in style, and Sabine Conrad would be irresistible to him, no matter what would be best for me. And so I was silent. For now. Someday, I would tell him.

But not today. I ran my hand down his chest, tangling my fingers in the wiry golden curls there, smiling up at him, and said, "At least stay with me a little longer. It won't hurt them to wait."

When I wrapped my arms around his neck, he rolled me onto my back and kissed me, and I felt the difference in the way he took me now, how the promises we'd made each other had gentled him. I missed the little cruelties he'd once inflicted upon me, but I was afraid to tell him I still wanted them. I was afraid to admit it to myself, because of what it meant—that despite my efforts and my promise to move on, it was taking longer than I'd hoped. And so I was gentle with him, and I held him close and whispered love words in his ear and told myself what was true: that I was happy, that this could be enough.

I WAS UP with the dawn, as I always was on Sunday, no matter how late I'd got to bed the night before. I'd told

Johnny months ago that I'd wanted to go to church again, and he'd looked at me suspiciously and said, "You ain't turning Methodist on me, are you, honey?" and I'd laughed and said I'd turned away from God long enough and I didn't see what harm a little praying could do. Though he'd been wary and watched me carefully for a few weeks, now that he'd seen I wasn't taking up a temperance cause or insisting on prayers before bed, he'd come to terms with it. It was a safe enough lie, though I felt guilty about it—I didn't believe Johnny would set foot in a church, and frankly it was a miracle that he hadn't yet found out about the choir. I knew it couldn't last, but I hoped to hide it from him as long as I could. Once the Palace was the theater he wanted, once real actors and singers took to that stage, the fact that I was a good enough singer to be part of a church choir wouldn't interest him.

This morning Johnny only muttered at me not to open the curtains before he turned over and went back to sleep, and I felt the familiar anticipation of singing come over me as I dressed and went to fetch Charlotte from McGraw's. She was still sleeping, as always; I saw the struggle in her expression— the same struggle I saw every Sunday, the wish to go, the wish to stay. I knew it was because of Robert Marsdon. She never admitted it to me, and I don't think she admitted it to herself. Hope was something new for Charlotte, and I was glad to think I was at least partly responsible for it.

The air was moist with the promise of rain, and a cold wind raced up the streets from the Sound. Our cheeks were whipped red by the time we arrived. Carriages and wagons lined the street in front: the congregation hurried inside—the weather did not allow for friendly greetings in the muddy yard.

Charlotte slipped into her regular place in one of the back pews, and I made my way to the vestibule, where most of the other choir members were already hanging their coats and cloaks, fastening the ragged robes over their clothes.

Robert Marsdon's head jerked up when I came in. He stepped up close to me and said in a low voice, "Might I have a word with you later?"

I knew it was about Charlotte, and I said, "Yes, of course." I'd suspected for weeks that he was gathering his courage to speak to me about her. But just then Mrs. Lapp and her daughters burst into the vestibule in a flurry of cold air, and Marsdon stepped away.

I put on my robe with the others and we went to our seats at the front of the chapel. I never listened to the sermon, or at least not much. For me, the sermon was there only to fill the time before the music started. I stared at the back of Mr. Monroe's head, barely restraining the urge to tap my foot in impatience. When we all rose to sing the first hymn, I burst out loudly and joyously over the beginning notes. Too much so. At Deborah Lapp's sideways glance, I caught myself, pulling back. But even that was enough. I let the solace I'd always taken in singing sweep over me, surge through me, swelling with every note. I glanced toward the back to catch Charlotte's eye.

And saw him there.

The shock of it made me falter; for a moment I lost the words and the tune. My mind would not believe it. Impossible. He could not be here. It was an illusion; it had to be. It could not be him.

But of course it was.

Miss Wright nudged me with her elbow, pointing hard at the place in her music where I was supposed to be, and with effort I called myself back. But now I was hardly aware of singing; a part of my mind knew the words and the tune, and that was the part that led me while the rest panicked.

I told myself he had not recognized me. But I felt his stare, and I knew any hope that I'd gone unremarked and unrecognized was a vain and foolish one. He looked different; his hair was long, to his shoulders, but I would have known him anywhere, just as he must have known me. And I knew without a doubt that I was the reason he was here.

The urge to run was almost unconquerable. I leaped through the possibilities for escape: how to get out of the church unseen, how far I could run before he caught me. Yet through it all was the knowledge that I would do none of those things. Because with my panic came relief, relief that it had happened at last, that the waiting I hadn't realized I was doing was over.

The song ended; we sat again, my view once more obscured by Miss Wright's head, for which I was thankful. I did not think I could resist the urge to look at him again, to see, to be certain, though I was already.

When next we rose, I did not think I could make a sound. But when I cast a quick glance, I saw he was no longer there— and that increased my panic. Where had he gone? Had I simply imagined him? I lost my place twice in the music; what peace I'd taken from it had completely disappeared, and I was trembling and bathed in sweat. I wanted nothing so much as to tear the robe off and run outside into the freezing air. It was all I could do to keep singing, to make it through the rest of the service, which seemed to last forever.

When it was finally over, I was hardly aware of leaving the nave. Suddenly I was in the vestibule, buffeted by the others as they removed their robes and hung them on the hooks. It took me a moment to think of where I was and what I was supposed to be doing, and with clumsy hands I took off my own robe. Robert Marsdon was at my side, saying, "A word, Miss Olson?" and I nodded absently, going with him because I could not make my own thoughts coalesce, and he gave me something to concentrate on, something to follow. He led me to the door that opened onto a small side porch. I slunk back into the shadow of the narrow roof overhang, crossing my arms, trying to look interested when my mind was reeling in a hundred different directions, trying to think something other than Where was he? Why didn't he show himself again?

"I'm sorry to have to involve you in this, Miss Olson, but I see no other alternative."

Marsdon's nervousness caught my attention, the dismay in his voice. For a moment, my apprehensions quieted in sudden interest, another dread. "Involve me in what?"

He stepped closer, as if afraid we would be overheard, though the narrow yard between here and the privy was empty. In the back, the canvas that sheltered the part of the church being expanded for the pipe organ flapped in the breeze. I could hear voices fluttering from the front, good-byes, the laughter of children running through the yard, the jangle of reins and squeak of carriage wheels.

"I am in despair," Marsdon said quietly. "I would not ask you this, but I think you know her heart best."

My dread eased. This wasn't about me at all. Of course it wasn't. I'd known that. But in remembering it, I grew impatient. I was no longer interested. I did not want to listen to this, not now.

As if he sensed my distraction, he took my arm, whispering ardently, "Miss Olson—Marguerite—you know how I feel. Could you be my advocate? Could you help me?"

"I—"

There was a sound, a footstep, the smell of tobacco smoke. I turned to see just as he came around the corner. My heart beat wildly; I lost all coherent thought.

He looked up—how blue his eyes still were—and drew on the cigarette he was smoking. I saw him look to me, to Marsdon, to the hand Marsdon still had on my arm.

"Excuse me," he said, all politeness, though there was irony below it. "I was looking for Miss Olson. I didn't mean to intrude."

The shock of his voice startled me. I had never thought

to hear it again, though it had never left my dreams, or my nightmares. I pulled away from Marsdon, who stiffened and stepped back, as if he too realized how compromised we were.

"It's no intrusion," Marsdon said, obviously embarrassed. He frowned and looked to me in question.

Faintly, I said, "Dr. Marsdon, I'd like you to meet . . . Gideon Price. Mr. Price, this is Robert Marsdon."

Marsdon offered his hand. "Pleased."

Gideon smiled wryly as he shook it. "Likewise."

Robert Marsdon glanced at me. "Well, I won't delay you. I'll see you inside at practice, Miss Olson." He opened the door to the church before I could stop him or say a word, disappearing inside. The door closed again with a thud.

Gideon exhaled; tobacco smoke stung my nose. I shivered and hugged myself close. In the church he'd been too far away to see well, but I saw him now: his hair dull, his eyes red-rimmed, as if he'd had little sleep. Though he'd always been thin, now he was frighteningly so, almost skeletal, his high cheekbones and elegantly planed face sharp beneath his skin, which was too pale.

But he was still beautiful. Despite everything, the urge to touch him came over me like a terrible fever, and on the heels of that came fear and anger. The combination lashed through me like a monster, dizzying.

He stepped onto the stair. "Marguerite. Is that what they call you now? Not what I would have chosen for you, but . . . I wonder, what does that make me? Faust? Or Mephistopheles?"

"They said it was to be five years."

He dragged on the cigarette and blew out the smoke in a cloud. "Is there somewhere private we can talk?"

"I have to be at practice in a few moments."

He lifted a heavy dark brow. "Practice? What for? Even in this godforsaken place they must realize you could sing rings around them on your worst day."

I swallowed. "I have an obligation."

"Do you meet all your obligations, then? What about the one you have to me?"

That arrested me—that I had one was undeniable, though I wished I could protest it. I hesitated only a moment before I gestured to the canvas-walled space at the back. "There. Will that do?"

He glanced to it and took a final drag on his cigarette, throwing it into the trampled mud at the base of the steps, grinding it out with his boot. He stepped back to let me go before him, and I did, my emotions in such turmoil I could gain no real hold on them. I dodged through the canvas flap. The wall of the church was only partially torn down, and planks had been nailed temporarily over the hole the builders had made. I stood near it, waiting while he came inside, and then the space seemed too small—how could it contain us both, as separate as we were now?

He said, "Is Marsdon your lover?"

The question was so absurd and unexpected that I gaped at him. "Robert? Dear God, no."

"Someone else then?"

"Why should it matter to you?"

"So there is one."

I shook my head, rattled, uncertain.

Again, that wry smile. "Liar."

"Why do you ask, if you choose not to believe me?"

He made a derisive sound. "Because I can't help myself. Why else? These last four years, I've tortured myself with thoughts of you. How can I stop now?"

"Please . . . don't," I said.

"Don't what? Don't say the truth? Wasn't that the problem, Bina? That we never said the truth to each other?"

"I don't know what you mean."

The look he gave me seemed to strip me bare. "The hell you don't."

"Have you come only to berate me? Is that why you're here?"

"No." His gaze swept my scar. The past hovered palpably. Quietly, he said, "Did he do that to you?"

I could only nod.

He cursed beneath his breath, reaching into an inside pocket of his coat, pulling out a small leather pouch. He opened it; I watched him roll another cigarette with fingers that seemed to be trembling slightly. But the light was dim; I might have been imagining it. When he was finished, he put it in his mouth and took out a match. He stuffed the leather pouch away and struck the match on the heel of his boot.

"You're smoking," I said unnecessarily.

He lit the cigarette and picked a loose bit of tobacco from his lip, flicking it away. "What of it?"

"You never did before. What about your voice?"

He laughed shortly. "When was the last time I sang?"

We both went quiet. It was strange and awkward, especially as there seemed to be so much to say. Perhaps that was the problem—there was too much. The smoke he exhaled filled the space between us. He was standing close, closer than I wanted, but it seemed an expanse. I wished he would go, but the thought that he might go . . . that frightened me too.

He said, "You didn't really think I wouldn't come after you."

"There was to be another year."

"I was paroled. Mostly it was because they discovered I could play the piano. They had me play in the chapel on Sundays. Thank God for that, and for Willa's visits. Otherwise the silence would have done me in."

The sound of my sister's name stunned me. "Willa?"

"She was at the trial. She wrote to me at Sing Sing."

"She's still in love with you," I said—and despite myself, I heard the bitterness in my voice.

I saw he heard it too, but he only said, "She helped me find you."

I laughed. "How did you convince her to do that? I can't imagine she wanted me found."

"She knew I wanted it."

"Of course. So she did it for you. How sweet."

"Do her reasons matter? I couldn't hire the Pinkertons from prison myself, so she did. I told her what they should look for."

"Which was what?"

"I didn't think you'd be able to give up singing. I kept waiting for you to emerge. In Chicago, or New Orleans. Even Denver. When you didn't . . . it occurred to me that maybe you couldn't sing, that you'd been hurt too badly"—he exhaled almost violently—"or that you were afraid. After that . . . I knew the things you'd taken with you. It was just a matter of looking for them."

"The jewels I sold," I said.

He nodded. His smile was small. "You left a solid trail until Cheyenne. After that it stopped."

"That was where I sold . . . the last piece." I didn't say what that was; if he'd found it, he already knew.

"The Pinkerton agent thought you'd gone to San Francisco."

"No," I said tightly. "Not there."

"I've been here two weeks looking for you. Four days ago I saw you at the Palace. I've been following you since."

I tried not to show how shaken I was that he'd seen me there, that I had not noted him. "How did you know to come to Seattle?"

"The agent had a friend in San Francisco. Some theater owner—no one I knew. He'd received a letter from a man here asking questions about a woman who'd shown up in Seattle four years ago. One thing led to another, and . . . well, I thought that woman might be you. The moment I got out, I came here."

A theater owner in San Francisco. A letter from Seattle asking questions. I cursed beneath my breath.

He looked at me sharply. "Who was asking questions?"

I met his sharpness with my own. "What do you want of me, Gideon?"

He hesitated. Then he said, "Vanderbilt's grown tired of waiting for them to give him a box at the Academy. He's building a new opera house. The Metropolitan. They're going to need singers to fill it. They're going to need you."

"Me? Are you mad? Look at me. They'd never have me. The scandal—"

"The scandal will only make you more popular than ever. They won't be able to resist coming to see you. The great Sabine Conrad, who's been in hiding all this time after her manager murdered a French impresario. . . . How sordid it all was. They'll line up in droves."

The thought startled me. I had thought my career on the stage gone forever. To think that it was not . . . "But the scar—"

"The scar only makes it more fascinating. They'll fall over themselves speculating. It will make you irresistible. We can make the most of it, Bina. Even my time in prison will help. Together we're notorious, and notoriety fills the world's biggest stages. The scandal will bring them back. Your voice will keep them there. It'll take a few months of practice to break you of your choir habits"—this said with a sneer—"but after that, you can be what you were before. More than that. You can have the world."

"You already promised me that."

"And I gave it to you, didn't I?"

"Not Europe."

He went still. He threw his cigarette into a puddle made by a leak in the canvas. "Things have changed. We don't need anyone to get us there. I can do it myself."

"If I say yes."

He met my gaze. "Can you say no?"

I had thought it all gone. I had never expected it to be a possibility, not ever again. I had meant to live without it. But now that he'd told me I could have my life back, I was stunned at the yearning that surged through me. The stage. The footlights. The audience. My voice, mine alone.

Dear God, how I wanted it.

But then I looked at Gideon and I remembered. The things I'd done . . . I could not live with who I'd become, who he'd made me, and now that I'd seen him again, I knew nothing had changed between us. I was more afraid of him than ever. I'd run three thousand miles to put it all behind me. I wanted to keep it there. I had a new life now.

"I can't go back," I whispered.

"You can't." He repeated the words as if he didn't understand them.

"I won't."

He frowned. "What?"

"I don't want to go back to that life. I'm . . . happy here."

Now he looked as if I'd struck him. "You're happy? You're singing in a church choir! You haven't done that since you were sixteen. You're working in a boxhouse. Christ, have you looked around you? This miserable town . . . you'd trade everything for this? Sabine . . . you could have it all back. You could have everything."

"I've changed," I said weakly. "I don't want those things anymore. You should go back to New York. I'm sure . . . Willa . . . would help you find your feet again. There must be other singers. Perhaps Herr Wirt has some other little girl in his choir—"

"Don't be stupid."

"Leave me alone. Go away. Go . . . back. I'm sorry for what happened. I am. I didn't mean for you to . . . I didn't mean for any of it."

His expression went grim. "Didn't you?"

"No. I—" I struggled to remember, to think. I was miserable with my refusal, desperate to keep to it. His presence overwhelmed me. "I was frightened. I didn't know what to do—"

"You thought I deserved it. At least be honest with me about that."

"No, I . . . yes, I did. I did. I was glad when they arrested you. I was happy when they put you in prison. It kept you away from me. Is that what you want to hear? Now will you leave me alone?"

He was quiet. Outside, the wind came up, snapping the canvas walls around us. I heard the scatter of drops across the top, and I looked up involuntarily and was caught by his eyes.

"I'm not leaving without you," he said.

"Then you'll be in Seattle a long time."

"I think I can bear it."

"Marguerite!"

We both started at the sound of Charlotte's voice as she called from the yard beyond. "Marguerite! Where are you? They're waiting for you!"

"I have to go." I started to move past him.

He caught my arm. His touch was charged. I froze.

He said, "I'm at the New Brunswick Hotel."

The irony of that was too much. The old Squire's Opera House. I laughed—a short, raw expulsion of breath. "Of course you are."

"Meet me there tonight."

"Marguerite!" Charlotte's voice was coming closer.

"I can't. I have to work."

"Then tomorrow morning."

"No."

"If you don't show up, I'll come looking for you," he said, his voice smooth and unperturbed, the threat he intended unmistakable. "Is that what you want? Perhaps I'll find whoever was asking questions—"

"Marguerite!"

"You owe me," he said. "Don't forget."

As if I could. As if I could forget any of the obligation or the guilt that had haunted me since I'd left him. As if his not being here had made his presence any less felt or real.

I nodded reluctantly. "Very well. Tomorrow morning."

He released me and stepped back. I said nothing else; I fled the canvas shelter, leaving him behind, hurrying into the yard, where Charlotte was just turning the corner.

She stopped short. "Where were you? Robert said he'd left you with some man, and I was afraid. . . . "

"Don't worry," I said, going up to her, taking her arm, leading her away from the canvas, back toward the church door, trying to reassure her. "I just needed a bit of air."

She frowned. "You all right?"

"I'm fine."

She stared into my face as if she could read the truth there, and I worked to keep my expression even. I saw the moment she believed me. She nodded shortly and turned back to the church.

I followed her to the step, to the door. It wasn't until we were inside that I could draw a breath, but I couldn't relax. He was still all around me, his presence like a brand that marked me. I smelled the smoke from his cigarette in my hair, I felt his touch on my arm. But mostly I heard his words like a relentless echo: *You could have it all back. You could have everything.* And that was worse, because their temptation mocked me; they threw the truth into my face, and I knew it was not just him I had to be afraid of—it was myself.

From the Journal of Sabine Conrad

JANUARY 16, 1877—Last night I went with Alain to Mrs. Stevens's New Year's soiree. He is the dinner guest *du jour*— how the society ladies love all things Continental, and a Frenchman most of all! They were quite jealous of me for commanding so much of his attention. It is true; he is very ardent and considerate, and though I have grown weary of these parties, where each hostess tries to outdo the other with their ostentation, Alain made it all seem amusing. He told me that Mrs. Parr looked like a horse decked out for the New York Circus, and that the cloud of perfume hovering about Mrs. Williams barely disguised the stink of her constant flatulence, and then he whispered in my ear that the orchids looked very like a woman's cunny, and he never came near one without the urge to bury his face in it. As obscene as it was, it made me laugh and choke on my champagne. He says things that others are thinking but don't dare to voice, and he is always surprising me.

He is also an excellent dancer, and he held me very close during the waltz, planting a secret kiss beneath my ear when no one was looking, and asked when I was going to leave my guard and come away with him, and I laughed and told

him I was ready to go to France whenever he was, and had he
any plans for when that might be?

He didn't answer me; he never does. He only says he is
not quite ready yet . . . he's looking for a mezzo now. But
when I teased him that I was beginning to despair that I shall
ever see Paris, he swept me off the dance floor and pulled me
down the hall to an empty parlor, and he closed the doors behind us so we were in darkness. Then his hands were all over
me, and his mouth too, and I let him unbutton my gown and
lift my breasts from my corset and bury his face between
them. I even helped him. All I could think was how much
Gideon says we need the money Paris will bring us, and how
much I want to be there. And I like Alain very much and find
him handsome, so it was not unpleasant.

Then I heard a sound—a maid passing in the hallway who
could no doubt hear us, because she made a great commotion
with a tray of glasses, and suddenly I thought of the whore on
my birthday and Leonard Jerome and McAlester's pale white
body thrusting against mine and I was confused and repulsed. I was afraid of myself.

So I pushed Alain away and told him I could not.

He seemed very offended. When I tried to soothe him, he
said he wondered if I was the prima donna he needed after all
and then he stalked away. So there I was, in a gown half unbuttoned and falling open, and no one there to do it up for
me, and I could not go back out to the party that way. It took
me some time of peeking out the door before I saw another
maid come down the hallway and asked her to restore me. It
was humiliating.

When I went back to the party, I could not find Alain anywhere. Mr. Stevens said he had seen him leave. Mr. Parr offered me his carriage home, which was exceedingly kind.

Gideon was in his room, going over receipts, no matter that
it was very late, and he looked tired and disheveled and there
were great circles beneath his eyes. My heart hurt to see him
so, but still . . . I did not want to come near him suddenly.

I was afraid that he would touch me, though I wanted that too. I wanted him to kiss every part of me that Alain had touched, to erase him, and yet I knew if he did I would forget myself, and I did not want that either.

He asked me if I had enjoyed the ball and said that by this time next year we would be in Europe, and I would be charming the people of Italy and Germany and England too.

That confusion I'd felt with Alain came over me again. Gideon motioned for me to come sit upon his lap, and when I hesitated he frowned and asked what troubled me. I could not tell him—how could I explain the things I'd been thinking? I do not even understand them myself.

I could not think of an excuse not to go to him, and there was a part of me too that said to just go, that it was easier to forget myself and not think too hard. So I sat on his lap and he kissed me and said how magnificent I was.

Europe is so close—it is what I have wished for; it is what Barret wanted for me. I am already as high as I can climb in America. Should I just stay here and wait for other singers to supplant me? Gideon is right; Europe is my future.

Now I am nervous that I have offended Alain past bearing. Tomorrow, I shall write him a note to apologize.

JANUARY 17, 1877—Alain has answered my note with a very lovely one of his own, apologizing for his "boorish behavior," and saying that I am sometimes so lovely it is all he can do to keep his distance. So I am forgiven. Thank God.

FEBRUARY 8, 1877—Tomorrow is Ash Wednesday, and the end of the season, so there will now be fewer parties and balls until the summer, when everyone goes to Newport. I was invited to the ball at the Vanderbilts', which will be the last of the season, but I have declined to go, and Gideon has sent a note to Alain saying I have a fever and must rest. It will do Alain good to miss me tonight; I think he is becoming far too certain of me and he is not as attentive as formerly.

Also, I admit here and nowhere else: I am relieved to not have to be charming for a few hours. I so rarely have an evening to myself that I am quite looking forward to it.

* * *

N.B. I have asked Gideon to take me to dinner. I cannot bear my thoughts when I am alone. I cannot bear to write them.

MARCH 5, 1877—This morning I woke early, and Gideon was still sound asleep beside me, and he looked so beautiful in the morning light that I could not keep from touching him. I felt when he started awake, but he didn't move and just lay there and let me run my fingers down his chest. Then I pressed my hand flat over his heart and he took my fingers in his and kissed the very center of my palm, and I shivered at how pleasing it was.

Then he whispered that Alain had told him he'd found the mezzo he was looking for: some woman from Chicago whom Gideon had never heard of, but he told me I was still Alain's favorite.

There came a great lump into my stomach and I thought I might cry, and when he rolled me beneath him I held him so close he very nearly could not withdraw in time, and still I could not let go. Finally he pried my hands from around his neck, laughing at me until he saw my tears. He asked me what was wrong and I said nothing, and then he frowned and made to get out of bed. I grabbed him back and begged him to stay with me just a little longer. He was confused, I know, but he obliged. He cradled me in his arms, and I buried my face in his shoulder. Then he asked very, very quietly if Alain had done something to offend me, and if I wanted to give up Paris. And I was filled with the most horrible panic. I said no—I think I almost screamed it—and his arms tightened about me and he sighed and said in that case I shouldn't worry. He would make certain we got there, and there was a look in his eyes that made me say I would do what I could to keep Alain's interest, and I doubted any little mezzo from Chicago could compete with me.

MARCH 24, 1877—Today I went to the theater to practice, except that Gideon was not there as we'd agreed. He'd sent a man to say he was running late, and I was to wait for him. So I wandered the wings, and I was walking past one of the practice rooms when I heard voices inside—two singers from the chorus, I think, though I didn't recognize them. The door was open, and they were talking about someone, and I stopped and stayed out of sight because they were speaking quietly, and it was so obviously gossip, and I was bored. Then one of them said, "Everyone knows how she did it. It's all the talk." And the other one answered, "Perhaps. But her voice doesn't hurt either—I've never heard its like." And then the one said something about how liaisons with people like Jerome and Belmont could do more for a career than talent, and she wished she had thought of fucking a European impresario, and her friend answered that it didn't seem to be working. "She's not in Paris, after all," and the other said, "Oh, she'll work it to her advantage soon enough. See if she doesn't. Some people will do anything to get what they want," and they laughed and I realized they were talking about me.

I felt sick to my stomach, and I told myself to walk away, but I couldn't. Because then the one said, "Well, I'd give just about anything for a manager like Gideon Price," and the other said, "I'd give anything to know what goes on between the two of them. It's strange, don't you think? The way she jumps to do his bidding?" and the one snickered and said, "My guess is she's jumping on something else of his as well."

That was when I made myself walk away. I nearly ran past the open door and to the exit. I wasn't even thinking—all I wanted was to get away from their talk and the horrible way it made me feel, because it was true, all of it, and that was the worst thing. I was near tears, and the gossip was ringing in my ears and as I went outside into the sunlight I remembered Willa standing in my hotel room, telling me what they called me in Kleindeutschland.

I hardly saw anyone or anything. I didn't know where I was going and I didn't care. All I wanted was to get the voices out of my head. Then suddenly a drover called out to me to watch out, and I looked up to see I was blocks from the theater, and there were peddlers in the street pushing their carts and wagons blocking the road and I realized I was near Washington Market.

I saw all those stalls and all the things for sale and for a moment I wanted just to be the Sabine Conrad who'd gone with Mama every week to the market, the girl who sang in the church choir and in the Völksstadt. I had not been to the market for so long, and it seemed so far away from everything, and that's what I wanted, though it was stupid, I know. So I walked the market, and for a few minutes I was my old self, and then it all changed. I was at a stall selling oranges from Cuba and they were so bright and sunny-looking that they made my mouth water. The peddler recognized me and of course he knew nothing of the gossip. He only knew I was the famous Sabine Conrad. He chose the very best for me and said, "You do me a great honor, Miss Conrad," and pressed the bag into my hands and refused my coin. And I was very glad I was not the old Sabine Conrad after all. Then I realized a crowd had come around me so tightly I could not move. They were trying to touch me and pushing to get to me. Men and women and children, and I heard my name on their lips so it was a constant whisper that sounded like the breeze coming off the Battery. Then a little girl, pushed by her mother, reached up to touch the ruffle of my gown, and I smiled at her, though I was feeling a little nervous at how neatly I was trapped, and then her mother called, "Hurry now, Jenny!" and the child grabbed one of the buttons that went in a line up my sleeve and jerked so it came loose in her hand. She yelled, "I got it, Mama! I got it!" and before I could do anything, she vanished into the crowd.

After that it became quite uncontrollable. Someone tore the ruffle from my skirt, and someone else took the feather from my hat. They had me backed into the peddler's stall, and I dropped the bag of oranges. They went rolling, and everyone raced after them as if they were golden coins. I am quite used to such things, but usually Gideon is there to direct and protect me, and I missed him very much and was frightened. Some of the people were wild-eyed as if they might tear me apart.

The peddler came in front of me with a broom and threatened to beat them all and call the police if they did not leave me alone, and finally they did, though they did not dissipate completely, and I hired the peddler's son, who was a large, strapping boy, to walk me home. I had been trapped there for more than an hour.

I stepped into the lobby, and the first thing I saw were the two police watchmen who are sometimes there, and Gideon with them looking frantic. When he saw me, he hurried over and I saw him take in my disheveled state and he turned to the peddler's son and asked if there were any reason he should not directly turn him over to the police.

It took me some time to calm Gideon and explain. He was furious. He called me foolish, and told me I was not to do such a thing again, and how was he to protect me against my own nature? And all I could think was what that nature had brought me. All I could hear was the talk of those two stupid girls saying that I jumped to do his bidding, and I stood in that lobby and listened to him chastise me and knew how true it was and how it will always be that way, because I want so much and Gideon knows how to get it, and I love him so it's like a disease in my soul and I grow more and more sick with it every day.

APRIL 2, 1877—I hear Barret's voice all the time now— sometimes it's so real and loud that I turn, expecting to see him, hoping I don't, because I don't want to see the disappointment on his face. I know what he would say; he says it in my head all the time. "This isn't who you are, Bina. He makes you forget yourself." And then he whispers, "You must leave him before he destroys you."

But I can't leave him. I don't want to. I don't. Without him, what would I do? Where would I go? He has made everything possible. He created Sabine Conrad. Everything I love has come from him: the singing, the fame, the money. He promised me he would make my dreams come true, and he has. They don't exist without him. I would not exist. I'm afraid if I were to leave everything behind there would be nothing left of me.

APRIL 6, 1877—Yesterday was the Grand Easter Charity Ball given at the Academy, and as I'd told Mrs. Murray several weeks ago that I would lend my name to such an attractive festival for children (and of course, because August Belmont, who is treasurer, had kindly suggested to her I might), I went and made myself very agreeable.

It was very nice, with a Carnival and a Grand March with Russian Cossacks and a procession of Tyroleans who danced the Tyrolean Waltz. There was even an Esmeralda in a golden coach drawn by four goats (who were decorated better than half the people there). I sang with the Juvenile Orchestra, who had all dressed in costumes of Mozart's day. They were charming, if a little uneven.

By the time the Grand Ball started at ten, I was exhausted from smiling so much and being so kind to all the little children, as delightful as they are, and so when Gideon suggested that we get some champagne and he and Alain and I should go back to the hotel, I was more than ready to do so.

Alain and Gideon were half drunk, and I was annoyed because they were having so much fun. So when we got back to the Fifth Avenue, I drank some champagne from the bottle. The bubbles fizzed up my nose and ran down my chin and

I coughed and Alain and Gideon laughed until I thought they would burst. Then Gideon grabbed me about the waist and twirled me around the room and gave me more champagne to drink until I was a little drunk myself.

Alain called that we should waltz, and so Gideon began to hum a tune and Alain waltzed me about the room quite clumsily. We were all laughing and very gay, and soon we had all drunk so much that we were stumbling. Then Alain took a bottle of laudanum and poured some into my champagne, and when I told him no, he said he did not realize I was such a staid old maid, and was I going to put a pall on the evening? And so I took the champagne and drank it to prove I could have as much fun as they.

After that I do not remember very much—only a few things, like images from a dream. I remember that Gideon pulled me to him and kissed me so deeply I moaned, and then suddenly Alain was there, and Gideon let me go into his arms, and Alain was kissing me too, and they passed me back and forth until I could hardly tell them apart. And though I thought how bad it was to be doing this, I didn't stop, because it was only kissing, and I knew that I must make certain I was Alain's favorite. I made myself think of Paris.

Then Gideon grabbed the laudanum and went to stretch out on the settee. He took a long drink and looked at me, and I knew what he wanted me to do, and knew too that I would do it, and the laudanum made everything seem all right.

Alain gave me more champagne, and the next thing I remember I was lying on the bed in only my chemise and my corset unhooked to expose my breasts, which Alain was nuzzling in a sleepy way, and I felt so languid and the world was so soft—it was as if I were locked inside a dream. I did not even mind his mouth on my breasts, though I knew I would mind it very much when I woke. Gideon was still on the settee, and when he took another drink of the laudanum, it roused me and brought me a little into myself, and I thought I should not be here, and that if I did not leave now I might not ever, so

I rolled off the bed, dislodging Alain, who only made a mild sound of protest and collapsed back again.

I thought I must be sleepwalking—I was very unsteady, and the floor was like walking on pillows. Gideon grabbed my hand as I passed him and pressed it to his mouth, and whispered "You still love me?" or perhaps he said "You still belong to me?" The world was in a fog and his voice was very low and I could not be sure. It didn't matter. The answer to either question was yes, and when I told him that, he let me go, and I went to my room through the adjoining door and locked it behind me.

And now I feel very sick, not just from the champagne and the laudanum, but at how willing I was to "jump" at Gideon's request. The only reason I did not fuck Alain was because he'd had too much laudanum—and I would have done it in front of Gideon too, and who knows what would have happened then? Perhaps there would have been the two of them together . . . which makes me so ashamed I do not think I can look at either of them. And so I have locked myself in my room, and when Gideon came to take me to lunch I told him to go away. I am afraid of who I am when I am with him, and of how much I want to please him. I am afraid of what I will do.

MAY 10, 1877—Alain has gone to Boston, and Gideon and I are in Chicago, as I am performing for two weeks in concert. The crowds have been large and wonderful. Each night has been full of suppers and cotillions held in my honor, and Gideon and I are feted wherever we go.

But he is not happy and I am desperate, because since that night in April, Alain has not mentioned Paris, and has been rather cold. I fear I may have lost his interest, and Gideon frets that Alain will find some new soprano in Boston. He has heard of two who are very much loved there, both younger than me and rumored to be quite pretty.

I am not sleeping well. I only lie there and listen to Gideon breathe, and deep into the night I find myself crying. I think of those two women gossiping at the theater and everything I've done so that Gideon and I might have what we want. The question torments me: if I were to leave him, could I return to myself? Or have I already given too much away to retrieve it? I remember how Barret told me there were other ways to have what I wanted, but I don't know what those ways could be, or if I could find them alone.

JUNE 3, 1877—Gideon and I returned to New York City yesterday, and Alain has not yet returned from Boston. This morning Gideon went to the theater to rehearse the new tenor. I have felt very unsettled and restless, and so I went to the Ladies' Sitting Room for tea, and Mrs. Burbage, who also stays at the hotel, said she had heard my "dear Friend M. DeRosier" was in the city last week squiring about some "lovely little nightingale he said he brought from Boston." I pretended I knew all about it. I told her Alain was auditioning for the troupe he intended to take to Paris. But I drank my tea very quickly and came back here to my room.

When Gideon returned I told him all about it. He was very quiet, and I did not miss how he looked at me, with such speculative eyes. And so I said that when Alain returned, I thought I would invite him to a private supper in my room.

When I said it Gideon slammed a desk drawer shut so hard my penknife rolled off and the ink bottle rocked, and he said I must do what I would, that he couldn't get me to Paris without Alain, and then he stalked out, and I do not know where he has gone.

So it is decided. When Alain comes back, I will make him my lover. It has been inevitable from the start, and I was a fool to tell myself otherwise. Gideon expects it. Even I have known all along it was coming to this.

And now I wonder: how many more times will I be so obliged? After France, there will be England, and then Germany and Italy. There will be new impresarios for every one.

No, I will not. Alain will be the last. I promise myself: Alain will be the last.

JUNE 28, 1877—Alain has sent a telegram saying he will be back next week in time to celebrate my birthday, and I have decided: when he returns, I will ask him to take me to Paris alone. I am going to leave Gideon—the thought makes me miserable, but I can see no other way. It will only go on like this forever and forever if I do not. After Alain, there will only be someone else I must seduce, and someone after that, and someone after that. . . . There will only be a long line of things I must do, and of course I will do them. All Gideon has to do is look at me, and I will do whatever he wants, and I am frightened. Thank God we never married. I no longer believe I have the will to deny him anything.

I cannot stay. It will destroy me to stay.

JULY 15, 1877—It is very late. Alain is delayed. He now says he won't return to the city until August.

Gideon and I celebrated my birthday very soberly. There was no performance tonight, and so we went to dinner in the hotel, and I ordered my favorite things and we had champagne. He had another diamond star added to my brooch, which made me cry—he thought it was for joy, I'm sure, but it was out of guilt and misery for what I mean to do. He gave me too some sapphire and diamond earrings to match. Then we went back to our rooms. Gideon kissed me and said Happy Birthday and that he could not stay because he must pay some bills and write some letters, and I am so weak and despairing at the thought that I must leave him soon that I pulled him to me and kissed him like a wanton in the hallway, and I had unbuttoned his vest and had my hands on his shirt before he stopped me and said, "Not tonight, Sabine."

I am such a fool! I started to cry, and that of course made him feel guilty, and so he came into my room and took me to bed, though he was impatient and did not seem to notice how sad I was, and he left just after.

Now I am thinking of Barret, and the drinking and opium eating he could not give up. Gideon is like that for me. I think I shall have to go very far away to cut him from my heart. At least I still have singing. If I had to give them both up, I think I would shrivel up and die.

AUGUST 16, 1877—Tonight is the night.

Alain returned last week, and he has been very flirtatious and on his best behavior. He is now talking about returning to Paris very soon, but he still will not say when, and by the way he looks at me, I know I am the one who will make up his mind. At dinner last night, when Gideon went to speak to someone across the room, Alain leaned very close and took my hand, and beneath the table he ran his thumb along the inside of my bare arm until he raised shivers on my skin. His eyes grew very dark, and he said he dreamed of my breasts and when would he have the chance to see them again, because it was the only reason he had returned to New York. "You do not mean to disappoint me, do you, chérie?" he asked, and I told him that I had planned a special supper in my room for us alone whenever he wished, and he said, "Tomorrow."

So it is done, and my stomach is upset thinking of it.

I told Gideon that the dinner is tonight, and he has been short with me all day, which is what I want. I think if he were kind I would lose my courage. There is a part of me that cannot bear the thought of never seeing him again. But there is another part—a bigger part—that tells me I must save myself. And he no longer needs me. He is a brilliant impresario and everyone knows it. There are singers who would do anything to work with him. The rest of the company love him. He will be a success even without me.

He is gone to the theater now. He told me he will take the others to supper and not return until very late, though neither of us will admit the reason for him to stay away.

I mean to ask Alain to hide me at another hotel until he can arrange for passage out of the city, because I know Gideon will not let me go so easily, and I do not trust myself to hold to my purpose if he were to try to dissuade me.

So much depends on tonight that I have taken special care. I am wearing my dressing gown of pink silk, which is Gideon's favorite, and the corset that matches it and very fine silk stockings with ribboned garters and slippers with little jeweled bows. I brushed my hair until it gleamed so golden in the light it did not look real. I am wearing four strands of pearls, and I spent a great deal of time arranging them so that they emphasize my breasts and let one of the strands fall inside the lace of my corset so that Alain will feel compelled to follow it there.

The dinner I've ordered up is oysters and strawberries and grapes and capon stuffed with sweetbreads and a silken custard and wine—there is a great deal of wine.

I am nervous, though I think I have no reason to be. Alain wants me desperately; I think he would do anything for me. I know he will be happy to take me from Gideon—how could he not? I am Sabine Conrad, after all, and I mean tonight to satisfy his every desire, and perhaps some he doesn't realize he has.

Now all that remains is the waiting. He will be here soon.

After tonight, my new life will begin.

CHAPTER 18

Seattle, Washington Territory—January 1882

I drank three shots of whiskey in quick succession, nearly choking as the last one burned its way down my throat. Duncan frowned at me. "You all right, Marguerite?"

"No," I snapped, pouring another.

I glanced at the stage. Annie and Lil were up there now, dressed in trousers and shirts as they sang their ribald song, grinning knowingly at the audience while the men hooted and laughed in reply. For the years that the Palace had been a box-house, I'd watched these girls and listened to the music and managed to inure myself to it all. But that was impossible to-night. I felt the lure of that stage, as simple as it was—new now, and larger, but still plain, with holes drilled in the apron for footlights that had not yet been installed and no curtain or drop or single bit of scenery. I saw the sweat glow upon Annie's skin and the way Lil's eyes shone when she bowed, and I remembered how it felt to be up there. The stage in the Völksstadt had been simpler than this, and I had loved every moment upon it, and the memory of that came so hard and fast I was unprepared. Gideon's words had done that. For more than four years, I'd managed to hold the barrier between the world I lived in now and the one I'd left behind, and it had taken only a single sentence to collapse it. *"You could have it all back.... You could be what you were before. More than that."*

Sarah bounced up to the bar, her sleeve slipping from her shoulder, her hair prettily disarrayed. "Mr. Ryan says he needs you at his table, Miss Olson."

"Tell him to solve his problems himself." I drank the fourth shot in a single gulp. Still, the numbness I'd hoped for didn't come. I looked at the bottle, wondering if I would have to finish the entire thing. "Better yet, you go over there. Suck whoever you must to calm them down."

Sarah looked startled, but she left again quickly, and I saw her whisper something to one of the other girls heading toward the bar. The girl glanced at me and turned around again.

Duncan said, "Ain't many drinks getting sold."

I knew what he meant; that I was the reason for it, standing there as I was, glowering at everyone who came near. I grabbed the bottle of whiskey and the glass and said, "I'll be in Johnny's office."

Once I was inside, I shut the door with my hip and slammed the glass onto Johnny's desk. Then I took the bottle and went to stand at the window, leaning against the weathered wooden Indian with his handful of cigars that Johnny kept there. The scent of tobacco wafted up to me; in a sudden fit of pique I grabbed two cigars and snapped them in half, dropping them to the floor and grinding them beneath my foot. The smell was even stronger then. I saw him before me, smoking his cigarette as if the very fact of it wasn't a change, watching me with those long blue eyes. . . .

"You could have it all again. You could have everything."

I closed my eyes, and the memories rose through the haze of alcohol, soft and blurry and alluring. The feel of a stage floor beneath my feet, the glare of the footlights, that growing nervousness as I waited in the wings, as I raised my forehead for his kiss and his words, *"In boca al lupo."* The feel of my voice, full strength, not held back, not blending with nine others, my own distinct sound. The straining of my lungs, the push of air from my diaphragm, the sense that a single note might sear everything away—

"What the hell are you doing?"

The door thudded against the wall hard enough to slam shut again. I turned slowly from the window.

Johnny strode to me, jerking the whiskey bottle from my hands, throwing it to the floor. The neck broke off, and the bottle rolled crazily into the corner, spilling whiskey all the way, and all I could do was watch it in dismay.

"I wasn't done with that," I said.

He trapped my chin, forcing me to look at him. "You got a meeting tonight. Or have you forgotten?"

Portland. "You can have it without me."

"What the hell has got into you?"

"Whiskey," I said with a nasty smile. "And there would have been more of it if you hadn't spilled it."

He let me go so quickly I stumbled. "Lyman Kerwin is sitting out there at a table right now, waiting for the both of us. He ain't going to be disappointed."

"I'm not going out there."

"The hell you ain't." Johnny's expression was grim. He grabbed my arm, hard, and I thought, *there will be bruises there tomorrow, and then what will Gideon say?* and then I was angry with myself for thinking of him at all.

"I'm in no mood to seduce a man tonight."

"You don't got to seduce him. You only got to be your charming self."

"I can't do that either."

"Well, ain't it a pity you got no choice. You knew he was coming tonight. If he has to wait 'til tomorrow, my bet is the whole thing's off. So put on a smile, honey, and get ready to charm the fuck out of him. Oh, and Prosch is here as well."

"The newspaper editor?"

"Kerwin's idea. He wants an 'objective viewpoint' on whether Seattle can 'support culture.' " Johnny's voice was mocking. His fingers tightened; he opened the door and escorted me out, whispering, "Smile."

The whiskey was roiling through my veins; my feet were unsteady. But I did what he asked—even drunk as I was, I knew how stupid it would be to challenge him. He led me through the bar, a riot of noise and motion I could hardly focus on. Johnny took me to the farthest table and said, "Mr. Kerwin, meet my partner, Miss Olson. And I believe the two of you are already acquainted, Prosch."

"Delightful to see you again, Miss Olson."

I blinked, trying to focus. Mr. Prosch's large forehead, prominent ears, larger than I remembered. Something warned me to be careful; I was too addled to remember why. I looked at the other man. Lyman Kerwin. He had a long face, thinning hair, full lips beneath a mustache that was scarcely there, and a straggling Van Dyke beard. He rose—his eyes seemed very close together, too close . . . had he one or two?—and bowed slightly. "Miss Olson. How pleased I am to make your acquaintance."

Johnny pulled out a chair, nearly pushing me into it before he took one of his own. Sally was at my shoulder as if she'd suddenly appeared out of vapor, and I jumped a little. "How about a drink?" she asked.

"Bring a bottle," Johnny said shortly. "And three glasses. Miss Olson ain't drinking."

"Like hell I'm not," I said. "Four glasses, Sally," and when she left and Johnny glared at me, I broadened my smile and ignored him and scooted my chair around the table until I was sitting next to Mr. Kerwin, and then I said, "What can I do to convince you to join our circuit?"

Johnny looked thunderous. "Now, Margie—"

Kerwin waved his protest away. "No, no, Langford, it's all right. It's a fair question, and I appreciate Miss Olson's frankness. My concern is whether we can get the acts we need, even with San Francisco involved."

"The city is growing day by day," Prosch said. "*Faust* made an impressive showing, better than I imagined."

"A one-time treat will always draw, of course. What about a regular diet?"

"We're ready for it," Johnny said. "I'm thinking something big to start, something that shows we ain't playing around."

"A combination act," Prosch suggested. "Or perhaps, if I might make a suggestion, something like *Uncle Tom's Cabin*."

Johnny snorted. "Christ, if I have to see another production of *Uncle Tom*. . . ."

"An opera singer, then. In concert," the newspaper editor suggested.

The warning buzzed again in my head. I wanted another drink. I glanced around for Sally, wondering where the hell the bottle was.

"You might be able to get Ellen Siebert," Prosch said.

"Who the hell is Ellen Siebert? That ain't the kind of big I'm talking about," Johnny said.

Kerwin smiled. "She's good enough. Who else do you expect to get in this city? Pauline Lucca? Sabine Conrad?"

Sally brought the bottle. I nearly tore it from her hands. I poured myself a shot, ignoring Johnny's warning glance, and drank it, then poured another. Johnny took the bottle and poured for the others.

Prosch leaned forward. "That maybe isn't so far-fetched, you know. I've got a friend in New York. A fellow newspaperman. He says Conrad's manager got out of prison several weeks ago."

I could not even breathe. I clutched my glass and thought of Gideon, only a few blocks away, if they could have known it.

"So what?" Johnny asked.

"So . . . there are some of us who think he'll go to wherever she is."

"You think he knows where she is?"

"Who better?"

"So where is he now?"

Prosch shrugged. "No one's seen him. Not yet. But someone will. Men like that don't stay hidden. He'll turn up again."

I wanted to leave, but even as drunk as I was I knew that would only raise Johnny's suspicions, so I stayed. The talk went on, but I did not hear anything they said. All I could see was Gideon's face before me, all I could think of was more whiskey. I drank another, and another. And then, I couldn't think of anything. I hardly knew what I was doing, or what I was saying. At one point, I found myself draped over Kerwin's shoulder while he and Prosch laughed and he told me some obscene limerick, and the lights and sound in the Palace were nothing but a big kaleidoscope swirling around me, and I think that was when I slipped my hand between the lapels of Kerwin's vest and looked brazenly at Johnny, wanting to see jealousy in his eyes, daring him to stop me. His careful expression pricked at me—not what I wanted. No banked passion, no promise of something darker, no hidden games, and I leaned closer to Kerwin, brushing my lips against his cheek.

Johnny stood and said something, but whatever it was got lost in the kaleidoscope. Suddenly Kerwin wasn't there. Suddenly I was on my feet, and Johnny had hold of me, and I was stumbling after him through the Palace and up the stairs to his room, trying to catch my balance against the flimsy curtains of the boxes lining the hallway. When he opened the door and we went inside, I was glad. This was what I wanted—jealousy, punishment. I wanted him to take away the mocking blue eyes, the thoughts of my other life. I turned to him, pressing my hands against his chest. He was so solid. All muscle and brawn. Not thin from four years of prison—

I felt for the buttons at his trousers. Johnny grabbed my hands, stilling them, his fingers strong about my wrists. He threw me to the bed, and I sprawled upon it like a whore, my hair falling down around my shoulders. I waggled my fingers at him.

"Come here," I said.

He turned away, heading for the door. "Sleep off whatever's got into you."

It took me a moment to realize he was leaving. I struggled to get off the bed. "Johnny, no, stay—"

"I thought we were past all this," he said impatiently. "Who is it you want, Margie? Me? Or Kerwin? Or someone else?"

His words cut through the fog of my drunkenness. I could only stare at him.

He said, "You want to fuck Kerwin, just say the word. I'll have him brought up. I'm sure he'll be happy to oblige."

I could not answer; it was so far from what I'd intended— what had I intended? To make Johnny jealous, to use him to forget. To make today disappear. Suddenly I wanted to cry.

At that moment, the whiskey turned, my stomach grabbed, and I jerked myself over the edge of the bed, vomiting.

Johnny said, "I ain't here to clean up your messes," and left me there.

In the morning, I woke alone, sprawled on the mattress with the stench of vomit heavy in the air, and I groaned and crawled from bed, my head pounding, feeling sick again as I nearly slipped on the pool beside the bed. I tiptoed around it, going to the basin, pouring water, gulping it down with trembling hands before I plunged my face in and let the cool water do its work. I washed myself as carefully and thoroughly as I could, trying not to think of why I was taking such care, wincing at every too-loud splash.

When I was finished, I cleaned up the vomit and opened the door to the little balcony so that the cold wet wind rushed inside, and only then did I feel better. I did not think about last night, not about Mr. Prosch's words, not about what I'd done. The morning was far advanced; there was someplace I had to be. I was possessed with the urge both to hurry and to delay.

I grabbed my cloak and crept from Johnny's room. The Palace was dark and quiet, smelling of whiskey and smoke and the lingering stench of sweat. I heard my own footsteps echo as I went down the stairs. Johnny was nowhere to be seen, but Duncan was behind the bar, and he looked up in surprise and said, "You're up early."

"Where's Johnny?"

"Sleeping in his office."

I went to the back door. "I'll be back later."

"He'll ask where you are."

"Breakfast." I braved a smile; it seemed to split my skull. "With Charlotte."

Duncan nodded, and I slipped out the back door, breathing a sigh of relief.

I had not realized how nervous I was until I was outside. I took a deep breath of the cold air, but it did nothing to ease how tightly I was wound. The rain was light but steady, the clouds so low it seemed one could reach up to touch them. There was a delivery wagon across the street, a drover unloading barrels, and I drew up the hood of my cloak, pulling it forward in an attempt to disguise myself. Though I doubted anyone would take the time to notice me, I did not want it getting back to Johnny that I'd made a morning visit to the New Brunswick Hotel.

I told myself to slow, but my nerves sent me racing onward. I was jangled and unsettled when I reached Commercial Street and the old door of Squire's Opera House. I glanced up at the sign reading NEW BRUNSWICK HOTEL before I went in and climbed the stairs.

The lobby was still wide and open, though not so much as before, because there was a desk there now, behind which a man stood, and behind him a row of cubbyholes holding keys.

He looked up as I came in, and I approached him and said, "I'm looking for Mr. Price's room."

"Around the corner to your right, number ten," he said, and I nodded my thanks and went past him, following his direction, into the hallway that had once been the theater, sliced up now, the ghost voices from *Faust* imprisoned behind pine boards and wallpaper. The hallway was dim, the gaslight turned low. The closer I got to his room, the more my footsteps faltered. I was at number ten before I was ready. I stood there for a moment and then I knocked lightly, tentatively—perhaps he would not hear.

But then I heard his steps, and the door opened, and I was blinking in the light from the room that seemed too bright after the dim hall.

"You've come," he said.

"Did I have a choice?"

He stepped back, motioning me inside, shutting the door, and I was thrown so far back into the past it was as if there were no present to be had or as if I did not exist in it.

The room was small and not elegant, like every hotel we'd stayed in during those early tours. His clothes were strewn over the back of a chair, and there was a folio on a desk, thick with sheaves of paper—music, I knew, because such a folio had always been present, everywhere we'd gone. A pair of mud-spattered boots by the door, and on the small table by the bed a lamp and a book and two framed photographs. The one of me in the blue silk dress and pearls, taken in San Francisco, and beside it the one of the two of us together.

I heard myself make a noise, a little moan, and I turned again to the door. "This is a mistake." I reached for the door-knob, suddenly desperate to get out.

He set his hand against the door. "You're not going anywhere."

"I'm not staying."

"Where's the brave girl I used to know? My Sabine was never afraid of anything."

"I'm not *your* Sabine. And stop calling me that. It's no longer my name."

"It's who you are. That won't ever change."

"It already has."

"Not for me."

"You're the past," I said. "And that's where I want you to stay."

He said, "You don't get what you want this time. I've just spent four years in hell for you—"

"Four years is hardly enough time to make up for everything."

"For everything?"

"For Alain," I spat. "And the rest too. Leonard, San Francisco. All of it." I let my anger grow, a safer emotion than fear. I threw the words at him. "I did whatever you asked of me. Whatever you wanted."

He laughed disbelievingly. "Whatever *I* wanted? My God, what a story you've told yourself."

"I never would have been in that hotel room if not for you. You told me we needed Alain. You told me we couldn't get to Paris without him. You told me to convince him."

"Convince him, yes. Not kill him."

"You wanted me to take him to bed." I felt a surge of satisfaction when he flinched. "I did it all for you."

"Don't fool yourself, Sabine. You had your own aspirations in mind every moment."

"I don't want to be that person anymore. I don't want to be who you made me."

He looked at me with an expression that was both familiar and not, and for one moment, he was not Gideon at all, but a stranger, and I faltered, uncertain, suddenly more afraid of what had changed about him than of what I knew. "Then don't be," he said.

"How easily you say that now. What would happen, I wonder, the first time a theater manager refused to pay our percentage? Or when some son of the Four Hundred decided to take an interest in my career?"

"What do you want me to say? That I'd keep you out of it, when you've such a talent for persuading men to your way of thinking?"

"You trained me well," I said bitterly.

He shook his head. "That was nothing I taught you, Sabine. That's simply who you are. It's who you've always been. That hasn't changed, has it? I've watched you in that boxhouse, you know. Promising everything with your eyes. Confusing those poor miners so they can hardly see straight—"

"It's not the same," I protested, once again disconcerted that I'd never noticed him there.

"It is, and you know it. You use it easily enough when you want something. It's only when it doesn't work out as you wish that it's someone else's fault."

"Ah, I see. I was to blame. It wasn't you who told me to have a private dinner with Leonard Jerome. It wasn't your plan to have me persuade him to give us money."

"A dinner. I didn't tell you to go to bed with him."

"What else does a private dinner mean?"

"He was enamored of you. He would have given you the money without your becoming his mistress if you'd pressed him."

"How disingenuous you are! You knew exactly what would happen when I went to that hotel."

"I knew what you would probably do," he admitted. "You were like a bludgeon when a tap on the shoulder would do. After all, it takes effort to lead a man along and keep his attention without meaning to fuck him, and you were never one for effort."

"You said we needed the money."

"We did. But I didn't ask you to whore for it. You had to see how jealous I was. You had to know how I hated sharing you. God knows I didn't try to hide it. But none of that mattered to you, did it? You knew exactly how much power you had—all I did was give you permission to do the things you would have done anyway."

His words were like little stones. I refused to feel them. "Oh yes. And you were so faithful yourself."

"More so than you."

"What about Leila? Or Pauline Lucca? Do you mean to tell me I had no reason to be jealous of them?"

"You had no reason."

"You're a liar. Don't tell me you weren't fucking them."

"It wasn't what you think. It was never what you thought."

"What was it then? Chaste little affairs? Flirting and nothing more? Do you really expect me to believe that?"

"Whatever I did, I did for us."

"For us?" I laughed shortly. "How good of you to make such a sacrifice. Forgive me if I don't thank you for it. I should have listened to Barret. He was right about you."

"Barret was a fool."

"He tried to protect me, and you wanted him gone. If not for you, he wouldn't have died."

"You wanted him gone as much as I did," he countered angrily. "He was useless as a manager. We couldn't afford for him to run things. But he could have worked for us in other ways instead. I never wanted him to die. Who tried to stop him from killing himself more than I? You? You ignored what you didn't want to see. Who was it who fished him from the brothels? Who went out in the middle of the night to bring him back from whatever hellhole he wandered into? I kept him alive for years longer than he should have been. You were willing to give him up to get what you wanted. At least admit that."

"You smoked opium with him."

"Of course I did. How was I to know he would take to it the way he did? It was a lark at first. After that . . . I went with him to keep him safe."

"And I suppose you had nothing to do with Willa either? You betrayed her and seduced me. What choice did I have? I was only sixteen—"

"How self-righteous you sound. 'I was only sixteen,' " he mocked. "Ah yes, what a little innocent you were. Following me around with those big blue eyes, pushing those breasts against me as if you didn't know exactly what you were doing. Poor Rinzetti never had a chance, did he?"

"It—it wasn't like that."

"It was exactly like that. Lie to yourself all you want about what happened between us, Sabine, but you can't lie to me. I was there. Yes, I wanted you. But you wanted me too."

"I was too young to know what I wanted."

He laughed. "Everything, as I recall. You wanted me to get it for you, and I did. You were more than willing to do what was required."

He was too close. His words were too loud. "I was a child," I protested weakly.

"You were too young for me," he conceded, and the admission seemed to calm him. "I tried to stay away from you. But you were no innocent." He sighed. "You and me, Bina, . . . we know what we want from the world. I won't apologize for it. If you feel guilty . . . well, you'll have to find a way to live with that. You can run away from me all you want, but you can't run away from what you are."

"I left you because I was afraid of you. I was afraid of what I would do for you, of what I had done. I'm afraid of you still."

"You don't understand, do you?" He stepped back to put space between us, shoving his hand through his hair. "I love you, Bina, but—"

"You love what I can do for you."

His head jerked up. I saw the flare of anger in his eyes, and then with almost rigid calm, he said, "I won't pretend that I don't want something from you, or that I don't think you owe it to me. I do. I want my life back. I want *our* life back. I've spent the last four years thinking of how it could be. I thought . . . it could be different this time." There was something in his eyes—sadness, I thought, and it surprised me and snagged uncomfortably at my heart. "I love you, Sabine, whether you believe it or not. But my days of absolving you are over. I won't be the one to take all the blame. Accept your part. We'll be equals in this, or we won't . . . go on."

My discomfort bloomed and spread. I could not call back my anger. I felt the inexplicable urge to cry. "Why am I here? Why did you ask me to come?"

"Those are two different questions," he said.

I said nothing.

"I don't believe you don't want it." His words were a whisper, as seductive as he must have known they would be. "You loved it. I know you miss it. This time it could be even better."

I looked away as if it could somehow diminish the fierceness of my yearning. I did not want him to see it. "Better? They would never leave me alone. There are reporters *still* looking for me. Dear God, it was bad enough before the scandal."

"I wasn't aware you disliked the attention. I would have said it was the lack that offended you."

"They would never let it be. You know what it would be like. All those questions—"

"You needn't answer them. Let it remain a mystery. They'd only be dissatisfied with whatever you told them, in any case. It would never measure up to what their imaginations provide."

I swallowed hard.

He said softly, "Believe me, Bina, I know. My own imagination has tormented me."

"I've put it all behind me. I'm not going back."

He was quiet for a moment. I knew he was waiting for me to tell him, but I could not. I could not bear to think of it, even now.

Finally he sighed and crossed the room to his dresser. He pulled open the top drawer and took something out, a book, along with something small, wrapped in a handkerchief.

He turned to face me. "These belong to you."

I was afraid again, swept by a panic I didn't understand. "I don't want them."

He came over to me, holding the book out. "They gave everything that was in the room to your family when they took me away. Your jewels—what was left of them, anyway— and your clothes. This. Willa brought it to me."

"I don't want it," I said.

He pressed it into my hands. "Perhaps it would do you good to read it again."

It was my journal. I thought of myself bent over these pages, night after night scrawling on them by the flickering light of a candle first, and then later by a rather ornate oil lamp, the constant scratch of the pen nib on the rough paper. I pushed it back at him. "The stupid ramblings of a very stupid girl."

He made no comment to that, but his full lips curved in a slight smile. He didn't take it. Instead he held out the other thing, the size of his palm, wrapped in a handkerchief. "This is yours too."

This I wanted even less. I had no idea what it was, but it felt dangerous. I shook my head.

He took my other hand and forced the thing into my fingers. It was heavy, round, and flat, and I felt a dread so large and overwhelming it seemed impossible that it might be caused by something so small. I let it lie there in my flattened palm, making no claim.

"Look at it," he whispered.

When I made no move to do so, he pulled back the folds of the handkerchief to reveal a filigreed circlet of gold, close-webbed with sapphires and a large pearl for a moon and nine diamonds—one for each year we'd been together. The last time I'd seen this had been in a pawnshop in Cheyenne, in the owner's dirty hand. I had never thought to look upon it again.

"How did you get this?" My voice sounded flat and far away.

"Pinkertons. When the agent told me he'd found it, I had him buy it back for me."

I stared down at the brooch. I could not look at him.

"You saved it for last," he said quietly. "It must have meant something to you."

I curled my fingers tight around it until I felt the press of the diamonds against my skin. Then I forced myself to release it. I held it out to him. "You should keep it. I think it matters more to you."

He laughed a little. I heard his disappointment. But he didn't take the brooch. He pushed my hand away. "Come back to your life, Sabine," he murmured. "Please."

CHAPTER 19

I tucked the brooch and the journal away beneath rolled stockings in the far corner of the dresser drawer. I thought of what he'd said, *"It would do you good to read it again,"* and my reluctance to do so rose solidly before me. What did the scribblings of the girl I'd been matter? I had already lived through it, and I remembered it too well. Why remind myself of the regrets I had, when all I wanted to do was leave them behind?

It was already time to return to the Palace. I knocked on Charlotte's door and got no answer; she must have already gone. The thought made me hurry. When I got to the boxhouse, there were men gathered around the poker tables, but it would be a slow night, I knew from experience. Mondays always were. I didn't see Johnny, and that was a relief.

I found Charlotte just outside the dressing room, adjusting the ruffle at her bodice. I pulled her aside and said in a low voice, "Have you seen Johnny today?"

"Not yet. I only just got here."

"If he asks, tell him I was with you this morning."

"All right."

I squeezed her arm. "Thank you," I said, starting to move away.

"Why are we lying to him?"

I looked back at her. Now was my chance to tell her the truth. I'd meant to do so eventually, someday, but I realized I wasn't ready to tell her or anyone else about Gideon or what he'd offered me. I felt too unsettled. So I made myself smile and said, "I'll tell you later. I'd best get back to the floor."

I spent the next hour at Jim Ryan's table, trying to make up for my neglect the night before. I forced myself to concentrate on the part I played as if it were a role and I were on a stage, as if the girls singing were the chorus, and the men sitting at the tables and playing cards were scenery. And I found myself watching for him, waiting for his arrival, thinking that at the end of the show I would find him backstage the way I always had, a smile on his face, criticism or praise ready on his lips. *"You were perfect tonight, Sabine. No one plays Marguerite as you do...."*

Then I saw Johnny hovering near the bar, and I remembered last night with Kerwin, and the truth of who I was and what I was came back hard enough that I sank into the nearest chair with the force of my disappointment.

He wandered over. "Feeling all right, honey?"

I shook my head tightly. "Like hell."

"No wonder." He pulled up a chair, straddling it.

"What happened to Mr. Kerwin?"

"At his hotel."

"He hasn't gone back to Portland?"

"Not yet."

"So I didn't ruin everything?"

"Not quite. Thanks to the fact that I got him drunk enough that he's mostly forgot the evening."

I let out a sigh of relief. "Thank God."

"God had nothing to do with it." Johnny's gaze was thoughtful. "He's staying another few days. You want to try again with him? I'd say tonight, but he seems worse off than you."

"You still trust me with him?"

"I don't know. Suppose you tell me what last night was about."

"I was just . . . stupid."

"Ah. Talk it all out at the docks this morning with your tall friend?"

I frowned at him. "The docks?"

"Ain't that where you went so early?"

It took me a moment to remember that I'd asked Charlotte to lie, to realize that he'd spoken to her. "The docks. Yes."

"So now you got it worked out? Whatever was eating you?"

I nodded. "You won't see me that drunk again."

He let out his breath and rose, twisting the chair back into place. "See that you keep that promise." He paused; I felt his gaze hard on my face. "I didn't know you had a fondness for watching ships."

My smile was wooden. "Didn't you?"

"Something new to know." He bent to kiss me, and his lips were soft and warm, and I felt guilty. Yet not guilty enough to keep him there, and I was relieved when he stepped away.

THAT NIGHT, WHEN the last customer left, and Johnny was in his office, I went up to the orchestra loge to bring down the beer glasses the musicians always left behind. There was an empty bottle of whiskey turned onto its side on top of the piano, sitting in a pool of spilled drink, and with a sigh, I picked it up and wiped at the whiskey with my sleeve.

I sat on the piano bench, setting the bottle aside. I raised the lid and laid my fingers gently enough upon the keys that they didn't depress, and I looked down at my hands and saw Gideon's instead. His long fingers, knobby jointed, spreading and jumping over the keys without effort, as if they moved separate from his thought, so quick and sure they were.

Slowly, I depressed a key, a low, resonant E that seemed to vibrate into the floor. When the sound faded, I heard some of the girls talking below, readying to leave.

I pressed another key—a G this time, and then higher, to a B and then an A, and when I hit the A I let out the air from my lungs in a matching hum—so softly I barely heard myself. One, two, three. A, C, F. My voice was breathy and quiet, for myself only. *"Vanderbilt's tired of waiting for a box at the Academy. He's building an opera house." "They need singers." "Notoriety fills houses."* Little temptations hiding in every note, in every catch of breath. *"It could be different."*

I felt the desire, coiled hard and tight, not the same as it had been before, when the church choir had been enough to quiet it. This desire could not be assuaged by choral music and hymns so easy to sing I could do so in my sleep. It quivered now, waiting, hungry with possibility, needing adoration and acclaim, anticipating joy.

I hit the G; my voice wavered.

C, A, D. My fingers pressed harder. The notes jarred. I hit a sharp. I stopped humming.

Impatiently I slammed the lid back down and rested my elbows on it.

I don't know how long I sat that way. When I heard the soft step up the stairs, I thought I had imagined it. Voices were still murmuring downstairs. But then she settled her hand upon my shoulder, and I wasn't the least bit startled.

"Duncan wants to know if you're going home or staying with Johnny."

I looked up to see her standing behind me. "I don't know."

"He's tired, Marguerite. He wants to go now."

"Then you should go ahead. I'll stay here."

She hesitated. Her fingers tightened on my shoulder. "Why don't you come home tonight? You said you'd tell me where you were today."

"I was . . . nowhere. I went for a walk."

She sat down on the bench beside me, forcing me to move over. "Maybe you can get Johnny to believe that shit, but I ain't Johnny. You ain't the kind to go promenading by yourself. Where were you?"

"That is where I was," I said irritably.

"Walk down by the water, did you?"

"Yes, as it happens."

"I'm surprised I didn't see you. I happened to be promenading myself." Her voice took on a mockingly aristocratic tone. "With the good Dr. Marsdon."

"Were you?"

"I never thought to like a respectable man so well." She sighed, a soft breath of air, scented with the watered-down whiskey we gave the girls. "You know, I been thinking. Maybe . . . if this place goes the way you and Johnny say . . . I don't know . . . maybe I could . . . give up the whoring."

She was waiting; I felt it. She was telling me something important, and I knew I should listen. But all I could hear were Gideon's words in my head. All I felt was my own longing. "I suppose."

She went quiet. She traced the keyboard cover with her finger, leaving a greasy streak behind. "You learn to play this from your musician?"

I said without thinking, "The first time I saw him, he showed me how to play 'Hot Cross Buns.'"

"The first time you saw him?" she echoed.

I nodded.

"He had a piano there on the street under your window?"

Too late I heard the flatness of her voice. Too late I remembered the lie I'd told her. "I meant . . . the first time . . . face-to-face. The lesson."

She rose. I felt the loss of her warmth, which made me shiver. "How much of it was true, Marguerite?"

I could not answer her; I could not look at her.

She went down the stairs, and I heard her call out to Duncan, "She's staying with Johnny tonight," and I heard his quiet assent and the cross of her footsteps to the door, the open and close, and then the silence she left behind.

I WOKE SWEATING, haunted by a nightmare I could no longer remember. I was too distressed to care about waking Johnny as I slid from beneath his arm. I went to the window, pushing aside the curtain of fading, dusty calico to stare out onto the street. It was just past dawn; I'd been asleep for only a short time. Below, it was quiet, only a crow pecking at something lodged in the mud, cawing raucously as his fellows joined him.

I knew I must make Gideon go. If nothing else, the despair I felt at the thought should convince me how necessary it was. I wanted what he offered too much, but I could not let myself forget what had led to my own hands covered with blood and the scar that marked me. I had meant to leave him. I had been desperate to do so. The girl I'd been had known what was best; I could not let four and a half years of distance tell me otherwise. I looked over my shoulder at Johnny. I had another life now. A life I meant to be happy in.

I stood there gathering my courage and my resolution, and then I dressed and went to the New Brunswick Hotel and knocked upon his door.

He did not seem surprised to see me. He was only partially dressed—it was early, after all, and I supposed I'd been lucky to not find him still abed. His shirt was open to reveal his long underwear beneath, his hair tousled from sleep. He'd obviously been shaving; he wiped at his face with a towel as he stepped back to let me in. He missed a bit of shaving lather. I reached up to wipe it away with my thumb—a reflex born of habit, a quick flick that I wished I had not done the moment I did so. His skin was warm, the hardness of his jaw familiar. I curled my thumb into my palm and stepped quickly away.

He seemed hardly to notice. He flung the towel to the top of the dresser and asked, "Did you read the journal?"

I'd forgotten all about it. "No."

"Have you changed your mind?"

I shook my head.

"Then why are you here?"

"I came to convince you that I mean what I say." I sat down at the desk. The music folio was there, stuffed full, the curled edges of the sheets peeking from between the covers, and the hunger to see that music again made my mouth water. I rested my fingers on the smooth, worn leather. "I'm not going back. I want you to leave. It's a waste of your time to stay."

"Let me be the judge of that."

"You've wasted so much time already." I drew my finger down the soft leather, down the side, over the edges of the pages. "Four years. I should think you would hate to waste more."

I meant to be cruel; I couldn't help myself. I expected him to make some cutting reply and was surprised when he didn't. He came up behind me.

"Why don't you look at it?"

I glanced at him over my shoulder. "Look at what?"

"The music."

I drew my fingers from the folio. I shook my head.

He said, "Come, Bina. You know you want to."

"I've seen it all before."

"The mad scene from *Lucia*'s there, and the Fountain Song," he said softly. "Music from *La Trav*, and your Marguerite, the *Barber*, *Il Trov*—"

"I don't need to see."

"*Aida, Don Giovanni, L'africaine*—"

"I've never really liked that one."

"*Sonnambula.*" He was almost whispering. "*Ernani.*" He was closer now, leaning over me, pulling the ribbon of the folio so it slipped loose, then opening the cover. On top was *The Barber of Seville*, Rosina's aria. Despite myself, I looked at it. The notes jumped off the page and into my brain like an electric current, the little notations above written in familiar pencil, the notations he'd made for me. This was the music we had practiced with in the past, his commentary on where I should embellish and where I should not, his always brilliant assessment of the music and how it should best be sung.

Each note leaped free and into my head, long remembered, never forgotten. My eyes raced hungrily over it, and the room disappeared before me, fading until what was real was the illusion cast over it, a glamour of white satin beneath my fingers and silk flowers in my hair, the smell of the gas footlights and the too-fresh paint of scenery strong in my nose. "*Una voce poco fa,*"—"a little voice I heard just now. . . ."

I reached to turn the page. One after another and then the next, not pausing until I came to the reconciliation duet from *Ernani*, and then I stopped, suddenly breathless.

"'*Tu, Perfida.*' Remember?" he asked softly.

I nodded. I felt him against me, though the back of the chair was between us. He bent to read the music over my shoulder, his hair brushing my cheek.

"I think it's when I first fell in love with you," he said. "Onstage, watching you sing those words to me. I remember thinking you were either the best actress I'd ever seen, or that you were in love with me too."

I could barely get the words past my throat. "I wasn't that good an actress."

"One night Barto was watching from the wings—did I ever tell you this?—and he pulled me aside and told me what a lucky man I was. He said that if he'd been twenty years younger and you had looked at him that way, he would never have left your side."

"You never told me that," I whispered.

"I suppose I didn't want you to know you'd snared another one." He laughed lightly. His breath stirred the pages. "There was already enough competition."

The memories were there again, shifting back, shrouded and drifting. . . .

"When I saw you in Rinzetti's arms . . . I wanted to kill him, you know. It was all I could do to let you be with him."

"You had Follett," I said tightly. "And Willa."

"Yes. I told myself that mattered. But it didn't, Bina. You know it didn't. Because I had that duet too. I think I would give anything to hear you sing it again now."

And then he began to sing his part, lightly, teasingly, against my ear. His voice was gravelly and unused, rough with smoke, but still his, the voice I remembered, not good enough for real fame, but one that had disguised very well and for a long time his real talent, and I closed my eyes and remembered looking at him across the stage, his eyes kohled and his reddened lips, his dark hair gleaming red in the footlights. I remembered pretending he meant those words he sang, and how much I wished they were true. And with that memory came another one, hazy, as if through smoke and distance. The way I'd leaned into him as he played piano during practice. The way I'd deliberately put everything I felt into my eyes when we sang together, how I'd meant for him to know I meant to have him.

The realization startled me. Hoarsely, I said, "I know what you're doing. I'm no callow girl any longer. Your seduction won't work this time."

"Won't it?" His lips brushed my hair. "Remember, Bina? Remember the way it really was? It was good, wasn't it?"

"Some of it," I admitted.

"Most of it." He drew back, and I felt him tug my hair, twirling a loosened strand of it about his finger. "I miss your yellow hair."

I tugged gently away. "That's no longer who I am."

His pale eyes flared. "It's who you'll always be. You belong up on Vanderbilt's stage, Sabine. And not just there, but at La Scala too, and Covent Garden, the Theatre Italien. . . . Take back your place. They'll come in droves to see you. You barely realized your promise. There was so much more to be had."

The things he made me see, the things I wanted . . . I shook my head desperately. I jerked away from him, on my feet so quickly the chair rocked. "And you would be right there beside me."

He frowned warily. "Yes."

"Guiding me. Managing me."

"Yes. Yes, of course."

"Telling me what to do—"

"Christ. What do you think you are, some biddable child?"

I turned away from him with a cry of frustration. "Dear God, why did I even think to come here?"

"Because you know what you want, even if you won't admit it to yourself. You know what I can give you."

"Oh yes. The reputation for being a whore. The return of a scandal I've spent years running from."

"If you would embrace it, Sabine, no one could use it against you."

"I don't want it! Don't you understand? I loved you and you used that to manipulate me."

"You did some manipulating yourself, as I recall. You weren't the only one who suffered. D'you think I enjoyed it? Watching Barret destroy himself? Seeing you go everywhere on Jerome's arm instead of mine? Letting all those men fawn over you because I was supposed to be your manager and nothing more? Christ, if just telling you no would have ended the torment, I'd have done so in a moment."

"You never even tried," I accused.

"*You* weren't listening." He was breathing hard, as angry as I was. "You never did."

I spun on my heel, heading for the door. "There's no point in this. I'm leaving."

"Go then," he snapped. "Run away. Keep running."

I had my hand on the knob. But I paused; I could not make myself turn it. As angry as I was, I did not want to go. Instead I turned back to him, uncertain.

He was there in a moment, as if he'd known better than I what we were moving toward, what we were waiting for. He pinned me to the door, shoving his hand into my hair so roughly it fell loose, and there was no subtlety in our kiss. It was open-mouthed and starving and still it was not enough. I had missed him. I could not satisfy my craving for him; there was no way to bring him close enough.

He lifted me onto the edge of the desk, and then his hands were beneath my skirt, pulling it up, running over my bare skin. The desk was too small, the music was in the way, and I pushed it, too far; the folio slipped to the floor and the pages scattered everywhere, and I didn't care. I cared about nothing but having him. And when he was deep inside me, one hand grasping my hip and the other entwining with mine as together we braced ourselves against a desk that rocked and jarred beneath our weight, I heard the music of him, vibrating into my body like a struck chord, a note held and blooming into fullness, harmonizing, and I burst and was gone, cast into a net of my own making, tangled irrevocably once more.

He trapped me as I made to leave. He kissed me, his lips against mine as he murmured, "Meet me here in the morning. We'll begin practice."

"I'm not coming back," I said.

CHAPTER 20

Everything had turned upside down, my entire life upended. I could no longer keep the past and the present separate—or, more accurately, the past would not stay the past. I was angry with myself for falling so spectacularly into the trap he'd laid for me, for failing to send him away, for not saving the life I'd worked so hard to make.

But mostly, I was furious with myself for *wanting.*

The past was there now, in my head, at every turn. I could not look at the Palace stage without yearning for it myself. I could not watch those girls singing without wanting to show them how it was done. I could not be Marguerite because Sabine was so much stronger, and the efforts I'd made to quiet her were unraveling, leaving me scrambling to catch the threads before they came completely apart.

The only thing I knew for certain was that I could not trust myself around Gideon, and therefore I would stay away from him. He could not tempt me if I did not see him. I would not go back to the hotel. I would not meet him tomorrow. And I would not—no matter the temptation—let him practice me.

I could go back to the way things were if I stopped now. It hadn't gone too far, not yet. I could still hold this life together if I tried. I had to. Today had shown me just how weak I was. I wanted to be Sabine Conrad. But being her had nearly destroyed me.

I glanced across the saloon to where Charlotte hovered at Lee Blotsky's table. She was laughing with some burly lumberman, and I remembered last night, how she'd come to me in the orchestra loge, how I'd disappointed her. I thought of how she'd brought me to the choir—had it only been six months ago? It seemed a hundred years—and how much she'd sensed of me even through my dishonesty. *"What makes you happier than singing?"*

I turned away, taking up the skirts the seamstress had mended and dropped off that afternoon, hurrying down the darkened hall behind the stairs toward the dressing room.

"You in another world tonight, honey?"

I jumped and dropped the skirts at the sound of Johnny's voice. I felt the blood rush hot into my face at the thought of where I'd been that morning, of what I'd done.

"Why, it seems you are," he said with a laugh. He kicked the skirts aside and pushed me into a darkened corner, kissing my ear. "Now I wonder, could it have anything to do with this morning?"

"This morning?"

His lips were at my throat. "You were gone before I woke. Not even a good-bye. Why, honey, I was worried."

I put my hand to his chest. "I went to breakfast. I was hungry and you looked as if you meant to sleep the day away."

"Hmmm." Johnny pressed close. "Where'd you go?"

"Only a few blocks away."

"By yourself?"

"Why, yes, as it happens."

He drew back, studying me.

"What is it?" I asked. "Why do you look at me that way?"

"Where was your tall friend?"

"Charlotte. In bed, I suppose. It was early."

"Now, ain't that odd," he said. "She said she was with you. That you went to Miller's."

Charlotte had lied for me. I was uncertain whether to be angry that she'd put me in this position, so neatly caught, or to feel relieved that, after last night, she still felt enough affection for me to protect me. Desperately I tried to stall. "She told you?"

Johnny's gaze was dark. "Where were you this morning, Margie?"

"I . . . I thought she meant for it to be a secret, that's all."

"Why should it be secret?"

I scrambled for a lie he would believe. "Why . . . because she'd arranged to meet with a man at Miller's, but she was afraid to go alone. So I went with her."

"Why's that a secret?"

"She'd met him here. I thought she didn't want you to know. I'm surprised she told you."

"She didn't tell me. She said she went to Miller's with you."

"She was afraid you would be angry that she was bedding him for free."

He was quiet for a moment, assessing. "Damn whores. I can hardly wait to be rid of them."

"Are we still to meet with Mr. Kerwin?" I struggled to keep my voice even.

"Not tonight. I'm going to show him around town. Show him Seattle potential." He laughed a little. "Such as it is."

"You don't need me?"

"Not yet." He paused. "You lying to me about all this, honey?"

"Why would you think that?"

"Because you did earlier."

"I'm not lying now." I put my arm around his neck, drawing him down, kissing him, appeasing him, reassuring myself.

When he was gone I knelt to gather the skirts I'd dropped. I pressed them to my face, inhaling the odors of musty satin and sweat and sex, and in my head I heard that desk rocking against the wall. Rocking and rocking, my breath a staccato accompaniment, his offer to practice me a haunting song.

WHEN I HAD composed myself enough to return to the floor, Charlotte was behind the bar. I went up to her with trepidation, afraid she was still angry with me—though how angry could she be, really, if she'd lied to Johnny on my behalf?

"I'm sorry about last night," I told her in a low voice.

She shrugged.

I glanced around. Johnny was up near the ticket booth. "Thank you for . . . for what you told Johnny. Though I wish you'd said something to me. I nearly ruined everything."

"I didn't get a chance to tell you," she said in a clipped tone.

"It was all right. I just had to manage him a bit. I didn't know what you said, and . . . I ended up telling him you were seeing someone in secret. Someone you'd met here, and I'd gone with you because you were nervous. Just remember that if he asks you." I pulled up a glass and poured.

"Walking by yourself again?"

I grabbed onto the excuse, too exhausted by my efforts with Johnny to come up with anything else. "Yes."

"Robert said he saw you down by the New Brunswick."

"Robert?" I looked at her in surprise. "Robert Marsdon? When did you see him?"

"I told you already. I went walking with him yesterday. Now why don't you fucking tell me the truth about something for once?"

"There's nothing to tell."

With careful precision, she arranged the glasses on her tray. Her voice was so quiet I had to strain to hear it above the orchestra and the singing and the noise. "You and me got to talk, Marguerite. You going home tonight? I'll come to your room. I'll henna your hair."

"I miss your yellow hair."

I tried to swallow the lump in my throat. "I can't. Johnny won't be here. I need to stay around."

She gave me a quick look. "That the only reason?"

"Yes. Of course."

I focused on pouring the whiskey, on making certain not to spill a drop. I felt her waiting. Tentatively, unable to help myself, I said, "Charlotte—have you ever wanted something . . . have you ever wanted something so badly you thought it would kill you not to have it?"

She frowned. "Ain't nothing worth having that much."

I looked away, filled with a disappointment I could not measure or quite explain. "Yes," I said quietly. "I suppose you're right."

I SPENT A restless night, tossing and turning, dreaming I was in San Francisco, walking down the street with Gideon and Barret while the crowds hindered our passing, and then suddenly the people were gone, and I was worried, and Gideon reassured me, "They'll return when they see your scar." Then Barret went running off, and when Gideon started after him, I stopped him, saying, "Let him go. There's an hour before rehearsal. Come back to the hotel with me." And then we were tangled together beneath the sheets, yet it wasn't Gideon at all, but Johnny saying, "Only fifteen minutes. We can't be late. There's five hundred people waiting for a piece of you."

I woke with a start to find Johnny shaking me. "Shut up! You woke me twice."

I mumbled an apology, still blurry from the dream, and got out of bed, slipping on my chemise and drawing a blanket around me, leaving him to turn over and go back to sleep. I left the room and went down the hall to one of the boxes, pulling aside the curtain. The only furniture was a chaise lounge, and I lay upon it, pulling the blanket up to my chin, trying not to smell the smoke and musk of the little room lingering in the upholstery and the heavy curtains, the pervasive scent of sex.

But my dream returned as I lay there—my worry when the crowds dissipated, Gideon's promise, the way I'd dismissed Barret so easily, Johnny's comment. *"There's five hundred people waiting for a piece of you."* And through it all, the lure: *"You could have it all back." "There was so much more to be had."*

I closed my eyes and tried to ignore those haunting little voices. I made myself remember other things: Leonard Jerome smiling up at me and Barret's despairing protests, Alain covered with blood.

Alain covered with blood.

All that morning and into the afternoon, I focused on resistance. On staying here. On being Marguerite. And every single thing I did seemed to erode it just a little more. It was as if the past had been waiting for a door, and now that one had cracked open, it was slipping through, insidious, attacking when I least expected it. Going through the girls' costumes to find rips and stains, I thought of taffetas and silks, of wools so fine they were a pleasure to touch, of silk corsets in many colors and jewels that seemed to draw life and depth from one's skin. As I set up glasses, I saw crystal goblets, champagne bubbles. When the music started, I heard instead a sublime piano; keeping silent was so painful it was hard to breathe. When Charlotte arrived, it was all I could do to smile back at her greeting, because the yearning to go out the door she'd just come in had me moving halfway toward it before I caught myself.

The saloon was crowded. I looked for Johnny and saw him at Jim Ryan's table, talking with Lyman Kerwin, who was playing poker. I reached beneath the bar for the bottle of good whiskey and poured a drink, swallowing it quickly, closing my eyes, shutting it all away.

"I'll have one of those too."

My eyes flew open. Gideon stood before me as if I'd somehow conjured him. His gaze was bold and knowing as he took
a drag on his cigarette.

"What are you doing here?"

He glanced down the bar to where Duncan stood laughing
as he poured drinks for one of the girls, too far away to hear,
even if the music and singing on the stage had allowed it.

"I came for a drink," he said.

"There are fifty saloons between here and the hotel."

"But none so well regarded as this." He exhaled smoke and
reached into his pocket, pulling out two coins, shoving them
across the bar. "And I know someone who works here. A
whiskey. Please."

I poured. The neck clanked against the glass, betraying my
nervousness, which I saw he noticed. "Drink it and go."

He took a sip. "I thought I'd stay for a while. Maybe play
some poker."

"You don't gamble," I said.

"Oh, I gamble all the time. That's why I'm here now, in
fact. Gambling."

"On what?"

"On the fact that you don't want me here. That you're
afraid I might figure out who wants to know who you are
badly enough to send a letter to San Francisco."

I refused to look for Johnny, though the temptation to do
so was terrible. "What do you want?"

"You know what I want."

"Gideon—"

"I waited all day for you," he whispered.

"I told you I wasn't coming back."

"Don't be a fool. Why are you punishing us both this way?"

"You could leave if it troubles you so much."

He said softly, "Bina, don't do this. Practice with me. What
can it hurt just to practice? Once you're back in voice, you can

decide what to do. If you still don't want to perform then, I'll believe you. I'll leave you alone."

I thought of his fingers on the piano, my voice stretching, warming. . . .

"I promise." He anchored his elbow on the bar and leaned forward. "I'll swear to it, if that's what you want. I'll swear by . . . by that mole above your breast. I assume it's still there. I regret I didn't get a chance to see it yesterday."

Despite every single thing I knew, I went hot. "Stop it. Don't say those things. Not here."

"Who's listening?" he asked. "The half-breed's flirting with that pretty blonde. Everyone else is attending that singer—who's excruciating, by the way. I thought you had a better ear than that."

"She'll spread her legs for two dollars. And her breasts are large enough that no one's listening to her sing."

"How it must torment you to listen to them. How do you do it? How do you watch them up there getting all the admiration and not go up yourself, knowing how much better you are?"

"Because I don't want to."

He smiled and took another drag of his cigarette before he threw the stub into the spittoon below. "You never saw a stage you didn't want to be upon."

"I want you to leave."

He picked up his drink and turned to survey the house. "Not without you."

Desperately, I said, "I don't want you."

He looked back at me. "That's not what I saw yesterday morning."

There was a movement across the floor. I glanced up to see Johnny rising from Jim Ryan's table.

"I want you to go," I said evenly.

He downed his drink and set the empty glass on the bar, flicking it so it skidded toward me. "Maybe you could try begging. Perhaps you could unbutton your bodice. Or, better yet, go down on your knees." His eyes darkened. "Isn't that always how you get your way, Bina? God knows it's how you managed me. Perhaps I'm just as easily commanded as I always was. Would you care to find out?"

I felt myself flush. "How you twist everything!"

"I'm not the one doing the twisting."

The girl onstage finished her song. There was dutiful applause. I saw Johnny look up and glance toward me. Whatever he saw in my face gave him pause. I saw the way he took in Gideon, who was leaning too familiarly in my direction. I saw Johnny frown.

I felt almost sick with fear. "Please, Gideon. Just go."

Gideon's expression went wary and perplexed. "What is it?"

Johnny began to cross the room. A customer called to him, stopping him.

"What must I do to get you to leave?" I asked.

"Say you'll let me bring you into voice again."

"And if I don't?"

"I'll come back tomorrow. And the day after. And the day after that. Nothing you do will keep me away. Now that I've seen you, I know it's what you want."

"It's what *you* want," I said bitterly.

He inclined his head. "That too."

Johnny was coming toward us. I said, "Yes. Yes. Very well. Now go. *Please.*"

"Meet me tomorrow."

"Not in your room. At . . . at Gold's. It's a restaurant."

"I'll find it," he said.

He turned away, and I could not keep from saying, "How lucky you are. You've won your gamble after all."

He stopped. "You hold all the cards, Sabine. You always did."

He left then, melting into the crowd just as Johnny emerged from it. When Johnny reached the bar he glanced about, looking for the man I'd been talking to, I knew, though I pretended not to see it. Instead I smiled at him, taming my nerves, summoning every bit of my charm. "How's Mr. Kerwin doing tonight?"

Johnny's frown grew. "Where'd he go?"

"Who?"

"The man you were talking to."

I feigned bewilderment. "Which one?"

"He was right here," he said.

"I've been serving drinks to men all night, Johnny. Most of them talk to me."

"You looked . . . close."

I made a sound of impatience. "That's what I'm supposed to do, isn't it? You've said so yourself. If you're going to be jealous every time I smile at someone—"

"It wasn't that," he said, looking puzzled, glancing about, still searching. "Duncan!" When Duncan looked up, Johnny gestured for him to come over. "Did you notice that man Margie was talking to?"

Duncan shrugged. "Should I have?"

"You see?" I said to Johnny. I reached across the bar to put my hand on his arm. "Are you jealous, Johnny? Come here and let me show you you've no cause to be."

He looked down at my hand as if it confused him, and then at me as if I were a stranger.

My smile wavered. "Johnny?"

He grabbed me by my wrist, pulling me toward him, across the bar, holding me there while he kissed me, ravaging my mouth before he let me go. A group of men at a nearby table hooted and whistled, and I felt the blood rush into my face in embarrassment.

But it made Johnny smile. "Come on over to the table and talk to Kerwin," he said to me, squeezing my arm reassuringly, and then he strode off again, back into the crowd.

I tilted my head back, breathing deeply to calm myself, and as I did so, I glanced up at the boxes. One of the curtains was open—someone was watching the show—and that was surprising enough that I looked more closely, and saw it was Charlotte. Charlotte, leaning on the railing as she looked out, except that she wasn't looking at the stage, or at the crowd. She was looking at me, and though I could not see her expression, something about her posture troubled me, and I found myself wondering how long she had been watching. I wondered what she had seen.

I LEFT THAT night before Johnny came out of his office, though I knew I should stay. I thought the hour I'd spent at the table with him and Lyman Kerwin had smoothed away his suspicions, but I should be sure of it. I was stupid to do otherwise.

But then I heard Gideon's voice in my head. *"Isn't that always how you get your way, Bina?"* and I felt a sick dismay, and instead of staying I hurried to Duncan as he made ready to walk Charlotte home.

"I'm going to McGraw's."

Duncan looked surprised, but he nodded. "Let's go then. It's been a long night."

I felt Charlotte's thoughtful gaze and did my best to ignore it as I went out into the darkness with them, hugging myself against the cold.

"Feels like it might snow," Duncan said, clapping his hands together and glancing up at the sky, which was starless.

"It's cold enough." Charlotte's breath was a little cloud of fog.

When Duncan said good night and left us at the door, I hurried inside, racing up the stairs before her, but she was as quick as I was, and while I stood there, fumbling with my key, she stepped over to me.

"You want me to come in?" she asked softly.

I shook my head. The key slipped annoyingly through my fingers, falling to the floor. She bent to pick it up before I could.

"I don't understand you. What the hell is going on? What happened with Johnny? Who was that man?"

"What man?"

"The one you were talking to at the bar."

My vision blurred. I wiped angrily at my eyes. "You and Johnny and your suspicions. I've grown tired of the both of you."

"I ain't mistaking the way you talked to him. Is he the man Robert left you with the other day at the church?"

She was relentless. I grabbed my key from her hand and shoved it into the keyhole, twisting it. "Leave me alone!" I said viciously. "Why can't you both just leave me alone?"

She stepped back; I felt her surprise and her dismay and I didn't care. I went into my room and nearly slammed the door shut in her face, and then I leaned back against it, regretting already what I'd done, nearly turning again to open it, to apologize, to call her back—

And say what?

Do what?

I waited until I heard her footsteps recede, until I heard the open and close of her own door, and then I undressed quickly, leaving the candle unlit, and stood there in the freezing cold because as long as I was cold I could think of nothing else. Not the dismay I felt over Charlotte and Johnny. Not my secrets. Not how quickly I'd promised him that I would practice with him tomorrow, despite my resolution to stay away, despite everything—as if I'd only been waiting for him to force me to do what my own heart longed for.

CHAPTER 21

It had snowed during the night, as Duncan had predicted, enough to cover the rooftops and dust the trees like sugar, and the clouds were gone, the sun shining without heat, the sky a pale, thin blue.

The mud was frozen and hard, the puddles turned to ice, and ramps and boardwalks were slick and slippery as I made my way to Gold's. It was beautiful in a stark and harshly bright way, and the sun sent such a brilliant glare upon the ice and the street and the harbor that the world before me seemed a sheet of fire.

The moment I saw the restaurant, with its hanging sign and its glassed front windows, the apprehension I'd been burying all morning rose again. Determinedly, I opened the door, hearing the tinkle of the bell above my head. It was late enough that the place was not full, but I would have spotted him immediately in any case. He was sitting at a table, a cup of coffee before him, smoking as he read the eight pages that served as Seattle's newspaper.

He glanced up as I came inside. When I sat across from him, he gestured with the paper. "They mention your boxhouse in here."

I was hardly in the mood for idle conversation, but I made the vain attempt. "What do they say about it?"

"Why, that it's a nest of sin, just like all the others. They want to shut it all down."

"That will work until they need to pay for street repairs."

He closed the paper and stubbed out his cigarette on the table. "What a cynic you are."

"I've learned from the best."

The cook, Tommy, came out from the kitchen. He wiped his hands on his grease-stained apron as he approached. "*Klahowya*, Miss Olson."

"*Klahowya*. A cup of coffee, please, Tommy."

"Nothing else?" Gideon asked.

I shook my head. "I'm not hungry."

"I don't want you swooning." To Tommy, he said, "Bring her a ham steak and some potatoes. I'll have the same."

Tommy glanced at me in question. I waved my hand dismissively. "Whatever he says." When Tommy left, I muttered, "Always whatever he says."

Gideon smiled.

I said, "We shouldn't have come here."

"Why? Is the food so bad?" He took a sip of coffee.

"People know me here."

"What of it?"

"They'll see me with you."

"What does it matter if we don't give them something to note? As long as you can keep from ravishing me on the table—"

"You're not amusing," I said. "We should have gone somewhere else."

"I offered my room."

"Not there."

"Afraid I'll seduce you again?"

"Keep your voice down. You're provoking. I'm nearly ready to change my mind about all this."

"You're the one who's provoking," he said, leaning across the table, his eyes flashing. "It's waiting for what you want that you can hardly bear. You wanted to sing that music so badly you were shaking. You wanted me just as much. You still do."

I jerked back, rising from my chair so quickly it fell over. The crack of it on the floor was like a shot in the small room. I felt the sudden silence, the curious glances.

Gideon gave me a smug look. Beneath his breath, he said, "If they didn't notice us before, they do now."

Tommy stepped from the kitchen. "You all right, Miss Olson?"

I glanced around, smiling weakly. "Yes. My . . . my skirt caught—"

Gideon rose and came around the table, righting the chair. "Sit down," he said quietly.

I did, though I was trembling now. Gideon went back to his seat. Tommy brought out our breakfast and my coffee, and I looked down at the ham, swimming in grease, and the potatoes which were shining with it, and thought I might be sick.

"Eat." Gideon pointed to my plate with his knife. "You've lost all your color."

I pushed the plate away. "I can't."

"A few bites, Bina. Please. I won't provoke you any more."

"Don't make promises you can't keep."

He sliced into his ham. "What I can promise is that you'll be more impossible than you already are if you don't eat something. I remember that well enough."

"I think I would vomit if I ate just now."

"You will if you don't," he pointed out. Then he looked at me and sighed. "Some potatoes. Please."

Obediently, I picked up my fork. I took one bite. Despite their greasy coating, the potatoes were good, crispy and salty, and the moment I ate one my hunger returned. I felt him watching me for a moment, solicitous as a mother hen, and grimly I kept eating, and finally he looked to his own meal, and I relaxed. I was halfway through the ham when he spoke again.

"We'll need a piano."

I looked up, a forkful of ham poised at my mouth. "Oh. Yes, of course."

"There's one at your boxhouse."

"No," I said quickly. "Not there."

"Why not?"

"If we're to do this, I want it kept secret."

"Afraid Langford will discover how you've been lying to him?"

I looked at him in stunned surprise.

He put down his fork and pushed away his empty plate. "What does he know? Anything?"

Mutely, I shook my head.

"You want it to stay that way?"

"Gideon, please. You can't—"

"Then find me another piano," he said.

"There—there's one at the church."

"Could you persuade them to let us use it?"

"Persuade them?" I asked sharply. "How do you mean?"

"I meant only that you should ask them, Sabine. Just ask them."

I felt foolish then, too sensitive, and I bent my head to cover my embarrassment and picked up my coffee. "I will."

WHEN I LEFT him, I went not to the Palace, but to Trinity Church. Mr. Anderson was kind and understanding when I asked if I could use the piano for a few hours each day, and when I requested that he keep it secret, he assumed I was planning a surprise for Charlotte, and I didn't disabuse him. The piano had been moved to a storage room to keep it safe from the construction in the nave, but I assured Mr. Anderson I would not be inconvenienced, and his pleasure over my desire to use it rang in my ears as I left the church and made my way back to the Lava Beds. The lie I'd told him was equally loud. But through it all was the anticipation I'd been afraid of, that fierce, unrelenting joy.

CHAPTER 22

That night, I saw each time Charlotte meant to search me out, and I deliberately disappeared. I kissed Johnny when he told me that Kerwin had decided to join the circuit, and pretended nothing had changed. I felt guilty for both those things, but all I could think of was the next morning, and when it finally came, as cold and bright as the day before, I forgot everything in my rush to the New Brunswick.

The reflection of the sun glowed through the lobby windows, bouncing off the spittoons and catching upon the floorboards. I hurried past the man at the desk before he had time to ask if he could help me. When I was at number ten, I rapped impatiently at the door.

It opened almost immediately, as if he'd been waiting. The sun was too bright behind him where it came in through the window, turning the smoke rising from his abandoned cigarette into a glowing fog so it looked as if he stood in a hazy box of light. He wore only an undervest of wool flannel and trousers that hung low upon his hips—too large now, with how thin he was. His feet were bare, and there was the shine of sweat on his skin.

Too sharply, I said, "Get dressed. We've the piano now if we want it, and I only have a few hours before I'll be missed."

"Come in. I need only a moment."

I stepped inside, and he closed the door, and deliberately I stayed there beside it, not allowing myself to look at him as he caught up a shirt from the chair and shrugged into it. The bed was unmade—best not to look there—and there was music spread on the desk—definitely not there either, and finally I looked down at the floor and tapped my foot impatiently.

True to his word, he was ready quickly. He gathered up the music and tied the folio shut, shoving it beneath his arm, taking up his cigarette. When we were outside again, I breathed deeply in relief.

He didn't miss it. His glance was amused. "Almost too enticing for you, Bina?"

"I don't know what you mean," I said stiffly.

"Who knows what would have happened if I'd taken another five minutes? I confess I was tempted to find out."

"I'll practice with you, but that's all."

He gave me a sideways glance as he drew on his cigarette. "Is that so?"

I was flustered, ill at ease. "I can't leave everything just because you've found me."

"Ah, that's right. You have a new life now."

"Yes."

He threw his cigarette to the ground. "Sabine Conrad, singing in a church choir. Christ, it staggers the imagination. Your brother would never believe you've chosen to throw it all away."

We crossed the throat. A wagon was overturned, feathers everywhere, chickens squawking about, pecking disorientedly at the mud while other drovers, stopped completely by the mess, hurled obscenities at the driver.

I stepped around a tottering chicken. "Barret would be glad. He hated the life we lived."

"No," Gideon said. "He loved the life we lived. It was me he hated."

"I always wondered what you did to him. You were the closest of friends once."

"Hmmm." The folio of music slipped a little beneath his arm, and he shoved it back. "How old were you when we first went on tour?"

"Sixteen. As if you didn't know quite well."

"Sixteen, and sent off with two young men to watch over you—one of whom wasn't even a relative—with hardly a backward glance."

"You were family. You were my sister's fiancé."

"I'd never made her an offer."

"Everyone assumed you would. It had been two years."

"She perhaps made more of it than it was. I was hardly faithful to her, and she knew it."

"But it served your purposes well enough to make the rest of us think you were," I said acidly. "You're not so honest as you pretend."

"That's true," he admitted. "I wasn't honest. But I saw a fortune in you. The same fortune your family saw."

"I don't think they viewed it quite the same way. They wanted the best for me."

"How was the best for you sending you across the country with only me and your ne'er-do-well brother to tend to you?"

I stopped dead on the boardwalk, heedless of the people who bumped into me and then cursed at the obstacle I made. "Are you saying my family cared nothing for what happened to me?"

Gideon took my arm, propelling me steadily forward. "Of course not. But they sent you unprepared into a world you had no knowledge of, and then they disliked what you did to survive it, though they liked the money well enough. They were hypocrites. Barret was the worst of them."

I stared at him uncomprehendingly.

Impatiently, he said, "He wanted you to be a prima donna. He had to want it. But he saw what was happening between us, and he knew what I would do about it. He hated me for the influence I had on you. And he was unprepared for what you were."

"For what I was?"

"A woman who knew how to get what she wanted," he said—and there was a pride in his voice that surprised me. "And one who had the ambition and talent to go along with her will. Barret was no match for you."

"The way you make him sound . . . Barret loved me."

"Yes. But he would have preferred you to be a safe, biddable sister." He threw me a thin smile. "And as I've been trying to tell you, you're far from biddable."

We were both breathing hard, climbing the steep grade of Jefferson Street. The cold seared my lungs, and my corset pinched. I saw the ugly bell tower of the church ahead and found myself both wishing to be there and wanting a little more time. The things he'd said confused me; I had questions I could barely articulate, a sense that he was opening wide something that had been shut tight.

Then there was no more time. We were there. We paused outside to catch our breath.

Gideon hoisted the folio higher beneath his arm and looked appraisingly at the clapboard building. Then he looked at me and smiled. "Well then, enough of the past. Shall we begin the future?"

We went inside. The church was empty of those in contemplation, no doubt because of the noise of construction, which was a constant cacophony of hammering and sawing and the shouting back and forth of workmen to one another.

I led Gideon to Mr. Anderson's office. The door was open, but the choirmaster was nowhere to be seen.

"Where's the piano?" Gideon asked.

"In some storage room," I said. "Though I don't know where—"

Just then, Mr. Anderson rounded the corner. He was carrying music, and when he saw us standing there, he burst into a smile. "Miss Olson! And this must be the friend you spoke of."

"Gideon Price," I said, introducing them quickly.

As they shook hands, Mr. Anderson said, "Is that music you're holding?"

"We hadn't decided which selections to use," Gideon said. "It seemed best to bring it all."

"To find the song that will best serve is one of my most difficult tasks," Mr. Anderson said. "I've some music as well, if you care to look through it. In my office. My observation is that Miss Rainey seems to prefer the more joyful melodies."

"Miss Rainey?" Gideon looked at me in question.

"Charlotte, of course," I said, then, quickly, to Mr. Anderson, "I think I've only ever referred to her by her Christian name. I never think of her as Miss Rainey."

"Such good friends are rare indeed," Mr. Anderson said with a smile. "Well, I won't delay you. Please, follow me and I'll show you the storeroom." He turned to lead us down the hallway, and then turned to go down some narrow stairs I had never before seen. "As I told Miss Olson, you must forgive us the disarray. With the building going on ... the best place for the piano was here. In fact, it's the only place there's room."

At the bottom of the stairs was a dark space that held a broken pew, a coatrack, several crates. It smelled of dust and mold. Mr. Anderson led us to a door on the far side. It was dark as pitch inside, and I heard him scrabble about, and then the strike of a match, and he was illuminated. As he adjusted the flame of the oil lamp, the room came into view: shelves stacked with hymnals and Bibles, crates holding candles,

incense burners, and boxes of incense, so the room smelled of
dust and dampness and fragrance, of old paper and oil. In the
middle of it sat the piano, and all around it were crates holding other things that had been put here to save them from the
builders.

Mr. Anderson looked apologetic. "You see."

"It will do nicely," Gideon said. He set the folio on top of
the piano and smiled. "We could wish for nothing better."

I looked about in dismay. It was not that the room was terribly small, but it was full, and that made it closer than I liked.
Though the room was enough removed from the rest of the
church that it afforded us the privacy to keep a secret, it was
that very privacy I dreaded as well.

But I thanked Mr. Anderson for the privilege.

"If nothing else, it's quiet," he said. "You won't hear the
construction down here, and it's loud enough up there that no
one will hear you either. Your surprise should remain one."

Then he was gone, closing the door behind him, closing us
in. I heard his footsteps beyond on the stairs, the thud of the
upper door—not so much as a sound, but as a vibration.

Gideon asked, "Who's Charlotte?"

"A friend of mine. I had to tell him something."

"Does she know anything about you?"

"If you mean about my past, then no. She knows I sing in
the choir. She works at the Palace. She's one of the performers."

"A whore?"

"Well, yes. But she's who suggested the choir. She comes
every Sunday to watch."

"Are you close?"

I glanced at him sharply. "Why?"

He shrugged. "I find it curious. You've never had much to
do with other women."

"I suppose it helps that she's neither trying to upstage me
nor sleeping with my manager."

"You mean *attempting* to sleep with your manager." He turned to the piano, going around it to flip up the lid, trying the keys. "It's in tune," he said in surprise.

"It should be. It was in the nave until the organ came."

He sat on the bench, running his fingers over the keys, elegant and easy, the same run he did before every practice. How well I remembered it. How often I'd watched those fingers, mesmerized by them, by the memory of how they felt against my skin. . . .

I turned away to stare at the shelves, the boxes of incense, trying to contain emotions that seemed suddenly too raw.

He finished with a flourish. "Come. Shall we see how much damage needs to be undone?"

It was a relief, and there was an anticipation too that made me go quickly to stand on the other side of the piano, settling my hands upon the top, feeling the vibration of the notes as he took me through the warm-ups. For weeks now, months, I'd done things Mr. Anderson's way, but I fell into Gideon's routine as if there had been nothing in the interim. I knew exactly which warm-ups he wanted, how he would lead me through them, and my body responded with the habit of years; without thinking, it knew his voice and the sound of his fingers upon the keys, the exact press, the pause, the way I must breathe, and the last months, the last years, fell away. I was Gideon's again, and I knew with a soft dismay that no matter what other teachers I'd had or would have, his was the imprint that mattered—I was poured into the mold he'd set. I was helpless to resist his commands, I was anxious to please him. He spoke shortly, pointedly:

"Sustain that."

"Rounder please."

"Less breathiness."

Over and over again, for half an hour, forty-five minutes, an hour, each comment accompanied by a nod of satisfaction or a frown. I found myself taking more pleasure than I should at his nod, trying to impress him—short-lived, that, because he snapped, "Don't strain. You'll ruin everything. You're weeks away from that note."

"I can hit it in the choir."

"You can mark it there, you mean, when no one wants you singing with your full strength. You won't be marking it when you're singing the Queen of the Night."

"I hate singing the Queen. I won't sing her again."

"When I have you back, there will be no bothering with anything but the premiere parts. No one wants to see you sing Pamina. You'll be singing the Queen."

"*If* I decide I even want to perform again."

"As you say," he said, though there was a gleam in his eyes when he said it, and I knew he was only humoring me.

It made me angry. "And if I do decide to go back, I'll decide what I sing."

"Some things never change."

"What does that mean?"

"Only that here's what's familiar—arguing with you about the difference between what's best and what you want."

"You always won those arguments, just as you won everything."

"Did I? How is it then, that you ended up singing *Tann-häuser*?"

"What was wrong with that? I love *Tannhäuser*."

"Wagner's what's wrong with it. If you recall, you were un-available for anything else for two months after."

"People loved it."

"It wasn't your best," he said. "You're a coloratura soprano, Sabine, which you know very well. Let others throw their voices at Wagner. You haven't the stamina."

I was stung. "You always said that. It wasn't true."

"Indeed not. I suppose giving up the Peace Jubilee concert the next month had nothing to do with wearing yourself out night after night with Elisabeth."

I went silent, remembering. Coming back to the hotel each night hardly able to speak, exhausted beyond bearing. I remembered him arguing with me about cutting short my contract. My insistence that I not, and then two months of forced inactivity, restlessness, tempers while I recovered. He'd been solicitous, hovering, concerned even through his anger.

It was a strange memory. I had to admit he was right, but it wasn't that fact that had me feeling suddenly unbalanced. It was the realization that I had forgotten it. Uncomfortably I remembered the things he'd said on the way here. What else had I chosen to forget?

"In any case, you're further along than I'd expected," he said with approval, and my distress faded at his compliment. "Now let's try 'Vedrai carino.'"

"At least give me something with a little challenge to it. Why not Donna Anna?"

"You're too impatient. You always have been."

"You would have me singing Zerlina forever."

"She was your favorite once."

"When I was a child."

"We'll start off with her nonetheless. And Susanna, until you're ready for more. Eventually we'll get to *Faust*."

"Shall I have to sing Marguerite forever?"

He glanced up quickly, and I realized suddenly what I'd said, what he would read into it.

He said softly, "Not if you don't wish it."

The moment strung between us. The room seemed very small; he was so close. I could touch him by just putting out my hand. I curled my fingers hard into my palm. "Shall we go on?"

He hesitated. Then he said, "Let's try this."

He went into the opening chords of the Countess's "Porgi amor," and though it was a lament to lost love, I could not contest the joy I took in the music, nor the need to raise my voice to match it. I let the music wind its way through me, and I sang the cavatina I knew so well I had hardly to think about the words, they were a memory like a dream pressed into my flesh, a part of me I could not cut away, because to do so would be to stop breathing, to stop existing, to . . . stop.

I let my voice grow. I felt the pleasure of it swell inside me the way it had that day on the dock with Charlotte, and the sheer joy of releasing it was enough; whatever flatness or scratchiness touched it was immaterial. I felt myself falling away, and there was no saying where it stopped and I began, because *I* was only the voice, nothing more. I was nothing but music, and it seemed the very walls around me quaked and shivered with the pressure of that sound, as if they might burst and fall away, because nothing could contain it, and I was exultant, and he was there before me, just as he'd always been, and there was a joy in that too that I could express no other way. I sang "Porgi amor" for him. I looked into his eyes and sang for him as I always had, and then—too soon—it was over, my final note carried on a sigh, the last measures of the piano bringing it to a close, Gideon's hands resting on those notes, the gentle fade. All was quiet.

And I realized in that single moment what I'd done, what he'd meant for me to do, what he'd no doubt known all along would happen.

How could I go back to being Marguerite Olson now? How could I give this up again?

I backed away from the piano. I hardly saw what I was doing; I backed into a shelf, sending boxes of incense falling to the floor, one breaking open, scented cones scattering.

Gideon was on his feet in a moment. "Bina," he said, and when he came toward me I put up my hands, terrified that he would touch me—Dear God, if he touched me. . . . It was all tied up together. The music, my love for him. I could not separate it. To have one without the other was impossible, yet to have them both was more impossible still.

He pulled me into his arms and I was resistant, stiff, my hands at hard angles. And then I felt his kiss in my hair, and it was like a spell—I went pliable and soft, burying my face in his chest, putting my arms around him, pulling him close, holding him as I had not allowed myself to hold him, even two days ago in his room, when I had kept myself separate, giving in to desire but not to love. And still I knew how dangerous it was to love him, when he had control of me so completely, when I was his to exploit or use as he would, as he always had.

"Come back to the hotel with me," he whispered.

I shook my head violently against him.

"Bina, there are things I need to say—"

"I don't want to hear them."

His lips were at my ear. "We can't stay here. Come back with me."

His breath was warm, sending the tiny hairs at my temple shivering. I clutched him, unable to let go. I knew already that I'd surrendered. When he pulled away, when he picked up the music and took my hand, leading me from the storage room, pausing to blow out the lamp, to close the door, I went with him like a little child.

Mr. Anderson was nowhere to be seen, but as we went through the nave I heard him talking to one of the workmen behind the canvas wall. He didn't see us, and no one stopped us. I wanted to be stopped; I wanted the moment to change my mind, to tell him no and mean it even as I was afraid someone might give me the chance to do exactly that.

The sun was so bright I had to squint against it. Gideon didn't pause; he took me down the street, walking fast, dodging around the people and merchandise that crowded the boardwalks ramping up and down, pulling me after him until we were before the New Brunswick. My last chance to refuse him passed in an instant—by then I knew I was incapable of taking it even had it lasted longer.

There were the stairs, the lobby, then the hall, the strains of *Faust* loud now in my ears, Satan's deep call, *"Me voici!"* and Marguerite's seduction and destruction, and then we were in his room, and he was closing the door and I was stepping into his arms. His hand was hot against my still-cold cheek. His thumb slipped over my scar, the strange half-numbness of that touch seemed to invade my whole body.

He undressed me slowly before the mirror above the dresser, such deliberation, taking down my hair pin by pin. His hands seemed to erase the ugliness that shrouded me, and with every piece of clothing he let fall to the floor, something beautiful rose, something hidden away from the world, from myself.

In the mirror we were the only solid things in the center of a light that was too bright to be real, that both polished our edges and eliminated them. He led me to the bed, the crumpled sheets blindingly white and warm, and when he came down to cover me, it felt as if I were in the center of the sun, his heat all around me, inside me, burning me up, and I was sweating and suddenly urgent, my hands sliding over his skin, raising my hips to his, clutching him.

He ground himself against me, and I came with a cry, a release of breath, a sudden arching that had him gasping and shuddering too, groaning as he withdrew, and I felt the wet heat of him on my stomach, spreading between us as he collapsed upon me with a moan.

We lay there quietly for a few moments. I traced his spine, unable to resist touching him. It roused him, and as he made to draw away I made a little sound of protest and he captured my hip and brought me with him as he rolled onto his back, kissing me softly and lingeringly while his fingers trailed over my shoulder, through my hair, to my waist. His lips left mine to press against my jaw, my throat, and that was when I heard him, the broken hum, breathless, soft, the words not spoken but echoing hushed and muted in my head, *"Tu, perfida,"* and I was drowsy and sated, caught in the dream of his body and the winter sun. I found myself whispering back, my own voice breaking with the strain of singing so quietly, *"A te il mio sen...."*

He stilled. His fingers froze at my waist, his kiss went slack though he did not move his lips from my throat. I felt the strain of his listening, and the remembered pleasure of how he'd always done that, how he'd always listened to me with his whole body, blended with the pleasure I felt at it now, so I didn't allow myself to resist; I was so tired of resisting. I let the duet take me, and like today in the storage room, my voice reached for the notes the way a body stretches upon waking, slowly and with joy, like honey after salt, unbearably sweet and smooth and liquid, familiar and at the same time like nothing one had ever tasted before. And then my part was done, and I went silent, waiting for his answer, which came, his hand tightening against me, his song quiet and for me alone, and then the back and forth and our lines together, harmonized, and it was over, the last notes joining the sunlight to make it seem brighter and hotter, and he was looking at me with a kind of wonder in his eyes, so strange. It was such a reverent expression it made me laugh, and then he was smiling and laughing with me, wrapping his arms around me, pulling me down onto his chest so I felt the vibration of his laughter.

We laughed for a long time.

He said, "How beautiful you are when you smile. How I've missed it."

I felt my smile fade. I pressed my finger against his lips. "Ah, such flattery. You'll turn my head."

He caught my hand, holding it away. "I want to tell you something."

I shook my head, afraid, leaning down to kiss him, whispering, "I want you again already."

He laughed again, softly. "Still running away."

I twisted loose, running my palm over his too-prominent ribs, downward.

He caught my hand again as I trailed it across his hip, stopping me just as the tips of my fingers reached him. "Listen to me, sweetheart."

"Don't tell me. Please. I don't want to know."

He ignored me. "I know you intended to leave me that night. I know you meant to ask DeRosier to take you away."

"You . . . knew?"

"You're not very good at hiding what you feel. I'd known it for weeks. I meant to let you go. I stayed away long after the performance was over to give you time. When I got back to the hotel it was nearly four. And then, when I saw him there and . . . all the blood—I went a little mad. I tore the damn room apart looking for you. By the time I realized you were gone, I was covered with blood myself."

I covered my eyes as if I could blind myself to the image his words roused, then let my fingers drop when he continued.

"When they took me away, I said nothing about you. They thought I'd done it and I let them think it."

"I saw the newspaper reports," I whispered. "I always wondered . . . why."

He looked at me as if he didn't understand the question, as if it made no sense to him. "Because I love you."

I stared at him. "You took the blame because you loved me?"

"Of course," he said impatiently. "Why else?"

Why else? I had thought a hundred other things. He'd been caught; they didn't believe him when he told them the truth; something. But not love. Love had never occurred to me. How little I'd believed it when he said the words. They were easy to say, after all, meaningless. He had used me and manipulated me. But what he'd *done* for me. . . . Once again, I had the disquieting sense that he was not quite who I'd thought he was.

He sighed. "I want you to understand. Sing Sing is . . . there's no talk allowed there. Only the guards are allowed to speak. It's silent, but it's not quiet, and it's heavy—there were times when I felt as if I were suffocating beneath the weight of it. All these . . . hushed sounds. It's inhuman, somehow. I thought of you. I thought . . . somewhere she's singing, she's happy. I imagined it until I thought it was real. There you were, on a stage somewhere, smiling, singing. . . . It was what kept me sane."

I buried my face in his chest, and somehow that was worse, the power those words had in their rumble against my cheek, and I lifted my head again. I looked toward the window, where the sun was too blinding to see.

"Then Willa wrote. I asked her for news of you. I wanted to know where you were singing, what the reviews were like"—he laughed shortly—"even what you were wearing. And she wrote back and said there was nothing. That you had disappeared. That you weren't singing anywhere she knew, and that . . . that broke my heart, Bina. And made me angry. I'd made this sacrifice, and you had thrown it back in my face. You made it worthless. Four years of my life, thrown away. That's what I mean when I say you owe me. That's why I came after you. Because you weren't singing, and I wanted to know why."

I rolled away from him, onto my side, turning my back to him, and this time he let me go. I was sorry for everything, for his sacrifice, for the fear that racked me now that I knew the truth of it.

"What happened that night, Sabine?"

"You know what happened. I killed him."

He whispered, "Tell me."

He put his arm around my waist, pulling me back against him. His breathing was low and deep against my shoulder. I rolled again to face him. I kissed him, softly first, and then pressing, seducing, using my tongue and my lips to quiet him.

He took my face in his hands. "Tell me."

I shook my head. I trailed my hand down his chest, to his navel, lower. I stroked him. "I don't want to remember. I want you to make me forget."

"You can't ignore it forever," he said, but he kissed me, and in relief I gripped him, bringing him closer. Yet I did not recognize his kiss; there was something there that was unfamiliar, an intensity that woke an equal desire in me, and he made love to me as if he meant to take me into himself, to consume me, as if he could make of us a single person, as if he could make me whole.

CHAPTER 23

I meant to go to the boardinghouse, to be alone, but Johnny had other ideas, and so I spent the night with him. I let him touch me and I thought of Gideon, and when Johnny was asleep I lay there and knew I must end things. Now. Tomorrow. I would send Gideon away, I would tell him about the newspaper reporters Prosch had said were looking for him, looking for me, and ask him to lead them away from here. And then I would quit the choir until things were settled at the Palace. I had no choice, after all. The risk of discovery had grown too great.

I meant to do it too. The next morning, I told Johnny I had some errands to run: chloral to pick up for Duncan, a pile of gowns to take to the seamstress, and he did not question me but waved me away and went back to the accounts. I hurried to meet Gideon at the church with my hood over my head and drawn tight, checking over my shoulder for anyone following, nearly running in my haste to save myself.

He was already there. The storage room door was open; I heard the music as I opened the door to the basement and

came down the stairs. He was playing "By the Margins of Fair
Zurich's Water" as if he loved it. I shut the door behind me
and shoved my hood back with the same motion. He glanced
up at me and smiled, but he didn't stop, and I went to the
piano and looked down at his hands racing across the keys,
those lovely hands, and when he finished with a flourish, I
found myself saying, "How strange that I don't know . . . how
is it you learned to play?"

He gave me a bemused look. "You're asking this now? After
all this time?"

"I . . . never wondered before now."

He sighed. "My mother. She taught lessons to make extra
money. There was a piano in the sitting room of our boardinghouse. She made me practice every day."

He said it wistfully, and I saw it was a good memory for
him. I would have said I knew Gideon Price better than anyone on earth, but now I thought of all the things I didn't know
about him, all the things I'd never questioned. The kind of
child he'd been, for example, or what it had been like for him
to grow up without a father. The sudden yearning to know
who he was apart from myself took me aback.

The time for that has passed. This is dangerous. Just tell him to go.
I opened my mouth to say it. But then he said, "Shall we
begin?" and launched into Susanna's "Deh vieni" and instead
I sang, flirting with him as he flirted with me, and when the
song ended, he said quietly, "I used to dream of that look on
your face. When you sing, you're even more . . . radiant," in a
sweetly sincere way that surprised and confused me, and
I thought of Charlotte saying much the same thing and
then . . . I could not send him away, and I could not give this
up, no matter the danger. Not yet.

WITH FEBRUARY CAME the rain again, and I went to the
church nearly every day, and then went with Gideon to his

hotel after. I was miserable with guilt and fear, but I could not seem to stop. I had a hundred lies to tell Johnny, to tell Charlotte. The tales were varied and inventive, and I marveled at how easily they sprang to my lips and saw the strain of my deceit in my face whenever I looked into the mirror. I expected any day to be discovered. I knew I must make Gideon go, and soon, but each morning, I thought, *one more day. I'll tell him tomorrow.*

I tended Johnny the way I'd once tended Leonard Jerome, but I didn't stay with him as often as I had for fear he would see the lies in my face. I told Charlotte I was with Johnny even when I wasn't. But neither did I like to spend time in my boardinghouse room, because there was the journal Gideon had returned to me, and I was resisting it too. When I was there, I ran my fingers over the top of my dresser and thought of it and was afraid of what was in it, what it would tell me about myself, the things I did not want to know.

And if I was miserable with the deceptions, well . . . there was the music to make me forget. As always, it was the only thing that mattered.

"THAT'S ENOUGH FOR today," Gideon told me one day after we'd been coming to Trinity for three weeks. I watched him put the music in the folio and tie it shut, and I followed him to the door. He extinguished the lamp and put his hand at my waist to guide me, and just then there was a commotion on the stairs, the clatter of something against the walls, and two workmen came into the basement, carrying a pew.

The men were frequently down here; Gideon and I backed up to the wall to give them room to pass, and then one of them looked up, and I saw it wasn't a workman at all, but Robert Marsdon.

"Miss Olson!" he said, looking both pleased to see me and

puzzled. His glance went from me to Gideon, then to the proprietary hand Gideon still had at my waist. The confusion on his face grew more pronounced. "Mr. . . . Price, wasn't it?"

"You've a good memory," Gideon said quietly.

Marsdon and the workman set the pew against the wall, and Robert dusted off his hands and told the other man that he would be back up in a moment. As the workman went up the stairs, Robert said, "What are you doing down here?"

I stepped deliberately away from Gideon and gestured help-lessly to the storage room. "The piano—"

"Ah," he said, obviously no less confused.

"Mr. Price plays the piano, and I . . . we—"

"—were practicing," Gideon said. As if he hadn't noticed how intentionally I'd stepped away, he put his hand again at my waist.

Marsdon noticed. He said, "Practicing? Something for the choir?"

"You've heard her voice," Gideon said impatiently. "Do you really think—"

"Yes, a special hymn," I said. I shoved my elbow surrep-tiously into Gideon's chest, willing him to be quiet. "Mr. An-derson knows all about it, but no one else does. I'd appreciate it if you would keep it secret."

Marsdon frowned. "I see. Is it to be for the service then?"

"Apparently we're planning a surprise for Miss Rainey," Gideon said.

I sighed in relief. "Yes, a surprise. You won't tell her, will you, Dr. Marsdon?"

"Of course not," Marsdon said, though he still looked puz-zled. "If that's what you wish."

"Thank you," I said, giving him my broadest smile.

He gestured to the stairs, obviously flustered. "W-well then. The others are waiting for me. We needed to move some of the pews. . . . Good-bye."

He hurried up the stairs, and when he was gone Gideon pressed his fingers into my waist and said, "You *are* a witch."

It was a light comment, but I heard something in his tone, some disapproval that went beyond his teasing, and I was ill at ease. I didn't like that Robert Marsdon had found us. Although I believed he would keep the secret, I was uncertain just how close he and Charlotte had become—and that bothered me too, that I didn't know.

"Let's go," Gideon said, urging me up the stairs. But as we went back to the hotel and fell into bed, I was aware of that vague disapproval between us that I'd felt in the basement, and nothing I could do to him made it go away.

HE LEANED AGAINST the wall near the window, wearing only his trousers, smoking as he watched me dress. The rain was a cold and steady gray curtain beyond the glass that made me shudder when I thought of going out in it. I wanted to be drowsy, still in bed, curled against him.

As if he'd read my mind, he said, "Why don't you stay?"

"I can't. They're expecting me back."

"You'll be leaving there soon. What does it matter?"

I concentrated on buttoning my bodice.

"How long are we keeping this secret, Sabine?"

I swept up my hair, reaching for the pins in a little pile on the dresser.

He said, so quietly his voice was nearly lost in the sound of the rain, "Do you love him?"

I glanced warily at him in the mirror. His expression was clouded by smoke. "Love who?"

"Johnny Langford."

When I didn't answer, he said, "You'll be ready in another month. Six weeks at the outside. I can have you onstage in New York by June."

I closed my eyes. The hush surrounded me; the rain could

almost have been an audience, those few moments just after the curtain opened as they waited breathlessly for the start.

"We'll have to time it right—the newspapers will want their story. We'll pick a reporter; perhaps Simon Trask from the *Times*. He's always been taken with you. You can tell him how difficult your life has been these last few years. Build the public's sympathy and curiosity. If we do it correctly, there will be ticket lines stretching around the block."

"Gideon—"

"We ought to be able to name our percentage. There isn't a theater in Manhattan that won't want you. We'll have to discuss what our story will be, of course."

"You mean a lie," I said.

"Unless you want to confess to killing him." He ground out his cigarette on the windowsill. "Since I've already served the time, I wouldn't suggest it. We want you performing, not in prison." He glanced up at me. "It would be easier if I knew what really happened."

"I don't like to think about it."

"What did he do, Bina? Why did you kill him? Why won't you tell me?"

I shook my head blindly. He sighed. I heard him cross the room. Then his hands were warm on my arms, pulling me back into his chest.

"Here I am, here *we* are, as we always were. Practicing and then making love in secret while you go off with some other man. You're doing exactly what you want, Sabine, just as you always did, while I'm living in the shadows, making certain you never have to pay the consequences for anything. What are you telling people about where you come every day? Your friend Charlotte—does she know anything about this? About me?"

"No, but—"

"What about Langford?"

"No. No, I—" My words were trapped in my throat.

"Let me tell you what I want, Sabine," he said very slowly. "Or perhaps it's better if I tell you what I *don't* want. I don't want this"—he gestured about the room—"no more hiding, no secrets."

"You were the one who insisted on that before, not me."

"Things are different now. I've grown tired of pretending that I'm not your lover. I don't want to share you. It's time for you to grow up and choose: a life with me, or to stay here with him."

"How can I believe you?" I demanded. "The first time there was a Leonard Jerome waiting in the wings—"

"There will be no more Leonard Jeromes, not for my part. If you decide to play that game, you can do it without me."

I did not expect this. I found myself foundering, trying to find the Gideon I knew in this man who looked at me so intensely, who demanded so fiercely.

He said, "I don't want anyone mistaking what we are to each other. If you truly do love me, then I want you to make the choice. I want you to marry me."

I stared at him in stunned amazement.

"Marry me," he said again, as if it were only now dawning on him how serious he was, "or we leave each other."

And the temptation was there, as terrible as had been the one to sing again, to take to the stage. To marry him, to claim him as my own, to never live in secrets . . . The Sabine who loved him wanted it so badly. But the Marguerite who had run from him—she knew what marriage would mean. To be chained to him, bound to his will, forced not just by circumstance but also by law to do as he wished, when I was already so prone to do so. How would I save myself then?

"Are you so certain of the past that you'd deny me out of fear?" he asked. "Are you so certain it's not what you want? Is your life here with him so much better?"

"I need some time," I said, dismayed to hear the tremolo in my voice. "Just a little more."

"You have a week," he said.

THAT NIGHT I flirted with the men and kept my vigil at Jim Ryan's table when things got tense, and took my place behind the bar, just as always. I kept a smile on my face. I played my role as well as I had ever played it. But in my head, I heard Gideon's words like a song I could not forget. *"You have a week."* *"Marry me."*

I watched Johnny across the room. Everything he'd done for me, everything I'd made here, seemed built of sea foam, easily blown away, and the very fact of that frightened me, the kind of power Gideon had over me, the things he made me want. . . .

When Johnny came over, I smiled at him and tried to feel desire and it wasn't there, though I wanted it to be so badly I wished it into existence. I turned to kiss him and brought my hands to his hips, and he laughed a little and said, "I've got some things to talk over with the deputy tonight about the changes here. I won't be done until late. You'd best go on to McGraw's."

I was relieved and grateful, though I tried to hide it. Perhaps I wasn't as successful as I'd hoped, because his expression was a little too thoughtful as he looked at me; I felt suddenly exposed, as if he knew . . . but that was only my imagination. If Johnny had known about Gideon, he would hardly be this sanguine.

I left that night well before the customers; it seemed the walls of the Palace were closing in around me.

I sat on my bed, huddled into the corner, listening to the rain beat down upon the roof and against the window while Gideon's words seemed to beat in time with it. *"Are you so certain of the past that you'd deny me out of fear?"*

I glanced at the bureau. I wanted nothing more than to

keep my distance. But I found myself crossing the room, opening the drawer, pulling out the things I'd hidden so carefully. I
laid aside the brooch. Beneath it was my journal. Settled, as if
it belonged, as if it were four and a half years ago and it was
simply waiting in another drawer in another fine hotel for me
to open it.

I gathered it into my hands and closed the drawer again
with my knee, and then I laid it on the bed, and I lit the
candle on the bed table and settled back into my corner against
the wall.

The board covers were a little warped, as if water had spilled
upon them; when I opened the first pages I saw the stain of it
marking them, the slight smear of the ink where the water had
touched. The writing was fluid, scrambling across the page,
quick and impatient, sprawling in a race to the very right edge
and then cramping as if the letters were falling over one another
at a sudden stop, the edge coming too quickly, too unexpected.

Slowly, I brought my eyes to the top of the page.

*New York City, December 10, 1870—Gideon is back from the tour
at last!!!*

The emotions came bubbling up as if they'd been locked
away and these first words were the key to releasing them, and
I remembered: my excitement at seeing him again, my hopes
rising as he'd cajoled Mama and Papa into letting me tour, the
agreement that he and Barret should go with me, Willa's anger,
the words she'd flung at me. *"Everything this family does is for you!
I'm tired of sacrificing for you, Sabine, do you hear me? You'd take
everything from me if I let you!"*

I slapped the book shut without reading the rest, overcome,
my vision blurring. I shoved it beneath the bed so hard it hit
the wall. Then I blew out the lamp and huddled beneath my
blankets and stared into the darkness. I'd never asked Willa to
sacrifice. That was Gideon's doing, even then. *"I saw a fortune in
you."* That was the truth. I didn't need to read this journal to
see it. I had been there.

I was not asleep when I heard the soft rap upon my door, but I meant to pretend I was. I lay quiet and still, but she was not dissuaded.

"Marguerite?" I heard her call, and then the door creaked open, the shadow of her leaned in. "Marguerite? You awake?"

And I said, "Yes."

She came fully inside, closing the door behind her. Within the darkness she was a deeper shadow, and there was no moonlight to ease in through the window to make her real. She could have been a dream; I was half convinced she was until she sat on the edge of my bed and put her hand to my forehead, smoothing back my hair, which I had not bothered to twist or braid.

"I thought . . . you need to henna. You want me to do it?"

"No," I said.

Her hand shifted from my forehead, down my cheek, that strange half-numb touch at my scar. She hesitated, as if she'd touched it by accident and didn't know best how to proceed, then when I said nothing, she traced it down, from my temple to my jaw, the way a lover might, the way Gideon had.

I turned my face away. Her hand slipped to my neck.

"You planning to go off with him?" she asked—so quietly, as if she had to ask the question but was dreading the answer.

I didn't pretend shock that she knew. I didn't pretend anything at all. "I don't know," I whispered.

She sighed. "You remember that night on the wharf? With the phosphorescence?"

"Yes."

"You were happy that night, weren't you?"

I couldn't speak.

"You were happy here for a long time, before he came. Or were you just pretending?"

"I was . . . trying," I managed.

She was quiet. Then she rose. "I'll let you get some sleep."

I grabbed for her hand as she turned to go. I got her wrist, and wrapped my fingers tight around it, but once I had her I wasn't certain why I'd done so; I had nothing to say. She turned back to me and leaned down, kissing me lightly. "Good night."

I released her, and she straightened, and neither of us said anything more as she went to the door, where she paused and looked back at me, and I felt the weight of her worry in the darkness between us, and I could do nothing to appease it.

THE NEXT MORNING I went to the church with a heaviness in my chest I could not dislodge. Gideon was standing outside the front door, huddled against the wind with the folio beneath his arm, his hair blowing in his face as he smoked his cigarette. In that moment before he saw me, I paused, staring at him, soaking him in, and then he looked up.

"There you are," he said, throwing his cigarette to the ground. "You're late."

"I'm sorry. I didn't sleep well."

He gave me a sharp look; I knew he was looking for the reason, but he only stood back to let me go into the church before him, and together we went to the storage room.

Halfway through the warm-ups, he stopped playing. When I looked at him in surprise, he said, "Let's not do this today."

"What?"

"Let's not practice. Come with me. We'll take a walk. We'll have lunch. We'll go back to the hotel. Whatever you want."

"But . . . why?"

"Because you're unhappy," he said quietly. "I never meant to make you unhappy, Bina."

"I'm not unhappy."

"You don't want to leave him."

"I don't want to hurt him. But that's not it, really. It's—"

"Yes, I know. You don't trust me." He sighed, and I heard his disappointment and his pain in the sound, and that was different too. I meant to say something to soothe him, but he ran his hands over the keys before I could speak as if he knew my platitudes already and had no wish to hear them. It was just notes at first, and then they coalesced into a song, and one that he knew by heart. Of course he did. He'd played it a hundred times before. Nearly as often as I'd sung it.

"All Things Love Thee."

My heart felt squeezed. But when my turn came, I sang for the simple joy of it—this was no coloratura aria, and there was nothing difficult about it, but thousands of people knew me by this song. Since the day Mr. Wilson had given it to me to sing, it had been mine. It said Sabine Conrad as nothing else did, as nothing else ever would.

" 'When thou dost in slumbers lie, All things love thee, so do I. All things love thee, all things love thee, all things love thee, so do I.' "

It was over before I was ready. Gideon settled on the final chord, and then we both stayed there, still, listening as the echoing notes melted slowly away.

Then he said only, "Beautiful."

He stood up, gathering the music. The smile he gave me was heartbreaking. As he put the folio beneath his arm and went to the door, I wished he would hold me. I wanted him to tell me we were going for the walk he'd suggested, or to lunch, or back to the hotel.

He said none of those things. He blew out the lamp and opened the door. I followed him out. The door clicked shut behind us. Gideon stopped short. I nearly walked into him before I looked up, before I saw who was waiting at the bottom of the stairs.

It was Charlotte, with Robert Marsdon.

And Johnny.

CHAPTER 24

Johnny leaned against the wall, and when he saw me he pushed away, straightening. He clapped his hands in slow applause. "Well, well. That was beautiful, Miss Conrad. I heard you sing that once in San Francisco. I think I'd recognize your voice anywhere."

I threw a horrified glance to Charlotte, who gripped Robert Marsdon's arm.

Marsdon said, "Forgive me for not keeping your secret, Miss . . . Olson. But you seemed troubled, and"—he threw a wary glance at Gideon—"and I wasn't certain of the situation. Then Charlotte was so worried. . . . Well, I meant only to help."

Gideon looked at me. "Your friends, I take it?"

Dully, I said, "You know Dr. Marsdon. And this is Johnny Langford, who runs the Palace. And Charlotte Rainey. Gideon Price."

Johnny stepped forward, offering his hand. His eyes were like stone. "Ah yes, Mr. Price, I've heard a great deal about you. I helped run the Luxe Theater when you were in San Francisco last. Your company—and Miss Conrad, of course—was very popular, I remember."

Gideon shook his hand. He was rigidly courteous. "San Francisco was good to us."

"I remember watching them pull her carriage down the middle of the street," Johnny said. His gaze came to me. "The Angel of San Francisco, they called her. Of course, that was before that Frenchie's murder."·

"Johnny, please," I murmured.

He ignored me and said to Gideon, "How'd you like Sing Sing?"

Gideon's smile was wry. "It left a great deal to be desired."

"Sing Sing?" Charlotte said loudly.

Johnny said, "Why, Charlotte, how is it you don't know this about your friend? That ain't Marguerite Olson you're looking at, it's Sabine Conrad. Didn't she tell you that?"

"Sabine Conrad," Charlotte said flatly.

"The premier prima donna in America," Johnny told her. "Didn't she tell you the story? She and her manager here killed some French impresario. Mr. Price went to prison. She ran off. No one's seen her since. Don't you read the papers? Why, I heard she fled to Africa. Or maybe it was Turkey. Some far-off land, anyway. I'm disappointed she didn't see fit to share it with you. I guess you must not have been the friends you thought you were."

I saw the pain in Charlotte's eyes. I looked away.

"But then again, I been fucking her the last four years, and she didn't tell me."

I had not thought the horror could be worse. I felt Gideon stiffen beside me.

"Johnny." My voice sounded constricted. "Please don't do this."

"Don't do what, honey? What's wrong? Oh, were you planning to keep this all a secret? Pardon me. My mistake. You'll understand, though, why I might be a bit ... annoyed? What was it we were all talking about just the other night? And there you sat, mute as a stone. Well, now, I guess Prosch knew what he was saying, didn't he? Price got out of prison and ran straight to you."

I was horribly aware of Robert Marsdon's ashamed curiosity, and Gideon's stillness, and Charlotte's accusing stare.

"Could we talk about this somewhere else, Johnny?" I said weakly. "Somewhere . . . private."

"Don't you want him to know? Ain't he your manager? Or maybe . . . I guess he might be more than that. You only been practicing with him, honey? Or you been fucking him too?"

I shook my head desperately. In panic, I said, "No. We were only practicing. And he *was* my manager. He's not anymore." I heard Gideon's quick expulsion of breath. So did Johnny.

He looked at Gideon. "Is that so?"

For a moment, Gideon said nothing, and I remembered what he'd said to me, about not wanting secrets any longer, about showing the world what we were to each other, and I knew what I'd said hurt him. But I had no choice. I turned to him, hoping he would understand, but he didn't look at me, and I felt this break within myself, this fracturing, a barrier between us that had never been there before.

Gideon said, "I don't want anything to do with her." His voice was harsh and blunt and dismissive; I felt as if he'd struck me. He moved away from me as if he couldn't stand to be near, crossing to the stairs, and for a moment Johnny stood there, blocking the way as if he might not let him pass, and Gideon said, "I'm done wasting my time. Good luck with her. You'll need it."

Johnny moved aside, and Gideon went up the stairs.

"Gideon," I said, starting after him. "Gideon, no—"

Gideon didn't look back, and Johnny stepped to block me. I tried to push past him, but he grabbed my arm to keep me there and said, "You and me got some things to talk about, honey."

I heard Gideon's footsteps recede, and then he was gone, and it seemed that whatever had been holding me up had folded; it was only Johnny keeping me upright.

"I knew you were a liar," Charlotte said in an angry whisper. "I knew you never told me a true thing. How you must have laughed at me. All your damn *secrets*—"

"Perhaps it would be best if we went, my dear." Robert Marsdon took Charlotte's arm, nudging gently.

"What about your own secrets, Charlotte?" I asked nastily. Charlotte froze. I told myself to stop. I told myself not to say it. Still, I heard my own voice, hurt and bitter and angry. "Has Charlotte told you about those, Dr. Marsdon? Has she told you she works the stage and the boxes down at the Palace? Did she tell you she's a whore?"

Robert dropped his hand from her arm. He was ashen. He said, "Charlotte, is that true?"

Charlotte made a sound like a yelp; the look she gave me was horrible. She turned and ran up the stairs. When Marsdon followed, going after her like a dead man, I felt a kind of painful satisfaction, as if I'd bitten down hard on an aching tooth and then released it, the numb relief of after.

Johnny said, "You're a piece of work, Miss Conrad, ain't you?"

In that moment I felt a terrible horror at what I'd done, and I tried to jerk away from Johnny to go after her, to go after Gideon, I hardly knew which. Only that both were gone and I had forced them away, and I did not know how to live without them. But Johnny held me tight, his fingers pinching.

"Let me go," I said.

He said, "How you do wound me, honey."

And then I heard the pain in his voice, and I knew with dismay that I'd hurt him too. I'd wanted so to save him from it—*no*, a little voice whispered honestly, *you wanted to save yourself.* Gideon had been right when he'd said I'd always done just

what I wanted. It would have been better to tell Johnny out-
right. I had owed him that, if nothing else.

"I'm sorry," I said. "I'm so sorry."

"It don't help," he said curtly.

But I knew what would. I knew it with a sick apprehension, and a realization that the decision I'd been denying for
weeks was made—that, in fact, it had been made long ago and
I had been too selfish to heed it.

I met Johnny's gaze. "Call Thomas Prosch. Tell him you
found Sabine Conrad."

He frowned, and then I saw the moment he understood. I
saw the quick light of ambition in his eyes, the thing that had
always been stronger than his love for me. "You sure, honey?"

That he even asked was humbling and completely unde-
served. I swallowed hard the lump that rose in my throat and
nodded. "I'm sure."

AFTER THAT, EVERYTHING happened so quickly I could not
keep it straight. Johnny sent Duncan for Thomas Prosch, and
he was at the Palace within minutes. "I can't believe I didn't see
it," he said, seating himself at the table where Johnny and I
waited. "Why, it's clear as day now that I know!" His gaze
seemed to consume me—my hair, where the roots shone oddly
golden, the scar, the cheapness of my dress. He pulled a *carte
de visite* from his pocket and held it out to me with a hand vis-
ibly trembling with excitement. "It looks just like you."

"Because it is me," I said wryly.

"The scar is different, of course, and the hair, but did no
one ever suspect?"

"In the first months, yes," I told him, remembering. Too-
watchful Pinkerton agents hired by private interests who'd
chased me from Boston to Philadelphia before I lost them. A
reporter in Columbus, Ohio, who followed me from my hotel
room. Overzealous, anxious, clever. He'd cornered me and

threatened and I'd sold a ruby ring and fled on the next train. Then, in Texas, some little town, and a storekeep with a picture of me on his wall who'd begged an autograph and a hundred dollars to keep quiet, but only if I would sing. The way they all looked at me, with admiration and with something else too,. knowing smiles that said, *We know what you are. A whore who can sing. Nothing more.* My pedestal had crumbled. I was still afraid to face that.

But I tried not to think of it. "I didn't want to be found. I wanted to disappear."

Johnny leaned back, folding his arms across his chest. "God knows this is the place to do it."

Prosch took out his notebook and pencil. "You've been in Seattle all this time?"

"Four years," I said softly, and then, resolutely, "but now I'm out of hiding, Mr. Prosch. No more Marguerite Olson. And I'll be singing at the Palace next Monday."

Johnny nearly fell off his chair.

I smiled with satisfaction. "A command performance. We'll be selling tickets at five dollars each."

"Ten dollars," Johnny said quickly.

"Ten dollars," I agreed. "Please write that down, Mr. Prosch."

He did. "Well, there's the quality act you wished for, Langford. The return of Sabine Conrad—and to a Seattle stage, no less. You'll be the envy of theaters across the country."

Johnny smiled warmly at me. "It looks like Miss Conrad knows something about loyalty after all, don't she?"

Prosch said, "I have a hundred questions. What happened that night at the Fifth Avenue Hotel? How did you get that scar?"

I struggled to remember what Gideon had said. *"Tell him how difficult your life has been...."* *"We want you performing, not in prison...."* *"If you would embrace the scandal, no one could use it against you."* Dear God, I wished he were here. I needed his expertise. More than that, I wanted him beside me.

Johnny said, "I confess I'm dying to hear the story myself."

I saw Duncan lift his head from where he stood at the bar; I knew he was listening. I saw the light in Mr. Prosch's eyes. I felt Johnny's still and avaricious quiet. Their attention was so focused I thought nothing short of an earthquake could distract them.

And I remembered who I was, the things I'd sacrificed to get here, and the last of Marguerite Olson fell away. I was Sabine Conrad again.

I looked calmly at Thomas Prosch. "We were to meet M. DeRosier at seven. . . ."

WHEN THE INTERVIEW was over, and Mr. Prosch was gone, I knew I had only a few hours at the most. Gideon had said the notoriety would bring them in droves, and if the past were any indication, I knew already the crowds I could expect.

I said to Johnny, "I have to find Gideon."

He gave me a thoughtful look, but he jerked his head at Duncan. "Go on down to the New Brunswick. Fetch back Price. I don't give a damn if he's sleeping or not."

"No," I said. "I'll go myself."

Johnny poured two drinks and handed one to me. "I wouldn't advise it. Crowds'll be all over this place within the hour."

"I have to take the risk."

"Yeah." He laughed a little. "That don't surprise me, honey. But to go down there now is just plain stupid."

"I've done a lot of stupid things."

"No doubt. So what did happen that night, anyway?"

"It was a mistake."

"Most things like that are." He downed his drink. "You know, when you first came through that door four years ago, I suspected something, but never that. Either I'm the biggest fool in Seattle, or you got a rare talent for deceit."

There was a bitterness in his voice that I knew I'd put there. I didn't know what to say.

He poured another drink. "So did you know Price would come for you? All this time . . . were you waiting for him?"

"Johnny, please—"

"Why the hell didn't the two of you take the first steamer out of here?"

"He wanted to," I said. "I didn't."

"You wanted to stay in this hellhole."

"I . . . it's complicated."

"Too hard for me to grasp, hmmm?" Johnny took up the drink he'd poured me and came around the bar, pushing it into my hand. "Tell me: did any of . . . this"—a broad gesture, himself, the Palace—"mean shit to you? No, don't answer that."

"I wanted it to mean something," I said quietly. "I meant to stay."

My words fell into silence. I couldn't look at him.

Johnny laughed. "Now you're lying to yourself, honey. You don't belong here, and we both know it. Go on, drink up. You'll feel better."

"Nothing can make me feel better. After the things I said . . ."

"We all get nasty when we're cornered. It don't matter. By the end of tomorrow you'll have the whole world at your feet."

"I don't want the whole world anymore," I said, drinking the whiskey.

Johnny looked at me. "No one believes that, honey."

"But I'll do what I can to help you make this place what you want. I owe you that."

"You sure as hell do," he said. "You make sure Price knows it too." To Duncan, he said, "Take her with you down to the New Brunswick. And get her back in one piece."

I was grateful, and anxious. When Duncan handed me my cloak, I drew the hood up close about my face and hurried out with him into the mistlike rain. I'd always liked Duncan's ability to be quiet when he had nothing to say; just now I needed the silence to rehearse what I would tell Gideon. When we finally got to the New Brunswick, I was rigid with nerves and desperation. I nearly ran up the stairs, Duncan close behind, and crossed the lobby.

"He's gone, miss."

The desk clerk's words reached me before I'd turned the corner. I looked back at him—of course he'd recognized me; he'd seen me come here nearly every day for weeks. "What?" I asked.

"Mr. Price, miss. He's checked out. About an hour ago."

"But . . . he can't have!"

"Paid his bill and left," the man said.

I was too stunned to speak. Duncan stepped up beside me. "Where's he gone?" he asked the desk clerk.

"He didn't tell me," the man said.

Duncan said to me in a low voice, "Maybe's he's off to catch a steamer."

He didn't have to say anything else. I was down those stairs and running Commercial Street to the wharf, Duncan following as I pushed through the people on the boardwalk in my haste. My only hope was to find Gideon before he boarded. There were too many steamers; the Mosquito Fleet was made up of hundreds of boats. Who knew which one he would have taken?

But he was not at the ticket office of the *Eliza Jane,* nor at that of the *Arrow* or the *General Lee,* and no one remembered seeing him, and after an hour of checking every ticket office I knew, I had no choice but to admit the truth: Gideon was gone.

CHAPTER 25

I should not have been surprised. I'd told him I didn't trust him. I'd known when he had gone up those stairs in the church without turning back that he was leaving. I'd known I'd lost him.

Hadn't that been what I wanted?

With him gone, I had no reason to be afraid. The concert planned for Monday night, the return to my old life . . . Those things were mine again without the fear that Gideon would manipulate me. He could not use my love for him against me when he wasn't here. I could go on that stage and sing as I loved and welcome the world I'd left behind, the world that still wanted me; it looked increasingly as if every soul within it might crowd onto my doorstep. After all, I'd never meant to leave the singing behind. All those years ago, I'd intended only to leave Gideon, not my career.

Now it was done.

I sent Duncan to the boardinghouse for my things. I could no longer stay there; I did not even try to leave the Palace—the crowds were too large—and Johnny told me I could remain until things were settled. So I stood on his balcony and watched them gather. It seemed each held a copy of the newspaper, which had hit the streets that morning with its lurid headline:

NOTORIOUS PRIMA DONNA COMES OUT OF HIDING!

Seattle Saloon Owner Discovers Scandalous Soprano

The TRUE Story of the SORDID MURDER that Shocked America

"Four telegrams already," Johnny informed me as he brought up my possessions later that afternoon. Everything I owned was contained in a single crate. "I told you Portland would be first. The reporter will be here tonight."

"And the others?"

"Newspapers from San Francisco, New York City, and Chicago."

None from Gideon.

"It's a crush downstairs. Stay up here for a while, until I send for you."

I looked again out the window. "All right."

"How the hell did you get about before? You couldn't've gone anywhere without a mob on your heels."

"Gideon took care of all that," I said softly. "He was always there."

"Well, I don't got time to be your bulldog. I got a boxhouse to run." Johnny reached into the crate and drew out my journal, throwing it to me where I sat on the bed. "Here's a book. Why don't you read?"

I caught the book and clutched it. "Have you seen Charlotte?"

Johnny shook his head. "If I do, I'll send her up."

After he left, I sat on the bed, cradling the journal, listening to the chanting from the street outside. "SA-BI-NA, SA-BI-NA, SA-BI-NA . . ."

The attention I had always loved. That I had craved. I should be glad of it now. I glanced down at the journal. I heard Gideon's voice in my head. *"Have you read your journal yet?"* What had he meant me to find here?

I sat there, dreading it, caressing the cover with my thumb. "SA-BI-NA, SA-BI-NA, SA-BI-NA . . ."

Carefully, I opened it, turning to the first page, the first words: *Gideon is back from the tour at last!!!*

I took a deep breath and began to read.

WHEN I FINALLY emerged from my memories, the day was far advanced. I'd been reading for hours in the near dark, too involved with my life to think of stopping to light a lamp, and now there was a steady pulsing behind my eyes, though I didn't know if it was from the strain or tears.

I stretched and got to my feet, going to the window. There was still the crowd outside, and someone caught sight of my movement, and began to shout, and the chanting that had quieted started up again. "SA-BI-NA, SA-BI-NA, SA-BI-NA." Downstairs the music was loud and someone was singing.

I went away from the window and paused for a moment at the mirror Johnny used to shave with. My hair was loose and falling, and I shoved it back into place and fastened it with pins and then I went to the door and out, into the hallway, which was seething with girls and men and the heavy smell of smoke. I hesitated, but the men were bent on sex, and the two or three that noticed me backed against the wall reverently and politely to let me pass, blushing furiously when I favored them with a smile.

The words I'd read left me shaken. I wanted to be around people, I didn't care if they adored me or left me alone. Just to hear their voices, just to shut off the ones chiming in my own head, was all I wanted. So I went down the stairs slowly, hanging in the shadows, and the place was so full that I was hardly noticed, at least not at first. But by the time I reached the bar, I heard the murmur slithering through the crowd—"She's here. She's here"—and I was being touched, grabbed. "Miss Conrad, sing for us." "How'd you get that scar?" "Sabine, were you fucking that Frenchie? Is that how he got killed?"

"Run away," Gideon had said. *"Keep running."*

But I was tired of hiding, and I no longer wanted to run away.

A man grabbed my arm, and I said, "Please, let me pass," and smiled back at him with my practiced prima donna smile, and he stammered and released me, and then I pushed through the others until I was behind the bar. Duncan looked up from a keg and frowned at me. "Johnny bring you down?"

I shook my head. "I don't need a keeper."

He didn't look convinced, but the place was too busy for him to do much more than shove a beer to the customer who'd ordered it and tell Sarah, who was just leaving with a new tray, to fetch Johnny.

"You needn't have done that," I told him.

"Someone's gotta protect you from this mob."

"I was used to this," I said—even I heard the wistfulness in my voice.

Then Charlotte pushed her way up to the bar.

I heard her voice first. "Let me through! Let me through, you bastard," and then I saw her slender arm, oddly disembodied, clad in cheap bronze satin, the edge of her scar showing beneath a dirty ruffle of lace, and she followed. She came up against the bar breathlessly and then looked up to call out her order. When she saw me, she froze.

"There you are," I said, trying to smile, failing. "I was looking for you."

She glanced away. "I need four whiskeys and three beers."

I got out the glasses. "Johnny said he would send you up to see me."

"He told me," she said stiffly. "I been too busy."

I turned to pour the whiskey, one after another, and then the beers. I felt ill when I remembered what I'd done to her, what she no doubt would never forgive—just one more thing to add to my tally, another reason for guilt, another regret I could never atone for.

"Sa-bi-na, sing me a song!"

"SA-BI-NA, SA-BI-NA—"

I turned to put the glasses on Charlotte's tray.

"They sure love you," she said.

I nodded.

"They can't know you very well."

That hurt; I didn't pretend it didn't. "I'm sorry, Charlotte. I shouldn't have said those things, but . . . but I was angry—"

"Why the hell should you be angry?" she demanded. She leaned over the bar, bent low over her drinks so I could hear her voice through the noise. "I ain't the one who kept secrets. And they weren't small ones either, Marg—whoever the hell you are."

"What would you have said?" I snapped at her. "What would you have done if I'd told you—" I stopped short, looking around at the curious eyes, the men huddled about the bar, listening avidly, not even pretending otherwise. "I can't talk to you about it here. Will you at least hear me out? Can I explain?"

"It don't matter," she said. She picked up her tray and turned away, shoving back through the crowd, disappearing within it.

"SA-BI-NA, SA-BI-NA, SA-BI-NA!" The chorus was growing louder. I could no longer hear Sally singing onstage.

"Get out of my way, you sons of bitches!" Johnny's voice carried forward; like Charlotte, he burst through the crowd as if it had birthed him, one minute not there, the next before me. He was annoyed, more than that, angry. "What the fuck are you doing down here? You got 'em all riled up. That reporter hasn't shown yet either."

"I couldn't stay in that room another minute."

"I swear you don't got the sense God gave a rock," he said. "No wonder Price left."

"We were a matched pair," I said acidly. "He gave as good as he got, I promise you."

Johnny gave me an odd look, one I couldn't interpret, and opened his mouth as if he meant to say something before he snapped it shut again. Behind him, the crowd's chanting grew even louder. I glanced up to see Sally had quit trying. She was just standing on the stage, staring at the crowd as if she couldn't understand what was going on. The saloon was growing dangerous; I could feel the discontent. I knew it was focused on me.

Johnny put his hands to his ears. "Christ! Has it always been like this?"

"Since I sang Marguerite at the Academy," I said.

"How'd you live with it?"

"Gideon knew how to appease them." It was getting hard to hear and be heard; I shouted the last words.

"How'd he do that?"

"He let them see me, but he kept me apart."

The crowd surged; Johnny was shoved hard against the bar.

"Sing for us, Miss Conrad!"

"Sing!"

"We want to hear you sing!"

It was growing out of control. Duncan looked panicked, which he rarely had in the four years I'd known him. I leaned forward and yelled into Johnny's ear, "Let me sing for them."

He shook his head. "They can buy tickets."

"One song," I told him. "Let me sing one song. They'll quiet down, I promise you. Then I'll go back upstairs."

He looked back over his shoulder, calculating. Then he looked back at me and shook his head. "I want them hungry."

"I can keep them hungry," I said; already I felt my confidence welling. "Let me try."

"SA-BI-NA! SA-BI-NA! SA-BI-NA!"

Johnny took a deep breath, and then he nodded. "All right. One song, honey, that's all. Duncan! Help me get her to the stage!"

"I'll never get to the stage. Just help me onto the bar."

He looked puzzled for a moment, and then his expression cleared, and he nodded. He leaned back against the bar and kicked out, saying, "Get back! Get back and Miss Conrad'll sing for you."

They eased back, not much. Those close to us heard what Johnny said and immediately quieted; the danger I'd felt in them tempered.

"Duncan, come and help me up," I called, and Duncan was there in a moment.

"You sure about this?" he asked.

"Get her up on the bar," Johnny ordered. He caught sight of Sarah, coming back for drinks, and shouted, "You girl! Go on upstairs and tell the band to play"—he looked over his shoulder at me—"what the hell do you want them to play?"

" 'Jeanie with the Light Brown Hair,' " I said, because I knew even Billy would have no trouble with that one.

Johnny shouted it to Sarah, who turned again and headed for the orchestra loge. Duncan put his hands at my waist and lifted me onto the bar, and the moment I was up there, the "SA-BI-NA! SA-BI-NA! SA-BI-NA!" died. It took a little longer for the talk and the laughter to quiet, and then there was a hush.

Someone shouted out, "Were you there when that Frenchie got killed?"

I felt myself flush.

"Shut up, you son of a bitch!" someone else shouted. "Let her sing!"

"Did you help murder him?"

The memory pushed back. I tried to ignore it, to smile. I tried to remember what Gideon had told me. To embrace the scandal, to not let them use it against me, and I called out, "Do you want me to talk, or would you rather hear me sing?"

"Sing!" someone shouted, and then someone else, "We want to hear you sing!"

Johnny wrapped his hand around my ankle, meaning to reassure me, I knew.

The strains of "Jeanie with the Light Brown Hair" began, as tuneless and muddled as ever, and I felt the nervousness come over me as it always did, and I closed my eyes and imagined his kiss, his whisper, and it was enough. I opened my eyes again just as the introduction ended. And then I sang.

I held them there, rapt, drawn into my hand, breathing in time with me, leaning forward as if they could somehow join their souls to mine. I enchanted them with my voice and with a song so simple this could have been Völksstadt, and I fourteen years old again, bringing hausfraus to tears with "Ständchen," or "O Du Lieber Augustin." I even made them forget Billy's wretched playing.

I searched the crowd until I found her. There, Charlotte. Standing at a table with her arms around some burly lumberman's neck, staring at me as if I had changed into something else before her eyes, and I held her gaze and sang to her, putting all my apology into the words and my inflection, until I saw the shine of her tears.

When I was finished, the applause was so loud it felt it might lift the roof off the building, and I smiled at them and made my bow a seduction; I invited them to come on Monday and hear the full concert, and then I jumped down from the bar and whispered hurriedly to Duncan, "Get me away."

He took my arm, nearly pushing me into Johnny's office. The applause was still going. Whistles, catcalls, shouts. Duncan handed me the key, and the moment he went out I locked myself in.

Then I stood there, listening to them, breathing hard, feeling that rush in my blood that had been like an addiction, and the words I'd read only a few hours ago in my own journal came back to me, words I'd forgotten. Barret saying that he would serve as my conscience, since no one else would. That I did not need the things I'd thought I did, not fine trappings or rich patrons, that my voice was enough.

Now, I heard the applause beyond, and my brother's words took on a poignancy that nearly made me cry. Because I had not been singing on any fine stage, nor had I been dressed in satins. This was no pedigreed, high-society audience. And yet they had loved me, and I had loved singing for them. For those few moments, my voice had brought us together, and I had not cared who they were or what they might have done, and they had cared nothing for the fact that I was scarred and no longer beautiful, nor that I was notorious for a murder no one knew the truth of and that I claimed not to remember.

All that had mattered was my voice.

How had it been that in all that time, I'd never seen that Barret was right? How young I'd been. How stupid and young and selfish. How had I let my ambitions—and Gideon's—overwhelm my joy?

I had told myself I was running away from Gideon. He'd been part of it all; he was no innocent, but the truth was as he'd said, that I'd been running from myself, from the things I was willing to do. With shame, I remembered my meeting with Blakely Davis at the Occidental Hotel. My flirtation with Lyman Kerwin. The way I'd managed Johnny. What had Gideon said? That I'd been a bludgeon when a tap on the shoulder would do. I had been that. He was not blameless, and perhaps he had taught me things I should not have learned, but in the end, the decisions had been mine. I had been the one who wanted it all. I could have stopped it. I could have said no.

"*I don't want to be that person any longer.*"

"*Then don't be.*"

How easily he'd said it, as if simply saying it could make it happen.

I looked at the door; I heard the applause dying down, the music starting up again, some girl taking the stage, and I thought: What if he was right?

CHAPTER 26

I stayed in Johnny's office until it was very late. I fell asleep in the chair, starting awake when he knocked and said, "Honey, open up. It's me."

The saloon seemed fairly quiet; when I went to open the door, Johnny slunk in, closing it tightly again behind him. He looked me over. "You all right?"

I nodded.

"They're starting to trickle out," he said. "You were right about the singing. Too bad most of the tickets are already sold."

"You might want to add another show," I said.

He started. "Another show?"

"I'll do four," I said. "That should be enough."

"Enough for what?"

"To get Seattle and the Palace mentioned in every review in the country." I smiled. "Prosch is right, you'll have your theater before you know it."

He went very quiet. "You break my heart, Margie."

"I'm sorry for that too." I went up on my toes to kiss him, and he put his arms around me and held me there, tightly enough that I couldn't escape, and kissed me back hard, and when he let me go I had tears in my eyes.

"I'm going to miss you," he said.

"You can read about me in the papers. I don't doubt I'll be in them."

"Not for any more murders, I hope."

"Not unless they're in *Faust*."

He laughed a little. "Well, you were never boring, honey, I'll say that for you."

"Perhaps . . . perhaps I'll come back to see you sometime. Maybe you could even book me to sing here."

He shook his head. "Price will never take what I can afford to pay."

I looked away. "Perhaps it won't be up to him."

Johnny took my chin in his hand, forcing me back to look at him. "Truthfully, honey, I think he might be the only man in creation who can keep up with you—or who wants to. He'll get tired of being bored soon enough. He'll be back."

"I don't need him."

"Maybe not, but that you want him is clear enough." He smiled. "And God help us all if you don't get what you want."

THE NEXT MORNING I rose early. The reporter from Portland had not made an appearance, and Johnny said he'd be here later, along with one from San Francisco, but there was something I wanted to do before they arrived. I dressed and left the Palace, going out the back door to avoid the people already gathering at the front—only a half dozen yet, as early as it was, and some were muddy, as if they'd slept there. I drew my hood over my head and scurried down the back steps and took the roundabout way to the telegraph office, breathing a sigh of relief when I reached it without incident.

The telegraph operator was half asleep and paid me no attention as I scrawled out the message he was to send.

Coming home. Sorry for everything. Forgive me.
Sabine

He glanced at it when I handed it to him, and I was relieved when my name seemed to hold no interest for him. "Where to?"

"Willa Griswold," I told him. "First Avenue and Sixth Street. The Völksstadt, in New York City."

When it was done, it was as if a weight had been lifted from me—one whose heaviness I had grown so used to bearing that without it I felt almost untethered. But I'd only gone a few blocks before my next task settled itself in its place, and I made myself rush forward so I did not have time to think about it, to reconsider.

I heard some of the boarders gathering in the kitchen for breakfast as I went in the door of McGraw's; the smell of some breadlike thing, pancakes or something, greeted my nose, and my stomach rumbled with hunger, but I ignored it. Quickly I went up the stairs. Duncan had only retrieved my things, not told Mrs. McGraw I was moving out, and I meant to check to make certain he'd got everything, but it was not really the reason I'd come, and I was nervous enough without delaying. Instead I went to Charlotte's door and rapped upon it, waiting anxiously for her reply.

It seemed an interminable time before I heard her sleepy "Come in," and I eased the door open and stepped into the darkness. The curtains were drawn; there was only the faintest thin edge of light coming from around them.

"Good morning," I said.

I heard her jerk fully awake. "You?"

I went to the window and pushed aside the curtains, flooding the tiny room with the gray overcast light. She rose to one elbow, blinking, rubbing her eyes. I sat down on the bed, pushing my hood back.

"Why the fuck are you here?" Charlotte asked bluntly.

"I told you I wanted to explain."

"I don't need your explanation. I already know why you did it."

"Do you?"

"You were angry. You wanted to hurt someone, and I was there."

I looked down at my hands. "That's about right."

"I don't understand you, Marguer—" She broke off with a muttered curse. "What the hell should I call you?"

"My name is Sabine," I said quietly. "Sabine Luise Conrad. I grew up in New York City, in what they call Kleindeutschland. My papa owned a beer hall."

"So that part was true."

"Yes, that was true."

"Did you really sing there?"

"Yes. From the time I was eight. When I was fourteen I began taking singing lessons from the choirmaster at the Lutheran Church."

"But the rest was a lie, wasn't it? The part about the pianist."

I sighed. "Not . . . wholly. I met Gideon Price when I was fourteen. He sang in the church choir with my brother. When I was sixteen he arranged for me to go on tour. He became . . . my accompanist. My teacher. More than that."

Charlotte made a sound of derision. "I can't believe you're Sabine Conrad. I can't believe I was so stupid."

"You'd heard of me then?"

Charlotte nodded. "Who the fuck hasn't? And the murder was in all the papers."

I swallowed hard, twining my hands together in my lap. "The murder."

"I don't remember much about that either. Something about a trial, and your manager—your Mr. Price, I guess—going off to prison. And you disappearing."

The way it sounded coming from her mouth was terrible. I wondered how I could say it, how I could tell her the truth; already I heard in her voice condemnation. But I had come here to make amends, and I was tired of secrets. If she chose to denounce me there was nothing I could do about it; at least I would know I had tried.

"I was the one who killed him," I said.

"What?"

"Alain DeRosier. The man who died. I was running away from Gideon and I wanted Alain to take me to Paris. When he refused, I killed him. I didn't mean to—or maybe I did. I know I meant to hurt him. Then I ran. When I heard they'd arrested Gideon, I . . . I didn't say anything. I let him take the blame." I made myself look at her; I made myself see the horror in her expression even as I flinched from it.

"I don't believe you," she whispered.

"It's true. Believe me, it's true. I wish it wasn't. I wish . . . well, it doesn't matter. It's what happened. And . . . I came here to apologize for being such a poor friend to you. I wanted . . . I wanted to tell you I was sorry. For everything." I got it all out in a rush and rose from the bed. "I don't expect you to forgive me—"

"Why the hell not?"

I was halfway to the door. Her words made me stop and look back over my shoulder. Now it was my turn to be confused. "What?"

"Why don't you expect me to forgive you?"

I turned fully to face her. "I don't understand."

"It ain't my place to forgive you for murdering that man. It's got nothing to do with me. And Gideon Price is the only one who can forgive you for what you did to

him. But what you did to me . . . I can forgive you for that.
And I do."

I felt this little explosion of something like joy in my chest,
but it spread slowly, as if it were afraid.

Charlotte pushed back the blankets and came out of bed.
"It wasn't going to last with Robert anyway. I knew that.
Sooner or later . . . well, it ain't like I was expecting to have a
life with him or anything—"

"But you could have. And I ruined it."

"He ain't what I want," Charlotte said. "He would never accept what I am, and I ain't much for keeping secrets. What
kind of a life would that be, anyway?"

"No kind of life at all," I said.

"You see? It's all right. Or, I mean, it ain't all right, but I understand. You can be a selfish bitch, and you got a cruel streak,
but the fact that you're here now . . . well, that matters to me,
Marg—Sabine. *Sabine.* Damn, that's going to take me a while.
I still can't quite believe it."

"Charlotte. Thank God." I was crying; that joy in my chest
seemed to straighten its fingers, to stretch out, and suddenly
I was in her arms, and she was holding me tight.

We stood that way for a long time, and then, tenderly,
she drew away. "What will you do now? After the show on
Monday?"

"I've told Johnny I'd do four." I wiped away my tears.
"I owe him that."

"Yeah."

"I think it will help him turn the Palace into the theater he
wants it to be." I smiled wryly. "Though it will no doubt
mean you'll be out of a job."

"Don't worry about me. I'll land somewhere."

"Perhaps you could . . . perhaps you could come with me."
The idea occurred to me just at that moment, and I rushed on
when I saw her skepticism. "You could be my dresser. Or my

assistant. Or something. I could use you, truly I could. Sometimes I forget what's . . . what's right. You could be my conscience. I think I need one."

"You already got one," she said. "You just got to listen to it."

"Then you can make sure I do. I know for certain that I need a friend."

Charlotte hesitated. "What about your Mr. Price? I don't think he'd take kindly to hauling me around too."

I looked down at the floor, at warped boards, scarred and scuffed. "I don't know where Gideon is. I think he's left Seattle. In any case, I don't think he wants to manage me any longer. You heard what he said in the church."

"He was angry. He'll think better of it."

"Oh, I doubt it," I said. "You don't know him as I do."

Charlotte stepped away. She went to the window, leaning against the sill to look out. "What would you do if he was here? If he ain't gone?"

It was a rhetorical question, I knew. But still my heart set up a hammering beat. "I don't know."

"Don't you?"

"I don't think we're good for each other."

She looked at me. "Why d'you say that?"

"I'm not a good person, Charlotte. I've done things I'm not proud of and . . . and I've blamed Gideon for them. And perhaps I was wrong to do that all the time, but some of the time I wasn't. I don't want to be that person anymore."

"Then don't be," she said.

The echo of Gideon's words startled me. "That's what he said."

"How long was he in Sing Sing?"

"Four years," I whispered.

"You think he might have learned something from that? You think maybe he's changed?"

Marry me.

"And maybe you've changed too." Charlotte smiled. "I mean, look at you . . . you ever apologized to anyone in your life before now?"

I sank onto the bed.

Slowly, she said, "He ain't gone."

I froze. "What do you mean?"

"He's down the hall. In your room."

"What's he doing there?"

Charlotte said, "Why don't you go and ask him?"

CHAPTER 27

I stopped before the door, raising my hand to knock, then hesitated. Why he was still here, why he was *here*—I didn't understand any of it, and there again was that dissonance that troubled me, that sense that he was not quite what I knew him to be. I was afraid if I knocked he would tell me to go, or he would not let me in. But more than that, I wanted the advantage. So instead of knocking I turned the knob. Slowly, carefully, I opened the door.

It was dark. I thought Charlotte must be wrong, but in that same moment I felt him there, I heard his breathing. I didn't move, letting my eyes grow used to the dimness. The daylight crept around the edges of the drawn curtains, glowing through the worn calico. I could see him, sleeping in my bed. I closed the door behind me, a little hard, to wake him, and leaned against it.

He stirred, groaning a little. "Who's there? Charlotte?"

"It's me," I said softly.

He jerked fully awake, sitting up, raking his hand through his hair. "Sabine."

"The New Brunswick suited you better."

"I'm used to worse."

I winced. "Why are you here?"

"I wanted some time to think. I knew you'd go to the hotel to look for me eventually. I didn't think you'd come here, not after the half-breed came for your things."

"Duncan knew?"

He nodded.

"He never said."

"I asked him not to."

"I thought you were gone. I thought you meant what you said."

"I wasn't as ready to leave as I thought."

I didn't ask the question that burned, and I kept hope tamped down. Instead I crossed the room and sat on the edge of the bed. "I sent a telegram to Willa."

"Did you?"

"I told her I was sorry."

"That's . . . good."

I hesitated. Then, "I've told Johnny I'd do four perfor-mances at the Palace."

"Four?"

"I owe him something. It's the least I can do."

He leaned back against the wall. "It was clever, what you told the *Post-Intelligencer*. I couldn't have thought of something better myself."

"You liked it then? I wasn't certain you would. You said they should still wonder a little, so I did the best I could."

"Amnesia always works."

"Well, it does in novels. And in opera."

He laughed. I thought of the day we'd lain in bed and sung the duet, and I had to look away for the longing that rose in me.

"I haven't told anyone what really happened."

He went quiet. I felt him waiting.

"You were right. I *am* afraid of it. It was easier to blame you than. . . . It was easier."

He said, "Tell me."

Just like that, I was thrown back into the past. The flash of images through my mind like photographs. A broken teapot. A knife glistening with capon fat. Blood. Instead of squeezing my eyes shut and pushing them away, I let them come. It was time for both of us to face what I really was. It was time to remember.

When he came through the door and saw me he stumbled to a stop and smiled, and there was a look in his eyes that made me nervous. He said, "My dear Sabine, how beautiful you are," and then his smile became mischievous, the Alain I knew, and I was reassured both by it and his flattery. And then he came to me and took my hands and kissed me, and it was very gentle and sweet.

"I've ordered up dinner," I said. "And wine."

"The dinner I think will wait," he said, striding to the table. "But not the wine." He poured a glass of wine for me and one for himself, which he drank very quickly. He poured another and laughed at my little sip and said, "Come, chérie, drink up, so we can enjoy each other better."

So I did. I gulped the wine and felt its warmth move through my veins, and he came to me and he was so finely made, with his smooth dark hair and his green eyes and his handsomeness and I knew this would not be difficult. I liked him so very much, better even than I'd liked Leonard. I could even enjoy it. The decision to leave Gideon and go with him seemed right.

He kissed me and then he jerked me close to him, and I felt his cock against my stomach, already hard, and suddenly he was at my breasts, unhooking the top hooks of my corset and plunging his hands in to lift them free, suckling and biting my nipples lightly, and though I didn't like the biting much, it was bearable. As long as it pleased him, I would let him do it.

"Ah, how you've made me wait, chérie," he said, lifting his head. "But no longer."

His eyes were strange, which made me nervous again. He pushed me to my knees. When he unfastened his trousers and offered his cock to me, I did as he wanted. I listened to him moan and I liked that I had this effect upon him. I liked the power of it. Then he pulled me up and told me to undress but for the corset, and so I did that too. He told me to lie upon the bed and spread my legs in just those words—it was not very romantic. I asked him if he had a condom and said if he did not there were some in the drawer and he laughed and undressed and said, "I don't like them, chérie. I want to feel you. I want to feel all of you as I fill you to your lungs." And then he buried his face between my legs, and he was messy and rather disgusting, not how I liked it at all, and I felt myself grow cold, though I lifted my hips to him and moaned to please him. Now that he was here I wished it to be over and done quickly, and I made myself stop thinking it. I meant to go away with him; I meant to be his mistress, and so I must do this a hundred times more if he wished it. Instead I thought of France, of the Theatre Italien, of the crowds who would come, and after that it was all right when he finally raised himself up and thrust inside me, whispering obscenities in my ear, grabbing my breasts roughly, biting me. He twisted me this way and that, and he was crude and coarse and it was so different from what I'd imagined. This was wrong, not what I'd wanted, and as he turned me onto my stomach and pressed my face into the blankets and raised my hips to meet him, I felt like a whore. When he finally withdrew, spending himself onto my back, I was glad.

But Alain was unsatisfied. He bade me bring him to hardness again, and the second time it seemed to last even longer. It seemed forever before he collapsed onto the bed with a "You were better than even I imagined, chérie. How lucky Price is to have you at his beck and call."

The comment troubled me, and restored my resolve to put my proposition to him. Quickly I got out of bed and said, "Shall we have some dinner?" and he laughed and said, "Why not? A little sustenance before I fuck you again," and I tried to smile with him. I sliced some capon and offered it to him with some tea, which he pushed away and told me to get him wine instead. I said I wished to speak with him about something important.

He got out of bed and went naked to grab the other bottle of wine, and uncorked it. "What is it?" he asked me with a very impatient voice, so I was suddenly anxious, but I told him anyway. I said I meant to leave Gideon, and that I wanted to be with him, and would he take me away? I said it all very quickly, to get out the words without interruption, and he drank his wine and listened. I said that perhaps he could keep me in a small hotel somewhere until we could book passage to France.

When I was finished, he drank from the bottle, and then he shoved a strawberry into his mouth.

"I am so looking forward to Paris," I told him. "How soon before we can leave?"

He began to laugh, which was very confusing. I tried to laugh with him, but I could not because I didn't understand what was so amusing. And then he looked at me with that strange expression again and said, "I'm not taking you to Paris, you stupid cunt. Not you or your pimp of a manager."

I thought I had imagined the words. I could only stare at him. Then he said, "You've beautiful breasts, chérie, that's all."

"But . . . you said you were looking for a soprano."

"I found one. A pretty little seventeen-year-old in Boston. I signed her yesterday. She's not as spoiled as you, or as demanding. And she doesn't have a manager to muddy things."

"I don't have a manager either," I said desperately. "I told you, I want to leave him. You could be my manager."

He sucked again at the wine bottle. "You're too much trouble, chérie. Stay with Price; he at least doesn't mind your stupidity."

"But you said you were taking me to the Theatre Italien. You promised it!"

He shrugged. "I wanted to fuck you." Then he smiled meanly. "So sorry to give you the wrong impression."

"You son of a bitch," I screamed as I grabbed the teapot and threw it at him. He yelped as it caught him on the hip and crashed to the ground, shattering, sending hot tea splashing everywhere, onto his legs, so he jumped back with a cry. "You stupid whore!" he shouted. His face went red. He picked up a shard of the teapot and leaped over the chair toward me, and I turned and ran, but there was nowhere to run to. He was on me in a moment, jerking me around to face him, his face murderous and only inches from my own. I struggled to free myself, but he held me fast, gripping my chin so hard it hurt. He lifted that shard of the teapot close to my eye.

"You think your beauty and your voice can get you anything, don't you? What a spoiled little bitch you are. Has no one ever punished you?" He pressed the sharp point of the shard to my temple, and I gasped and cried out, and that made him smile. He held me still; I could not move an inch as he drew that shard down my face, deeply, slicing, the pain like a terrible burn. The tears came to my eyes; the blood ran fast and heavy, and his grin was sadistic and cruel and I hated him. When he reached my jaw he threw the shard aside and pushed me hard to the bed. "Let's see if you can get anything you want now."

He turned to leave. I was heaving and crying, my face burning, the blood falling into my eyes. When he bent to retrieve his trousers, I pulled myself up. I crawled across the bed, half blinded, toward the table at the end of it. The knife I'd used to slice the capon was just there. I grabbed it just as he turned around, as he saw what I had. He lunged to take it from me just as I lunged for him, but he was stronger. He grabbed my wrist, twisting my arm behind my back, forcing the knife to fall useless to the bed, and then he pushed me forward, onto my stomach. I cried out and he shoved his knee between my legs, and said, "Shall I teach you another lesson, chérie, as the first seems so hard for you to learn?"

He was on top of me then. I tried to buck him off, but he was heavy and I was hurt, and he kept a firm grip on my arm. And then he was probing at me with his other hand, his fingers shoving into me hard and insistent, hurting, and then suddenly his fingers were gone, and his cock took their place, but not into me where he should, but where no one had ever been, and the pain was like fire; I could not keep from screaming. He told me to shut up and shoved my face into the comforter until I could not breathe and he thrust and thrust, and I was crying and shaking, and then I heard him groan; I felt him go still with his release, and in that moment of his vulnerability, I reached for the knife still glittering on the coverlet; I twisted beneath him. I didn't think; I only reacted to how much I hated him. I was half blind with blood and tears. I thrust the knife. I didn't aim, I hardly knew where I'd stabbed him. I only felt a great satisfaction as I felt it plunge in, as I heard his gasp of surprise, and then there was blood everywhere, everywhere, splashing into my face, covering my hands and my skin, and Alain fell limp on top of me.

In panic, I shoved him off, and he thudded to the floor. It wasn't until then that I saw where I'd stabbed him—in the throat. It wasn't until then that I saw the way the blood pulsed as it spurted, or the shocked disbelief in his green eyes. He reached for me once, weakly, and then again, and then his hand went still, and I rushed to the basin and poured the water with shaking hands and listened to his final, drowning breath.

I went quiet, my voice breaking on the last words, scattering, motes of sound that meant nothing, that said nothing, already gone, leaving the memory behind, untouched, unabated, as much as I wished it to be changed, to be gone. But there was relief there too, in finally saying it, in releasing it, in telling him the truth. The burden of that secret was one I wished no longer to carry, no matter that it might turn him from me forever.

Gideon said nothing. He was very still, and I was afraid to look at him. I was afraid of the repulsion I would see in his face.

I said quietly, "He was right, what he said. About my being a whore. About my depending on my voice and the way I looked to get what I wanted. I did those things. I was that."

"You think you deserved what he did to you?"

I clasped my hands tightly to keep them still. "Didn't I?"

He cursed beneath his breath. "Bina, for God's sake . . . Why did you listen to him? DeRosier was a son of a bitch. He was no better than we were. He meant to hurt you—and me."

"You?"

Gideon's face was stark with pain and anger. "Listen, there's . . . there's something I never told you. You didn't want to hear about the finances and I obliged. But I should have told you. I should have."

I began to feel cold. "Told me what?"

"DeRosier and I had been arguing for months. He wouldn't budge on the damn percentages, and I wouldn't give in. We needed the money too damn badly. Hell, I was selling your jewels left and right to finance things as it was. He signed Elizabeth Masterson in Boston because her fool of a mother gave him what he wanted. She was a good enough soprano, but not in your league. DeRosier knew that too. He was settling, and he was bitter about it, and I only let you go to him that night because I thought he would take the opportunity to show me up. I thought he would take you away, and I knew it was what you wanted. But he wasn't as clever as I'd thought. He didn't see the chance when it offered itself to him. He was too angry with me. *Me*, Bina, not you. Those things he said to you meant nothing. That"—he gestured bitterly at my scar— "that was because of me. I took the blame for killing him without knowing what had happened. Now that I do . . . well, it seems only appropriate that I was punished for it."

"*I'm* the one who killed him," I said. "Whatever he might have deserved, it wasn't that."

"You'll pardon me if I disagree. If I'd known . . ." He looked away, as if trying to control himself, and then looked back at me. "The point is that we've both been in prison, it seems. Now I'm out. It's your turn to set yourself free. It's been long enough, don't you think?"

I met his gaze. "I know what I am."

"So do I," he said softly. "That is, I know what you were, Bina. I know what I was too. Shall we just accept it and move on?"

I wanted to cry with relief and hope. "Yes. Oh yes."

He took me in his arms then, and kissed me and whispered that he loved me, and I let myself dissolve against him. I climbed into the narrow warmth of my own bed beside him, and he held me close that way he used to and I felt his lips against my hair and his breath in my ear and saw the future laid out before me the way it should be, the way we would make it, and I was not afraid.

CHAPTER 28

I twisted, trying to see my whole body in the tiny mirror—impossible. The pale blue silk I wore shimmered in the sunlight coming through the windows of Johnny's bedroom. I had not felt silk against my skin for four and a half years, and I could not keep from smoothing it, touching it, even though the roughness of my fingers snagged upon it.

"I can't see," I complained, twisting again in an attempt to see the bustle with its lace-edged train. "Damn Johnny for a cheap bastard. Why hasn't he a proper mirror?"

"It looks perfect," Charlotte assured me, adjusting the fall of lace over the bodice. "You're beautiful."

"My hair is wretched. Look at it: it's striped."

"I'll agree with you about that," Gideon said from where he sat at the table, watching. "We might have to do something about it before we get to New York."

"I look like a skunk."

Charlotte laughed. She glanced at Gideon. "Is she always this way before a show?"

"Nothing but nerves," he said. He rose and stepped over to me, leaning to kiss my bare shoulder above the cascade of lace. "Charlotte's right. You're perfect."

"You are going to play for me?" I asked him for the twenti-eth time. "You're certain?"

"Of course."

"Billy ain't even here," Charlotte assured me. "Johnny's told him to stay out of the Palace the next four nights."

"Two nights too many," Gideon said dryly. "There aren't enough people in this town to warrant it."

"You're just angry because he won't give up the percent-ages," I said.

"He's a shrewd businessman, I'll say that for him."

"Johnny never met a dollar he didn't like."

"I'm going out," Charlotte said. "I want to get my seat. Hell, even the city founders came. The Yeslers *and* Mr. Denny too."

I felt the jump of nerves in my stomach. "I had an invita-tion from Sarah Yesler for tea tomorrow."

Charlotte laughed. "Ain't you the favorite now?"

She kissed me lightly on the cheek and whispered good luck and then she slipped out the door. When she was gone, Gideon reached into his pocket and pulled something out.

It was the brooch. Sapphires and a pearl moon. Nine dia-monds. "Will you wear this tonight?" he asked me, and I took it from him with a smile. I held it for a moment in my hand.

"You'll have to add another diamond."

"Five of them," he corrected. "When we can afford it again."

I mused, "Five of them. You'll have to have some of the sap-phires removed. Soon it'll be nothing but diamonds."

"That's my intention," he said. He kissed me again. "Are you ready?"

I went still, listening. I heard the crowd, the hushed talk so different from a usual night at the Palace. Downstairs, I knew, were not the usual miners and lumbermen, but what passed for high society in Seattle, who had scrambled all over themselves to buy tickets for tonight's performance. There were reporters there too.

I swallowed. "Very well then. Let's go."

He held out his arm and I took it, and then he led me from Johnny's bedroom and down the hallway, past the boxes, which contained not whores tonight, but chairs set up specially, and the best of society who were more than willing to ignore the chaises shoved to the back for the illusion of exclusivity. It was no Academy of Music, but it would serve. I smiled as we went past them and down the stairs. Johnny had taken out the tables and lined the Palace with chairs, and there was hardly room to move.

Someone hissed, "Here she is," and then the whisper was taken up. I saw their heads turn as they followed us along the aisle to the stairs that led to the orchestra loge and the stage. I felt the panic, as familiar as the rain, and at the bottom of the steps, Gideon paused. He kissed my forehead and rubbed the spot with his thumb, and then he smiled and said, *"In boca al lupo,"* and the nervousness went away. I watched him climb the stairs to the loge, two at a time. I heard the scrape of the piano bench as he pulled it out, and then I took a deep breath and went onto the stage.

The crowd went silent. I felt their eyes on me as I moved to the center of the proscenium; that hushed anticipation I loved. I could not live without it. It astounded me that I had ever tried.

The piano began. The opening bars, beautiful, sublime. I looked out over the crowd.

And then the moment was mine, and I seized it. I seized it with joy and triumph. I sang, and my voice flew from my head and my heart, illuminating the shadows in this building that had been my refuge for the last four years, and my soul went with it, spreading to the hearts and minds that lay open before me, until the gift I gave them circled back to become the one I gave myself, the voice I thought I'd lost forever, my own song for the angels.

Acknowledgments

Many thanks to my editor, Suzanne O'Neill, whose comments on this manuscript were both insightful and inspiring, and Heather Proulx, Dyana Messina, and everyone else at Crown/ Three Rivers Press for your enthusiasm and support. As always, I am forever grateful for the efforts of Kim Witherspoon, Julie Schilder, Mairead Duffy, and the rest of the staff at Ink-well Management. I'd also like to thank Kitsap Regional Library, for supplying me with a weekly dose of opera (much to my children's dismay), as well as for providing access to the historical *New York Times,* and the Seattle Public Library and the University of Washington Library for their incredible online resources. And, as always, I owe a great debt to Kany, Maggie, and Cleo, for their patience, understanding, and love.

Sometimes truth is the greatest illusion of all.

THE SPIRITUALIST *(A Novel)*
$14.95 paper (Canada: $16.95) / ISBN 978-0-307-40611-8

O N A COLD January morning in 1856, Evelyn Atherton's husband is found murdered after attending an exclusive séance. Caught in a perilous game in which she is equal player and pawn, predator and victim, Evie finds there is no one to trust, perhaps not even herself. As her powerful in-laws build a case against her, and with time running out, Evie must face the real ghosts of her past if she is to have any hope of avoiding the hangman.

THREE RIVERS PRESS · NEW YORK

Available from Three Rivers Press wherever books are sold
www.crownpublishing.com